South Asian Diaspora Narratives

South Asian Diaspora Narratives

Roots and Routes

Amit Sarwal

RAWAT PUBLICATIONS
Jaipur • New Delhi • Bangalore • Guwahati • Kolkata

ISBN 978-81-316-0790-9

Published by
Prem Rawat for **Rawat Publications**
Satyam Apts, Sector 3, Jawahar Nagar, Jaipur 302 004 (India)
Phone: 0141 265 1748 / 7006 Fax: 0141 265 1748
E-mail: info@rawatbooks.com
Website: www.rawatbooks.com

New Delhi Office
4858/24, Ansari Road, Daryaganj, New Delhi 110 002
Phone: 011 2326 3290

Also at *Bangalore, Guwahati* and *Kolkata*

Typeset by Rawat Computers, Jaipur

Printed at Chaman Enterprises, New Delhi

For
Reema and *Mishank*

Contents

Acknowledgements

The development and completion of this research would not have been possible without the financial support of the Australian Government. I would like to thank the Endeavour Asia Programme (Department of Education, Employment and Workplace Relations) that enabled me to visit Monash University, Clayton, in 2006–2007. I would like to thank the staff of New South Global International Projects who managed the Endeavour Asia Programme. My special thanks to Dr Andrew Hassam and Dr Tseen Khoo for hosting me at the National Centre for Australian Studies and School of Political and Social Inquiry, respectively. I also thank Professor Rae Frances (Dean of Arts, Monash University) and the staff of School of English, Communication and Performance Studies and Matheson Library (Monash University).

I am indebted to Dr Andrew Hassam for encouraging me to apply for the Endeavour Asia Award. His friendly advice, constructive criticism, and a first-hand introduction to the Australian way of life helped me formulate the theoretical framework for this study. Without his friendship and initiation, I wouldn't have made so many more Australian friends with such ease!

This book would not have been possible without the institutional support of Centre for Citizenship and Globalisation (CCG), Deakin University, and feedback of my fellow researchers: Professor David Walker, Professor Fethi Mansouri, Dr Vince

Marotta, Dr Yin Paradies, Dr Danny Ben-Moshe, Dr Benjamin Isakhan, Dr Michele Lobo, Dr Sally Percival Wood, Dr Amelia Johns, Dr Liudmila Kirpitchenko, Dr Masa Mikola, Ms Paula Muraca, and Ms Cayla Edwards.

I owe wholehearted thanks to Professor Santosh K. Sareen, Professor Makarand Paranjape, Professor Harish Narang, Professor G.J.V. Prasad, Professor Kapil Kapoor, Professor Saugata Bhaduri, Dr Navneet Sethi, Dr R.K. Verma, Dr S.N. Sharma, Dr Meeta Mathur, Dr Tasneem Shanaz, Dr Rita Mehra, Dr Usha Shourie, and Dr Usha Sharma for their invaluable support and recognition of my work. I greatly benefited from their lectures, discussions, and encouragement. I must also thank the staff of CES: Rawat ji, Radhe ji, Bhagwati ji, and Karamchand ji for their administrative help.

Thanks also to the editors and reviewers of *South Asian Diaspora*, *Lemuria*, *Rupkatha Journal on Interdisciplinary Studies in Humanities*, *Dialogue*, and *Journal of the Department of English* (Vidyasagar University). Special thanks to Professor David Lowe, Dr Ajaya Kumar Sahoo, Dr T.P. Mukhopadhyaya, Dr Tarun Tapas Mukherjee, Dr Indranil Acharya, Dr Anida Basu Roy, and Mr Shalaj Mittal (Readworthy Publications), for permitting me to reprint my research papers as chapters in this book.

It is a pleasure to thank the many people who made this research possible with their wise advice at various junctures of time: So many people have provided assistance to me in countless big and small ways at various junctures of time: Late Professor J.V. D'Cruz, Late Professor Bruce Bennett, Professor C.T. Indra, Professor Anisur Rahman, Dr Eugenie Pinto, Professor David Lowe, Professor Hema Sharda, Professor Yasmine Gooneratne, Professor Bill Ashcroft, Professor Stephen Muecke, Professor Vijay Mishra, Professor Brij V. Lal, Professor Satendra Nandan, Professor Richard Nile, Professor Marika Vicziany, Professor Malati Mathur, Professor Didier Coste, Professor Paul Sharrad, Professor Devleena Ghosh, Professor Marie de Lepervanche, Professor John Webb, Professor Laksiri Jayasuriya, Dr Chandani Lokugé, Dr Lachlan Strahan, Dr Kama Maclean, Dr Richard Hosking, Professor Ghassan Hage, Dr Sonia Mycak, Dr Toni Johnson-Woods, Dr Geetha B., Dr Nathan Hollier, Dr Margaret Allen, Dr Suvendrini Perera, Dr Lisa French, Dr Larissa Jane McLean Davies, Dr Sissy Helff, Dr Michiel Baas, Dr Alice

Ingram, Dr Sharon Rundle, Dr Bernard Whimpress, Dr Selvaraj Velayutham, Dr Manas Ray, Dr Pramod Nayar, Dr Russell Blackford, Dr Indranil Acharya, Dr Nicholas Birns, Dr Nathanael O'Reilly, Dr Sophie Loy-Wislon, Dr Agnieszka Sobocinska, Dr Vikrant Kishore, Dr Jaydeep Sarangi, Dr Goldie Osuri, Dr Sharon Rundle, Dr Jean-François Vernay, Dr Nalin Sharda, Dr Mala Pandurang, Dr Ishmeet Kaur, Dr Alex Naraniecki, Mr Sunil Badami, Ms Malathy Anandavalli, Mr Anupam Sharma, Ms Kumud Mirani, Mr Chris Raja, Ms Lily Petkovska, Mr Parichay Patra, and many other scholars with whom I had the pleasure and honour of working. I am grateful to everyone and especially to those whose names are not mentioned here!

Thanks also to my colleagues at the University of Delhi, Dr Vijay Laxmi Pandit, Dr Jafri S. Abbas, Dr Vrasha Gupta, Dr Chander Shekhar Singh, Dr Bharti Sharma, Dr Harish Dahiya, Dr Saurabh Mishra, Dr Rajesh Kumar Jha, Dr Gautam Chakrabarti, Dr Sumita Pal, Ms Gorvika Rao, Mr Ved Mitra Shukla, Ms Kanch V. Arora, Ms Pawan Oberoi, and Mr Mithuraaj Dhusia.

Personally, I am grateful to Suboohi, Ehsan, Anthea, Fiona, Rakesh, Tupur, Ashrut, Smriti, Jyothi, Phani Raj, Alex, Sonja, and all other friends who have made me feel at home in Australia. My thanks and best wishes must also go to my dear friends from JNU, especially Gunjeet, Pradip, Aniruddha, Deepa, Swati, Rhythma, Shantanu, Amrita, Parul, Aditi, Swapnil, Divya, Deepti, Amit Ranjan, Prateek, Moola Ram, Geetharani, Sami, and Devapriya.

A very special thanks to my dearest friend Dr Aneeta Rajendran for her guidance and advice during the various stages of this research.

Many thanks to members of Australia-India Interdisciplinary Research Network (AIIRN), Indian Association for the Study of Australia (IASA), and Asian Australian Studies Research Network (AASRN) for their support and feedback during various conferences.

Tons of thanks to Ms. Rini Barman (Delhi) for copyediting and fine-tuning this book.

To the publishing team, who have handled the editorial and production work on this volume with professional skill and finesse, a very big thank you!

My love and thanks to my parents, parents-in-law, brothers, my entire extended family (in India, United States, United Kingdom, Germany, and New Zealand) and all my in-laws for their constant care and unconditional love.

Most importantly, I would like to express my most profound love, appreciation, and thanks to my wife, Reema, for her generous praise, advice, encouragement, guidance, proofreading, and love. I would be lost without her! I dedicate this book to Reema, our son – Mishank, and the writers of South Asian diaspora in Australia.

Melbourne, 2016 **Amit Sarwal**

Introduction

Roots and Routes

Makarand Paranjape in his Afterword to *Shifting Continents/Colliding Cultures: Diaspora Writing of the Indian Subcontinent* (2000) notes that:

> (...) instead of the diaspora writing India, I wanted India to write the diaspora. While, the diaspora, out of its own needs, compulsions, or expediencies, seems constantly to write India, I wanted India to offer its own response to such diasporic imaging of itself. (p. 228)

This statement initiated my journey to chart out the – roots and routes – geography, needs, compulsions, or expediencies of South Asian diaspora in Australia and to locate South Asian-Australian fiction in the larger rubric of South Asian diaspora writing. The present study aims to fill the paucity of not just critical material but also lack of awareness about South Asian-Australian diaspora creative writing both in South Asia and Australia. It delves into the frameworks and trends of this writing in order to analyse the politics of location – both spatial and sensory – as reflected in the short narratives while also referring to Australian government policies, blogs, websites, and newspaper reports. These narrative and cultural productions also form a part of the larger rubric of the sociocultural-economical-historical 'narratives' produced by the South Asian diaspora around the world, as they also show how multiple locations become a part of the broader question of negotiation within the community and the self.

The nature of this study is interdisciplinary because although it is primarily an analysis of short stories produced by South Asian diaspora writers in Australia, it depends heavily on data from sociological, anthropological, and historical studies as secondary sources. In fact, the coupling of the metaphors 'roots and routes' used in the title of this study has been employed in a large number of sociological and anthropological studies on transnational migration to 'capture the ways' in which refugees and immigrants 'consciously balance their ethnic and new national identities in understanding themselves, their lives, and how they represent themselves to others' (Mosselson, 2006: p. 22; see also Mosselson, 2002). For the purpose of this book, the title 'Roots and Routes' reflects the processes of 'rooting into a culture' and 'routing out of a culture'. It is the diasporic peoples search for '*roots* located in a specific place of origin', as J. Eade (1999) observes, that 'gives way to an increasing sense of *routes* along which people have moved and continue to move' (p. 26; emphasis added). This interrelation of the roots and routes couplets, according to Mosselson (2006), privileges the individual experiences of the immigrant in understanding their adaptive processes to the hostland. Building on this and borrowing further from Paul Gilroy's (1991) work on origins and orientation, the metaphors 'roots' and 'routes' reflect past ethnic experiences (roots) and future ethnic expectations (routes). Thus, it also echoes the processes of adjustment and negotiation that the immigrants make after a successful transplantation.

The aim of the present study, as suggested by the title, is to analyse the metaphysical and poetical notions of 'roots' and 'routes' as most of the 'diasporic journeys are essentially about settling down, about putting roots 'elsewhere' (Brah, 2003: p. 616). The central questions raised in this book are those of roots and routes of South Asian-Australian diaspora, which constitute their 'politics of location'. Even in contemporary times, globalized world diasporans who stay far away from their homeland or roots seek to return or create routes of return to the time when they left it.[1] Cindy Horst (2002) observes that 'Moving has always implied uprootedness, but it could also be interpreted as 'being at home in the world' (p. 12). Feeling 'at home', just like the imagined 'return' is not an easy task for the immigrants and the diasporic location of individuals is suspended in a struggle between their roots and routes, as in the myth of *Trishanku*, who hangs midway between the earth and paradise, or like transnationalism that is apparently becoming 'a Janus-faced phenomenon' (see Ballard, 2001).

Most of the South Asians abroad (moving on to different places) have realized that it might be the mind and heart that matter but the country where one survives on a day-to-day basis, constantly engaging and negotiating with its complexities – local and global, does affect the mind and heart. This study also aims to provide resourceful background information – historical and sociological – a knowledge that provides indispensable aid in analysing the various images of South Asia and Australia that materialize from the South Asian-Australian diasporan short stories presenting the rich subcontinental cultural heritage. The framework of analysis of the present study is not concerned with the writers' personal history and biographical details but with the characters and situations that enliven their stories. This approach also leads towards an exploration of the 'otherness' created for the readers in their fiction both in terms of people/characters and geography/living spaces.

A key theme of this book is the constitution of *location* – spatial and sensory – through both movement (routes) and attachment (roots). I am fascinated and intrigued by the ways in which the idea of the politics of location circulates and the ways in which South Asian diaspora produces multiple contexts or categories that problematize the same. Analysing the ways in which diasporans define themselves in relation to these locations helps us understand South Asian diaspora and its creative output better. Thus, it is precisely through carefully situating the selected literary narratives in their literary, social, class, and other contexts that we can help 'capture both their specificity and their relevance to other contexts' (Hage, 2005: p. 495).

Locations

It is said that 'when a man travels, or when he moves, he takes with him what he can, but his baggage cannot hold everything' (Scott 5). Structurally, according to A. Wylie (2003), a *location* is marked by the above-mentioned parameters of social inequality along with sexuality and geopolitical location and their attending subject positions of identification and disidentification, material conditions, privileges, and feelings as well as 'conceptual resources (...)

to represent and interpret these relations' (p. 31). However, major researches on South Asian diaspora in Australia have failed to incorporate and address the politics of location – the 'locations' they inhabit, reproduce, and transform. According to the present study, this does not only help in the reconfiguration of 'identities in an ongoing quest for self-determination and power' (K. Butler, 2001: p. 212) but also helps in, according to Chandra Talpade Mohanty (1987), a better understanding of 'the historical, geographic, cultural, psychic and imaginative boundaries for political definition and self-definition' (p. 42).

The word 'Politics', as used in the *politics of location*, comes from the Greek word *politika* and examines the acquisition and application of power structures. The word politics covers a very wide range of phenomenon. It is used here to describe, what Erik Olin Wright (2001) refers to as the 'power relations within micro-organizational settings' (p. 18) – as in the discussion of power relations embodied in a set of practices that individuals engage in a diasporic condition. While the word 'location', according to Floya Anthias (2007), represents:

> (...) social spaces defined by boundaries on the one hand and hierarchies on the other hand. Therefore when we think of our located identities we are forced to think of them in relation to each other and also in terms of some of the contradictions we live in through our differential location within the boundaries in terms of hierarchies. (p. 17)

The notion of location recognizes the importance of 'context' and the 'situated nature of claims and attributions and their production in complex and shifting locales' (Anthias, 2007: p. 17). Avtar Brah in *Cartographies of Diaspora* (1996), for example, explores the politics of location in the context of migration 'as locationality in contradiction' (180). According to her, migrants and members of diaspora simultaneously experience situatedness in 'multi-axial locationality' (1996: p. 205) and engage in 'movements across shifting cultural, religious and linguistic boundaries' (1996: p. 204). In relation to this, Purnima Mankekar (2003) notes that a 'politics of *location* entails the examination of how one's perspective and subjectivity are shaped by one's complex positioning' (p. 53; emphasis added) at both the old and new homes subsequent to migration. The term *location* thus captures a number of aspects that contribute in the making of a diasporic consciousness. So, by politics of location, I here refer to a migrant's position within power hierarchies created through sensory and spatial factors. This affects and shapes the relationship in between the homeland and the hostland – thereby providing a more useful way of thinking about the potential found in diasporic processes resulting from immigration.

Immigration or 'separation of people from their native culture either through physical dislocation' or through 'the colonizing imposition of a foreign culture' is considered 'one of the most formative experiences of our century' (Bammer, 1994: p. xi). Immigration also signifies a situation of interaction between two cultural systems and in some cases between a traditional and a modern cultural system, like South Asian and Australian. It also means 'a change in the existential conditions of immigrants with all its implications for the change in their consciousness' and further represents 'a turning point in the lives of immigrants to confront a strange new world and to make sense of it' (S.L. Sharma: p. 60). It also involves a possibility that immigrants and their subsequent generations may 'modify' and 'reconstruct' their diasporic world in the hostland. And although the situation of the migrant and particularly a diasporic writer 'does create a sense of identity, such an identity is renegotiated from time to time in relation to the regional or national contexts within which it operates' (Assayag and Bénéï: pp. 10–11).

Adib Khan, the noted Bangladeshi-Australian writer, in his essay 'Trends in Australian Fiction', observes that in the last couple of decades 'the universe in Australian fiction has begun to creak open, but not without protests and frenetic writing about the perceived threats to mainstream culture' (2002: p. 1). Khan obviously is referring to a shift in Australia's literary landscape, that is, from Anglo-Celtic towards a multicultural one (see Helff, 2010). Taking on this as my reference point, this section is concerned with the theoretical ways in which this shift is accelerated in Australia's literary landscape by the South Asian diaspora writers who engage in the question of *locationality* in diverse forms and dynamic contexts. It also focuses on South Asian diaspora's widely agreed 'ability to recreate their cultures in diverse locations and locates the elements of the liminal within the nitty-gritty of this changing history' (Ray, 2003: p. 34).

It has been argued that migration has ambiguities of its own, based on two dialectics, that is, of 'belonging' and 'longing'. According to Peter van der Veer (1995), 'the theme of belonging opposes rootedness to uprootedness, establishment to marginality', while the 'theme of longing harps on the desire for change and movement, but relates this to the enigma of arrival, which brings a similar desire to return to what one has left' (p. 4). In this play between belonging and longing and as people of the twentieth century we all have been somehow marked by the experience of *dislocations*. It has played such a prominent role in 'the operative theoretical paradigm with which we have attempted to understand and explain the human condition and conditions of knowledge in our times' (Bammer: xii). Keeping in mind, the concepts of belonging and longing and the link between displacement, location, and fiction/story, it has been suggested by Wendy Walters (2005) that 'displacement creates a distance that allows writers to encode critiques of their homelands, to construct new homelands, and envision new communities' (p. viii).

A question that arises in mind is what are these *locations*? Locations, as discussed earlier, does not merely refer to geographical locations but, *locations* rather, provide 'a critical angle or perspective on cultural formations and emerging cultural capacities' (Chambers: p. 27) of the South Asian diaspora in Australia. Avtar Brah's distinction about 'borders' as metaphors and 'part of the discursive materiality of power relations' (1996: p. 198) can also be applied to these multiple *locations*. These *locations* like spaces thus can be understood as social and cultural characteristics (see S. Hussain: p. 104). These postmodern and postcolonial locations are 'stretched across multiple ruptures' between 'here and there' or both 'here *and* there and neither here *nor* there at one and the same time' – movement in space, movement in time, and movements in internal external consciousness (Bammer, 1994: p. xii).

So, whether the presumed South Asian migrant (subject/protagonist) is a student, a worker, a professional, a refugee, or in exile, his *location* 'depends on the routes and temporality of diasporic movement and determines the production of class, racial, and ethnic positionality' (Shukla: pp. 565–566).

According to Sissy Helff (2013), 'the way people live, move, and behave within a particular domestic space characterizes their social status, gender roles, and right to belong to this place at any particular moment' (p. 3). This in turn creates new room for dialogues on the nature of memory and space in the South Asian diasporic short stories or a new politics of sensory and spatial locations. The socio-historical experience of difference and construction of a subject is also done on the basis of these multiple locations. Because it is not just the 'historical subjectivity of a diaspora which holds the key to its cultural life' (Ray, 2003: p. 21) but also the locations and its politics that is played out between the majority and minority communities, this point warrants emphasis because 'the very strong association of notions of diaspora with displacement and dis*location* means that the experience of *location* can easily dissolve focus' (Brah, 2003: p. 615; emphasis added). My purpose in the next sections is to situate various discussions and theories in order to formulate a critique of politics of location*s*: memory and space.

Defining Racism

> It can hardly be denied that ignorance and prejudice towards Asian nations, cultures and peoples has figured prominently in our history. (Walker, 2007: p. 313)
>
> (...) the whisper on Asian streets, in cities, towns and villages, is that Australia is a racist country. (D'Cruz and Steele: p. 81)

Australia – the world's largest island and smallest continent – is easily, and most often, distinguished from the rest of the world by its history – 'a colony populated by people whom Britain had thrown out (but who) proved to be so loyal to the British Empire for so long' and its geography, 'red earth and its alien flora and fauna' (see Ferguson, 2003). The history of Australia is marked by an important phenomenon in the history of mankind – migration. Australia has, through migration, developed into one of the world's most culturally diverse societies. This increased diversity has brought with it many new cultural experiences and has undoubtedly made Australia a more vibrant and multicultural place. We know in a settler society, 'everyone is either a migrant or a self-conscious descendant of a migrant' (van der Veer: p. 2). This ethnic and racial diversity in Australia has also resulted in some cases Australia's confrontation with racism or negative stereotyping of the 'Other', as is reflected from observations in the above quotation. In Australia, the Chinese, Afghans, Jews, Greeks, Lebanese, and Vietnamese communities have at one or other time have been attacked by racist fundamentalists. Is it now the turn of South Asians?

Van Thanh Rudd, leader of the Revolutionary Socialist Party, and nephew of former Australian Prime Minister Kevin Rudd, openly proclaimed that most of the Australians are racist. He notes,

> There is a culture of racism that comes from our schools, our education system. The dominant culture in Australia is a racist culture. As a son of a Vietnamese mother, I too experienced racial abuse in school. (quoted in P. Sharma, 2010)

Despite these scathing comments, the original argument that was circulated by Australian media in the wake of 2007–2009 racist or opportunistic attacks on Indian students was that the whole thing was the brain child of the strongly sensationalist Indian media, which hyped the whole thing out of proportion. So, around 2010, Australian government and its various agencies working towards public and cultural diplomacy started using Indian media for an image correction process, as can be seen from the number of advertisements on promoting Australia as safe and tourist friendly destination. This has also resulted in a serious introspection and acknowledgement that racism is still a serious problem in Australia. The latest being on ABC-2 TV titled 'Dumb, Drunk and Racist'.[2] In this documentary, Australian journalist Joe Hildebrand was on a three weeks tour of Australia with selected Indian contestants to change their opinion about Aussies as dumb, drunk, and racist. According to journalist Michael Madigan (2012), we just need three words to describe everything:

> England is 'Superior, Conservative, Stoic,' America is 'Brash, Confident, Successful,' Italy is 'Exuberant, Festive, Food,' France is 'Cultured, Intelligent, Rude,' Switzerland is 'Staid, Pretty, and something about Chocolate,' Canada is 'Solid, Progressive, Tolerant,' while the image of Australia has changed from 'Friendly, Coarse, Irreverent' to Joe Hildebrand's 'Dumb, Drunk, and Racist.'

This image according to Hildebrand originated in Indian call centres where team leaders and staff were specially instructed by managers that Australia was the stupidest continent, populated largely by technologically backward drunkards or racist bastards. This book also uses three words 'Racism, Prejudice and Indifference' to explore the complex relationship between Australia and its Indian immigrant population – Westernized yet conservative in many ways (for a detailed discussion, see Jupp, 2001).

We know in a settler society, 'everyone is either a migrant or a self-conscious descendant of a migrant' (van der Veer, p. 2). This ethnic and racial diversity of Australia has resulted in some cases a vicious confrontation with racism, which is perpetuated by the negative stereotyping of the 'Other' (see Castles: p. 53). Today, social prejudice and racism are the two very unpleasant practices that are prevalent in both multicultural and monocultural societies throughout the world.[3] Perhaps, in contemporary times, 'this is a communal reaction to fear, a backlash against globalization that is perceived to be a threat to national identity' (A. Khan, 2001). Therefore, a diverse or cosmopolitan society founded on migration does bring with it a range of ever-changing issues and challenges.

The crucial question here is: Is Australia a racist country? According to Chris Gilligan (2009), everyone agrees that racism is 'a scourge, a malignant cancer which eats away at the body of a healthy society'. But we don't all agree about what racism is. Well the perception towards racism also depends on which dictionary definition you take into view. Defining racism in the Australian context is a difficult task as it is not a static notion:

- According to the *Oxford English Dictionary*: racism is a belief or ideology that all members of each racial group possess characteristics or abilities specific to that race, especially to distinguish it as being either superior or inferior from other racial group or racial groups.
- According to the *Merriam-Webster's Dictionary*: racism is a belief that race is the primary determinant of human traits and capacities and that racial differences produce an inherent superiority or inferiority of a particular racial group, and that it is also the prejudice based on such a belief.
- According to the *Macquarie Dictionary*: racism is the belief that human races have distinctive characteristics that determine

> their respective cultures, usually involving the idea that one's own race is superior and has the right to rule or dominate others.

Racism or social prejudices are a lived reality for many people in this part of the world, but it remains largely a silent or invisible issue.[4] According to the Australian government, there is no real evidence that racism as 'ideology' or as a 'belief' or as a 'dominant attitude' or as a 'state policy' (like apartheid) is increasing in Australia.[5] But in the past few years, it has been expressed in more open and violent ways towards Asians particularly the Indian subcontinental students (see Castles, 1992; Dunn, 2003; Hassan, 2005; Ghosh, 2009).[6] What we need to enquire here is precisely this – Is it necessary that racism be institutionalized?[7] Going back once again to the academic/scholarly definitions of racism, some sociologists have defined racism as a system of 'group privilege' – prejudice plus power.[8] The perpetuation of racism, as Ghassan Hage (2002) points out, is a collective social act and not the responsibility of individuals only:

> Violent racists are always a tiny minority. However, their breathing space is determined by the degree of 'ordinary' non-violent racism a government and culture allow to flourish within it. (p. 247)

Similarly, in *Portraits of White Racism* (1993), David Wellman has defined racism as 'culturally sanctioned beliefs, which, regardless of intentions involved, defend the advantages whites have because of the subordinated position of racial minorities' (p. x). Sunil Badami (2008), an Indian-Australian short story writer, recollects his growing up years in Australia being one of only three Indian kids at school, who were often called by diverse names such as 'Curry-muncher, towel-head, abo, coon, boong, darkie, nig-nog, golli-wog' (pp. 9–15). The assertions of white dominance, apart from these derogatory terms, have also resulted in 'curry bashing', which refers specifically to racist activities in which a section of Australians have engaged in the past few years – beating up or opportunistic attacks, totally unprovoked and random acts of violence that not necessarily involve robbery on Indian students or towards South Asians as common to this (see Baas, 2009). This race-based prejudice, violence, and dislike towards a particular minority group denote 'racism'.[9] However, there also exists significant protest against such incidents and support for the South Asian community (see Northrop, 2010).[10]

The ambiguity of such a situation is clearly reflected in the words of Sangeeta, one of the interviewed second-generation Indian women in Vijaya Joshi's book *Indian Daughters Abroad* (2000):

> I think to be accepting of other people is a typically Australian trait. (...) Australians are *willing to accept all the different cultures*. I know people will disagree with me on that point. (pp. 139–140; emphasis added)

She also adds:

> Maybe now *they're not so accepting* because economic times are bad; competition is greater. Now maybe they're starting to begrudge the fact that people from other nations are coming in, doing better. That is leading to some negative things about migrants. (p. 140; emphasis added)

Although an 'accepting' nation, but the sudden realization in the times of economic recession has made Australians suspicious of 'people from other nations' that are 'coming in'.[11] This sudden realization takes us directly into the psychological definition of racism that is also related to the growing visibility of South Asians today in almost every city of Australia that as a phenomenon was absent say three to four decades ago (see also G. Hassan, 2005).

So, is racism an 'attitude' or an irrational form of bigotry that exists apart from the organization of social structure in some fringe groups only? With reference to this, Ghassan Hage (1998) has persuasively suggested the utility of the binary concepts of 'spatial managers' and the 'spatially managed'. The 'spatial managers' are those who feel empowered to express an opinion about the country, and about who belongs, and who should be allowed into the national space. The spatially managed are those who have opinions expressed about them, where they should be put, what they're doing, where they should be sent back to, and so on.[12] Recent events tend to indicate that some groups of Anglo-Australians acted as spatial managers by reviving racism using symbols of 'white supremacist' views that are relics of the past and cultural hegemony for presenting a tendency of opposition and intolerance towards multiculturalism and multicultural symbols of state policy.[13] It is a known fact that all communities use symbols to make themselves visible (or audible!). But nations 'don't make symbols: people do'. The symbols that 'seek to foster unity within Australian society' are 'sometimes used to discriminate between who is Australian and who isn't' (Harper and White: p. 2). Similarly, the earlier colonial way of symbolizing nonbelonging or representing the South Asian migrants was that they were 'heathens, lazy, cunning and quarrelsome', who

> tended to cling tenaciously to their culture in order to make up for the loss on economic front or to cope with their status loss on the social front; that they were so carried away by their desire to grab wealth and power that they had no compunction at throwing the natives out of employment and power in the latter's own hands; and, that their difficulties in foreign countries were largely of their own making. (S.L. Sharma: p. 45)

This representation or negative labelling is a sad excuse to justify racial abuse, exploitation, and ignorance about 'Other' communities' positive role in the development of a nation (see Alatas, 1977). These situations have in some cases made migration to Australia from South Asia an increasingly complex phenomenon, as many migrants have to overcome psychological and sociological barriers, whether erected by passive tolerance or difference blindness, in their quest to make Australia their home.

The South Asian diaspora in Australia today is 'still developing, growing in number and diversity almost by the day' (Voigt-Graf: p. 142). As discussed in detail in Chapter 1, South Asians have migrated to Australia as workers, professionals, and students – for better studies, infrastructure, jobs, a better life, and a better future.[14] Compared with other migrant groups, South Asians have not formed ghettos in Australia and till a few years back were not 'subject of direct racial abuse' (Joshi: p. 18) or racial violence. But despite the two-centuries-long history, race now has started acting as a problematic issue, 'with its complex manifestations' in the daily lives of the immigrants and sometimes 'it goes unacknowledged, let alone articulated', the result being 'a blind, often intense racism' and unfounded racial prejudice towards the South Asian community (Bhattacharjee: p. 176; see also Stratton and Perera, 2009).

This blind racism, prejudice, and ignorance towards South Asian community has also sparked a debate on popular networking website Facebook (see J. Ghosh, 2009), reminding one of the 1981 'Blainey Debate'.[15] To reputed historian Geoffrey Blainey, immigrants and their multifarious cultures appeared to receive favoured treatment over native-born Australians. He further warned his fellow Australians of the danger of continued high levels of Asian immigration and particular unease over increased South Asian migration (see Langfield: p. 36). The fear of the 'Other' has also been effectively transformed into political capital[16] by the notorious Pauline Hanson[17] and her One Nation party – who tried to homogenize the official narrative by enforcing the idea of one nation, one culture (see Gopalkrishnan and Babacan: p. 3).

According to Monika Fludernik (2003a), these 'hate crimes are the reverse of a medal whose obverse portrays individuals who define themselves as representative of their respective (diasporic) communities' (p. xxii). The recent racist attacks on Indian students and taxi drivers, often stereotyped as representative of the South Asian community in Australia, or hostility towards recent immigrants from other ethnic communities, as already pointed out above, is an ambiguity. I would like to ask here, whether Benedict Anderson's (1983) claim that 'nation is imagined as *limited*' fits well for the Australian state too? Because Australian state that proposes to understand its various communities and at least a section of its people, who ironically belonging to both the majority and minority groups, fail to understand the 'finite elastic boundaries, beyond which lie other nations' or 'imagined communities' within Australia. It also fails or pretends not to understand that '(U)ltimately it is (the) fraternity that makes it (nation) possible' (Anderson: p. 7).

In Australia, the contemporary forms of racism and discrimination have shifted their focus away from biological notions of racism to cultural notions.[18] These are referred to as 'new racism' that includes cultural dimension, ethnic linkages, and assertion of certain religious beliefs (see Gopalkrishnan and Babacan: p. 5). Renata Salecl (1994) observes that old racism was a direct form of slotting people into essentialist categories so that the 'Other' was really a threat against 'Us'. In new racism, cultural difference is highlighted and it acts as a 'natural' determinative force that 'locks individuals and groups a priori into their cultural genealogy' (p. 12). It is then not a product of ignorance in the way it used to be earlier. Today racists blame their socio-economic environment for their acts, thus projecting themselves as victims of circumstances.

According to Chik Ling et al. (2004), 'the main problem with Asian-Australian communities and politics' is that they are 'largely voiceless' (p. 152). And thus 'accepting their political position of powerlessness, the Asians quietly pursue their occupations' (Tinker: p. 11). The silence has been there in spite of a long presence and various success stories in Australia.[19] In Australia, migrants from the Indian subcontinent represent a highly qualified group engaged in professional occupations (see Voigt-Graf: p. 155). Also, South Asia has been targeted by Australian educational institutions, 'often organizing aggressive marketing campaigns', and efforts have been 'successful' as far as 'India's bourgeoning middle class is concerned' (Voigt-Graf: p. 153). Moreover, Salim Lakha (2006) notes that 79 per cent of Indian residents in Australia take up citizenship (see pp. 385–387), which is applicable to other South Asian groups as well. The recent racist attacks on Indians in Australia have made the South Asian diaspora come out of the shadow, become visible, and voice its concerns.[20]

The question of 'how visible' South Asian diasporas or its writers are in Australia is very important (see Gelder and Salzman: p. 49). As majority of the South Asian diaspora writers examined in this study, except for a few, are probably 'little-known in the Australian literary community', which testifies to show 'how Anglo-Celtic, and Anglo-Australian', the 'community has been and still is' (Gelder and Salzman: p. 49). However, these writers and stories represent the growing heterogeneity of South Asian-Australian diasporic voices, thus reminding the scholars of diaspora and multicultural studies that 'racism is not the whole story, but neither can it be expunged from the story' (D'Cruz and Steele: p. 66).

Although my central concern, much narrower, in this study is restricted to an exploration of the politics of location in the genre of South Asian diasporic short stories in Australia, it is well worth exploring the process of immigration and the social attitudes of

Australians (both majority and minority groups) towards South Asians particularly post-recent racist (or 'opportunistic violence' as it was referred to by the concerned Australian authorities) attacks on the students from the Indian subcontinent. In an interview, Arnold Zable (2008), son of Polish-Jewish refugee parents, responding to the question on the anti-Greek riots in Kalgoorlie during World War I, notes that because of such violent attacks and hate crimes the islanders who came to Australia felt that they are really not a part of the Australian society. He further says:

> These riots are among our hidden narratives, darker episodes in Australian history that have been overlooked or conveniently forgotten. The riots, related incidents, and general distrust towards 'foreigners' did alienate many immigrants and it took a long time to build a sense of trust and belonging.[21]

White Australian literature[22] abounds in examples of 'darker episodes in Australian history', which helped in a nationalistic self-definition through racially stereotyping the 'Other' – in major cases the Asian (see Broinowski, 1992; Walker, 1999). This according to Graham Huggan (2007) is so because 'for all the ideological force of white Australia, Australian literature has no more been a relentless propaganda-machine for the production of racial and cultural stereotypes than has any other national literature' (p. 26). Similarly, the Australian government,[23] police,[24] and media's response[25] to the racist attacks on South Asians present how quickly they have created a 'well-fortified psychological defence mechanism' (Nandy, 2003: p. 6). The hypocrisy of the Australian authorities on racial and human rights violations has been well pointed out by D'Cruz and Steele (2003). They observe a huge 'gap between white Australian rhetoric on human rights violations outside Australia (say, in Asia) and its own failure on human rights issues within Australia, especially towards Aboriginal and Torres Strait Islander people (...)' (p. 9). This according to Hodge and Mishra (1991) is the continuing history of racism in Australian society and culture that is marked by the best known Australian mainstream writers' inadequacy and skirting of the issue of racism in their works and thereby confirming to social prejudices and a cultural amnesia as a 'defining quality of the Australian mind' (p. 14; see also Huggan: p. 31). Furthermore in Australian media and mainstream literature, South Asia is inscribed, 'positively or negatively', according to Australia's 'definition of itself, past, present and becoming' (Jose: p. 9).

So, are South Asians becoming 'victims of circumstances in the lands where they settle' (Tinker: p. ix)? Is the hard work and resulting affluence of South Asians becoming a problem for a section of Australian population? And are the diasporans 'regarded in terms of "images" or 'stereotypes'? The roots of contemporary racism are deeply steeped in historical processes. Contemporary racism and intolerance of specific cultural groups in Australia is likely linked to historic constructions of Australian national identity (see Rajkowski, 1987; Rizvi, 1996; Dunn, 2003). David Walker in *Anxious Nation* (1999) presented an examination of Australian responses to Asia (1850–1939) and demonstrated how the idea of 'Asia' then was essential for an 'invention' of an Australian nation. Today, in the era that is historically postcolonial, colonial attitudes and representations continue to circulate in Australia (see Alatas, 1977; D'Cruz and Steele, 2003). Graham Huggan's question – Is Australia still postcolonial? – becomes relevant under present circumstances. Australia is a product of British colonialism, a settler society, populated by people whose ancestors travelled from elsewhere during and after the colonial period (Stratton and Ang: p. 135). Its 'cultural, political and economic ties with Britain remain strong' (Huggan: p. 27). So, the 'virus of Australian racism', according to D'Cruz and Steele, arrived possibly 'as an unwitting cultural inheritance of the British imperial and racist mantle in the 18th and 19th centuries' (p. 59). They further note that the

> lava of racism is always there in Australia and for some periods it may be publicly inactive; mostly it splutters and simmers below the surface. From time to time the lava of Australian racism bursts forth, singeing mainstream Anglo relations with Aboriginal and Torres Strait Islander and Asian others, before again receding to a quite simmer. (p. 66)

Moreover, racism in Australia has been documented since the arrival of Europeans in 1788 – in fact 'settlement was based on racism'. White settler opposition and racism was seen also in the violent riots of 1857 and 1880s.[26] According to Stephen Castles (1992),

> In the colonial period, *settlement was based on racism and genocide* against the aboriginal population, while the colonies were integrated into the British Empire as suppliers of raw materials, such as wool, wheat and gold. The imperial state took an active role in providing workers for expansion through convict labour, assisted passages, and the encouragement of free settlement. When the surplus population of Britain was insufficient for Australian labour needs from the mid-nineteenth century, Britain supported Australian employers in their demand for cheap labour from elsewhere in the Empire: China, India and the South Pacific Islands. (...) Hostility towards Chinese and other Asian workers took on a violent character. The exclusionary boundaries of the emerging Australian nation were drawn on racial lines, and one of the first Acts of the new Federal Parliament in 1901 was the introduction of the White Australia Policy. (pp. 53–54; emphasis added)

Immigration control through Immigration Restrictions Act (1901), popularly known as the White Australia Policy, was in many ways institutionalized racism. This tradition of racism towards non-Europeans and any non-British nationalities was carried forward for a long time. It must be remembered that the granting of citizenship[27] to Aborigines (1967) and the abolition of the White Australia Policy (1973) are still events in recent history and the 'deeply ingrained racial stereotypes – such as the concept of the "yellow peril" – have yet to be overcome' (Castles: p. 68) by Australians. Also, the various census figures clearly demonstrate that Australia will remain 'a predominantly European country' with respect to its ethnic composition well into the twenty-first century. The demographic facts are indeed 'a far cry from the myth of "Asianisation" of Australia arising from claims made by One Nation and other groups such as Australians Against Further Immigration' (Jayasuriya and Pookong: p. 21). This threat or fear of 'Asia' or mass generalizations about the 'idea,' which is Asia and of 'Asian hordes' is well commented upon by the noted Australian historian David Walker in his in-depth and critical study *Anxious Nation*. Walker reveals an unfounded fear of 'Asianisation' of Australia. In the cases that recently happened in Australia, it can be said that 'it is easier to come from immigrant stock than to be an immigrant' (M. Israel: p. 376).

As a settler society, Australia depended on sustained immigration for its economic development and national security (see Stratton and Ang: p. 151). W.M. Hughes stated in 1901 that: 'our chief plank is, of course, a white Australia. There is no compromise about that! The industrious coloured brother has to go – and remain away' (quoted in Langfield: 31). On the issue of South Asian immigration, James Jupp (1988/2001) has rightly observed that it has been 'a constant theme in Australia since 1788 but has often been curiously overlooked or under-stressed by historians' (p. 3). The White Australia Policy's infamous European language test was partially devised with Indians (who were known to be fluent in English) in mind. The question then is, does racial prejudice still remain a feature of Australian society, that is, despite the existence of antidiscriminatory legislation, various multicultural policies, and 'the rhetoric about equity and access' (Langfield: p. 37; see also Hugo: p. 136)? The Australian state now, according to Stratton and Ang (1998),

> shamelessly flirts, for economic reasons, with the idea of 'enmeshment with Asia', the cultural status of Australians of Asian descent in 'multicultural Australia' is still a fragile one. While (...) migrants of Asian region are now considered an integral part of Australia's ethnic mix, these groups are still collectively racialised whenever a wave of moral panic about Asian immigration flares up. At such moments, the old collusion of race and culture is reinstated. (p. 159)

One of the common assertions of contemporary times that 'Australia has always been a multicultural society' is both 'trite and historically misleading' (Stratton and Ang: p. 157).

Rowan Ayres (1997), a former BBC producer resident in Australia, puts the Australian concern and anxiety in these words:

> Australians still think their territory is being eroded. Strangers, foreigners, whatever you like, are beginning to take over the country. And I think that is turning them into a slightly anxious, slightly frightened and slightly racist kind of nation. (p. 7)

On the same issue, writing from a different perspective, Australian social researcher Hugh Mackay (1993) concludes that underlying the widespread sense of 'anxiety' about their cultural identity, which a large number of Australians suffer as they adapt to life, is a symptom of the 'age of redefinition' (pp. 16–17; see also D'Cruz and Steele: p. 34). So, keeping in mind the above arguments and debates, it is not wrong to say that 'except perhaps in South Africa, the ideology of racial superiority was probably more powerfully developed and imposed in Australia than in any other settler country' (Melleuish and Stokes: p. 113).

Juxtaposing two very different pictures, sadly, while South Asians were and are being episodically targeted by racist attacks in Australia, significantly, 'voices of many Australians remain silent, and among these are some recognized in Asian cities soliciting favours in business dealings of various types, including educational and development projects' (D'Cruz and Steele: p. 11). So, predominantly, racism still persists in the common psyche of Australians because the privileged community have not pressurized the government and other organizations to undertake strict measures to maintain racial harmony. On the other hand, this lack is subsumed by the kindness or positive action of some and assertions, like Rajender Singh Gabbi's (1998), that

> Australia is a 'lucky country' as it is free from any social infighting or unrest and it is safe. It is a country of opportunities and anyone who has self-confidence and determination to do better, can be successful. (p. 185)

There have been similar claims by smaller groups who have also successfully carried out campaigns through e-mails and popular networking websites such as Facebook for racial harmony and tolerance (see Northrop, 2010). These people (of both South Asian and Australian origin) reflect a positive image of Australia: 'Australia (that) provides migrants with a secure environment, freedom from political persecution, opportunities for education and training, and the possibility of a better life' (Langfield: p. 28), thus presenting how Australia represents future opportunities for students, businessmen, and professionals. But the proponents of 'closer trading ties with Asia' often face 'vociferous and often vituperative opposition from Australian nationalists' (Walker, 2007: p. 320).

Another significant question worth our concern was also raised by D'Cruz and Steele: Why do Australian textbooks, particularly history textbooks, often fail to highlight the positive contributions made to Australia by South Asians? During Prime Minister John Howard's national speech on 26 January 2006, he called for a 'root and branch renewal of the teaching of Australian history in schools' and also talked about a 'coalition of the willing' to undertake this task. His concerns related to the limited time devoted to Australian history in the curriculum and a focus on themes and issues at the expense of chronology and narrative. However, South Asian diaspora's capacity to contribute on an equal footing to Australian cultural life was again neglected. As Deborah Henderson (2004) notes,

> Given such global and regional realities it seems puzzling that the Howard government does not advocate the study of Asia in the education system and support education policies for future generations to be inter-culturally skilled. (p. 9)

She further notes that Australian students 'must be prepared for the rewarding and complex challenge of engaging with the Asian region and Australia's Asia-knowledge base should be supported by specific school-based Asian cultures strategies' (p. 10).

Notably, with an ever-increasing knowledge about Australia in South Asia, regarding economic opportunities, the volume of South Asian migration to Australia has been augmented since 1980s. There is a 'combination of push and pull factors: the push of inadequate opportunity in South Asia and the pull of better prospects' in Australia (Tinker: p. 10). And 'the positive and negative experiences' of international students and workers from South Asia while studying in Australia cannot but 'impinge on broader relations between Australia and the Asia-Pacific region' (D'Cruz and Steele: p. 77).

One is here reminded of Pandit Jawaharlal Nehru's declaration in Singapore on 18 March 1946:

> India cannot forget her sons and daughters overseas. Although India cannot defend her children overseas today, the time is soon coming when her arms will be long enough to protect them. (quoted in Kudaisya: p. 84)

Furthermore, Nehru explained the complexity of the hyphenated identities of Indians to the Indian Assembly on 8 March 1948. He said:

> Now these Indians abroad, what are they? Are they Indian citizens – are they going to be citizens of India or not? If they are not, then our interest in them becomes cultural, humanitarian and not political. (quoted in Kudaisya: p. 84)

Postcolonial India's policy towards its diaspora was deeply informed by Nehru, who was also the Foreign Minister. In the realm of foreign policy, he enjoyed the greatest freedom of action. With his wide vision and cosmopolitan background, he was a visionary of the cosmopolitan ethos and was convinced that it was in the 'best interest of overseas Indians to integrate into their host societies' (Kudaisya: p. 86). He repeatedly argued for them to 'identify themselves with and integrate in the mainstream of social and political life of the country of their domicile' (Kudaisya: p. 86).

However, William Safran (1991) opines that this forceful integration has resulted in mistreatment of the 'members of diaspora communities' by the groups of people in the host country as 'strangers within the gates' or their exploitation for 'the sake of the domestic and diplomatic interests of the host country' (p. 92). In addition, this threat or attitude towards new migrants is also heightened by the influence, participation, challenge, and pressure that the government of homeland yields on hostland. Such an example was seen in the case of Indian government's attitude in recent racist and opportunistic attacks on South Asian students in various cities of Australia – a direct result of Australian government's 'unwillingness to engage with immigration policy issues relating to recruitment or settlement' (Jayasuriya, 2008: p. 1). Although India has been unable to push forth the issue, its engagement with Australia significantly started since Hawke–Keating era (1983–1996). This is also because

> While oil and water are the most important physical factors of international politics at the beginning of the twenty-first century, the most important human factors are population and migration. (McLaren: p. 36)

Thus, concerns about the well-being of migrants have also been expressed in some of the other Asian countries.

Much has changed in Australia and South Asia in the last few decades. The issue of migration to Australia has become more 'controversial at both ends of the migration chain' (Sullivan and Gunasekaran: p. 157). The composition and volume of the recent migration stream has shifted significantly. This new wave of migration has a number of positive characteristics focusing on occupation, language skills, and educational background – students, skills, professional, and entrepreneurs. But, in recent years, many people in Australia believe that they see in migration, particularly, of South Asian students (with intention to settle permanently) and people a threat to their Anglophone (or the dominant) culture and society (see Dunn, 2003). This threat is heightened by the presence of alien dresses, languages, smells, literature, and code of behaviour (also see M. Israel, 1991). This 'cultural shock' is not one sided, it is equally important in the case of new migrants who plunge into unfamiliar behaviour patterns, sociocultural values, and morals. This presence not just as 'Little Indias' but also in the mainstream jobs and localities challenges the comfortable and stable world of individuals who thought the country to be 'their' home or conceived themselves as being Australian. With the presence of large number of 'highly educated and skilled professionals and business people among the "new" migrants', the prejudiced section of Australians must very soon do a 'rethinking' of the 'theoretical frameworks' (Inglis and Wu: p. 195).

As discussed earlier, Australia as a country has always depended on immigration for its population, but as in the early years of settlement, each successive wave was given time to settle and be absorbed before the next one arrived (Banchevska: p. 177). Today, with the incoming of a large number of students, workers, and refugees from South Asia and people from many more countries within the existing population, it has become difficult to understand the 'Other' vis-à-vis assimilation at such a rapid pace. But on the other hand, it can be argued that we are living in an age when it is more than ever possible to overcome barriers of language and culture and communicate with 'Others' on the same ground. It is an age where divergence has taken the form of multiculturalism, that is, a favourable and enlightened response towards 'Other' cultures existing within Australia (Manning: p. 178).

At present, the Australian national objective, to which the government is committed, is to focus on multiculturalism and encourage what is called 'unity within diversity'.[28] Obviously, a question arises about the motives that led Australia to go for multiculturalism during 1970s. According to John Clark (1997),

> Understanding cultural flows necessitates paying a lot of attention to the type of cultural flow, to what is produced, and who produces it. But we should also look at the receivers, or gate-keepers for reception. If egalitarian openness may characterise the attitudes of some recent migrants, in immigrant cultures closedness more often characterises the long settled. Being in control of the already established cultural values is a good way of privileging the long settled over both newcomers and the new and the best way to keep control over those values is not to tell newcomers what they really are. Australia does not have a universal and public set of common values deriving from traditional society nor is it based on the historical disjunction of a war of independence with its legitimating revolutionary myths. Access to either would give immigrants ideological claim to challenge the long settled. (p. 207)

This particular attention towards the type of 'cultural flow' and other related issues present before the Australian government in the shape of migrants from Asian and other continents resulted in understanding multiculturalism as solely a policy.

Australia's going in favour of a multicultural policy during 1970s was the result of incoming stream of migrants post-World War II, when a large number of migrants came to Australia as new settlers and refugees. This gradually created new larger diasporas among various cultures. Vijay Mishra (2002) observes that for the people in these new diasporas 'race and ethnicity are linked to questions of justice, self-empowerment, representation, equal opportunity, and definitions of citizenry' (p. 236). Some particular concerns in relation to their contribution to providing a concrete shape and identity to Australia are its society, culture, and economy. Skilled labour and competent professionalism have been both vital factors in giving shape to the Australian multicultural policy.

It was Al Grassby, the Minister of Immigration, who in 1970s argued in favour of increasing the 'diversity of the Australian society' that was till now considered to be a strongly traditional Anglo-Celtic or a white-dominated society (see Huggan: p. 129). So by 1989, a *National Agenda for a Multicultural Australia* was adopted. The policy of multiculturalism was also comprehensively used to refer to the cultural diversity more largely counting the diversity represented by Australia's Aboriginal and Torres Strait Islander peoples. It incorporated three principles for multicultural policy, which are as follows:

1. *Cultural Identity*: the right of all Australians, within carefully defined limits, to express and share their individual cultural heritage, including their language and religion;
2. *Social Justice*: the right to equality of treatment and opportunity, and the removal of barriers of race, ethnicity, culture, religion, gender, or place of birth;
3. *Economic Efficiency*: the need to maintain, develop, and utilise effectively the skills and talents of all Australians, regardless of their background. (*National Agenda for a Multicultural Australia*: p. 14)

Later on, the opinion makers and academicians started mounting stress on 'civic values' and on Australian 'citizenship' as one of the strongest unifying symbol in this culturally and linguistically diverse nation. According to Alaistair Bonnett (2000), the institutionalized versions of anti-racism are concerned with racism 'as a destabilizing influence upon "good community relations", "social cohesion" and "national unity"' (pp. 4–5). It also aims to regulate and control destabilizing influences, assert moral norms, chastise and punish transgressors, and prescribe etiquette. Australian government presents integration and tolerance as antidotes to socially disruptive racism (see Gilligan, 2009). But this pressure, according to Ghali Hassan (2005), has often resulted in a shallow multiculturalism that is being promoted by politicians and the media, creating an impression of ghettoized and marginalized communities 'not living together but living next to each other' and against each other.

Even if we assume that people of South Asian origin, particularly the second and third generations, have integrated publicly into the mainstream, while keeping certain aspects of their cultural life alive at home, what about the postassimilation mainstream Australians' attitude towards them? According to Fazal Rizvi (1996),

> Australians have been asked to make a decisive ideological shift in their thinking, away from the colonialist frame that has

> traditionally informed their perceptions of Asia to a post-colonial outlook which challenges the racist assumptions of cultural dominance and superiority. Yet most of their attempts to revise their thinking have at best been clumsy, with the new practices of representation failing to make a decisive break from the residual racist expressions that had rendered Asians as a homogenised mass, socially inept and culturally inferior. (p. 173)

So, the closest designation that we currently have for this attitude of neglect and indifference towards a particular community is racism – 'a reduction of someone from a particular group to the stereotypes, negative or positive, we have of that group' (Chow: p. 27).

There is of course much more that could be written about the logic of racial (in)differences, and the ways in which racial tensions can be resolved.[29] However, this issue will provide a constant backdrop to my discussion of these selected narratives (in Chapter 6). Australia has however accepted its failures to save its multicultural legacy and has taken responsibility for any 'hate/opportunistic attacks' on South Asian and other migrant groups. It also aims to educate the future younger generations to foster respect for multi-ethnicities in cultural formations.

It is difficult to proceed much further without indicating more clearly, what words such as diaspora and South Asianness mean, as these are the themes and issues that also go into the creative processes and are very much essential to diasporic literary studies. Drawing from the subjects of anthropology, migration studies, cultural studies, sociology, and political science, this study will examine the politics of location and problem of diaspora–hostland–homeland relationship as reflected through the medium of short stories by South Asian diaspora.

Defining Diaspora

> If change of residence were the chief criterion of *diaspora*; if, moreover, crossings, migrations and travel are a part of the history of all humanity; then a clearer notion of boundaries will be required to distinguish the different kinds of dis*location* we suffer. (Paranjape, 2000: p. 229; emphasis added)

Modern era is an era of unprecedented human mobility, global migration, and scholarly discourse on migration and in this respect it may be said that it is an era that belongs to South Asia as it features significantly in the dynamics of migration not only in Asia but also in the world (see Haque, 2005). While for some 'the societal diversity created by global migration is a cause for celebration, for many others the growing presence of "foreign" peoples give rise to concerns about the ability of national societies and national citizenship to cope with and to accommodate cultural differences' (Nagel: p. 231). There has been a veritable explosion of interest in diasporas since the late 1980s. But the term *diaspora* acquired a scholarly currency only in 1990s. Diaspora as a concept has travelled beyond communities, disciplines, and generalizations. It is an historical formation that has caught the attention of a number of scholars and has 'become a breeding ground for new sociological concepts within scholarly work' (Y. Hussain: p. 5). Through a continuously growing theoretical literature, scholars across national spaces have responded to the concept and discourse of diaspora from different academic locations. In what seems to be a controversial statement, Vijay Mishra (1996a) says: 'All diasporas are unhappy but every diaspora is unhappy in its own way' (p. 189). We are reminded by Robert Sellick (2004) that diaspora is:

> first and foremost a political process, beginning with decisions taken by European governments to establish colonies, for whatever reasons. It was not only people who were dispersed across the globe, but also assumptions and attitudes, structures and institutions that had their origins in various 'homelands'. (p. 1)

There is attached a multidisciplinary nature to diaspora studies, as James Clifford (1994) notes that the diasporic language 'appears to be replacing, or at least supplementing, minority discourse' (p. 311). Today, research on diaspora is conducted from numerous academic perspectives as debates on diaspora are spread across a range of disciplines, encompassing sociology, anthropology, geography, human geography, migration studies, culture studies, politics, international relations, race, multiculturalism, postcolonialism, political economy, and communication (see also Karim, 2003).

My aim in the following discussion is to chart out and explore various theoretical approaches and analytical possibilities of conceptualizing the term *diaspora* that can supplement the narratives of South Asian diaspora in Australia as diaspora is a particular 'way of imagining, inventing, constructing, and presenting the self' (Klimt and Lubkemann: p. 146) in different ways from the mainstream society. Today, the notion of diaspora, as opposed to 'collectivities of immigrants or people living outside their homelands, used first in classical world, has acquired renewed importance' (R. Cohen, 1996). Therefore, any study related to the diaspora must begin by qualifying this term, with its chequered and complex history, as a point-of-entry.

Diaspora evoked the dispersion of people linked to political misfortunes or to commerce. The word derives from the Greek words *dia* ('through' or 'over') and *speiro* ('dispersal' or 'to sow widely'), also implying 'dispersion' or 'forcible dispersion' as found in Deuteronomy (28:25). First used in the *Septuagint*, the Greek translation of the Hebrew scriptures explicitly intended for the Hellenic Jewish communities in Alexandria (circa third century BCE) to describe the Jews living in exile from the homeland of Palestine, diaspora suggests a dislocation from the nation-state or geographical location of origin and a relocation in one or more nation states, territories, or countries. The term *diaspora* then has religious significance that pervaded medieval rabbinical writings on the Jewish diaspora, to describe the plight of Jews living outside of Palestine (Braziel and Mannur: p. 1). In religious terminology, this scattering of people was seen as a punishment to those who had forsaken the righteous path and good old ways. For a long time, it has been associated specifically with the violent dispersal of the Jewish people – that filled them with anxiety and distrust (R. Cohen, 1996: p. 512). However, post-1948, when Israel became a nation for Jews, the land 'promised' to them in the Biblical myth, diaspora no longer remained a term used only for the displaced Jews. A large number of Jews preferred to stay on in their countries of adoption or refuge due to the political turmoil of Israel and its relations with the neighbouring countries. As a result, diaspora as a term could no longer refer to Jews alone as in theory at least, they could 'go back home'. The usage of the term has been subsequently extended, changed, and expanded to other violent and forced human dispersals such as those of the Armenian and African people. People of African origin, with the painful history of slavery, descendants of indentured labourers, people of Chinese origin displaced through cultural revolution, and many others who had been transported, displaced, or exiled due to the workings of the European imperialism also began to be seen in the same framework of the diaspora. Finally, voluntary migrants and their descendants, the second generations, were also included.

Increasingly, however, the word, diaspora, has come to refer to the resettlement of identifiable communities of people across the globe, not necessarily violent or forced and the present study employs the term in this larger contemporary meaning. Diaspora has not just itself become a much-contested term, but has led to problematization of other terms such as nationality, ethnicity, and hybridity (inbetweenness or antibelonging). The most widely held view about the Indian subcontinental diaspora is the one adopted by Rabindranath Tagore – 'The civilization of India, like the banyan tree, has shed its beneficent shade away from its own birthplace. (...) India can live and grow by spreading abroad – not the political India, but the ideal India' (quoted in Tinker: p. iii). As D. Dayan (1988) observes, 'diaspora' is more of an

> intellectual construction tied to a given narrative. (...) incarnations of existing discourses, interpretants of such discourses, echoes or anticipations of historical projects. (p. 110)

The metaphor of the living tree or the banyan tree that Tagore has used provides a sense of centre and rootedness. It can be argued that it has been so often used by the intellectuals for the diasporic condition, that it now seems a cliché, mere decorative jargon overlooking the pain and unhappiness of dislocation and other aspects of migration. According to Mohit Manoj Prasad (2005),

> The diaspora is much a product of history as it is a performance of the narrative acts of inscribing place, people, event, incident, accident, coincidence, causality and the official record in contradictory practices of living/dying, dis/location, and of dying/living and dis/location as cycle. (...) Diasporas begin with moments of displacement with its insistent reasons for causality that begins

the remove of a people, of place, of identities and representations. (p. 12)

In the works of major immigrant authors, diaspora stands for traumas and pains of human displacement.

Khachig Tölölyan (1994) has tracked applications of the term that include references to 'corporate diasporas' and even an 'egg cream diaspora' (p. 235). There are several other views regarding the contemporary significance associated with this dislocation and relocation of people around the world.[30] In his famous article titled 'Diasporas in Modern Societies' (1991), discussing the concept of formation of diaspora and the application of this term to other than Jewish communities – most notably 'expatriates, expellees, political refugees, alien residents, immigrants, and ethnic minorities' (p. 83) – William Safran highlighted nine key points or 'common features' of the diasporic phenomenon. These are as follows:

1. Dispersal from an original homeland, often traumatically, to two or more foreign regions.
2. Alternatively, the *expansion* from a homeland in search of work, in pursuit of trade or to further colonial ambitions.
3. A *collective memory* and myth about the homeland, including its location, history and achievements.
4. An *idealization* of the putative ancestral home and a collective commitment to its maintenance, restoration, safety and prosperity, even to its creation.
5. The development of a *return movement* which gains collective approbation.
6. A strong ethnic *group-consciousness* sustained over a long time and based on a sense of distinctiveness, a common history and the belief in a common fate.
7. A *troubled relationship* with host societies, suggesting a lack of acceptance at the least or the possibility that another calamity might befall the group.
8. A *sense-of-empathy-and-solidarity* with co-ethnic members in other countries of settlement.
9. The *possibility of a distinctive yet creative and enriching life* in host countries with a tolerance for pluralism. (p. 83; emphasis added)

As some of the definitions have been rather restrictive in defining diasporic communities across the globe, Khachig Tölölyan in 'Rethinking Diaspora(s)' (1996) suggests a tighter definition of this concept and puts forth the following criteria:[31]

1. The diaspora has its origin in the fact that a large number of individuals were forced to leave their country by severe political, economic, or rather other constraints.
2. Before leaving their country, these people already shared a well-defined identity.
3. Diasporic communities actively maintain or construct a *collective memory*, which forms a fundamental element of their identity.
4. These communities keep more or less tight control over their ethnic boundaries, whether voluntarily or under constraints from the host society.
5. Communities are mindful to maintain relations among themselves.
6. They also wish to maintain contacts with their country of origin, provided it is still in existence. (p. 16; emphasis added)

Here too, diasporas differ from other migrant communities or people by their desire to maintain relations with their own location or ancestral land through a 'collective memory'. So, one of the key points in considering a diasporic community is 'group consciousness' or retention of 'a collective memory, vision, or myth about their original homeland, its physical *location*, history, and achievements' (Safran: p. 83; emphasis added; see also Safran, 1999). In the words of French social scientist Michel Bruneau, this can be summed up as 'a conscious and factual claim to an ethnic or national identity' (quoted in Dorais: p. 4).

Also, diasporas have largely been identified or defined in terms of social or economic power they yield, that is, the development of a triadic political or economic relationship. Vijay Mishra in the diaspora double issue of *SPAN* offers a three-tier definition of diaspora as a corrective to the original OED (1989 ed.) related to the dispersion of the Jews.

1. Relatively homogeneous, displaced communities brought to serve the Empire (slave, contract, indenture, etc.) co-existing

with indigenous/other races with markedly ambivalent and contradictory relationship with the Motherland(s). Hence the Indian diasporas of South Africa, Fiji, Mauritius, Guyana, Trinidad, Surinam, Malaysia; the Chinese diaspora of Malaysia, Indonesia linked to high (classical) Capitalism.

2. Emerging new diasporas based on free migration and linked to late capitalism: post-war South Asian, Chinese, Arab, Korean communities in Britain, Europe, America, Canada, Australia.
3. Any group of migrants that sees itself on the periphery of power, or excluded from sharing power. (quoted in Paranjape, 2001b: p. 3)

Being a diasporan, 'based on free migration and linked to late capitalism', is a win-win situation or a 'privileging situation' in economic terms according to Paranjape, which is not any longer 'an anguished state' because of further possibilities of 'bi-culturalism' (Preface: p. vi).

With reference to bi-culturalism, diaspora can be 'minimally defined' according to John Docker (2001) as 'a sense of belonging to more than one history, to more than one time and place, more than one past and future' (p. vii). He further observes that

> Diaspora suggests belonging to both here and there, now and then. Diaspora suggests the omnipresent weight of pain of displacement from a land or society, of being an outsider in a new one. Diaspora suggests lack and excess of loss and separation, yet also the possibility of new adventures of identity and the continued imagining of unconquerable countries of the mind. (pp. vii–viii)

Although there are complexities of defining a diaspora or possibilities of 'new adventures of identity', no fixed definition of diaspora related to a particular geographical location can be offered or reached to. Kim D. Butler (2001) has proposed 'shifting the defining element of diaspora studies from the group itself to a methodological and theoretical approach to the study of phenomenon of diaspora in human history' (pp. 193–194). For this, Butler has provided the following five dimensions that are unique to diasporas to facilitate research and studies:

1. Reasons for, and conditions of, the dispersal;
2. Relationship with the homeland;
3. Relationship with hostlands;
4. Interrelationships within communities of the diaspora, and
5. Comparative studies of different diasporas. (p. 195)

The historical discourse of the diaspora then may be seen as 'a way of replacing or supplementing the majority/minority binary discourse' (Dorais: p. 6) in life and literature. Isidore Okpewho (2001) further defines diaspora as 'a global space, a worldwide web, that accounts as much for the mother continent as for wherever in the world her offspring may have been driven by the unkind forces of history' (p. xiv). This diasporic discourse based on a methodology using historical framework also provides a meaningful dimension to the whole transnational experience and further develops solidarity with co-ethnics in other countries (Dorais: p. 7).

It is clear from the discussion above that 'Diasporic discourses frame terms of argument rather than terms of definition' (Klimt and Lubkemann: p. 148). Taking into account all the definitions of diaspora, it can be said that there is a very fine line between transnational migration and pure diasporas. The term *diaspora* can be restricted to, according to Glick Schiller, 'dispersed populations who attribute their common identity, cultural beliefs and practices, language, or religion to myths of a common ancestry' (quoted in Dorais: pp. 7–8).

It can also be noted that the metaphorical figure of the diasporan occupies here a 'third space' and is therefore considered to be a link between homeland and hostland. But if we study closely, there is always a push and pull factor involved in it. Homeland with its sociocultural aspects tries to attract these diasporans towards itself, and similarly the hostland with its 'opening' policies, incentives of monetary gains, and equal status situations tries to push these diasporans into its own politics and culture. Resulting in what John A. Armstrong (1976) distinguishes as the 'mobilized diasporas' (the elite) and the 'proletarian diasporas' (the exploited).

Figure 1 *Circular Model of Settling in the Hostland*

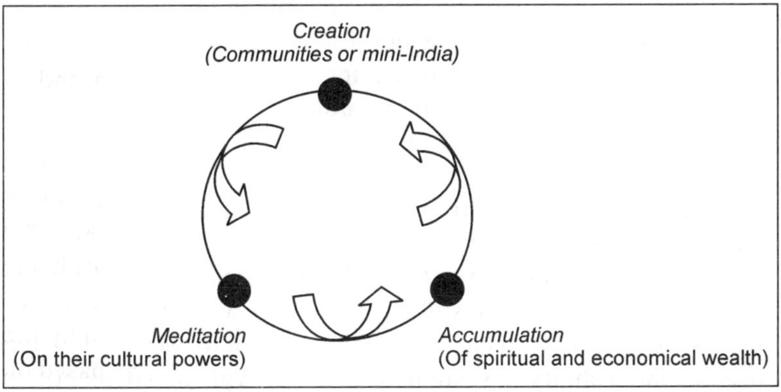

Using the framework of diaspora studied so far, I would like to propose a simple point in relation to the movement and settlement of the diasporans in various hostlands – What happens when the diasporans start to cross over the 'transit' points after some years/generations rather than living in between? They in this hypothesis, just like the original Hindu myth of Trishanku, must initiate new flows and movements and start a new cycle, which continues with every new diasporan's arrival into the hostland, as he or she brings something 'new' and 'valuable' in terms of his/her sociocultural baggage. This process of settling down in hostland can be explained with the help of Figure 1 that results in a *paraspara* (mutual and equal) contribution towards both the homeland and hostland. In the proposed concept of *paraspara*, migration is 'a two-way process' that does not involve the migrant alone, it also 'involves those who make up the environment (physical and social), that the migrant is now part of, unobtrusively and gently, or violently and relentlessly, in appositive, negative or neutral manner' (De Jong: p. 3).

As an immigrant leaves his or her homeland and arrives in the hostland, the process of 'Creation' starts as he or she feels a need to settle down comfortably in this new land with known things or referents of the past. So, he or she tries to create mini-homelands or similar communities as existed in the homeland. As the communities start building up, these diasporans start the next process, that is, of 'Meditation'. Now, they strive to assert their cultural powers in the hostland and get the best bargain in terms of equal rights and status. This assertion benefits them not only in the emotional and spiritual areas in the hostland but also in the economic standing. Finally, the diasporans feel ready for the last process, which is 'Accumulation' of wealth and its utilization in protecting and promoting the core values of Indian culture in both the homeland and hostland.

This is a kind of bi-culturalism or double cultural orientation – towards both the country of origin and the country of adoption, which is not a contradictory phenomenon as it initially looks to be. Actually, some people postglobalization, now with homes and businesses in two (or even more than two) countries, are showing an astonishing ability to sustain 'double' or 'hyphenated' identities or diaspora consciousness, with strong cultural ties and contributions towards both homeland and hostland. These are the people who now travel more frequently and for longer distances are spreading out (see Massey, 1994; Paranjape, 2001c). This has also led to a new category of highly mobile diasporans, better known as 'Transnationals', who are moving in and around the metropolitan centres of the world, resisting a precise definition. These are the groups who are really in a sense, in charge of 'time-space compression', who can really use it and turn it to advantage of the diasporic community, whose power and influence it very definitely increases (Massey, 1994).

How, then, might one clearly define or establish a concept of diaspora? Having reviewed the changing meanings of diaspora its differences and tensions, I use the term *diaspora* with care to refer to historical and contemporary presence of people of the Indian subcontinent with common national origin or ancestry who reside outside a claimed or an independent home territory in other parts of the world. They preserve their diversity as a transnational ethnic community and contribute positively towards both the cultures. So the concept of diaspora, while focusing on transnational processes and commonalities, does so by deploying a notion of ethnicity, which privileges the 'point of origin' in constructing identity and solidarity (see Anthias, 1998). A point also made by James Clifford (1997), when he suggests that the immigrants think globally but live locally. This constant negotiation with one's roots and routes through memory, nostalgia, history, and most of all through metaphoric *journeys* or *locations* is one characteristic of the diasporic communities, which makes it possible and pertinent to study diaspora-diasporic literatures as a separate category. The diasporic discourse in this context becomes stronger in terms of the four-part process of 'displacement, detachment, uprooting and dispersion' (Kirshenblatt-Gimblet: p. 339), while at the same time it is crucial to take into account the unique and multifarious causes that inform this process ranging from colonial migration, political exile, professional ambition to simply the desire to cross the seas in search of a 'better life'. A view very similar to Stuart Hall's (2000), who writes:

> Diaspora does not refer us to those scattered tribes whose identity can only be secured in relation to some sacred homeland to which they must at all costs return (...). The diaspora experience as I intend it here is defined, not by essence of purity, but by the recognition of a necessary heterogeneity and diversity. (p. 235)

Hall's emphasis on the terms 'heterogeneity' and 'diversity' is important to the focus of my study. I am not looking for commonalities of expression in the short stories of South Asian diaspora, but I am more interested in analysing the ways in which they write or interpret their multiple *locations*. As already discussed, the term *diaspora* in the classic theoretical framework and analysis of diasporic literature is concentrated more on the reasons and conditions of migration, as well as on integration and assimilation issues in host societies.

Defining South Asianness: Social and Theoretical Identities

> The identity of South Asians (throughout the world) has proved to be problematic, both for the self-identification of the group and for the identifying institutions and popular perceptions of the host society. (Koshy, 1998: p. 285)

The term *South Asian Diaspora* allows for the 'encompassing of a wider range of people and experiences' (Selvadurai: 5) and diversity of region, language, religion, custom, and tradition of the Indian subcontinent. It also provides some measure of inclusion within Australia, even if it is almost meaningless within South Asia itself. According to Vijay Prashad (1999), the cultural commonalities between the dominant migrant groups of the Indian subcontinent – Indians, Pakistanis, Sri Lankans, and Bangladeshis – draw them together, and 'the moniker "South Asian" allows them to feel solidarity despite their different national origins and religious commitments' (pp. 186–187).

As noted above, South Asia is not a homogenous region, which makes the South Asian diaspora a 'complex and variegated' (V. Lal, 2004) zone of engagement that includes diasporans with diverse social, political, economic, and cultural backgrounds. South Asia, home to a well over one-fifth of the world's population, typically consists of India, Pakistan, Sri Lanka, Bangladesh, Bhutan, Nepal, and the Maldives. A clubbing of countries, essentially mostly encompasses countries that were part of the former British Indian Empire. The terminologies 'Indian Subcontinent' or simply 'The Subcontinent' are also in common usage to denote South Asia, as well as the 'South Asian Subcontinent'.

On the wide currency of the term *South Asia*, Shiromi Pinto (2004) notes that it appears to

> have become the preferred descriptor when referring to the dances, literatures, cultures, even people, originating from these regions (i.e. South Asian countries which are not, otherwise, in a formal or informal, economic or political block) (...) a concept that is said to underlie a panoply of cultural, artistic and political products, including identity construction in the diaspora. (p. 3)

And according to Sunil Khilnani (2004), 'South Asia' is a 'bureaucrat's phrase'

> In the US map of the world, post-partition India came to be designated South Asia, and its new states were clubbed with the Near East (again a State Departmentism), to form the Bureau of Near Eastern and South Asian Affairs. Exactly what South Asia encompassed has always had some indeterminacy to it. Even after the creation of a separate Bureau of South Asian Affairs within the State Department (which only happened in the early 1990s), debate has continued over which countries exactly to include. (p. 19)

And by 'containing division and rivalry', he writes further:

> 'South Asia' conjured the idea of a common space of community – perhaps temporarily in abeyance – that seemed to transcend national boundaries, and promised a kind of irenic description and identity for a subcontinent that seemed in reality to be driven by national, religious, ethnic and other divisions. Superbly anodyne, it seems to offer a benign transcendence of these conflicts. As a term of self-description, for members of the diaspora, 'South Asian' might also be seen as a gesture toward safety. (p. 20)

The question of 'identity of South Asians' negotiates a rethinking of the question of South Asianness in the diaspora. According to Brij V. Lal (2006a), due to its 'varied origins, divergent patterns of migration and settlement', and further 'different degrees of absorption or integration' into the culture of the hostland, the Indian subcontinental diaspora 'defies easy categorization'. It is moreover 'a complex confluence of many discreet cultures, languages and histories' (p. 10).

In the case of the South Asian diaspora in Australia, people who belong to different communities or groups in homeland blend into a new identity of 'geographical ascription'. The supposed 'identity' of South Asians is 'merely mythic'. The Indian subcontinent is also 'divided denominationally' – Hindus, Muslims, Christians, Sikhs, Parsis, and Buddhists, and moreover the Indian caste system separates people further (see Fludernik, 2003a: p. xx). Thus, South Asia or South Asianness can be defined as a field of inquiry that explores cultural consequences of migration from the Indian subcontinent. And it can be seen that even 'within single diasporas, simultaneous diasporan identities are possible' (K. Butler: p. 192).

For Makarand Paranjape (2000), South Asian diaspora is 'a part and symbol of the larger' Indian subcontinent 'not just in terms of its physical boundaries but also in terms of its mental dimensions' (p. 243). As the term *South Asian diaspora* connotes people who have at some time in the past come from all the countries that comprise the Indian subcontinent, yet without the emphasis on forced expulsion that Jewish or black diasporas have conveyed (see Boyarin, 1992; Gilroy, 1993). Avtar Brah's (2003) question: 'Can we speak of a "South Asian diaspora" other than as a mode of description of a particular cluster of migrations?' (p. 617) is very insightful to the study of South Asianness. She further suggests that 'it is the economic, political and cultural specificities linking these components that the concept of diaspora signifies' (p. 617). This means that 'multiple journeys may configure into one journey via a *confluence of narratives* as it is lived and re-lived, produced, reproduced and transformed through individual as well as collective memory and re-memory' (p. 617).

As noted earlier, the situation of South Asian immigrants in Australia is ambiguous. A related and much politicized issue has been that of South Asian 'racial identity'. Sucheta Mazumdar (1991) opines that for South Asians, 'questions pertaining to racial identity and skin colour have had a particularly convoluted history' (p. 25). It is worth noting that although South Asians think in terms of class, caste, religion, and region wherever they go, upon arrival in Australia, from 'being persons with no tangible race' they 'become people of color in this society', as South Asians do not think of themselves in racial terms (Rudrappa: p. 85). Through mass media, South Asians now have 'a fair inkling about race' structures in Australia, still 'they are unprepared' and 'cannot conceive of the ways in which their self itself will be challenged' (Rudrappa: p. 87). Thus, South Asian migrants with their affluence become the visible minorities in Australia.

The very notion of a 'South Asian identity' or 'South Asianness' promotes a 'unity and solidarity' among the 'imagined community' of the South Asian diaspora. And 'people from its various South Asian cultures have been treated typically as one monolithic people by the West' (Y. Hussain: p. 2). South Asian culture is not one monolithic category, yet the term *South Asian* 'functions as an umbrella term', that is often 'abbreviated to "Asian", to unify diverse peoples against common obstacles, in the name of empowerment and coalition-building' (Y. Hussain: p. 2).

It has been observed that the number and proportion of people of South Asian descent living outside South Asia is small in relation to other migrant populations, such as Chinese, the Jews, the Africans, and the Europeans (see van der Veer: p. 1). Moreover, as already observed, there are a number of differences within these ethnic groups, for instance lifestyles, dress, diet, and language. Furthermore, their responses to new social and economic environments are also different, with diverse employment patterns and marriage practices for example (see Y. Hussain: p. 2; Ballard, 1994).

We have already noted in the above discussion that there is no essentially 'homogeneous' South Asian cultural identity but because of 'our common imperial past' we are bound, apart from sharing common ocean, ecology, rivers, and cable cultures, by 'a common legal, administrative, and constitutional framework' (M. Desai: p. 300) at one level. And similarly, at another level 'centuries of migration and movement within South Asia and intermarriages have made its people similar' (M. Desai: pp. 298–299), thus helping the concepts laid down for the transnational identity and the South Asian-Australian diaspora by giving them tremendous opportunities in various fields

Transnationalism or rather a global South Asian diaspora, according to Lord Meghnad Desai (2005), can be imagined only when we in South Asia break our 'barriers (built) against the flow of goods and people' (p. 289) created against each other. Because of these barriers and restrictions, we have emphasized our 'separateness, rather than (our) similarity' (M. Desai: p. 289) to the rest of the world. What we need are speedy reforms in the Indian subcontinent – sorting out crucial political problems, stopping infighting within the South Asian Association of Regional Cooperation (SAARC), exploiting common advantages, creating a common market and free movement of people (see M. Desai: pp. 290–292). Our mind and energy is great and what we need in South Asia is strong leadership – political and economic – which could help cooperation in various fields such as trade, transport, movement of people and goods, and most important of all on the lines of the European Union (EU), a South Asian Monetary Union (M. Desai: pp. 292–293).

It can also be added here that the South Asians, for example, Indians abroad have facilitated and galvanized in building India's and the subcontinental image in a far better way than they could have done from the country itself. Repatriation of foreign earning by the diaspora also plays a significant role in the economic development of the homeland. Lord Desai calling South Asian community a 'successful business community' writes that

> South Asians abroad have shown that they can make a success in any country they go to. In most countries in the West, the South

> Asian groups which have settled there have succeeded against most adverse circumstances. (p. 290)

Facing all odds in terms of economic, social, political, and cultural spaces, as first-generation immigrants, these diasporans have created variant hues on Australian multicultural landscape.

Contributing through various societies, associations, lobbies, religious, and spiritual bodies, they have collaborated within and outside community to cultivate India-Australia ties successfully. And their various attempts, as seen in these narratives undertaken in this study are just part of the various 'means', as Erez Cohen (2003) feels,

> by which migrants come to understand and experience their life in a 'new' place. Such attachments are not merely an act of nostalgia or part of the effort to maintain culture, as depicted by multiculturalism. Rather, relations with the homeland are part of the ambiguity of 'home and away' that constitute the life experiences of many immigrants and construct their various ways of generating 'communities' in their new context. (p. 38)

These short stories or narratives from South Asian diaspora in Australia thus play an important role in promoting the Australian and South Asian connections by acting as a gathering of colourful perceptions, experiences, and reflections. There is a continuous need to re-enter these narratives, not just for the purpose of making analyses, but also to provide the diaspora discourse with new continuities, visions, and issues in terms of transnationalism, multiculturalism, and biculturalism, based on questions related to social, political, cultural, and economic vis-à-vis a new issue, as proposed here, in terms of commercial–cultural benefits that are reaped by the diasporans both at homeland and hostland.

On the use of the word 'Indianness' for the people of the Indian subcontinent, Bharti Mukherjee (1985) observes, 'Indianness is now a metaphor, a particular way of comprehending the world' (p. 3). The very use of the term *Indian* encapsulates diversity and brings into play various contradictory viewpoints, in relation to identity and, cultural dimensions. The divergence of viewpoints, in fact, related to any 'identity', be it the Indian or the much larger South Asian one, can also be noted in the different ways in which the term *diaspora* has been theorized by various academics in their dialogues.

A major trap in a study of such proportion is that the definition of South Asianness or South Asian diaspora in academics sometimes reeks of Indianness to the exclusion of all else, momentarily excluding all other South Asians except Indians. The discussion of South Asianness is problematic as it presupposes a 'unifying force'. Though there is still vast scope for a serious debate about the internal hegemonies implicit within the term South Asian, according to Crispin Bates (2001), a genuine pan-South Asian ethnicity, that could 'realistically begin to address the material and spiritual inequalities of the subcontinent and its satellite communities throughout the globe, may therefore be an ambition that awaits a different generation, and a different set of circumstances to that of the present' (p. 39).

In spite of the difference in the migration points, that is, the point of arrival of these writers from the Indian subcontinent show a common sensitivity and consciousness. This is the result of the idea of Indianness that is not made up of any particular geographical border in our diasporic imagination. This is also because, as Satendra Nandan (2000) observes

> Unlike some other diasporas, the Indian consciousness of India is not linked by a single region or transferred institutions, nor by colonial hierarchies transplanted, nor by politics or economics or military considerations. Indeed not even by language. It is essentially and vitally one of *cultural imagination*. (p. 54; emphasis added)

The people of South Asia have carried on a tradition of internal and international migration as traders, indentured labourers, skilled workers, and professionals. Despite a shared history of uprooting, South Asia is not a homogeneous entity and there are inherent tensions that exist within it. South Asia with its several independent nation-states has certain commonalities and continuities because of a shared culture of 4,000 years with stratifications or subcategories on the basis of region, religion, language, dialects, politics, economics, caste, class, and culture. South Asians have suffered, survived, and prospered in various countries of their settlement. As Paranjape observes,

> all over their areas of migration, South Asians have been mistreated and discriminated against (...) it is South Asians who have borne the brunt of injustice, oppression, and racism the world over. Deprived of their rights in South Africa and Canada, driven out of Burma and Uganda, upstaged in the Caribbean and Fiji, and still discriminated against in most Western countries, South Asians have nevertheless not just survived, but prospered. (2001b: p. 2)

So, it is this prosperity of South Asians that adds a curious facet to their writings. It would be wrong to homogenize or generalize the South Asian diaspora and similarly their experiences in terms of hostland, that is, Australia. This is primarily because the situation, location/dislocation, and perceptions within and outside the Indian diaspora changes in relation to various host nations. And, not always is a diasporan position to be pitied at as it may be considered 'a richer and a more complex way of being that is equally at home and abroad' (Paranjape, 2001a: p. vi), which to a larger extent is also true about the writers, intellectuals, academicians, and professionals who migrated voluntarily and are part of the Australian egalitarian multicultural life and enjoy the wider horizons of improving and shaping their identities in relation to homeland(s)/hostland(s).

Through its struggles and experiences, in this way, the South Asian diaspora will finally emerge as, what David Walker has termed, 'Australia's Asian future – who would develop the country' (1999: p. 7) and that will finally lead South Asia and Australia into a more intellectual and social constructive dialogue. For this to happen, undoubtedly requires the involvement and a collective effort on the part of South Asian and diaspora thinkers, artists, politicians, business people, policy makers, and concerned citizens (see M. Desai: p. 297). Therefore, every artistic involvement or testimonial on the subject, constructive dialogue, and discourse – academic, political, or public – in the present interlinked world, then merely is a step towards it, as a result forming change in perceptions and attitudes by creating a knowledge and interest base in this field. The South Asian diaspora in Australia will ultimately share a dynamic key role in all areas of Australian society with its steady growth and prosperity. An area of abundant cultural and literary potential, it will contribute towards global peace and trade that are vital measures of world reconstruction.

Chapter Divisions

> (...) to write is, of course, to travel. It is to enter a space, a zone, a territory, sometimes sign-posted by generic indicators (...) but everywhere characterised by movement: the passage of words, the caravan of thought, the flux of the imaginary, the slippage of the metaphor, 'drift across the page.' (Chambers: p. 9)

Migration in this rapidly globalizing world has not just spread the roots of diasporic literature deeper but has also made it relevant on a global level by concretizing it as a natural and inevitable result of the migration process. So, I shall begin by drawing limits. This study is chiefly concerned with short narratives written in English. It is also concerned with a deep rooted question: What does it mean to study the work of writers who have migrated from their homes? These short narratives or stories are like 'conversations' – a 'set of smaller narratives' introducing characters who have migrated to Australia. Gelder and Salzman (2009) point out that: 'Some Australian literary fiction has continued to turn to Europe for its themes and influences; other literary fiction travels more widely and engages with identities-in-process in relation to various conceptions of Otherness' (p. xi). Keeping the above point in mind, this study and the themes with which these authors engage in has certain urgency since the current migration debate, particularly about South Asian diaspora in Australia impinges on areas of literary, social and cultural practice. It has been well argued by Ghassan Hage that 'literary texts can enter into better "dialogue" with other discourses' (2005: p. 494) and I have therefore taken an interdisciplinary approach to question memory and spatial identity – issues close to the theme of politics of location. As a result, any work on/from postcolonial perspective or postcoloniality will have to deal with interdisciplinarity, historical and political contexts, race and power relations, and contemporary sociocultural experiences.

Monika Fludernik (2003b) sees literature (novels, short stories, and narratives) by South Asian expatriates as falling into four groups, which are as follows:

1. the novels of immigration and cultural exile that concentrate on an individual's private journey of assimilation;
2. multicultural novels;
3. diaspora novels in which the collective identity of Indian migrants, expatriates and second or third generation immigrants is at stake; and
4. cosmopolitan novels in which South Asian expatriates are portrayed as individuals (outside a diasporic community) and in which the process of assimilation either has been successfully completed or is not focused on the binaries of India vs America/Britain (Australia). In these novels (short stories) the main South Asian protagonist is frequently married to a Westerner or person from another (non-South Asian) nationality and ethnicity. (p. 265)

This study attempts to begin to fill this gap by analysing and calling upon a wide range of works in this field – from historical, anthropological, sociological, cultural, and literary studies – engaged in new research and a study of the politics of these constant shifting locations. This book analyses a number of short stories written by known and not so known South Asian Australian writers. The themes that emerge on my reading these works include such as those closely related to the study of politics of locations – sensory and spatial.

I here seek to map out a neglected oeuvre, South Asian diasporic short stories, and propose that there is a slow but steady process of South Asian literary development going on in Australia. Further, I also propose to conceptualize, through my close reading, the theme of location as an important and complex category in relation to South Asian migration to Australasia that has deep impact on the processes of family and class structures and individual/community memory and nostalgia as reflected in these narratives and when read through the theories of diaspora, postcolonialism, and race relations (see Hage, 1998). My focus is directed at short stories produced by South Asian – middle class and professional – postcolonial immigrants to Australia and see the 'ways in which this community's members imagine and represent themselves' (Ganguly: pp. 27–28).

Why should one deal with the topic from a literary perspective? After all, the diaspora would appear to be a sociological, economical, and historical fact (Fludernik, 2003a: p. xxviii). The question is: Do imaginative writings attempt to find satisfaction by releasing preoccupied thoughts? This study accepts the fact that individuals reveal themselves in whatever they read and write (Y. Hussain: p. 3). The South Asian identities and issues expressed in the works examined in this study are the collective concerns of authors who have roots in South Asia and are living in Australia. The issues include migration, settlement, identity, family, marriage, and children – important to these authors regardless of their being Indian, Sri Lankan, Pakistani, or Bangladeshi. These short stories are 'essentially products of individual imaginations' and can also be taken as 'eyewitness accounts: not literal autobiographies, but representations of aspects of the lived experience and preoccupations of each author which she recognized as relevant to lives other than her own' (Y. Hussain: p. 3).

Some happy occasions, such as the 1995 Commonwealth Writers' Prize for Best Book to Bangladeshi-Australian author Adib Khan, 2008 Man Booker Prize to Indian born Australian writer Arvinda Adiga, and the 2013 Australian Prime Minister's Literary Award for Fiction to Sri Lankan-Australian author Michelle de Kretser, have definitely boosted the self-confidence of other South Asian-Australian writers in Australia. But little attention is given to South Asian-Australian short story writers particularly by Australian critics. Australian literary criticism has been relatively slow to address the South Asian Australian literary studies and its examination of literature. Short stories by prominent South Asian writers have tended to concentrate on a number of key topics and themes. By identifying these common themes and the different ways they are addressed in these creative works, we can uncover some of the major issues in the South Asian diaspora in Australia. I hope to throw some new light on problems of politics of location and conflict it causes.

South Asian-Australian writers included in this study are Vijay Mishra, Brij V. Lal, Satendra Nandan, Sudesh Mishra, Shrishti Sharma, Mena Abdullah, Renuka Sharma, Manik Datar, Rani Jhala, Rashmere Bhatti, Chandani Lokugé, Manik Datar, Chris Raja, Christopher Cyrill, Grace Mackie, Ruth Van Gramberg, Michelle De

Kretser, Neelam Maharaj, Radha D'souza, Sunitha, Yasmine Gooneratne, Suvendrini Perera, Derek Bartholomeusz, Adib Khan, Subhash Jaireth, Beryl T. Mitchell, Shelagh Goonewardene, Sunil Badami, Sushie Narayan, Karobi Mukherjee, Madu Pasipanodya, Sujhatha Fernandes, and K.C. Paramanandam. These writers through their short stories and autobiographical narratives present 'the clash of the new and the old worlds' (Paranjape, 2007: p. 354). They also enable an understanding of the a diaspora culture and its outstanding contribution towards the cultures of both the home and the hostland vis-à-vis the diaspora cultures of the world. They are thus able to make possible the celebration of the achievements of the South Asian-Australians in their involvement in the process of building a liberal world.

The study argues that the narratives of South Asian diaspora writers produced from Australia deserve a special status in analyses of the social-cultural-economical-historical 'narratives' produced by the South Asian diaspora around the world. It further argues that a clearer notion of politics of location will be required to distinguish the different kinds of 'dislocation' the diasporans suffer psychologically and sociologically (see also Paranjape, 2000) because literature acts as an instrument for the deployment of these often 'complex discursive strategies' (see Huggan, 2007). The study points out that the authors explore the processes of displacement and dislocation of identities through migration, journey, settlement, and nostalgic returns and their character's struggle to negotiate locations within Australia. In turn, these migratory experiences have created diasporic locations – of nostalgia and spatial identity – that need to be read and explored in one interpretative framework, that is, politics of location. This helps in examining the position of the migrant as a subject influenced by political, economic, cultural structures, and processes in his/her environment, thus affirming a community's genuine right to self-identification.

The first chapter, 'South Asian Diaspora in Australia: History, Research, and Literature', engages with the existing research in this area. The study uses historical, social, political, economic, cultural, and personal contexts as means of widening the scope of research, analysis, and writing. Researchers examined in this chapter consciously provide a new direction to the dynamic field of research on the South Asian diaspora in Australia and its social, cultural, political, economic, and literary participation in the Australian society. It also provides a brief history of migration from South Asia to Australia and Australian immigration policies towards various South Asian countries. Briefly overviewing South Asian diaspora writing in Australia, it also provides resourceful 'background' information – historical and sociological – a knowledge of which provides indispensable aid in analysing the various images of South Asia and Australia that materialize from the South Asian-Australian diaspora short stories presenting the rich subcontinental cultural heritage.

The constant yearning for ones 'roots' – sensory and spatial locations – has become a phenomenon for different immigrant groups. The short stories analysed in Chapters 2 to 5 attempt to provide an understanding of the variety of interpretations of the sensory and spatial locations. In Chapter 2, 'An Element of Romanticization: Sensory and Spatial Locations', we can note that in most of these stories the immigrants try to bring the Indian subcontinent to Australia with them by using myths, legends, and historical facts. These immigrants besides using myths also display a prized possession of nostalgia, which reminds them constantly of home. These objects or icons or elements from the past, which the immigrants carry with them as cultural products, are used as helpers in making a sense out of the alien situation presented before them. The chapter concludes with the assertion that Indian-Australian short stories act as an important expression of the Indian way of life in Australia and may also effectively help in removing misconceptions and better understandings of local conditions, thus encouraging fellow Australians to see differently within the cultural context of India and Australia. Chapter 3, 'A Journey through Places: Politics of Spatial Location', analyses the postcolonial and postmodern experiences in the light of spatial identities. This chapter is mainly concerned with the theoretical ways in which a shift is accelerated in Australia's literary landscape by the South Asian diasporic writers who produce and cover the dynamics of politics of location in different contexts. It also focuses on South Asian diaspora's widely agreed 'ability to recreate their cultures in diverse locations'. The politics of sensory and spatial locations that act as one of the core features joining Indian diaspora across continents stresses that these stories are not just of spaces but also of a promising future for the South Asian diaspora in Australia.

South Asian diasporic writing as a genre in Australia encapsulates the collective social and psychological anxieties of whole dispersed generations and their children living on the margins. In diaspora literature or marginal literature, most homes are constructed through the memories of the migrants. This construction of home through memory raises an important question: How do representations of lost home shape the lives of the diasporans? Home (real, imagined, and mythologized), as a place of origin, becomes a key site of a displaced migrant's experiences and connections with past. Chapter 4, 'Real, Imagined, and Mythologized: (Re)Presentation of Lost Home', looks at the (re)presentation and perceptions of re-visiting 'home'. I focus on how this (re)presentation and (re)anlyses of lost home in these narratives helps the diasporans in moving, with their eternal diasporic cultural baggage, towards their Australian future (discussed fully in chapter 7). A diasporic author who is unable to go back home again views the past through the pieces of a broken mirror, as discussed by Rushdie, which inevitably distorts the memory one has of a 'homeland', making it idealized so that only certain memories and ideas are highlighted. This remembrance of 'the best bits' is a powerful impulse of the memory that awakens a longing for the past, about the unrealized dreams of the past in a lost home and often leads to the yearning for the lost homeland, the re-presentation or re-creation of South Asian spaces in Australia and a reflexive appraisal of the homeland, and its cultural values and norms. In Chapter 5, 'Acts of Remembering and Forgetting: Reflections through Nostalgia', I examine the formation of ideas such as (lost) home, nostalgia, sense of belonging, and diasporic identity represented through the ideas of time and journeys of the authors through memory, that is how 'roots' can be constructed by nostalgia. I further explore the melancholia of diasporic loss and the place of longing and memory in the renegotiation of a lost home in the selected short stories of South Asian diaspora in Australia. I conclude by suggesting, how a nostalgic return to past or homeland can be a means of establishing roots in the hostland or one's new home.

Today, as the certitudes of the nation-state are eroded under the pressures of globalization, social prejudice and racism are prevalent in both multicultural and monocultural societies throughout the world. The case in point here is Australia, which has, through migration, developed into one of the world's most culturally diverse societies. This increased diversity has brought with it many new cultural experiences and has undoubtedly made Australia a more multiculturally enriched place. In the wake of 2009–2010 'opportunist violence' or 'race attacks' on students from the Indian subcontinent in Australia, Chapter 6, 'An Australian Learning Experience: Prejudice, Racism, and Indifference', attempts to critique racism, prejudices, and indifference as represented in the short stories of South Asian diaspora in Australia. It argues that multicultural literature is an important forum for negotiating these issues and concludes with the assertion that for Australians and its various migrant groups, an understanding of their diversity and tolerance of difference is required to resolve racial tensions and build a stable and secure future.

Chapter 7, 'Another World, Another Future', argues that twentieth-century South Asian immigrant narratives in Australia need to be understood as inherently and essentially 'spatial stories' – stories of movement and stories of different *homes*. The South Asian-Australian writers' postcolonial and postmodern experiences as presented in the narratives analysed here support this statement. In this chapter, I analyse narratives in the light of questions and issues concerning the spatial identities the diasporans carry – Where are you from? Who is an Australian? or What makes a person Australian? This chapter deals with the issues of complexity of setting up home and how diasporans imagine themselves and their future in the Australian social and national space. Further, these stories decipher that Australia and its literatures do not just inhabit an Anglo-Celtic space but 'there also exists other voices, bodies, worlds' and the 'possibility of another place, another world, another future' (Chambers: p. 5).

The last section or the Conclusion, titled '*Thoda* Indian, *Thoda* Aussie', puts together the observations and analyses of the previous chapters to show that these short stories dynamically present the cultural diversity within the South Asian community in Australia. These stories not only emerge as a dynamic, prolific, and innovative group of writing but also present South Asian diaspora and its literature in Australia as an acknowledgement of the stage that South

Asian studies and dialogue are essential for national productions and knowledge. The Conclusion also outlines possible areas of further scholarship in this area and as such, studies of South Asian diaspora and its literature in Australia are important for not only literary studies but also the policy makers of both India and Australia.

Notes

1. See Clifford, 1997; Friedman, 2002; Braakman, 2005; Braakman and Schlenkhoff, 2007. The 2013 *Mapping Social Cohesion* national report by Scanlon Foundation, Australian Multicultural Foundation and Monash University, reported through its survey that among the immigrants from South Asia some 44 per cent indicate that they visit their home country at least once a year, a close to 51 per cent watch television from their former home countries on cable or satellite, and read news reports on the internet from their former home countries at least several times a week as a way to stay connected with their roots (Marcus p. 4 and p. 48).
2. See "Dumb, Drunk & Racist" poll where 44% people said yes to the question "Are Australians Dumb Drunk & Racist?" (http://www.abc.net.au/tv/dumbdrunkracist/).
3. D. Mellor (2004) notes the complexity of racism and demonstrates how everyday racism occurs through a range of means by a range of players.
4. See Sydney gang rapes, Ashfield gang rapes, and Cronulla riots involving ethnic Australians as perpetrators.
5. See "85% Australians Feel Racism Exists in Australia" (2009). Also, the India's High Commissioner to Australia Sujatha Singh had acknowledged that there had been 'a racist element' to the attacks on Indian students in Melbourne ("Racism Confined to 'Minority' of People", 2009).
6. According to reports, in Victoria alone in 2009–2010 'an astonishing 1,447 people of Indian origin were punched, kicked, raped or robbed' (see Bolt, 2009).
7. A study on racist attitudes conducted by a team led by Dr Kevin Dunn of the University of New South Wales in 2003 found one in eight Australians interviewed admitted they were prejudiced, particularly towards Muslim Australians. The study also found some Australians were living in denial of such prejudice though 80 per

cent of those surveyed recognized racism was a problem. Unfortunately, the problem has been promoted since and continues to contribute to decrease in the process of integration.

8. According to Phil Griffiths (2005), '(R)acism towards Asian people was grounded in *strategic feras*' (p. 163) that were highlighted strategically by the ruling class for serving their own interests and hold on working classes in Australia.
9. In Melbourne and Sydney, Indian students protested against what they claimed were racist attacks. The protesters also accused police of 'ramrodding' them to break up their *dharna*. Former Australian High Commissioner to India John McCarthy agreed that there may have been an element of racism involved in some of the attacks on Indians, but they were mainly criminal in nature. See also "Nepalese Student Bashed in Sydney" (2010).
10. See Facebook group 'I am Australian and I would rather Immigrants Living here than Racists', 'Australians against Racism & Discrimination', and also various standup spots related to Australian racism done at the '2010 Melbourne Comedy Festival Gala', available at www.youtube.com.
11. The development of racist movements has also been linked to the crises that many of the countries face as global economic decisions cause societal changes.
12. For a detailed discussion on the dynamics shaping racism in Australia (see Dunn, 2003; Griffiths, 2005; "Racism in Australia", 2010; "Racial Violence in Australia", 2010).
13. Lake (2010) observes that the power of Anzac mythology is still working at the symbolic level in Australia today. Earlier it has been used "to serve as White Australia's creation myth" (p. 1). She further notes that the Chinese colonists also joined the celebration of Federation in 1901, "even though they were subject to systematic racial discrimination" (p. 3). She further observes that it is "inappropriate" for Australia, a "modern democratic nation to adopt an Imperial, masculine, militarist event as the focus" of its "national definition in the twenty-first century" (p. 3).
14. India has become the third largest source of international immigrants and second largest source of skilled migrants and international students to Australia (see Bhandari, 2008).
15. See "The Blainey Debate on Immigration – Newspaper Clippings."
16. On the rise and fall of anti-immigrant and racist parties and major policy shifts in the last years of the century (see Jupp, 2003).

17. Recently Hanson said that 'a multicultural country can never be a strong country' and supported this assertion with a number of widely publicized remarks about Asians not assimilating and living in ghettos, and more recently about Africans bringing disease (particularly AIDS) into Australia.
18. According to Andrew Bolt (2010), many of the attacks on Indians (students and taxi drivers) in Victoria and elsewhere seem to have been carried out by members of recently arrived racial minorities, whether African, Middle Eastern, Maori, Pacific Islander, or Asian. While the Australian and Indian media along with Victoria police have been very reluctant to admit such things, they blame the attacks on whites.
19. Australia's first Asia-born Cabinet minister, Penny Wong, former Federal Climate Change Minister, said that racism in Australia was confined to 'a minority of people' with extreme views: 'On the whole I think Australians are tolerant'. However, Wong had a few years back recounted her 'pretty difficult' childhood facing racist remarks while growing up in Adelaide ("Racism Confined to 'Minority' of People", 2009).
20. It is also interesting to see how migrants re-define or 'make use of the strict immigration regulations in Australia in ways different from those intended by Australian policy-makers' (Voigt-Graf: p. 143; for an interpretation of the ways in which migrants challenge the structures of the system, see Ballard, 1994).
21. See Zable's interview with Mark Rubbo at http://www.readings.com.au/interview/arnold-zable.
22. The invasion narrative added with conspiracy theories and taking over of the vacant fertile Australian land by the Asiatics formed 'a sub-genre in the narratives of racial conflict' in Australia (see Walker, 2007: p. 315).
23. Describing the seriousness of Australian government towards growing attacks on Indian students, the then Prime Minister Kevin Rudd said that an assault against any international student was 'one assault too many'. Nonetheless, he pointed out that if compared with international criminal data, Australia would still be safer than the United Kingdom, France, Italy, and the United States. He further observed that 'In any relationship, there are bound to be problems. Let's not take this out of context' (quoted in R. Srivastava, 2009).
24. Victoria's Chief Police Commissioner Simon Overland said, 'Some of these crimes are racially motivated; however I also believe that

many of the robberies and other crimes of violence are simply opportunistic' (quoted in Bhandari, 2009).

25. There are often discrepancies in how the media (in South Asia and Australia) reports 'racial' violence. The Australian media has been accused of using stereotypes to that groups' detriment. According to BBC journalist Stephen Evans (2009), Australians attitude, particularly media attitude and reporting, towards casual racism needs an urgent 'self-questioning'. And according to journalist David Penberthy (2009), 'Addressing our casual racism would require a total change in our national psyche'.
26. Hate crimes and racial violence are not a new concept in Australia. Violence against the Chinese community is an early example in Australia's history of mobs attacking Chinese miners (see also De Lepervanche, 1975).
27. A result of early Aboriginal campaigns and struggle demanding full citizenship thus extending 'the Australian principle of equality' (Lake: p. 3).
28. See DIMIA, *National Agenda for a Multicultural Australia* (1989).
29. Internationally known Indian filmmaker Mahesh Bhatt, recounting his film unit's alleged mistreatment and harassment by the Australian authorities (particularly Melbourne City Council) while shooting for a film on racial attacks against Indian students – *Crook: It's Good to be Bad in Australia*, says: '(...) after what has happened to me and my team at ground zero there, that it is agreed that Australia is a great place and all that, but there is still there a great section of society that has a very clear and pronounced bias against us. It has been a nightmare for me' (Prabhakar: p. 95). Contrary to what Australian government has publicized, Bhatt feels that apart from suffering huge financial losses the whole thing has left him traumatized.
30. The critical interest in this diaspora and its study is largely post-1990s, which coincides with the period of globalization and political interest in home countries to strengthen their foreign policy and relations with the host countries through diasporas (see P. Cohen, 1999; Kalra et al., 2005).
31. See also Hall, 2005: pp. 543–560.

Chapter 1

South Asian Diaspora in Australia

History, Research, and Literature

People have been migrating since the dawn of humanity. Many of today's diasporic groups, particularly the Africans, Chinese, Palestinians, Armenians, Jews, and South Asians, to name a few, have had long histories of travel away from original homelands. However, during the past 100–150 years these diasporas have been recorded, documented and analysed for their economic, political, and cultural impact (see also Jupp, 1998; Bates, 2001). Migration in this rapidly globalizing world has not just spread the roots of diaspora deeper but also put it on a global level by concretizing it as a natural and inevitable result.[1] South Asian-Australians have played an important role in the spreading of new ideas and thoughts. This can go a long way in making diasporic cultures more interesting. A matured understanding of the achievements and the contributions of the South-Asian Australians to the home/hostland cultures can help build a liberal world.

Despite this fact of nearly simultaneous migration, the Indian subcontinent has been 'a blind spot to most Australians during the one hundred and eighty years of their history' (J. D'Cruz, 1973: p. 31). Australians were present in South Asia as advisers, technicians, teachers, diplomats, journalists, but most of all as soldiers and seamen for the Empire (see Walker, 1999). They engaged with their neighbours – the South Asians – through travel, study, art, and literature (see Macintyre: pp. 207–208), and hence this blind spot is not the result of lack of access to the subcontinent. The History of migration from South Asia is also rich in stories and metaphors of our civilization and, to borrow a phrase from Judah Waten (1952), its 'imperishable peoples' immense arc of influence that lies far beyond their own subcontinental shores, like the metaphor of the 'banyan tree' spreading its roots in several soils. The banyan tree and its branches taking 'root' in different soils have been consistently used as metaphors by scholars across time to represent this human movement or transplantation across borders. According to Bhiku Parekh, a malleable migrant '(F)ar from being homeless, (...) has several homes, and that is the only way he has increasingly come to feel at home in the world' (quoted in Mahanta: p. 13). Noted Indian writer and poet Rabindranath Tagore perceived 'the Indians going overseas as taking their Indias of the mind with them, and recreating new Indian colonies in the lands of their adoption' (quoted in Tinker: p. ix). Tagore writes:

> To study a banyan tree, you not only must know its main stem in its own soil, but also must trace the growth of its greatness in the further soil, for then you can know the true nature of its vitality. The civilization of India, like the banyan tree, has shed its beneficent shade away from its own birthplace (...). India can live and grow by spreading abroad – not the political India, but the ideal India. (quoted in Tinker: p. iii)[2]

Yet, the controversial writer, Salman Rushdie ridicules the very idea of metaphoric roots in his novel *Shame* (1983), when he writes: 'to explain why we become attached to our birthplaces we pretend that we are trees and speak of roots. Look under your feet. You will not find gnarled growths sprouting through the soles' (p. 86). For Rushdie, 'roots', are 'a conservative myth, designed to keep us in our places' (p. 86). This debunking of the metaphor of roots, as a culturally constructed idea, supports the view that human beings were, are, and will remain mobile and rootless (see Jin: p. 22). However, as Sissy Helff (2009) notes, this view cannot accommodate the characterization of migration as a life and death prospect for many South Asian migrants. For some migrants boarding the ship and crossing the *Kala Pani* (black waters) meant transgression[3] and thereby a loss of cultural identity – 'the sorrow of the passage across the black water' (Paranjape, 2007: p. 354). Furthermore, Rushdie (1985/1991) being a migrant himself is more ambivalent on the issue of loss of cultural identity and suffering than the earlier quotation allows us to surmise:

> A full migrant suffers, traditionally, a triple disruption: he loses his place, he enters into an alien language, and he finds himself surrounded by being(s) whose social behaviour and code is very unlike, and sometimes offensive to, his own. And this is what makes migrants such important figures: because *roots*, language and social norm have been three of the most important parts of the definition of what it is to be a human being. The migrant, denied all three, is obliged to find new ways of describing himself (...), new ways of being human (...). (p. ix; emphasis added)

While these theoretical approaches to diaspora and diaspora consciousness are relatively new, migration is an old phenomenon in the history of South Asia – be it internal or external. The contemporary migration of people from South Asia to Australia is marked by much cultural traffic – there is the exchange of ideas that takes place on large scale through festivals, art exhibitions, film screenings, and others – as well as 'academic traffic' – exchange of students, research scholars, and faculty members through various exchange programmes, seminars, MoUs, academic associations, personal visits, awards, and scholarships, writers-in-residence programmes, joint publications, and so on.[4] These two trends – cultural traffic and academic traffic – have also resulted in producing a more refined or nuanced awareness and common knowledge base about South Asia, which though known to Australia for centuries was consciously overlooked as it belongs to the group of countries that are part of what is pathetically called 'the third world'.

According to Vinay Lal (2004, 2009), the South Asian or third world diaspora is an 'incontestable fact of contemporary history'. But many Australians had and still have mixed feelings about South Asia and therefore about the inward bound streams of migrants (refugees and asylum seekers included). It is, however, an undeniable fact that Australia has been built on migration with people from over 230 different countries, speaking more than 300 languages, and practicing more than 100 religions constituting the 'fair dinkum Aussie' of today. Migrants from South Asia, the most populous region in the world, comprising India, Pakistan, Sri Lanka, Bangladesh, Bhutan, Nepal, and the Maldives, have contributed enormously to the rich cultural life and diversity of Australia at both the local and national levels. They also continue to enhance progressively the nation's economic and political landscape by adding to its cultural mix through involvement and achievements in businesses, literature, educational, and other related activities.

Under the pull of capitalism, all countries in South Asia have experienced migration since the early nineteenth century. One of the challenges in writing about the South Asian diaspora in Australia is the nature of the beast: what are the various migration and entry points into Australia. In the next section, I will focus on typology of migration patterns to Australia from individual South Asian countries.

South Asians in Australia: A Brief History

Migration is the most dominant feature of Australia throughout its history – be it the arrival of Captain James Cook in 1788 or later the coming of free settlers, voluntary migrants, indentured workers, and so on.[5] The earlier groups, apart from the British, were Irish, Germans, Scandinavians, Poles, Hungarians, European Jews, Greeks, Italians, Lebanese, Latin Americans, Dutch, Yugoslavs, and Turkish. Most of these 'groups' were running away from religious persecution (see Jupp, 1998), or were in search of better living standards, or were free settlers, or entrepreneurs attracted towards the Gold Rush, mining, railways, vast 'virgin' untilled lands and other Australian industries, while a large number came from poverty-ridden or troubled (war ridden) countries as 'displaced persons' (see Jupp, 1998). The coming or intake of indentured workers from South Asia and China began at the same time, but has gone unnoticed till the advent of the 'Asian' economies on the global arena since the globalization of South Asia. The South Asian diaspora in Australia refers to the scatter of people of Indian subcontinental origin who are living in various parts of the world outside of the Indian Subcontinent (Clarke et al., 1990: p. 1).

To begin with India, the largest number of people of Indian origin[6] has migrated to Australia only since the 1980s. But if we look at Australian history, its earliest inhabitants, the Aborigines arrived from the Asian continent via the islands of Indonesia and the Malay Archipelago 40,000 years ago.[7] They probably originated in South

India and from here they made their way to Australia via Ceylon, Malaya, and Indonesia, thus making the Veddas, the original inhabitants of Sri Lanka, a possible connection in the migration chain (see Weerasooria, 1988; Flannery, 1994; Smith, 2007). According to C.D. Narasimhaiah (2000), Australia's first inhabitants the Aborigines are 'our (South Asians') common ancestors' (p. 24). Arguably, they can be considered the first South Asian immigrants, if not diaspora; however, the time lag makes these ancient connections a matter for archaeological study, far away from the realm of literary or narratival probing. Nevertheless, even the more recent immigration history of South Asians and more particularly Indians in Australia with accurate statistics, data, and evidences is yet to be written.

Indian immigration to Australia[8] began largely as the result of a desperate shortage of labour. Adrian Mitchell (2000) observes that Australia-India connection

> begins of course with the First Settlement, with the transport of ships heading off to India when once the convicts had been off-loaded; and soon after that the foundling colony was sending off to India for grain, both to feed the colony and for grain seed. By the 1890s there was a small informal immigration programme under way – which is to say politely that India was supplying cheap labour to private individuals. Indians were working as builder's labourers in Albany as early as 1835–36. A number of British who had been in India settled in Australia and brought the household retinue with them (...) the physical presence of Indians developed throughout nineteenth-century Australia, and we find the evidence of that here and there – growing maize in Gippsland or as hawkers throughout the rural districts, confused by undiscriminating Australians with the Afghanistani camel-drivers. (pp. 19–20)

It is an oft repeated observation that the first South Asians to reach Australia travelled on Captain Cook's ship in 1816. A significant number of Indians were brought to Australia in the early nineteenth century to work as labourers – on agricultural lands and in the gold fields, as domestics and hawkers. Many more Indians were brought to Australia thereafter to run the now famous 'Camel trains', which transported goods and mail on camel backs in the desert. These Indians, part of the first wave of migration to Australia, were important in keeping the communication and supply line open between Melbourne and Central Australia. Many of the earliest Punjabis (chiefly from the northwestern Punjab region) arrived in late nineteenth century and also took part in the rush for gold in Victoria. Punjabis, comprising mostly the more enterprising Sikhs, came to work on the banana plantations of Southern Queensland. Today, the descendants of these migrants have their own banana plantations and farms and are fairly rich. The establishment of the Sikh community would not have been possible without the welcome, tolerance, and even encouragement of the existing Australian community.[9]

According to Makarand Paranjape (2007), 'Punjabis came to Australia about the same time that they went to Canada, that is, around 1907. Apparently, the regiment that was destined for Canada, actually went via Australia. When they returned to India, they brought back stories of unlimited stretches of land waiting to be farmed and settled in two continents' (p. 349). This second wave of migrants arrived around the World Wars I and II respectively. Indian soldiers were present in Gallipoli (1915) fighting for the British armed forces alongside the Australians. Also, after India's Independence from Britain in 1947, another important group of South Asians, namely Anglo-Indians, migrated in large numbers to Australia. They arrived on the scene as 'British subjects' exercising the choice to settle permanently in Australia.[10] It has been noted that Anglo-Indians were present in Australia from the earliest years of European settlement, including a few convicts. The Anglo-Indians have been immigrating to Australia in relatively large numbers since the early 1960s and were, in fact, among the first Asians to immigrate in the 1960s–1970s with the relaxation of rules for entry of persons of mixed descent to Australia.

The third wave of migrants began arriving in Australia immediately after the whites only policy (Immigration Restriction Act, 1901) was abandoned in 1973 and adaptation of the Multicultural Policy in 1975. Australia's political, economic, and social stability proved magnetic for these new migrants, who saw Australia as a land of opportunity. They consisted mostly of teachers, doctors, engineers, businessmen, software, and hardware professionals, the Fiji-Indians, who came in large numbers to Australia after the two coups in Fiji and finally, the relatives of settled Indians in search of greener pastures.

An independent Indian-Australian writer and documentary filmmaker Surinder Jain accidentally traced the antiquity of the South Asian diaspora in Australia. While working on his documentary in 2005 on the 'places of spirituality and places of pilgrimage in Australia', he discovered a cave that looked like an ancient place of worship most probably used by South Asian Hindu labourers or pioneer immigrants. He says about the experience:

> I was wandering in the hills of Ex-Mouth when I was stopped in my tracks by a snake. An eagle (Garuda) came to my rescue and led me to a cave. I went into a state of trance when I entered the cave and noticed God Vishnu and Goddess Laxmi along with Ganesh in its central chamber (...). I noticed a face on the side of the hill. It was also perhaps a natural formation of stones but looked like a Dwaarpal (temple guard) of the temple that I had just visited.

This amazing discovery of, which may perhaps be, an old Cave Temple, on the 9 August 2005, in the remote hills of Western Australia inspires us to trace the antiquity of South Asian diaspora in Australia. Jain is not sure till date if what he 'saw was an ancient temple in ruins or just a natural rock formation with a spiritual force', but this discovery does hint towards the antiquity of the Indian presence in Australia – the labourers or some earlier Indian or Sri Lankan immigrants.[11]

A connected history is that of the Pakistani-Australian diaspora, a group whose origins in Australia are co-mingled with the Indian history due to accidents of history peculiar to the subcontinent, like the Partition of India first into India and Pakistan and then further of Pakistan into Pakistan and Bangladesh. So, the history of migration from Pakistan[12] to Australia in search of opportunities begins from undivided India. A large number of migrants presently known as 'Pakistani-Australians' have their origins in India, that is, their ancestors migrated before the partition of India in 1947. As has already been mentioned, Indian immigration to Australia has a longer tradition in Australian history that goes back to around 1800 when a small number of Hindu labourers, from various northern regions, were brought into the country for contractual work. Late in the mid-1860s, the Afghans or popularly-called 'Ghans' in Australia came from Karachi, Punjab, and Kashmir (the parts that are now in Pakistan) as camel men. They made a very crucial contribution to the exploration, development, transport, and building of the first overland telegraph line across the continent from Adelaide to Darwin and of the trans-Australian railways across Australia's far-flung regions – a contribution that is well noted in Pamela Rajkowski's *In the Tracks of the Camelmen: Outback Australia's Most Exotic Pioneers* (1987). The immigrant population from what is now Pakistan subsequently dwindled because of the White Australia Policy, as many left Australia and returned 'home'. Post-partition Pakistani migration has a relatively recent history. Pakistani nationals started coming to Australia in the 1960s but a large number came in the late 1970s and 1980s as students, professionals, and their dependent families under various plans and schemes of the Australian government – under the Humanitarian Program and the Skilled and Family Migration Streams (see Rajkowski 1987; Deen, 1992). Immigration from Pakistan increased significantly in the 1990s and by 1996 the Pakistan-born population had more than tripled. However on the other hand, scholars like Abdur Rauf believe that migration from Pakistan is inseparably linked with the arrival of Muslim traders in Australia since Pakistan's port cities, especially Karachi, served as link routes to Australia from the Middle-East countries and further deduce that Pakistanis themselves must have accompanied or followed these traders into Australia. In other words, this school of thought dissociates the Pakistani migration pattern from that of pre-partition India by linking it with the migration of Muslims to Australia from around the world. According to Abdur Rauf (1994),

> The exact date when the first Muslim arrived in Australia has not been ascertained so far. However, the remains of settlements and cemeteries of the sixteenth century Macassar Muslim fishermen have been discovered in the southern coast of the continent.

More concrete evidence to support the claim is yet to be found. Today, the majority of the Pakistani-Australians are making a substantial contribution to the process of development of the Australian continent.[13]

Next to Indians, the largest numbers of migrants who have made their presence felt are from Sri Lanka.[14] As mentioned earlier, the first recorded Sri Lankan immigration to Australia was in the year 1816 aboard Captain Cook's ship, with the transportation of Drum Major William O'Dean (a Malay) and his wife Eve (a Sinhalese) from Sri Lanka. It was in the late nineteenth century that the first significant number of Sri Lankan immigrants came to Australia (1870s), under the category of labour migration, specially recruited to work on the cane plantations of Northern Queensland, in the gold-mining fields in New South Wales, and as pearlers in Broome, Western Australia.

Following Sri Lanka's independence in 1948 and the political ascendancy of the dominant ethnic group, the Sinhalese, minority Sri Lankan groups such as the Tamils and the Burghers felt endangered and began migrating to various countries including Australia as humanitarian entrants or political refugees. During the 1960s, Burghers comprised the largest number of Sri Lanka-born migrants to Australia. By 1986, there were 22,519 Sri Lanka-born persons in Australia. While many were fleeing the political instability because of the conflict in Sri Lanka between Tamil separatists and the Sinhalese, a fairly large number of professionals were also compelled to migrate because of a stagnant Sri Lankan economy and unemployment. The case of the Sri Lankan Burghers,[15] the most Westernized and English educated of the ethnic groups in Sri Lanka, resonates in some ways with that of the Anglo-Indians. They are a Eurasian ethnic group, descendents of European colonists (mostly Portuguese, Dutch, and British), from the sixteenth to the twentieth centuries, who intermarried with local Sinhalese and Tamils. During the last few decades, the number of Sri Lankans entering Australia has been steadily increasing, with the majority of Sri Lankan-Australians located in Victoria, Western Australia, and New South Wales. They prefer to identify themselves based on ethnicity, for example, Sinhalese-Australian, Tamil-Australian, or Burgher rather than the putative homogeneous group identity 'Sri Lankan-Australian'. Sri Lanka-born immigrants are over-represented in professional and clerical occupations particularly in health and community services.

Australia did not consider South Asian countries such as Bangladesh, Nepal, and Bhutan to be of any strategic value in the past. But because of the recent migrations of professionals and skilled labourers from South Asia, the structure of Australia's population intake from these countries has increased relatively. Australia on its part is now also supporting the national governments and civil society organizations in various sectors in the South Asian region in relation to projects dealing with HIV-related research, education, human resource development, water purification, environmental sanitation, institutional reforms, good governance, and so on.

Migration from Bangladesh to Australia began in the 1970s due to the War of Independence from Pakistan in 1970, and Bangladeshis were first counted separately in the Australian census in 1976.[16] By the early 1980s, there were perhaps approximately 200 migrants in Australia from Bangladesh, nearly all professionals. In the mid-1980s, they were joined by some students pursuing tertiary studies. Between 1991 and 2001, there was a dramatic increase in the number of arrivals from Bangladesh, with the number growing to 9,000. While some arrived as a result of Skilled and Family Migration, others were accepted under the Humanitarian Program.[17] The 2001 Census estimates that as a consequence of recent relaxation in immigration policies, particularly relating to students, this number must have now grown to about 13,000–14,000 (approximately). The majority of Bangladeshis live in Sydney with a smaller though significant population in Melbourne, Canberra, and other regional capitals as well.[18]

One of the most beautiful countries of South Asia, Nepal is also making an inroad to Australia with its migrants.[19] The door to Nepalese skilled labour was opened in the 1980s, long after the abolition of the White Australia Policy. Sydney saw the influx of skilled migrants and private fee-paying students from Nepal. Australian universities also encouraged Nepalese students to come to study in Australia on scholarships. The number of private Nepalese students studying in Australia has been on the increase with 24,500 enrolments in November 2009, predominantly in vocational studies. Some Nepalese families migrated to Australia looking for a safe home after the outbreak of the insurgency in Nepal. Thus, the Nepali community grew tremendously over the years and is still growing. According to Basundhara Dhungel (2000), one of the important experiences of migrant families from

Nepal in Australia is the spotting of 'new opportunities, new lifestyle, new intimacy and companionship' (p. i). Australia and Nepal celebrate 50 years of diplomatic relations in 2010. Nepal-Australia interconnections are mostly based on tourism, education, and Australian assistance in various activities since 1960s. Many Australians have also visited, as tourists and foreign aid workers, the only Hindu Kingdom in the world and have returned home with a great fondness for the Nepali people, their ethnic culture, and culinary culture. The first and so far the only man-made cave temple dedicated to the Lord Shiva, the Mukti Gupteshwar Mandir, also known as the Minto Hindu temple, was made by the Nepalese community in Australia. To make the bonds between the two countries stronger, there exist a few associations in Australia. Foremost among them is the Nepalese Australian Association (NAA) established in Sydney in 1976, which has helped Nepalese-Australians with a range of issues, from emotional and humanitarian ones. Its other objectives include assisting the newly arrived Nepalese, whether they are students on scholarships or short-term visitors, and to act as an unofficial embassy in providing information about Nepal to Australians.[20]

Similarly, a small but fair number of tertiary educational scholarships for Bhutan have provided Bhutanese students with an opportunity of visiting Australia and pursuing various professional courses.[21] Initially Australia agreed to resettle Bhutanese refugees from Nepal under the Humanitarian Programme over a number of years as part of a coordinated international strategy. According to the recent census, the Bhutanese community in Australia is very small. To date, more than 750 Bhutanese have resettled in different parts of Australia. On 13 May 2009, approximately 300 Bhutanese gathered at Olympic House at Franklin Street, South Australia, showcasing their food, culture, dance, and singing to celebrate the first anniversary of their arrival in Australia. The community's progress in Australia has been phenomenal and for the children, teenagers, and youth the future holds a lot of promise.[22]

For some South Asian migrants, Australia was only the journey, not the end, being 'a stepping stone on a route eventually reaching the United States, a country which continues to be the ultimate desired destination for many Indians' (Voigt-Graf, 2003: p.

143). However, recent changes made in Australia's migration policy will make access to a good education and opportunities possible for deserving students (Valentine, 2010). So it is worth concluding this history of the South Asian's migration to Australia with Vinay Lal's pertinent observation in the "Diaspora Purana" (2003). Lal thinks that the South Asian diaspora has

> come out of the shadows in recent years, and its largely forgotten history, which encompasses narratives of displacement, migration, the cross-fertilization of ideas, and the emergence of new cultural forms and practices, is increasingly being viewed as an important and intrinsic part of the story of late modernity and humanity's drift towards globalization, transnational economic and cultural exchanges, and hybrid forms of political, cultural, and social identity.

It is these hitherto ignored histories of South Asian migration to the antipodes that this collection will recuperate and assess.

Researches on South Asian Diaspora in Australia

South Asians in Australia, as noted above, still only make up a small proportion of the population as a whole, although their total numbers have grown rapidly since the early 1990s. South Asian diasporic literature has, according to Tamara M. Athique (2006) 'in a relatively short space of time, achieved commercial and critical success' and 'come of age' (p. 1). Today, critics and reviewers speak of 'unprecedented attention'. This high profile is also related to South Asian diaspora's 'visibility in other areas of cultural production, notably in film, music and fashion' (Athique: p. 1). Although critical books on and by the South Asian diaspora are not many – small but significant researches have steadily increased in number akin to the achievements of the South Asian diaspora during the last decade. This is attested by the plethora of recent publications and conference calls for papers, and academic interest in the South Asian diaspora. Some well-organized and thoughtfully conceptualized historical studies of the South Asian diaspora by academics often belonging to South Asian communities or led by scholars belonging to other racialized minority groups in Australia have helped to reveal the complex historical processes and the limitations of past research done by Anglo-Australians.

Today, nothing can alter the fact that South Asians have become an integral part of the Australian social order. The diaspora has helped in opening up borders between cultures and has inspired various critics and scholars to theorize the diasporic condition in relation to its historical, social, political, economic, cultural, and personal contexts (see A. Sarwal, 2006). The dilemmas of the migrants 'become more poignant when migrants find that despite all their new opportunities, they still remain aliens at their destination' (Ballard, 1994: p. 9) and no attention is paid towards ethnic issues such as the achievements of their communities or to the multicultural education of their children.

The study of South Asian diaspora, in recent years, has emerged as an important branch of both social sciences and literature. In India according to N. Jayaram (2004), the study of overseas Indians has evolved through three phases:

1. *The cultural perspective phase* that focused on the study of cultural dynamics of the diasporic community, particularly on the questions of cultural continuity and change, identity, and integration, and resilience and adaptation.
2. *The structural perspective phase* with its focus on the study of structural dimensions such as gender in Indian diaspora, caste in Indian diaspora, regional identities in Indian diaspora, and the issues of racial discrimination.
3. *The political phase* that focuses on the role of the Indian state and its diasporic policy. Three questions in particular: (a) What has the Indian state done for the Indian communities in various parts of the world? (b) What has the Indian diaspora done for or against the Indian state? (c) What should the Indian state do to cultivate and harness the Indian diaspora as a resource for Indian development? (pp. 15–43)

Similarly, critical literature on South Asian diaspora in Australia can be distinguished into three major groups: historical, anthropological/sociological, and literary analyses.

Sociological and Anthropological Researches

There are relatively more historical, anthropological, and sociological studies available on the South Asian diaspora in Australia, most notably *Indians in a White Australia* (1984), *The Anglo-Indian*

Vision (1986a), *The Lotus and the Rose* (1986b), *In the Tracks of the Camelmen* (1987), *Complexities of the Sri Lankan Migrants in Australia* (1987), *Indians in Victoria (Australia): A Historical, Social and Demographic Profile of Indian Immigrants* (1988), *Links Between Sri Lanka and Australia* (1988), *From India to Australia* (1992), *Proud and Prejudiced: The Story of the Burghers of Sri Lanka* (1995), *Caravanserai: Journey Among Australian Muslims* (1995), *The Hindus and Sikhs in Australia* (1996), *Sikhs in Australia* (1998), *Indian Daughters Abroad* (2000), *A Punjabi Sikh Community in Australia: From Indian Sojourners to Australian Citizens* (2001), *The Muslims in Australia* (2002), *My Journey Behind the Veil: Conversations with Muslim Women* (2002), *Australia for Pakistanis: Where Cultures Meet* (2003), *A Passage from India: Anglo-Indians in Victoria* (2004), *The Anglo-Indian Australian Story: My Experience – A Collection of Anglo-Indian Migration Heritage Stories* (2004), and *Colonial Cousins: A Surprising History of Connections between India and Australia* (2010).

Pamela Rajkowski's *In the Tracks of the Camelmen: Outback Australia's Most Exotic Pioneers* is a ground-breaking study that records the contribution of the 'Afghan' camelmen or cameleers – mainly men from northern India and Afghanistan – in the opening up and development of the Australian colonies (pp. xi–xii). She writes:

> They were a network – bringing together the many dispersed settlements around the gold-mining fields of Western Australia and connecting them to larger supply and coastal service centres; connecting the sheep properties of South Australia's far north; passing up the Strzelecki, Birdsville and Oodnadatta Tracks and over the borders into the Northern Territory; connecting the region of New South Wales west of the Darling River with southern and western Queensland. (p. xi)

Rajkowski sees the coming of Indian and Afghan cameleers to Australia as a 'movement of one group of colonists to another colony within the one great empire, the British Empire' (p. 1). The word 'Afghan' or 'Ghan' was given as a title to these cameleers to differentiate between the two groups of Indian migrants – one working on camel strings in the desert region and the other working on coastal plantations and farms. She notes that the 'work done by the Afghans and their camels (...) was commemorated by the naming of certain improvements and paddocks after them' (p. 33). The book is a lucid account of the contribution of the Afghan and Indian camelmen to the 'economic development and indeed survival of many of the outback settlements' of Australia. It is 'a tribute to their efforts and a record of their lives and achievements' (p. 184).

Purushottama Bilimoria and Ruchira Ganguly-Scrase's *Indians in Victoria (Australia): A Historical, Social and Demographic Profile of Indian Immigrants* is a pioneering monograph published on the Indian community, contributing in a significant way to furthering an understanding of the intricate features that characterize the Indian community that has settled in Victoria (Australia). While the study is extremely interesting, both authors are aware of its limitations in the absence of insufficient historical, social, and demographic information on the Indian community. The basic concern of this study is to collect relevant information and detail with respect to the pattern of settlement, adaptability, linguistic and cultural integration, educational and professional status, cultural orientation, and welfare issues. In this light, it can be counted among the best in the archive of documentation generated in the 1980s on ethnic minorities in Australia.

From India to Australia: A Brief History of Immigration; The Dismantling of the 'White Australia' Policy; Problems and Prospects of Assimilation as the name suggests is an historical account of Indian migration, white Australia policy and assimilation models employed in Australia. In his Introduction, the editor S. Chandrasekhar surveys the land, the mountains, the rivers, the fauna and the flora, the climate, and the weather along with the Aborigines, economy, Indian contract labour in Australia, and Immigration Restriction Act (1901). The book is a collection of well-conceived articles engaging with historical and political issues of Indian migration to Australia.

Vijaya Joshi's study *Indian Daughters Abroad: Growing Up in Australia* tells the 'stories of the real-life experience of marginal groups' particularly about the second generation. She writes that it was her own ethnic identity that prompted her to undertake this research, which through interviews with second-generation Indian women in Australia, assesses their status and lack of power within the diaspora and Australia. The book 'maps some of the socio-cultural themes which frame a second generation Indian woman's life in Australia' (p. 1), particularly studying the construction of gender roles within Indian culture. She concludes that for 'the women, understanding their gender roles within their family and community were intertwined with their cultural role. They were not women within the Indian community, but *Indian* women' (p. 202). So in her work South Asian diasporic woman becomes a location for traditions that others have abandoned.

Joyce Westrip's and Peggy Holroyde's *Colonial Cousins: A Surprising History of Connections between India and Australia* traces the real story of the links between India and Australia and presents through an Australian perspective an 'Australian Tale' of connections. According to the authors this is 'a personal exploration into an Indian-Australian landscape, a subject largely ignored or overlooked by recorders of social history, novelists and the media' (p. 3). The authors use archival material and interviews with people all over Australia, who are linked in one way or other, to the two countries and 'share their memoirs, diaries and reminiscences of India experiences' (Hayes: p. IX). Westrip and Holroyde write that their 'long quest for elusive connections', fell into three sections:

1. that of affinities, conjectured and real, which we certainly, and others in their own way, could affirm. This became the bedrock of the text.
2. research into documented evidence long since absorbed into state archives or forgotten private memorabilia. Both of these provided a context and a framework of history for the third area.
3. the anecdotal, based in the taped reflections, the immediate linking of people, many still alive, who can trace memories back through several generations, or who still travel between India and Australia as their forebears did from the earliest days of settlement. This was the oral history. (p. 7)

This book 'traverses a period of history involving the movement of Anglo-Indians from India to Australia and is the first time anyone has recorded such a comprehensive social history covering one group migrating from India to Australia over two centuries' (Hayes: p. XI). *Colonial Cousins* is the story of India and Australia, not of the British Raj. It is 'another story' – 'a real down-to-earth Australian version of experience in and with India from the very first days of settlement by the white British' (p. 1). The authors note that the connections between Australia and India were quite different from that between Britain and India, as 'India and Australia often suffered together under the watchful paternalism, and maternalism in the latter part of Victoria's reign, of the mother country' (p. 1). The book not only traces the human links but also geological, anthropological, architectural, and mythological similarities between the island of Australia and subcontinental India. The authors are aware that the records referred to in this book are 'incomplete or require further research' but since this research has been funded privately such limitations are acceptable. Through their book, the authors 'have managed to blend the unusual story of the "colonial cousins" in historical times with more recent developments in the India-Australia relationship in terms of trade and business' (Hayes: p. XI). Although Westrip and Holroyde, both over 85 years of age in the book, present their 'deep understanding and genuine love of India and Australia' (Hayes: XII), their passion as Australians for the India subcontinent once again reminds us of the necessity of more researches based on the same format by younger researchers who have professional backing and proper resources (p. 8).

Some ethnic migrant communities in regional Australia have been the focus for relatively constant studies by anthropologists. In White Australia, 'Sikh' and 'Punjabi' were almost synonymous words. Marie De Lepervanche in *Indians in a White Australia: An Account of Race, Class and Indian Immigration to Eastern Australia* embarks upon an anthropological fieldwork journey. Her study of the Punjabi community of Woolgoolga, undertaken in the 1970s, provided the basis for understanding how the white Australian ideologies, policies, and practices affected the community. Through her interaction with the Punjabi community in the villages, she recorded the fascinating story of their community development, successful establishment of the Punjabi settlers whose banana farming and cane-cutting jobs provided the source of income. The connections between these pioneer settlers with their home villages, and their arranged marriage alliances with partners from

India are also examined. She notes that this continuing contact with their culture and customs also provided a secure foundation for their adjustment to different social and cultural attitudes in Australia. De Lepervanche's doctoral fieldwork was also among Punjabi Indian settlers on the New South Wales North Coast, an enterprise that entailed a critical inquiry into the interrelation of race, ethnicity, and class in Australian society.

Purushottama Bilimoria's *The Hindus and Sikhs in Australia* is a part of the *Community Profile* series instituted by the Bureau of Immigration, Multicultural and Population Research. The main aim of the series is to provide a perspective on the Australian population through a description of the religious communities with which the people identify. The profiles tell a story of immigration and settlement. This book is a detailed account and examination of the religious beliefs and practices of Hindus and Sikhs in Australia. Some of the possibilities and challenges that Hindus and Sikhs face living in Australia's multicultural society are noted, the documentation of which will hopefully permit a better climate for engagement between the host populations and the newer immigrants. Bilimoria concludes that 'Hindus and Sikhs, like all South Asians in Australia, have endured many hardships, and experienced prejudices on account of their colour or religious background' but they have 'preserved despite social and cultural alienation (...)' (p. 73). To him in 'the broader context of mainstream Australian society, the Sikh *gurdwara* with its "Word as God", and the moon-domes of the Hindu temple with its myriad of gods, symbolise in their different ways the struggle of maintaining distinctive communities within a decidedly multicultural and ethnically plural environment' (p. 74).

R.S. Gabbi's *Sikhs in Australia* is dedicated to the 'Pioneer Sikhs in Australia who did not lose their heart under discriminating and unbearable conditions and gave the footings to the present Sikh community in Australia' (p. 3). It is a brief but reliable history of Sikhs in Australia and shows Gabbi's knowledge of Sikhism and community life. His work differs from others as he exclusively chooses Sikhs, while most of the earlier works focused more on Hindus. The book helps us understand the contribution the Sikhs have made in the development of Australia while working under unbearable conditions in the nineteenth and twentieth centuries. According to Gabbi,

> Sikhs had a very distinctive life in the late 19th and the early part of 20th century. They were not willing to assimilate or even integrate with Europeans but European children were always happy to play with them. Most of the Sikhs were single as very few could bring their wives into Australia or get married to Aborigines or European women (...). (p. 110)

Gabbi's book also contains a plea to present generations of Sikhs to 'set up such an image of a Sikh so that coming generations feel proud to be a Sikh and Australians will hold them in high esteem' (p. 189). In his conclusion Gabbi, to join others in the task of related research on Sikhs in Australia, suggests to all Sikhs to 'see directories under "SINGH" when they pass through or visit any town or city of Australia and try to establish a branch of "Australian Sikhs Historical Society" in each state with an Australian based headquarters. For a long time to come, such information will become an authentic reference and a source of positive thinking about the place of Sikhs in Australia's past, present and future' (p. 189).

A Punjabi Sikh Community in Australia: From Indian Sojourners to Australian Citizens, edited by Rashmere Bhatti (co-ordinator and community settlement services officer at the WNC) and Verne A. Dusenbery (a scholar of Sikh communities in multicultural societies outside of India) was developed as a project[23] over a number of years in response to local, national, and international curiosity about the Punjabi Sikh community in the Woolgoolga-Coffs Harbour area and how they came to be established on the north coast of New South Wales. Bhatti writes about her own experience in the community: 'As an Australian born Punjabi Sikh, I value the unique experiences that I have had with both Punjabis and non-Punjabis, at both a professional and personal level, in this community. My being bicultural – at home in both worlds – is what has made this project possible' (Preface).

The Punjabi Sikhs in Australia today are highly diverse in terms of their migration biographies, their cultural and social lives, their economic activities, and their transnational kinship ties. This book is a 'a portrait of a Punjabi Sikh community having weathered the era of the White Australia Policy and coming to terms with evolving Australian multiculturalism' (Preface). The story of how Sikhs, as Indians (a restricted race), entered and ultimately settled in a white Australia is unique. According to Bhatti and Dusenbery, it came about as a result of the political, social, and economic changes taking place in both Australia and India and because of the link these two countries had as members of the British Empire. Importantly, the Punjabi Sikh community's settlement reflects this country's growth from a white Australia to a nation embracing Australian Multiculturalism as an ideology. The book also analyses the roots that Punjabis have planted in Australia and how they have managed to retain many aspects of their traditional culture and religion, the establishment of *gurdwaras*, arranged marriages, retaining of property or ancestral land, maintaining close contacts with relatives in Punjab, community (ethnic) newspapers and radio programmes, and associations to celebrate festivals and other Punjabi recreational activities in Australia. The prominent contributors to this study – W.H. McLeod, Marie M. de Lepervanche, Carmen Voigt-Graf, Verne A. Dusenbery, and Ramindar Singh – through their anthropological fieldwork and sociological studies of the community feel that the times ahead bode well for a community as promising as the Punjabi Sikhs with impressive achievements, both in religion and in the world. This book is an interesting collaborative undertaking that not only provides considerable background information on Sikhs and white Australia ideologies, policies, and practices that affected the community in Australia but also opens up new issues of research related to gender and generation studies. The framework and methodology used in this project also inspires young scholars to research more on South Asian migrant communities and tell their stories.

Tania De Jong writes that she embarked on her study, *Complexities of the Sri Lankan Migrants in Australia*, 'as a hobby' and because of her 'strong interest in migration' (pp. ii–iii). Her study concentrates, she writes in her Introduction, on a set of human relations that are directly linked with the process of migration. She argues that this process is a particular significant component of the wider processes of social change and modernization. Her analysis of Sri Lankan migrants in Australia, according to her, 'proceeds diachronically, trying to understand human reality and relationships through the long journey which brought them to this current situation' (p. vi). She also surveys the condition of Sri Lankan migrants during the 1980s Australia. However, she feels that her synchronic analysis of the Sri Lankan community is severely restricted by the lack of sociological analyses, studies, data, and statistics on Sri Lankan-Australians. Hence, her study is to a great extent result of her own 'participation, observation, curiosity and questioning of those complexities Lankans face in Australian society (...)' (p. vii). She analyses Sri Lankan reactions within the Australian society in the socio-historical context of 1950–1982. She discusses Sri Lankan migration history to Australia and Australia's immigration policies and does a brief historical overview of culture and population. But her main focus in this short study is on Sri Lankan migrant complexities and processes of absorption, integration, and assimilation (p. 82). She concludes her study with a question: 'Whether they (Sri Lankans) will be recognized as a national and cultural entity, within the context of multiculturalism for all Australians, remains to be seen' (p. 83). Though the entire study is only a hundred pages long, but the depth of knowledge about the issues it covers and its anthropological approach are both quite fascinating.

In *Links Between Sri Lanka and Australia*, W.S. Weerasooria, a prominent lawyer, civil servant, diplomat, an academic, and former Sri Lankan High Commissioner to Australia and New Zealand, notes that the Australian Aborigines probably originated in South India from where they made their way to Australia via Ceylon, Malaya, and Indonesia. This argument thus makes the Veddas, the original inhabitants of Sri Lanka, a possible connection in the migration chain. His book is based on previous researches in collaboration with the researchers who have done major and minor researches on the community at various Australian universities. Writing (or compiling) this book on Sri Lankan migration to Australia, in Weerasooria's words, was 'a voyage of discovery' (p. 42).

Rodney Ferdinands' *Proud and Prejudiced* tells the story of the Burghers before the mass migration, their exodus to new countries after the war, and their experiences of assimilation in Australia with the help of historical records, interviews, recollections, and anecdotes. Both a sociological history as well as a personal account into the heritage of a group hitherto minoritized into a larger 'Sri Lankan' history and nomenclature, the book is full of hope for the descendants of Burghers who chose Australia as their new home. With English as their first language and their dedication to assimilate, their adaptation to Australian ways of life was considerably easier than the rest of the Sri Lankan migrants (particularly from non-English backgrounds). According to Ferdinands, 'Burghers do not think of themselves as on the margins of Australian society. They do not see themselves, in the political sense, as Sri Lankans. They have assimilated into mainstream (Australian) society. Politically conscious Burghers are already active in the wider community' (p. 262).

The migration of Muslims to Australia also forms the subject of a number of studies. The Muslim strength in Australia is an issue of debate, as there is no separate census data on Muslims and the diverse groups (belonging to different nationalities) within it. Bilal Cleland's study *The Muslims in Australia* tries to provide an account of progress of Islam in Australia. His story of Islam's journey in Australia starts long before the white settlement, stretching back to traders from Macassar with links to Aborigines in northern Australia. Cleland not only outlines the achievements of Australian Muslims but also reveals the problems that they have faced – from community misconceptions to divisions in their own rank. He writes of the 'despised men' (p. 1) – Afghan and Indian Muslim cameleers and hawkers. But later observes that 'Indian Muslims were not discriminated against (in Australia) on religious grounds during the course of the war (World War I)' (p. 52).

Hanifa Deen, a third-generation Australian of Pakistani-Muslim ancestry, an active Australian human rights activist, and a social commentator, in her prize-winning book *Caravanserai: Journey among Australian Muslims*, portrays the lives of Muslims in Australia. Its title, *Caravanserai*, refers to the central court of an inn where caravans pull in for the night. Caravans, or covered wagons, were the mobile homes of many Muslims who later came to Australia to make a living by hawking goods. She observes

> Caravanserai were not the place to maintain a social distance; travellers from different lands did not keep one another at arm's length. Everyone gathered together, sharing, exchanging, enjoying one another's company – unless you happened to be a blood enemy; though even then you enjoyed sanctuary in the caravanserai. (p. viii)

Deen further challenges the misleading stereotypes – images of veiled women, fierce bearded men, barbaric parents, rapists, and suicide bombers – that the Western media has spread. She notes that 'Muslims are highlighted as a "problem" with little in common with other Australians' (p. vii). Deen through her sensitive narrative provides 'Muslims a human face' (p. vii) and shows them as ordinary people who have their own little problems like everybody else, who have a mortgage to pay; who like sports and watching rugby matches; who worry about gaining weight; who send their children to school; who pay tax; who vote. She says that her book is not 'religious' or 'academic' or '*Who's Who* of the Muslim world in Australia' (p. vii). She concludes that there is 'enormous diversity among Australian Muslims' (p. 215) and with education and knowledge 'Young Muslims in the twenty-first century will be better equipped in terms of confidence and skills to reduce the social distance which exists between them and non-Muslims' (p. 217). Although in the second edition of her book published in 2003 after 9/11 attacks and Bali bombings of 2002, when she revisited the Muslim people she originally interviewed in Australia to discover how recent international events have affected their daily lives, she notes that Australia has shifted from the welcoming caravanserai that she had originally envisaged to a place that many Australian Muslims no longer see as safe for their families. Her book is a valuable contribution to the long and rich history of the books on Muslims and Australian life.

Kay Rasool's *My Journey Behind the Veil: Conversations with Muslim Women* draws upon the lives of women in Australia, India, and Pakistan and provides portraits of Muslim women from diverse backgrounds. The book is based on her documentary *My Journey, My Islam*, made for ABC TV. It explores the relevance of the veil in a modern world and the stories of the women who wear it. She says, 'My task is to give a human face to women who wear the veil, especially those who live in a Western society, and are not compelled in any way to cover their heads' (p. xiv). Thus, she is able to uncover a range of often opposing perspectives to personal belief and dispel stereotypes. The book will be a success according to Rasool 'if my readers can look at a covered head without surprise or wonder, as just part of the normal landscape of a multicultural society' (p. xv).

The dissertations submitted in the field of sociology outnumber the literary ones. Pandula Endagama's study "Sri

Lankan Material Culture in North-East Queensland: A Study of Acculturation" (1981) submitted at James Cook University; Sisiri Kumara Pinnawala's PhD thesis "Sri Lankans in Melbourne: Factors Influencing Patterns of Ethnicity" (1984) submitted at Australian National University; Rosita Joan Henry's PhD thesis "A Tulip in Lotus Land: The Rise and Decline of Dutch Burgher Ethnicity in Sri Lanka" (1986) submitted at Australian National University; Adrian Gilbert's PhD thesis "The Anglo-Indians in Australia: From Unsuccessful Caste Members to Attaining Immigrants" (1996) submitted at Monash University; Basundhara Dhungel's dissertation titled "A Study of Nepalese Families' Paid and Unpaid Work after Migration to Australia" (2000) submitted at The University of Sydney; Bianca M. Fijac and Christopher C. Sonn's research on "Pakistani-Muslim Immigrant Women in Western Australia: Perceptions of Identity and Community" (2004) submitted at Edith Cowan University; and Michiel Baas' PhD thesis titled "Imagined Mobility: Migration and Transnationalism among Indian Students in Australia" (2009) submitted at University of Amsterdam.

Pandula Endagama's study, "Sri Lankan Material Culture in North-East Queensland: A Study of Acculturation", focuses on Sri Lankans who immigrated to Australia after 1948 and also on some of the descendants of early pioneer migrant who came on the ship *Devonshire* in 1882. The primary objective of his study is to identify and analyse what these Sri Lankan immigrants had retained of their original ethnic culture and the ways in which the links with the homeland were maintained, which he does by way of a fascinating examination of a catalogue of personal possessions that the Sri Lankan migrants brought over, such as furniture, household items, dresses, objects of religious or caste significance, musical instruments, native plants, and the like.

Sisiri Kumara Pinnawala's PhD thesis "Sri Lankans in Melbourne: Factors Influencing Patterns of Ethnicity" is one of the most comprehensive researches on Sri Lankan migrants. He notes that some Sri Lankan immigrants, in the Australian context, prefer their ethnic identity, for example Sinhalese-, Tamil- or Burgher-Australian. He notes that most of the Sri Lankans who have settled since 1950s in Melbourne belong to the middle-class. His study of the Melbourne Sri Lankans is based on data from the Australian Bureau of Statistics, fieldwork, interviews and questionnaires, and discussions with officials of different clubs and associations and community leaders. His division of the Sri Lankan migrants into three sociological categories or groups, namely Ethnic Assimilationists (Burghers), Ethnic Intergrationists (Sinhalese and Tamil Christians), and Ethnic Traditionalists (Sinhalese Buddhists and Tamil Hindus), is quite interesting in the way Sri Lankan Diaspora sees itself in Australia.

Rosita Joan Henry in her PhD thesis "A Tulip in Lotus Land: The Rise and Decline of Dutch Burgher Ethnicity in Sri Lanka" considers the historical processes and human agency involved in the creation of a particular identity category, the Dutch Burghers of Sri Lanka, their rise and fall. She does so by reflecting upon Karl Marx's maxim that 'People make their own histories, but not just as they please'. Her thesis, like her other studies on the same theme, is homage to the Dutch Burgher migrants and their life experiences.

Basundhara Dhungel's dissertation "A Study of Nepalese Families' Paid and Unpaid Work after Migration to Australia" is a case study of 28 couple families, who migrated from Nepal under 'skill' or 'professional' category. Dhungel observes that the patterns of paid and unpaid work adopted by migrant families with dependent children are more or less similar to that of prevailing working pattern of men and women of Australian-born couples (whites). The only factor that differentiates working pattern of migrant families with Australian-born families (whites) is the experience of migration and their categorization as migrants. One of the important experiences of migrant families is that there are new opportunities, new lifestyles, new intimacy and companionship, and new sharing of work between husbands and wives after migration. At the same time, there are losses of extended family relatives, close friends, and cultural events, which affect their day to day lives. However, there are Australian-based friends who provided support in the initial period of migration but these families do not provide regular assistance or support that family relatives provided in Nepal.

Bianca M. Fijac and Christopher C. Sonn's research paper entitled "Pakistani-Muslim Immigrant Women in Western Australia: Perceptions of Identity and Community" explores the perceptions and experiences of impacting identity and community for Pakistani-Muslim immigrant women living Western Australia. Ten Pakistani-Muslim immigrant women, aged 40–50 years, who immigrated to Australia in the 1970s, were interviewed about their perceptions and experiences of their community. The findings indicated that the role of religion was a core component in the experience of community and the settlement process. Racism and exclusion, social support structures, and gender roles were other factors impacting the development and maintenance of the identity and community of this group.

Adrian Gilbert's PhD thesis "The Anglo-Indians in Australia: From Unsuccessful Caste Members to Attaining Immigrants" analysed the successful settlement and progress of Australian Anglo Indians. One of his most interesting findings is that Anglo Indians in Australia are doing better in both fact and perception than in Britain or, indeed, in India. Gilbert notes that the Anglo-Indians in Australia are doing better than people of Australian descent, although there are some areas of concern, such as the under-representation of Anglo-Indians in management positions and the lower hourly earnings of Anglo-Indians with higher degrees. Gilbert's is one of the important studies of Anglo-Indians who settled in Australia (see also Assisi, 2006).

Because of a recent increase in racist and/or opportunistic assaults and attacks ('curry-bashing') on Indian students in 2009, the issue of Indian students in Australia made headlines around the world. The incidents happened when Michiel Baas' thesis had already been completed and there was thus little he could do with this new development. His PhD thesis, "Imagined Mobility: Migration and Transnationalism among Indian Students in Australia", a result of being involved in the topic of Indian (overseas) students for over five years, focuses on the case of Indian overseas students who go to Australia not just to study but also to migrate there. Baas notes that by the end of 2006, there were nearly 350,000 overseas students (including 38,700 Indian students) enrolled across all educational sectors in Australia, making the country one of the biggest players in the world of 'offering/selling education'. This number continued to grow and reached new heights by the end of 2008. Because of the recent race attacks on Indian students, this increase in numbers has declined a bit but Australia still remains a popular destination for overseas study. He argues in his thesis that 'imagination is crucial in understanding people's desire to be transnationally mobile. This goes not only for understanding why people decide to migrate but also how they experience the process of leaving one's country of origin behind and making their way into a new one' (p. 3). Central to this examination are the questions: how do Indians experience the process of migrating abroad, aiming for an Australian permanent residency (PR), while being overseas students at the same time? He explores these questions with three interrelated concepts: imagined mobility, arrival points, and in-betweenness. Adrian Bailey (2001) has argued that: 'key questions of migrant agency and hybridity remain under-theorized' (p. 413) in migration studies. Baas' thesis ultimately fills this lacuna by bringing in migrant's agency into a study on migration and transnationalism. He examines the way Indian students experience the process they are undergoing (which for many is the underlying reason for having chosen Australia as a study-abroad destination) in light of the finding that studies of transnationalism pay little to no attention to the (individual) process of transnationalization itself (p. 10). His passion for the welfare of students, awareness of the ongoing events, and multiple dimensional possibilities for further research is reflected when he writes that 'I am still in active touch with many of the people who colored my fieldwork I consider my research as ongoing, likely to yield more data in the years to come' (p. 11).

Literary Researches

Very few studies have dealt with the subject – I have come across only a handful of literary researches on South Asian diaspora in Australia. This includes books such as *Celebrations: Fifty Years of Sri Lanka-Australia Interactions* (1997), *Celebrations! – Sinhalese and Sri Lankan Women in Canberra: Testimonies and Memories* (2008), Sissy Helff's *Unreliable Truths* (2013), and my edited collection: *Bridging Imaginations: South Asian Diaspora in Australia* (2013). Apart from my own MPhil dissertation, titled "Postcards from Trishankus: Images of India and Australia in South Asian-Australian Short Stories" (2006) and PhD thesis, titled "Roots & Routes: Politics of Location in the Short Stories of South Asian Diaspora in Australia" (2010) submitted at Jawaharlal Nehru University, I have come across

Glenn D'Cruz' PhD thesis titled 'Representing' Anglo-Indians: A Genealogical Investigation" (1999) submitted at University of Melbourne, Sharmini Kannan's MA dissertation titled "Pappadums in Paradise? – Journeys of Indian Migrant Women to Australia" (2002) submitted at Deakin University, Mohit Manoj Prasad's PhD thesis titled "Indo-Fijian Diasporic Bodies: Narratives in Text, Image, Popular Culture, and the Lived Everyday in Fiji and Liverpool, Sydney Australia" (2005) submitted at University of Western Sydney. Tamara Mabbott Athique's PhD thesis on South Asian Diaspora literature in Australia titled "Textual Migrations: South Asian-Australian Fiction" (2006) submitted at University of Wollongong; and Pauline Lalthlamuanpii's MPhil dissertation "A Study of Women's Characters in Yasmine Gooneratne's Novels *A Change of Skies* and *The Pleasures of Conquest*" (2009), submitted at Jawaharlal Nehru University.

Celebrations: Fifty Years of Sri Lanka-Australia Interactions, edited by Cynthia Vanden Driesen and I.H. Vanden Driesen, as the title suggests celebrates the contribution of Sri Lankans to Australia. This edited collection contains views on Sri Lankan diaspora and writers from Australia along with a few literary articles. This massive book of about 31 essays, biographical writing, fictional work, and poems was released to commemorate the 50th Anniversary of Sri Lankan Independence. Sri Lankan migration has steadily increased since World War II. *Celebrations* feature issues and personalities of national and international importance, and the stories from the community that provide insights into a range of life experiences. This book, intended for general readers (both Australians and Sri Lankans), is an informative and valuable contribution to an understanding of the Sri Lankan diaspora, its postarrival experiences, success, problems, and hopes in Australia. Contribution to this collection ranges across fields as varied as the academia, law, business, and sciences. In most of the stories collected here, the writers recount the day when they decided to migrate to Australia. Writing in the Foreword to this tome, Alison Broinowski (1997) says:

> They recall the date of their arrival, and the weather on that day. Being met by relatives, Sri Lankan or Australian friends, made the difference between feeling welcome and wishing they had not

> come. Small gestures of kindness from neighbours were worth much more than those who made them knew. (...) Some find a new vocation in working with other migrants, or with Aborigines. Others recognize some of the obstacles confronting them for what they are, protectionism, and they each find their own way to overcome them. (p. xvi)

This book makes an important contribution to multicultural Australia by showing us that 'it exists not only in a policy but in people's lives and the choices they make; (...) and the need for all of us to appreciate that diaspora involves coping with difference, indeed relishing it' (Broinowski: p. xvii). So the recurring note in this book is of celebration – 'celebration of Australia, their adopted land, for affording them the opportunity to reinvent themselves as it were and yet with this theme remains a nostalgic love and acknowledgement of the debt owed their original homeland, Sri Lanka' (vanden Driesen and vanden Driesen: p. xxi).

Celebrations! – Sinhalese and Sri Lankan Women in Canberra: Testimonies and Memories, edited by Thishanka Karunarathna and compiled by Badra Kamal Karunarathna, of the Sinhala Cultural Association under a project funded through the 2006–2007 ACT Women's Grants Program is an extraordinary collection of life stories presenting hopes, joys, and challenges of ordinary Sri Lankan-Australian women who have made their home in Canberra over the last two decades and as they establish themselves in a new country. Sri Lankans and Sinhalese make up a small but vibrant part of the ACT's population. By compiling and publishing this massive collection, Karunarathna has put to history the extremely important contribution and experiences of women from South Asian cultural background – housewives, academics, social workers, journalists, and others.

Sissy Helff's *Unreliable Truths: Transcultural Homeworlds in Indian Women's Fiction of the Diaspora* explores migratory histories of homemaking in South Asian Diaspora and globalized world. Chapter 4, titled 'Growing up in Transcultural Diasporic Worlds', analyses Suneeta Peres Da Costa's novel *Homework* (the only one for study in this book) as a novel of formation that charts a young person's development through complex fictionalized experience. Helff notes that although South Asian-Australian diaspora writing is 'still in its infancy, and there is little critical appraisal of it as yet' (p. 112) but there are some promising new voices and talent, who are working towards creating an oeuvre and providing new perspectives on Australia through their stories.

My edited collection, *Bridging Imaginations: South Asian Diaspora in Australia*, containing essays that are both informative and theoretically astute from eminent scholars from diverse disciplinary standpoints, is considered a foundational volume dealing with cross-cultural themes in Australia. According to Vijay Mishra, in his endorsement, the 'essays in the volume establish the parameters for any future study of the South Asian diasporic imaginary in Australia' (Back cover). It is an exciting collection that serves as a timely reminder of the extraordinary historical depth of the presence of the South Asians in Australia. It covers conversations combined together with a broad range of academic material under a variety of approaches: historical, sociological, film, media, literature, and politics. This book provides a splendid overview of South Asian Diaspora's way of living and covers varied topics of historic importance – from pioneering Indian coolies, hawkers, and labourers in the Queensland sugar plantations to students, academicians, and other professionals in more recent times.

Glenn D'Cruz's PhD thesis titled 'Representing' Anglo-Indians: A Genealogical Investigation" examined Anglo-Indian representations in the social sciences, literature, and films. In "Beyond the Pale" (2004), he says that he began his research as an academic to seek a better understanding and 'discover the historical and cultural factors' that shaped his Anglo-Indian identity in Australia (p. 226). Using the postcolonial theories of Bhabha, Spivak, and Said as an 'insight', he writes that his research helped him to

> come to terms with my cultural identity, it helped me to answer some questions about my family's odd quirks that had long perplexed me. In some instances these often personal eccentricities resonate with history in curious ways. (2004: p. 227)

He observed in his thesis that the social sciences continue to construct the Anglo-Indian as 'a rather pathetic figure' on the 'margins of legitimate society'. He writes that

> Anglo-Indians are the smallest, and possibly, minority group in India. They are the literal progeny of European colonization, and

> are often stereotyped as being 'more British than the British' because they practise Christianity, speak English as their first language and generally adopt British social customs. (2004: p. 223)

The result being, most frequent representation of the Anglo-Indian male as a social and cultural misfit, like a 'marginal man' whose problems exist because of 'an unrealistic self-image'. During the course of his research, he discovered that Anglo-Indians in British India had the reputation of being the best clerks – 'a natural vocation for Anglo-Indians' (2004: p. 227). So, to him

> It was, therefore, gratifying to recognise that in writing my PhD thesis I finally became a clerk of sorts. I sifted through fragments, organizing a mass of haphazard documents and records. The archival records told me quite a bit about Anglo-Indians, satisfying my inner clerk, but it was the critical analysis of personal artifacts I uncovered during the course of my research that I found most compelling, and most helpful in putting my life and my sense of subjectivity into context. (2004: p. 228)

With the help of archival material, he contested the 'various deprecatory stereotypes of Anglo-Indians that circulated in the literary and social-scientific texts' (2004: p. 228). Rather than simply dismissing the representation of Anglo-Indians in literary texts as offensive stereotypes, D'Cruz identifies the conditions for the emergence of these stereotypes through close readings of writers such as Rudyard Kipling, Maud Diver, John Masters, and Salman Rushdie and key works such as *Bhowani Junction* and *Midnight's Children*. As far as the representation in films and literature is concerned he explains that Anglo-Indians were often presented 'as feeble biological specimens prone to lax morality, melancholia and a wide variety of vices that led to poverty' (2004: p. 228). His thesis is the first detailed study of Anglo-Indian representations in literature and films. Glenn D'Cruz now finds value in things like *Cotton Mary* and *Bhowani Junction* – 'Not necessarily because they are good films, but because they are like rare texts which deal with Anglo-Indian culture, Anglo-Indian themes' (see Assisi: p. 2006). His thesis presenting a persuasive argument against 'image criticism' underscores the importance of contextualizing literary texts and makes a timely contribution to debates about the representation of

Anglo-Indian diaspora, 'mixed race' identities, minority literature, and Australian Multiculturalism.

Mohit Manoj Prasad's PhD thesis, "Indo-Fijian Diasporic Bodies: Narratives in Text, Image, Popular Culture, and the Lived Everyday in Fiji and Liverpool, Sydney Australia", examines 'modalities of identity and representation for the Indo-Fijian diaspora and its second shift diasporic remove in Liverpool, Sydney, Australia'. He also examines the 'Indo-Fijian Literature in English, Fiji-Hindi, Memoir form of Indo-Fijian diasporic writings along with representations of Indo-Fijians in other texts' to 'enable siting of various identities and representations' (p. 2). The Indo-Fijian diasporic identity and its representation is the core concern for this thesis in its manifestations in the literature, memoirs, and narratives on the diaspora, tourist ephemera, popular culture, and the everyday (p. 1). His arguments are well placed and theoretically sound for examining alternative practices of reading the Indo-Fijian diaspora, literature, and narratives about it, and their particular production, expression, and consumption of popular culture. His thesis not only helps us in understanding the politics of the retrieval of performative identities but also expands current research and scholarship on Indo-Fijian-Australian diasporic identity and representation.

My PhD thesis titled "Roots & Routes: Politics of Location in the Short Stories of South Asian Diaspora in Australia" raises the central questions of the concept of 'roots' and 'routes' – 'rooting into a culture' and 'routing out of a culture' – of South Asian-Australian diaspora which constitute their 'politics of location'. The nature of this study is interdisciplinary because although it is primarily an analysis of short stories produced by South Asian diaspora writers in Australia, it depends heavily on data from sociological, anthropological, and historical studies as secondary sources. The thesis argues that the narratives of South Asian diaspora writers produced from Australia deserves a special status in analyses of the social-cultural-economical-historical 'narratives' produced by the South Asian Diaspora around the world. It further argues that a clearer notion of politics of location will be required to distinguish the different kinds of 'dislocation' the immigrants suffer psychologically and sociologically because literature acts as an instrument for the deployment of these often 'complex discursive strategies'. The study pointed out that the authors explore the processes of displacement and dislocation of identities through migration, journey, settlement, and nostalgic returns and their character's struggle to negotiate locations within Australia. In turn, these migratory experiences have created diasporic locations – of nostalgia, spatial identity, gender, family, and class – that need to be read and explored in one interpretative framework, that is, politics of location that helps in examining the position of the migrant as a subject influenced by political, economic, cultural structures, and processes in his/her environment thus affirming a community's genuine right to self-identification.

My MPhil dissertation "Postcards from Trishankus: Images of India and Australia in South Asian-Australian Short Stories" is a selective reading of a gamut of stories, born out of the experiences of two worlds and cultures, produced by the South Asian diaspora writers in Australia and published in various journals, anthologies, and collections. Divided into two groups: the first group (titled 'Looking Back: Imagining Home') containing those short stories that look at the homeland or present an image of India and the second group (titled 'Present and Future: Imagining Australia') looking at the hostland or present an image of Australia, raised certain pertinent questions and relevant issues such as How important is physical location for an individual? How do these Trishankus construct or imagine the past for future's sake? How do they re-read their own country (homeland), now that they have left it and has the image of India changed in these works? How does the immigrant look at India in relation to Australia? Are these immigrants at a privileged position or is their status as 'Trishankus' a source of an irresolvable dilemma in relation to identity markers? It also argued that these short stories by South Asian-Australians have in some ways helped to situate the Australian short fiction in the world literature today by forming international literary links, which are needed by any literary culture to be considered successful and worth critical attention. The short stories under analysis presented the themes of emotional alienation, self-identity, cultural expectations, cultural displacement, and representation of difference, and so on, and also displayed a uniform thread of sensibility in taking up issues that remain the same in spite of the difference in the migration points, that is, the point of arrival of these writers from the Indian subcontinent. A significant number of the stories analysed here are by and about women who migrated to Australia, in some cases with their husbands and in some cases alone to pursue and see their dreams become reality. These women writers have in a very strong way contributed towards the 'powerful literary contribution' of women writing in 'contemporary Australian culture' as well as that of the pioneering immigrant male who have been till now projected as shouldering the responsibility of contributing towards the making of their homes and Australia. In conclusion, I observed that the South Asian immigrants present a gaze that analyses what happened to the protagonists/characters before they arrived in Australia or the motives of as to why they arrived in Australia leaving behind their homeland. In a sense, these immigrants never cease their efforts to reveal and construe the past.

Given the growing recognition of multicultural and Asian-Australian literatures, the study of South Asian-Australian cultural production now requires attention. Tamara Mabbott Athique's thesis on South Asian Diaspora literature in Australia titled "Textual Migrations: South Asian-Australian Fiction" responds to the gaps in the scholarship of minority literatures and makes a new contribution to diversifying the field of diaspora criticism. Athique examines the tactics employed in and around selected works of fiction – a set of 15 texts by Christopher Cyrill, Suneeta Peres Da Costa, Christine Mangala, Bem Le Hunte, Michelle De Kretser, Chandani Lokuge, Chitra Fernando, Ernest MacIntyre, Brij V. Lal, Sudesh Mishra, and Satendra Nandan. Her thesis also considers the productive limits and limitations of literary categorization. To consider the narrative detail of South Asian-Australian fiction, she looks into a set of questions: what types of stories do South Asian-Australian writers choose to tell and how do they craft them? And what are the effects of such narratives and how are their complex cultural locations conveyed? Through detailed textual and conceptual analyses from postcolonial studies, theories of diaspora and critical multiculturalism, Athique argues for an integrated theoretical approach to a set of texts that operate across local, national, and transnational literary contexts.

Sharmini Kannan's dissertation "Pappadums in Paradise?" on Indian migrant women in Australia is a work of creative nonfiction with real characters. Her dissertation has 'its genesis in the stories of eleven migrant women who now live in Australia' (p. 7). She notes in her Prologue that the 'blue glass is always the hardest to find' (p. 1) and her search for Indian migrant women is like a 'quest for the blue glass. It was not an easy task. It became a process of rummaging through other people's lives, searching for fragments and relics. Eventually I was able to fit pieces together to form a mosaic of their lives in that other time, that other place. And also in this present time, in this place they now call home, Australia' (p. 2). Her dissertation is a record of conversations, narratives, debates, songs, questions, and answers. Her study emphasizes 'the geographical and psychological borders and boundaries crossed in the process of migration' (p. 8). 'Pappadums' in the title is used as a metaphor for Indian women and suggests the ways in which a word from English 'can be spelt in any number of ways' – Pappadums, Pappadams, Pappadoms, and Puppodoms – and 'how different cultures have influenced the borrowed spelling of a foreign word' (p. 11). It is lucidly written in the short stories format and 'is a narrative about narratives' (p. 12). It is 'an exploration of stories and histories that recover the losses one is subjected to in migration and displacement' (p. 12). Her dissertation explores a process of transformation that is both enriching and challenging.

Pauline Lalthlamuanpii's MPhil dissertation "A Study of Women's Characters in Yasmine Gooneratne's Novels *A Change of Skies* and *The Pleasures of Conquest*" attempts to study three main issues in migrant writing by taking Yasmine Gooneratne's fictional work as a case study. First, it is a study of Gooneratne's concept of multiculturalism in the context of Sri Lanka and Australia. By presenting multiculturalism from a woman's perspective, Lalthlamuanpii observes, Gooneratne beautifully merges the public and the private sphere. Thus, family as a unit becomes a space where issues of racial purity and multiculturalism are negotiated. Gooneratne breaks away from stereotypes by showing multiculturalism as a space where women break away from traditional structures. Lalthlamuanpii further argues that Gooneratne is satirical when she portrays Australia as a multicultural utopian space. This sort of portrayal accentuates its flaws and weaknesses effectively. This awareness of its flaws shows Gooneratne's anxiety to create an alternate model for Sri Lanka. The problems in Sri Lanka made it impossible to talk about its multiculturalism in a positive light. Lalthlamuanpii is also able to establish the importance of Gooneratne in South Asian-Australian writing. According to her, Gooneratne's importance lies not only in how she has positioned herself as a Sri Lankan in Australia, but also in her stance as a woman migrant writer in Australia. So, unlike majority of first-generation migrant writers she does not confine her works to her ethnic community only. Her novels reflect a conscious attempt to move away from communalism to a more global outlook. In conclusion, Lalthlamuanpii sees the importance of Gooneratne in her conscious refusal to position herself as the 'Other'.

In spite of all the sociological, anthropological, and historical research to support literary studies, there are only nominal critical articles or dissertations on South Asian diasporic literature published in Australia and most themes remain underexplored, making the fate of South Asian diaspora writer suffer in the 'anxiety of invisibility' (V. Lal, 2009). Literary studies have yet to see a full-length published study of South Asian diaspora writing. The larger picture in the literary area is one of lack, that is, critical material is limited to book reviews and articles that are published in various journals and conference proceedings or anthologized essays dealing with Australian literature. Pauline Lalthlamuanpii's dissertation on Yasmine Gooneratne's novels is a good beginning, along with Tamara Athique's thesis, thus breaking away literary research on South Asia from Asian-Australian writing.

Other notable authors such as Mena Abdullah, Chandani Lokugé, Adib Khan, Chitra Fernando, and Christopher Cyrill also deserve full-length studies and research. It is imperative to note here that Mena Abdullah and her short stories are crucial in the literary history of both South Asian diaspora writing and Australian literature. Annette Robyn Corkhill in *Australian Writing: Ethnic Writers 1945–1991* (1994) and *The Immigrant Experience in Australian Literature* (1995), and Bruce Bennett in *Australian Short Fiction: A History* (2002) have dedicated a section on Mena

Abdullah, second-generation South Asian diaspora writer of Punjabi background. And according to Corkhill (1994), Abdullah's stories are

> crucial in the literary history of our immigrant writing, for their enthusiastic reception hailed the advent of a new age of critical enlightenment. Abdullah's regional writing was significant not only for the profound cultural variance expressed, for the fact of female authorship, for the setting of the stories (a sheep farm in Australia's New England), but also, and perhaps most importantly of all, for the autobiographically-based recording of life in a family whose religious tradition was alien to a monochrome society (the narrator's father was Muslim, her mother of Hindu origin). (p. 69)

Despite her crucial importance as the first major female author of South Asian origin, it is a pity that no full-length study on her life and works has ever been attempted. This is because, as Yasmine Gooneratne (1992a) notes,

> Although Abdullah is one of the very few authors of Asian background who have achieved substantial publication in Australia, her finely crafted stories have not yet received the attention from Critics that they deserve. This is possibly because, although she is Australia-born, the experiences she writes about place her inevitably on the 'periphery', and beyond the line that has hitherto lovingly enclosed Australia's 'traditional' authors in an enclave that is deemed 'central' to the nation's literary and cultural development. (p. 115)

The literature I have surveyed above consciously provides new directions in the dynamic field of research on the South Asian diaspora in Australia and its social, cultural, political, economic, and literary participation in the Australian society. As a young researcher, one appreciates the work that must have gone into it. These books tell us the story of 'a tenacious, persistent people; who in all kinds of circumstances have endured and survived' (Tinker: p. x).

It may be reiterated that the study of South Asian diaspora in Australia or any part of the globe is 'not a discipline by itself, but only an area of specialized study utilizing the data, concepts, methods and theories of many disciplines' (Jayaram: p. 33). The number of articles published in various journals and critical anthologies do cover, although nominally, as noted above, a wide range of South Asian-Australian socio-cultural and literary formations. These studies of South Asian diaspora in Australia is still a rich and impressive gathering. It is hoped that utilizing from the information and experience of previous research and data, more researches in the area of literary studies will emerge and present a dynamic community in transit.

Conclusion

The wide spectrum of writings that we see in Australian Literature today shows that it has come a long way from the days of Anglo-Celtic dominance to an era of a literary culture that is much more representative of Australia's migrant or multi-ethnic past and present. This has been made possible by multicultural writers asserting their own literary and cultural traditions in their work. These narratives/texts produced by authors belonging to diverse – both culturally and linguistically – ethnic backgrounds/communities have stimulated not only fascinating cultural dialogues but also a whole new area of critical perspective in diaspora and multicultural studies. In a certain special way, these writers and their writings have raised questions of re-defining and re-viewing the national canon. They have also tried to abolish categorizations and compartments of majority and minority literatures by making the mainstream accept their work as part and parcel of the truly 'Australian made' experience. However, the 'voices' of the early Indian subcontinental 'coolies' or pioneer migrants themselves, according to Marie de Lepervanche (2007), an authority on migration from Indian subcontinent, are for the most part silent documents. She notes that the early South Asian migrants did not leave any journals, diaries, letters, memoirs, or autobiographies and their lives as pioneer immigrants in Australia were very hard, often lonely, and isolated. Yet, she asserts, their contribution to the economic success of Australia's early industries, particularly pastoralism, must be acknowledged (see pp. 99–116)

The South Asian diaspora in Australia is continually growing and flourishing as one of the most prosperous communities, with an ever-increasing role and responsibility in all areas of society – law, engineering, the medical profession, literature, performing arts (music, dance, art, theatre, and films), economics, philosophy, sociology, history, and other fields. David Carter (1997) has noted that 'literature is not just a set of individual texts or authors but rather a set of institutions and institutional practices which regulate the making and transmission of (literary) meanings in a given society' (p. 18).

In conclusion, Indian diaspora is supposed to have achieved success when its people are in Bollywood and national politics. Similar sentiments were recently expressed by Professor Amitabh Mattoo, Director of Australia India Institute at the University of Melbourne, in an interview to a community newspaper, *The Indian Sun*. Commenting on the role of Indian diaspora in national politics, he noted:

> You know when a diaspora has come of age when it directly intervenes in the electoral process of a democratic county that hosts them. I think the fact that Indians are candidates in the forthcoming general election in Australia is health and reflects their mainstreaming and growing empowerment. ("Indian-origin Candidates ...", 2013)

A number of Bollywood films have been shot in Australia, and some Australian film makers have also used India as their location. India-origin actresses Maheep Sandhu Kapoor, Shubha Verma, Anusha Dandekar, Vimala Raman, Pallavi Sharda, and Japji Khaira have tried their luck and showcased their talent in Bollywood and regional cinemas of India. On the other hand, till now, South Asians in Australia were considered mostly politically silent or marginalized when it came to contributing to the electoral process (see also Kanth, 2013).

> Migrant communities have been slow to take their place at the table when it comes to politics. However, this election has proven to be a turning point. The Liberal Party was most generous with its seats for minority communities with six candidates. However, the Greens, Liberals and even the Palmer United Party fielded candidates of Indian background. (Kallivayalil, 2013)

In the 2013 elections, it was strongly believed by political *pundits* that Australian citizens of South Asian origin, along with other migrant communities from Asia, will certainly play a critical role in the outcome. Twenty-six South Asian-origin candidates – Bhupinder Kumar Chhibber, Sam Swami Nathan, Gurminder Sekhon, Indra Esguerra, Ammar Khan, Dinesh Jayasuriya, Ganesh Loke, Mohandas Balasingham, Raheam Khan, Kalpesh Patel, Mohammad Ashraf, Alex Kaur Bhathal, Ali Khan, Jatinder Singh, Nihal Samara, Kim Mubarak, Balwinder Singh, Bikhar Singh Brar, Manoj Kumar, Jag Chuga, Shilpa Hegde, Vashil Sharma, Vimal Sharma, Avtar Gill, Bill Gupta, Binoy Kampmark, and Suresh Rajan – representing various political parties, contested the 2013 election (see Dixit and Luthra, 2013).

Although, given the newness of the idea, these candidates despite their major political backing and support from local communities didn't stand a chance to win against political heavy-weights. They were not even close to be called game changers as some people in the local South Asian community media thought of it, but their spirit to work for the larger Australian community and fight the elections can be seen as a new beginning for people of South Asian origin in Australia. Tanu Kallivayalil notes in her piece, 'The Work has Begun' (2013), in *The Indian Sun* magazine:

> It's time for the community to withdraw and take a good look at how it can further its position within the various parties and make a more meaningful contribution to the political scene. It is truly a sign of successful integration if we are part and parcel of the political landscape of the country. One thing that we should keep in mind is that nothing is to be given for free, or to be taken for granted. We need to fight the good fight and learn how to do it right.

Participation of such a large number of candidates can be read as an acknowledgement of the South Asian presence in Australian political space and their ability to foster change in Australian society can only be nurtured by giving them key roles in national politics.

Finally, in the field of literature, all diaspora authors, wherever they are present, are our very own world travellers, who have set foot in every known region and society of the earth. And their journeys and experiences have generated bridges and influenced the historical, cultural, social, and academic perceptions of the ever-changing world society. Immigrants, who connect South Asia and Australia, are of special relevance to both the continents – especially to India, which has a centuries-old multicultural existence and continuous interaction/interconnection with its neighbouring (SAARC) countries combined with its plethora of languages, customs, discordant history, and religious and regional diversity. Thus, Australia, with its own rich and distinctive culture, provides space for the contribution of various successive immigrants and gives them political and economic stability.

Notes

1. The concept of globalization and diaspora formation is clearly an ongoing process related to global flows (see Kelly, 1998).
2. Rabindranath Tagore in a letter addressed to C.F. Andrews when contemplating a visit to Java.
3. As *Kala Pani* represents the taboo of the sea in Indian culture, the fear of crossing the *Kala Pani* also derives from the notion in Hinduism that it entailed the end of the reincarnation cycle, as the traveller was cut off from the regenerating waters of the Ganges. Migration across this has often meant losing one's caste privileges and having to reinvent oneself.
4. Student migration is an example where 'migrants become agents creatively opening routes into Australia using regulations that were put in place for other purposes' (Voigt-Graf: p. 155).
5. The 2011 Census reported that over one in four of Australia's 22 million people were born overseas. The number of settlers arriving in Australia from more than 200 countries between July 2008 and June 2009 totalled 158,021.
6. For a detailed discussion on migration from India, see Tinker, 1977; De Lepervanche, 1984, 2007; Rajkowski, 1987; Bilimoria and Ganguly-Scrase, 1988; Chandrasekhar, 1992; Bilimoria, 1996; Narasimhaiah, 2000; Joshi, 2000; Bilimoria and Voigt-Graf, 2001; Faria, 2001; Lakha and Stevenson, 2001; D'Souza, 2002; Ray, 2003; Jayaram, 2004; Prasad, 2005; Dale, 2005; Kenna, 2006; Sharrad, 2009; Baas, 2009; Westrip and Holroyde, 2010; "Indian Diaspora – A Short History"; "Indian-born Community in Australia"; "Jains in Australia"; "Hindu Council of Australia"; "Anglo-Indians – Family Tree"; "Indians in Australia (Anglo Indians)"; "Indian Arrival in Australia"; "Queensland Aust-Ind Association"; East Indian Club of Melbourne, 2004; "The Indian Diaspora: 2004–2005";

Sivasupramaniam, 2006; "The Indian Diaspora"; and DIMIA, "The Indian Born Community – Historical Background" and "Main Migrant source for Australia is India."

7. According to Associate Professor Richard Roberts from University of Wollongong, there is little consensus between researchers about the timing of this event, estimates pertaining to this initial occupation range from 125,000 years before present to as recent as 40,000 years ago, see "When did Australia's Earliest Inhabitants Arrive?" (2004).
8. The Australian Bureau of Statistics estimated resident population (ERP) at June 2011 was 22.55 million people. In the 2006 census, 153,579 Australian residents declared that they were born in India and this number increased significantly to 340,604 in the 2011 census, making India the largest group in Asia for overseas-born residents. For a detailed discussion on South Asian, particularly migration, see Hugo, 1992; McMahon, 1995; B. Lal, 1996, 2006a; Walker, 1999; Bates, 2001; Carter and Torabully, 2002; Kinsella, 2003; V. Lal, 2004; Australian Bureau of Statistics, 2006, 2007; "Immigration to Australia"; "Conference on Australasia's Diaspora"; "Regional South Asia"; and "South Asians are Forgetting Their Roots."
9. For a detailed discussion on Sikh migration from India, see Tinker, 1977; Bilimoria, 1996; Gabbi, 1998; Bhatti and Dusenbery, 2001; De Lepervanche, 2001; "Indian Arrival in Australia: Sikhs in Australia".
10. For a detailed discussion on Anglo-Indian migration and settlement, see Moore, 1986a, 1986b, 2001, 2007; Jupp, 2001; S. James, 2001; Z. Phillips, 2004; Blunt, 2005; Assisi, 2006; Crane, 2009; "Anglo Indians Pioneers and Prodigies".
11. The work of *Pratibimb* – Indian Cultural Community of Australia (ICCA), a nonprofit organization on popular networking website – is also commendable. Its membership is open to all and aims to be a reflection of the Indian population in Australia. The objective, according to its creator Navneet Choujar is to 'bring together talented individuals/groups under an umbrella to protect and promote them, and evoke the diversity of the rich Indian cultural heritage. There are no religious boundaries, no caste barriers; we do not speak about political affiliations or financial tie ups. Let us come together with a common cause – our culture!' ("Pratibimb" 2009).
12. For a detailed discussion on migration from Pakistan, see Tinker, 1977; Rajkowski, 1987; Rauf, 1994; Deen, 1995, 2003, 2005; Bates, 2001; R. Hassan, 2001; Rasool, 2002; Cleland, 2002; S. Hassan, 2003; Fijac and Sonn, 2004; Lal and Mahboob, 2006; Casimiro et al., 2007;

"The Urdu-Speaking Community in Australia"; "History of Immigration from Pakistan"; "Pakistani Australian"; "Pakistan Australia Friendship Association"; "Pakistan Association of Australia"; and FECCA, "Pakistan": 2005; and Victorian Multicultural Commission, 2008.

13. Pakistan-born Australians have also played a significant role within local Muslim organizations, and have contributed to the development of independent Muslim schools and language programmes throughout Australia. A number of Pakistani associations also support this community, the oldest being the Pakistan Australia Association (PAA) formed in 1959.
14. For a detailed discussion on Sri Lankan migration, see Endagama, 1981; Pinnawala, 1984; De Jong, 1987; Weerasooria, 1988; Vanden Driesen and Vanden Driesen, 1997; C. Vanden Driesen, 1997; C. Vanden Driesen, 2004; Sparkes and Shnukal, 2004; Karunarathna, 2008; Lalthlamuanpii, 2009; DIMIA, "The Sri Lankan Born Community"; "Sri Lankan Australian"; FECCA, "Sri Lanka"; Sivasupramaniam, 2006.
15. For a detailed discussion on Sri Lankan Burgher migration, see Ferdinands, 1995; Vanden Driesen and Vanden Driesen, 1997; "Burgher People"; and "Burghers."
16. For a detailed discussion on migration from Bangladesh, see Tinker, 1977; Bitel, 2005; "History of Immigration from Bangladesh"; "Bangladeshis in Australia"; "Bangladesh Australia Association, Canberra"; and Commercial Wing, Bangladesh High Commission, 2005.
17. For a detailed discussion of the changing nature of Australian Immigration Policy, see "An Overview of Australia's Migration Program", 2013.
18. The community has active social and cultural networks such as the Australia Bangladesh Council of Victoria (ABCV), which promotes Bangladeshi culture and supports newly arrived migrants. Similarly, the Bangladesh Australia Association, Canberra, is an integral part of the Canberra multicultural community that represents people of Bangladeshi origin. For more than two decades, the association has been a strong participant in Canberra's multicultural life and has actively promoted cultural diversity and harmony in the Canberra community. Bangladeshi-Australians have also lend a helping hand in the economic development of Bangladesh and in forging Australia-Bangladesh relations because of the repatriation of foreign earnings, highlighting key business areas in which Australian

entrepreneurs should be interested and by providing a platform for bilateral cooperation in other fields between the two countries.

19. For a detailed discussion on Nepalese Migration to Australia, see Dhungel, 2000; "Nepal Australia Friendship Association"; "Nepal: Country Brief"; "Nepalese Association of Victoria"; "Nepalese Australian Association"; "Nepalese in Australia Protest against Laxampur Dam"; and "Sagarmatha Nepali Restaurant."
20. Other prominent associations include the Nepal Australia Friendship Association (NAFA) formed in January 1989 in Queensland (a nonpolitical, nonprofit aid organization dedicated to assist communities and individuals with projects that improve the quality of life in Nepal), the Nepalese Association of Victoria (established in 1997, aims to promote the interests of all people of Nepalese origin living in Victoria and also to promote Nepali culture, heritage, and goodwill between Australia and Nepal), the Gorkha Nepalese Community and the Nepalese-Australian Welfare Association (both located in Sydney) have also been playing a key role in promoting awareness about Nepalese communities in Australia. On a lighter note, perhaps, one might note that the one 'Nepali' phenomenon that has most vividly registered upon Australia has been the Nepali-run restaurants in various states of Australia – Sydney, Canberra, Melbourne, and Brisbane – these have helped publicise, in however limited a fashion, the kingdom's rich cultural heritage in Australia.
21. For a detailed discussion on Migration from Bhutan, see "HM Birthday Celebrations in Sydney"; "Bhutanese Community Profile"; and "Question on Notice – Bhutan Refugees."
22. The Australia-Bhutan Friendship Association (ABFA) works hard to promote relations between Bhutan and Australia, with a very consistent, well defined, and focused programme of co-operation. Australia's support for a number of development programmes in Bhutan through its aid programmes and projects such as building roads, education, and providing better health care services has also brought the two countries together.
23. Available online at <http://www.apnaorg.com/books/sikhs-in-australia/>.

Chapter 2

An Element of Romanticization

Sensory and Spatial Locations

> The element of romanticization which is present in every nationalism is even stronger among nostalgic migrants, who often form a rosy picture of the country they have left and are able to imagine the nation where it did not exist before. (van der Veer: p. 7)

Sensory versus Spatial Locations

The 'element of romanticization' or the constant yearning for ones roots – sensory and spatial locations – has become a phenomenon for different immigrant groups. As 'Diaspora' do not simply refer to a geographical dispersal but it also defines 'the vexed questions of identity, memory and home which such displacements produce' (Ashcroft et al.: p. 218). Relationship between a diaspora and its homeland is an integral component of reading an immigrant framework for analysis. There are of course many diasporas in Australia and the 'concept of home' or 'roots' for these immigrants is 'as compelling as it is for those Anglo-Australians committed to the "core values" of a monolithic cultural nationalism' (Gelder and Salzman: p. 49). But it is the *politics of sensory and spatial locations* that act as one of the primary reasons that join Indian Diaspora across continents. For these immigrants, India is 'not simply a space on the map', but it has been 'the locus of *memory, longing, desire, and anxiety*' (Mankekar, 2003: pp. 52–53; emphasis added). As immigrants, these people draw on their memories of what has been left behind, a romantic past, and live in the present. This individual, his collective imagining or romanticization of the Indian subcontinent – its past, linkages, traditions, and attachments help him 'nourish a psychological appeal among successive generations of emigrants for the "mother" country' (G. Singh: p. 4). Further, it also acts as a security and emotional refuge against the sometimes hostile new environment.

According to the noted cultural critic Stuart Hall (2000), the crucial question related to a diasporic identity is not *subjectivity* but *subject position* or *location*. So, the Indian diasporic writers not only provide a fluidity of identity to their protagonists but also 'a constantly changing subject position, both geographically and ontologically' (Ashcroft et al.: p. 218). The politics of identity, memory and space, and the narratives (autobiographical or fictional or factional) that they shape are central issues in the short stories under critique in this chapter. It is important to note how diasporic individuals (and characters) exercise their *agency* – 'the temporally constructed engagement by actors of different structural environments (...) which through the interplay of habit, imagination, and judgment, both reproduces and transforms those structures in interactive response to the problems posed by historical situations' (Emirbayer and Mische: p. 970). Agency can further be understood as having three broad components based on its orientations:

1. *Iteration*: the capacity of persons to actively select and incorporate patterns of thought and social practices from the past, to give stability to their present situation so that they may cope with the temporal/spatial transitions of perhaps migration and immigration.
2. *Projective Element*: it refers to the imaginations of persons, that is, received traditions of thought and social practices from the past and recast in relation to the persons' hopes and desires for the future.
3. *Practical Evaluation*: the ability of people to make judgments among the various possible trajectories of action in response to present social situations in order to make sense of future. (Emirbayer and Mische: pp. 989–990)

Through 'agency' and 'reiteration', the past 'becomes a stabilizing influence that shapes the flow of effort and allows us to sustain identities, meanings, and interactions over time' (Emirbayer and Mische: p. 975). This reiteration also helps in imagination and identification with the spatial and sensory locations. So in a globalized world, the Indian immigrants imagine themselves to identity.

Further, in relation to agency and the analyses of location and its connection within a changing global social order, David Harvey (1993) points out that the 'real as well as metaphorical territories and spaces of power' or locations must be given equal weight (p. 3). But, what are these *sensory* and *spatial* locations? And, how does the agency affect these two concepts related to memory and space? Memory and space are 'neither a flat stage upon which subjects perform their historical task, nor a predefined volume through which they pass' (Papastergiadis: p. 52). Space is both 'a transformative force and a field that is transformed by the interactions that occur within it' (Papastergiadis: p. 52). Thus, by exploring the spatial politics of location in ways that 'articulate both mobility and displacement alongside location and positionality' (Blunt: p. 8) we can explore sensory productions of knowledge in the Indian diaspora. As situated within a range of imagined and real nations or locations, Indian diaspora in Australia embodies a set of (dis)connections between place, culture, and identity. This complex relationship or linkages between facts of geographical location – homeland or hostland – and notions of imagined or metaphorical geographies is thus addressed by spatial and sensory locations.

These connections or links with the 'homeland' and 'associated myths of origin', according to Crispin Bates (2001), 'often play a large part in identity formation amongst migrant communities' (p. 21). Even though the actual origins of the diaspora Indians living in the hostland can be highly diverse. He further notes that the

> experience of migration itself and, second, any racism to which they are subjected by indigenous population are often all that migrants have in common. A selective 'remembering' of the culture and traditions of home is therefore frequently employed to build a sense of community. (p. 21)

From this it can be formulated that 'the reconstitution of a memory, which veers between an imagination drawn back to the atavistic homeland', thus making Indianness or South Asianness as 'a set of inalienable values' bestowed by the country of origin and 'the constellation of signs spawned by the uneasy interaction of the exiled' Indian values with the cultures of the hostland (Carter and Torabully: p. 14). Salman Rushdie (1991) beautifully sums up this uneasy interaction and the politics of spatial and sensory locations by observing:

> Exiles or emigrants or expatriates are haunted by some sense of loss, some urge to reclaim, to look back, even at the risk of being mutated into pillars of salt. But if we do look back, we must also do so in the knowledge – which gives rise to profound uncertainties – that our physical alienation from India almost inevitably means that we will not be capable of reclaiming precisely the thing that was lost; that we will, in short, create fictions, not actual cities or villages, but invisible ones, imaginary homelands, Indias of the mind. (p. 76)

This theory cannot be explored without bringing into question the narratives and the ways in which Indian diaspora represents spaces of home, the hostland. The short stories analysed here attempt to provide an understanding of the variety of interpretations of the sensory and spatial locations.

The Element of Romanticization

Introducing the essays of Günter Grass, Salman Rushdie observed that literature of migration offers us 'one of the richest metaphors of our age' (1991: p. 278). Adding to this viewpoint noted Fiji-Indian author Satendra Nandan (2000) explains that the idea of a 'metaphorical being' is perhaps more true about 'a writer than of any other member of a society' (p. 35). He further says that a writer 'is almost always and everywhere either an exile or a migrant and, because of this distancing and distress, he may capture more vitally and vividly the very essence of our migratory experience' (2000: p. 35). The continuance of a dialogue with the past through 'plot, characters, actions', and a constant looking back by the diasporic authors, 'through memory, fantasy, narrative and myth' in their stories is to a larger extent the result of the notion of 'home' and its 'authority' as constructed over the mindscapes of the diasporic individuals. This is not to say that a diasporan will 'return' to the origin because there is no point of actual return for him or her. For noted postcolonial critic Vijay Mishra (1996b), this inability to return is one of the most dominant and distinctive characteristics of diasporas and he observes that 'diasporas do not, as a general rule, return' (p. 75).

Although the immigrants may not actually return home permanently, as they are now located in a new adopted 'home', they however do present an attachment towards traditions, customs, values, religions, and languages of the ancestral home, through the use of memory or sensory locations, as can be seen in the themes of their works. How they re-create their Indian identity under diasporic conditions through recreation, continuation, maintenance, and nurturing of their social and cultural uniqueness is often the product of their desires to connect with their country of origin, homeland, and with the other subcontinental diasporas present in different regions of the world, thereby giving it a true global unity and identity. In the words of Homi Bhabha (1994), this is the 'celebratory romance of the past' (p. 9). It is a result of the restrictions that migration has placed upon them and the creative possibilities it has offered. This romancing with the past is reflected in the creative output of the diasporic author and 'continues to depend on the bits and pieces of its origin to hold itself together in the face of the onslaught, rejection or domination by the "other," by the world which both frightens and fascinates' (J. Jain: p. 79). This 'fascination' with/for what has been left behind, or with the very 'home-idea' (Mishra, 1996b: p. 75) in relation to what is to be acquired in the hostland is the consequence of the migratory displacement. And this in turn makes the writer imagine home the way he or she wants it to be, that is, 'a romantic idealization that fossilises memories', and therefore it can also be referred to as the 'constant looking back syndrome' (R. Ahmad: p. 93). The return to home or roots, physically, is also not viable because of the other important incentives that are offered by the hostland. In the very act of returning/re-turning lies the problematic of losing identity and most important of all, losing the opportunity that has been procured through hard work in the hostland or places of migration.

Descendants of Indian indentured migrants, who are now twice displaced because of the coups in Fiji, constitute an important part of 'the mosaic of this Indian diaspora' in Australia (B. Lal, 1996: p. 167). From this part of the world, Satendra Nandan, Brij V. Lal, Vijay Mishra, and Sudesh Mishra have emerged as the most prominent Fiji-Indian voices in Australia. They belong to that special category of the diaspora authors who carry a double hyphenated identity, that is, of being Indian-Fijian-Australian. These authors, descendents of the indentured labourers, are preoccupied with reassessing their origins in the mini-Indias created by their ancestors in lands outside the Indian subcontinent.

Vijay Mishra in "Ni Sa Moce/Salaam Fiji" (1989) writes 'in remote Fiji, a displaced Indian migrant community clung onto traditions that the community brought with it from the India of the late nineteenth century (...) this India had effectively been frozen in time' (pp. 481–482). Brij V. Lal, in "Return to Bahraich" (1998), calls it the dilemma of the 'people caught in-between the tensions of culture and history'. He finds 'something strange, something incongruous' about the indentured people and the villagers and writes:

> Now in their mellow twilight, they seemed to be shipwrecked by fate in a place they did not, perhaps could not, fully embrace, and they could not return to a place they so dearly loved. They were a people caught in-between the tensions of culture and history, resisting assimilation into the ways of their adopted homeland by re-enacting archaic customs from a remembered past. (p. 92)

Satendra Nandan in his short story "The Guru" (1988) takes a very humorous view of this diasporan situation – 'caught in-between' and 'frozen in time' – and the Indian way of life away from India. He builds his story on the pattern, however not on the same scale and grandeur, of V.S. Naipaul's *The Mystic Masseur* (1957) and Cyril Dabydeen's *The Wizard Swami* (1985), two of the best known *Girmitiya* narratives. It is important to mention here that it was Naipaul who started the trend of a distinctive *Girmitiya* narrative or the narratives of the old labour diaspora by providing it with a form, style, language, ideology, and fantastic images and also in some ways made it consciously into a discourse to be comprehended and critiqued. According to Nandan in "Antyesti Samskara" (1996), 'Naipaul has given us a searing glimpse of our own unexplored, unwritten lives, roadless and rootless' (p. 420). Similarly, in "The Guru", Nandan presents Pundit Bhondu Maharaj, whose 'mumbling' of Sanskrit mantras makes 'the hair on his knuckles bristle with holy excitement' (p. 69). He exploits illiterate people and blind believers of Hinduism, its rituals, and traditions.

He and other indentured labourers, as Shyam Selvadurai (2005) has observed 'cut off from South Asia (...) were forced to recreate little self-conditioned South Asias and to draw meaning from their landscape' (p. 9). It is their common memories that have united the indentured people in a way that makes them distinguishable from other groups on the plantations. They have re-created a 'home away from home' and preserved the rich cultural, religious and social traditions of India over the years of their dislocation in Fiji and carried it to Australia too. This, according to Vijay Mishra (1991), is the construction of an 'imaginary belief systems for its own self-authentication, self-generation and legitimation' (p. 79) by the Indian section in Fiji. Despite the strictures against travelling overseas in the Hindu *shastras*, these early Indian immigrants were indentured as labourers to countries unknown to them. Soon their relationship with the Fijian landscape became solid and they accounted for more than half of Fiji's population till the coups of 1987 and again in 2000, as a result of which these people migrated to various other countries for safety. The protagonist of Nandan's story, Beckaroo, can obviously see that his parents, the Pundit and the other first generation or old immigrants are living with an invariable hope of making 'a trip to Motherland' (p. 77) because they are still, what Vijay Mishra calls, 'trapped in a cultural time-warp' (1991: p. 79).

Similarly, Sudesh Mishra in his autobiographical short story "Lila" (1994) describes in detail 'the time-warp' in the celebration and performance of Ram Lila by the Indian-Fijian community in Nadi, Fiji. A playing field is converted into a 'stage for this week-long enactment of Tulasidasa's *Ramayana*' in *shudh* (pure) Hindi (p. 650). Using *Ramayana*, its characters and the trope of exile, Sudesh Mishra discusses the politics of language – Hindi, English, Fijian, and Fijian-Hindi or Fiji-baat – in the diasporic context. The narrator's father can speak Fijian in Nadi dialect, and for him language is 'an evanescent butterfly and not a thing to cast in bronze. He speaks it and it is gone' (p. 653), whereas for the narrator, on the other hand, says that he 'plunge(s) the living butterfly into a vat of molten ore in search of an aesthetic that is durable' (p. 653). Fijian drivers, who work under the narrator's father, respect him for the 'use of their language as if it were his own' (p. 654). The narrator, having grown up travelling a lot, settles down in Australia but keeps his connection with Fiji and the language. He again sees the *Ram Lila* performance and notices 'Shudh Hindi has long been altered (...) so that his lines are no longer scripted by Tulasidasa. Instead, they are the lines of a diasporic self (...)' (p. 655). Sudesh Mishra's story is a celebration of Indian-Fijian culture and Fiji-Hindi – a diasporic language that encompasses within it the history, experience, and stories of indenture and shifting or recreation of home in Fiji.

Satendra Nandan in "Nandi" (1990), remembering the stories he was raised on, observes: 'We lived by such stories – first of our grandparents, then our mothers and fathers, now our political leaders. Our fate in Fiji had echoes of the *Ramayana*: exile, suffering, separation, battles, but no return' (p. 629). In "Nandi", Jagat Mahajan, the richest man in the narrator's village, who worships Lord Shiva, erects under the pandanus tree a temple. The narrator observes that there was a

> carved wooden statue of Shiva mounted on a clay figure of Nandin, Shiva's joyous bull. A mound of red earth symbolised Mount Everest, on which Shiva sat in meditation. These pieces of sculpture were grotesquely coloured and covered with hibiscus petals or small yellow marigolds. (...) Shiva looked strong, ominous as a mountain with a hidden volcano. (p. 620)

This temple, however 'grotesquely covered', represented the very memory of the sacred religious space – a temple – that the indentured labourers have left back in India.

For Nandan in "Antyesti Samskara", this re-creation of the 'lost' space and re-enactment of sacred customs and religious rituals is the very essence of the Indian-Fijian community. It is also a journey of 'going back – into oneself, one's family, one's country – the search for a history and identity' (p. 420). Nandan understands that by preserving the rich myths along with the cultural, religious, and social traditions of India over the years in Fiji, Indians blinded themselves from seeing the culture and value system in which they were transplanted. In Nandan's "Mangoes" (1992), the old man, who was once an indentured labourer, remembers the 'delicious, juicy and sugar-sweet' mangoes of his village Sultanpur in India notes:

> The Fijian mangoes, thick and fleshy, lacked the taste, the character of the fibre that made you suck the mango stone till it shone white like a piece of human bone. Mangoes in Fiji lacked the *mithas* and the people were no different: fruit and flower, fish and flesh reflect the nature of people in a place. (p. 307)

For the old man, the mango tree is also 'a symbol of this bountiful land' (p. 309) that he left. He is unable to find the same warmth in social life from the Fijian community. But for some immigrants, the small villages in which they settled in Fiji as indentured labourers with their families also became their home. The narrator's father, son of an indentured labourer, in Shrishti Sharma's "Saying Goodbye to the Mango Tree" (2003), looking at his family album remembers the 'best times' spent in his small village in Fiji. He observes:

> I enjoyed ... everyday, I went one step further ... no turning back ... had to ... that's how you get here. That was village life, see? There was the farm, and the friends, and the family ... but most of all the family. We went along with the simple things. Everyone did. Not enough of nothing sometimes. But the good things were there. In the people ... in the life ... in the soccer! Very little we had, but we had the open field ... different place, different time it was ... not anymore ... but *that was the life* ... the village .... (pp. 51–52)

One of the first Australian born South Asian writers Mena Abdullah (along with co-author Ray Mathew) presented in her short story collection *The Time of the Peacock* (1965), delightful and light-hearted descriptions of the transplantation of an Indian family in the outback or hinterland of Australia. According to Corkhill (1995), 'the beauty of these brief sketches of life in an alien environment lies in their clarity, simplicity and integrity' (p. 36). Growing up in New England, a region in New South Wales, and despite many odds the narrator never loses her 'optimism, joy and innocence' (p. 36). Despite their problems in this hinterland, the family becomes accustomed to the Australian soil and the landscape. The garden, representing the Garden of Eden, in "Because of the Rusilla", although like a place of exile, is also an example of their adaptation to Australian land:

> The garden was a strange place and lovely. It was our *mother's place*, Ama's own place. Outside its lattice walls was the farmyard

> with its fowls and goats (Sulieman the rooster and Yasmin the nanny), and beyond that was Father's place, the wool-sheds and the yards, and beyond that the hills with their changing faces and their Australianness. We had never been to them, and Ama (...) told us they were very strange. But everything was strange to Ama, except the garden.
>
> Inside its lattice walls grew the country that she knew. There were tuberose and jasmine, white violets and the pink *Kashmiri roses* whose buds grew clenched, like baby hands. The garden was cool and sweet and full of rich scent. (p. 12; emphasis added)

The garden, with its mix of tuberose and Kashmiri roses, is not just a symbol of India or the motherland, represented in the story as 'mother's place', filled with its representative flowers, it is also a security or defence mechanism that this family employs by recreating the environment of the homeland against anything hostile in their present. The garden 'provides an important sanctuary for the mother and a place to confine her children' (Tucker, 2003).

Three generations of a migrant family are portrayed in Renuka Sharma's short story "Paternity" (1994). Sharma writes that the grandfather, now a 96-year-old man, wore a turban and rode a horse 'to look at the land and talk to his descendants', that 'he had helped settle almost sixty years ago when as a foreman of the sugar company he was rewarded for his toil' (p. 154). The old man, has the 'curious sensation' that he has 'achieved' something in his life as a migrant in Australia, but 'never quite sure of what' (p. 154). The children from his two wives have merged into the Australian society and are now university educated and they live 'in the urban centre with long periods abroad' and come on 'infrequent visits' to meet him (p. 155). His only regret is that his youngest son doesn't believe in the traditions of India and in the eyes of the old man he is 'an infidel' with all his modern views:

> With much glee the son had told the father that he ate pork. A high caste Brahmin eating pork, the old man had been outraged and asked one of the lurking grandsons to bring buckets of water for his sons' cleansing, after the visit the house was scoured. (p. 155)

The old man, belonging to a Brahmin family, has, for the past 60 years, performed at various functions the role of a high priest and one man judiciary for his small community. Still, he cannot understand the feeling of loss: 'some valuable part of himself which he longed for in an uncertain way' (p. 155). The loss he feels is of the youngest son, who in all respects resembles the old man but with his foreign ways has distanced himself from his father and his traditions. He is a 'man toughened and hardened by circumstances' (p. 156) just like his migrant father, but representing modernity, while his father stands for traditions of India transplanted in Australia. It is the grandson who understands what his father and grandfather are truly feeling and muses that 'even in seeming opposites there are similarities' (p. 156) and in their 'acknowledgement of difference' there is present true love (p. 157). The grandson represents the third generation of Indian-Australians and says that 'he would be different, a real radical, a nihilist disagreeing with their ideas on tradition and modernity, going beyond' (p. 157).

Recent migrations are creating new displacements and this recreation of home has re-constructed the South Asian way of life and cultural values to produce a home away from home, which has resulted in what Makarand Paranjape (2001a) calls an

> astonishing cultural continuity (that is seen) when one crosses boundaries these days – one never has to leave India, so to speak, even as one leaves its shores. The same, or at least similar, music, food, clothes and people haunt one not just on the plane and through the transit points, but also at the final destination, whether it is America, Canada, Britain, or Australia. (p. vi)

Migration, diaspora, and exile offer diverse and complex environments for the renegotiation of social and cultural identities. These phenomena have become everyday experiences in our contemporary society in relation to cultural markers and intercultural negotiations taking place between individuals and nations.

Even in the compromises and acceptance made by the protagonists about their new identity as Australians, we see a celebration of the past through constant references to India. Manik Datar, who was born in Calcutta, confidently defines her roots through the kin networks and webs of social connection in Australia and India and uses the same theme in her fictional narratives about Indians in Australia. In her story "My Sister's Mother" (1995a), the younger sister living in Australia 'begins to understand that my sister's mother is different from my mother' (p. 76). The difference is not in terms of blood relationship but it lies deep inside the psycho-sociological conditions before and after the family's migration to Australia. The elder sister never migrated and stayed back in India – ' the country of (our) ancestors' (p. 76), where she proudly 'belongs as a native' (p. 76). The real shock for the younger sister is not the elder sister's feeling proud about India but lies in how her elder sister perceives even the internal migration taking place within India. She believes fervently that 'outsiders from other provinces in India should recognize they are guests and not demand equal rights as the local people' (p. 76). This statement shocks the younger sister and it is obvious because she herself is an 'emigrant in a country already taken from its local people' (p. 76). There are further shocks for her as the she faces linguistic problems related to the use of English – Indian English and Australian English. At other levels, the younger sister to preserve her authentic Indian image in Australia owns, as a proud possession, a 'white marble mortar and pestle' (p. 77) and because of it has suffered the jokes of her Australian friends to whom it looked like 'a piece of Taj Mahal' (p. 77). The elder sister does not need a mortar and pestle, as it is very old fashioned and she proudly says that 'in India we are quite modern; we can buy all masalas readymade' (p. 78). She, for the younger sister, is a connection between India and Australia (the past and the present) but unknowingly and quite happily is 'caught between two beliefs' – tradition and modernity (p. 78). While, on the other hand, the younger sister, who is also facing the same dilemmas as an immigrant, is still trying to balance and hold on to both the cultures for the sake of her future in Australia and because of this 'holding on' she is not rooted in either Australian or Indian identity. The younger sister is married to an Australian and going back to India is not a possibility for her. The only choices available to her are either to confidently strike a balance between her Indianness and Australianness or to merge in the mainstream Australian identity.

Conclusion

We can note that in most of these stories the immigrants try to bring the Indian subcontinent to Australia with them by using myths, legends, historical facts, and so on. These immigrants besides using myths also display a proudest possession, which reminds them constantly of home. These proudest possessions are 'iconic referents', which perform the signifying function of an icon and to a certain point act as a linkage between personal and national. These iconic referents or 'cultural symbols', according to Homi K. Bhabha (2006), 'ensure that the meaning and symbols of culture have no primordial unity or fixity; that even the same signs can be appropriated, translated, rhetoricized, and read anew' (p. 157). For the immigrants, in their everyday life in Fiji or Australia, everything depends on these representations or icons. Thus, the 'consumption' of particular commodities in the diaspora might lead an 'individual to remember the warmth and laughter surrounding family gatherings and celebrations in the homeland (rather than the conflicts and family politics surrounding them)' (Mankekar, 2005: p. 206).

The task is to keep the roots, history, and memory, of South Asia alive in Australia by conspicuous consumption. Satendra Nandan also notes this in his story, "Ashes and Diamonds" (1989) that for the first-generation immigrants, like his father, Air India, a connector between the subcontinent and Fiji or the outside world, represented 'the idea of India itself' (p. 65). This acknowledges how the 'experience of dislocation, modulated by a nostalgic longing for the familiar, is also deeply rooted in the creation of imaginary fictions' (Mannur 2007). For example in Rani Jhala's story "Life's Key" (1999), a rose plant becomes the symbol of 'love of today and the promise of tomorrow' (p. 21). However, it does not take time for the protagonist to realize that 'thorns are inseparable'. A 'white marble mortar and pestle' is the 'proudest possession' and an authentic one too for the younger sister to show her Indianness in Manik Datar's "My Sister's Mother". In Mena Abdullah's "The Time of the Peacock", narrator's mother has made her own garden full of Indian flowers, a connection with the old country or in other words with the Indian subcontinent inside their farmhouse – 'her own walled-in country'. Similarly, the white peacock, Shah-Jehan, in the same story is a reference to 'Indians' or migrants who are settling in Australia. Peacock as India's national bird symbolizes the national sentiments and an Indian way of life in the diasporas, wherever they are settled. A sentiment well expressed by the noted Gujarati poet Ardeshir F. Khabardar: 'Wherever there is even one Gujarati, there is forever Gujarat'.

According to Bruce Bennett (2002), the 'powerful hold of myths and stories brought with migrants, and retained in the new country, recurs in much cross-cultural fiction' (p. 158). These objects or icons or elements from the past, which the immigrants carry with them as cultural products, are used as helpers in making a sense out of the alien situation presented before them. As diaspora writers who are displaced and uprooted, according to Terry Eagleton (2005) usually 'clung to the values of order, authority, hierarchy and tradition more tenaciously than some of their less unsettled colleagues' (p. 259). Sticking with them and putting meanings inside these objects or referents in an alien environment can also be seen as, at the initial stages of migration, a way of legitimating their relationship with home from a 'third space' for future's sake. This in a way is the immigrants' strategy of providing these objects a dominant meaning in reference to homeland by articulating an ideological or socio-religious function different from what they had back home and thus establishing a privileged position. Thus, also creating works that deepen our understanding of the ways in which Indian diasporic communities define and use collective memory to negotiate their sense of origin. The Indian diasporic writers with their worldview appear and the cultural life provides other ways of viewing the world. As often, according to Amitava Kumar (2004), distances from homeland produce a 'shift in perspective' and 'the immigrant writers find that they are discovering not only the new country, but also the place that they have left behind' (p. xiv). In conclusion, Indian-Australian short stories, analysed in this chapter, act as an important expression of the Indian way of life in Australia. This genre may also effectively help remove misconceptions and foster a better understanding of local conditions, thus encouraging fellow Australians (and diasporans) to see differently within the cultural context of India and Australia.

CHAPTER 3

A Journey through Places

Politics of Spatial Location

> To see things plainly, you have to cross a frontier. (Rushdie, 1991: p. 24)
>
> The writers in the diaspora are a product of movement. They embody travel. The kind of language that these writers use, (...) conveys the variety of their translated lives. And in their writing they record the enormous richness, and pain, of displacement and loss. (A. Kumar, 2004: p. xvii)

Politics of Spatial Location

By politics of spatial location, I mean a migrant's positions within power hierarchies created through historical, political, economic, geographic, and other socially stratifying factors in the new homeland. Writing by immigrants is a culture-specific tool and has developed, as Sudha Rai (2002) observes,

> against the backdrop of issues relating to the movement between home country and country of immigration as geographical spaces; culture shock; attempted cultural recuperation through ethnic bonding; binary stereotyping of cultures traversed; the immigrant split-self; fantasies of return passages; and tentative stabilisations of identity. (p. 134)

The immigrants' search for the things lost and their efforts to rediscover, cherish, and bond with their past and culture alike often seems to the dominant majority, as nothing more than tactics of enclosure on the part of the new migrants. This was also noted, more than half a century ago, by John O'Grady (a.k.a. 'Nino Culotta') in his famous novel, *They're a Weird Mob* (1957):

> There are far too many New Australians in this country who are still mentally living in their homelands, who mix with people of their own nationality, and try to retain their own language and customs ... Cut it out. There is no better way of life in the world than that of the Australian. (p. 204)

This highly ambiguous Australian 'way of life' that O'Grady is talking about here was used initially as the line of attack by the Anglo-Celtic Australian public to 'discriminate against migrants' (R. White, 1985: p. 160). According to Stratton and Ang (1998), the Australian way of life 'was a vague discursive construct which lacked historical and cultural density, often boiling down to not much more than the suburban myth of "the car, the family, the garden and a uniformly middle-class lifestyle' (p. 153; see also R. White, 1985: p. 166). However, it can be seen that this same concept of an Australian 'way of life' as different from others was glorified in white Australian literature on the basis of its pluralistic, tolerant, and multicultural nature.

Immigrants, in turn, see attempts – both on the individual and on governmental levels – to initiate migrants into the culture and policies of the hostland as a ploy by the politically and linguistically dominant group to categorize them in some way or the other solely in the context of assimilation and multicultural policies. And sometimes, as pointed out by Janis Wilton (1985) in the case of Australia, the process of recognition of the 'otherness' as now part of the 'Australianness' can be slow (p. 24). Wilton notes that Anglo-Australians have taken a lot of time to 'recognise the richness and complexity of the experiences and traditions which have been brought to and re-created in Australia' by the migrants (p. 24). As a result, migrants viewed through the representations of literary and other mediums emerge to be seen as stereotypical, complex, exotic, marginal, eccentric bunch of characters. This accentuates the process of typifying them as highly un-Australian by virtue of racial differences. These archetypal viewpoints and prejudices are largely due to ignorance and lack of knowledge on the part of the dominant culture about the culture(s) of the incoming immigrants. This leaves the immigrants in a Trishanku-like situation of neither retaining their nationality of origin, nor being best assimilated, not-so-Australian Australians (see Parameswaran, 2000).

On the politics of home and spatial location, Rosemary Marangoly George (1996) reflects:

> Immigration and the fictions it engenders teach a certain detachment about 'home'. In these texts, identity is linked only hypothetically (and through hyphenation) to a specific geographical place on the margin. And yet, wandering on the margins of another's culture does not necessarily mean that one is marginal. Home in the immigrant genre is a fiction that one can move beyond or recreate at will. The association between an adequate self and a place to call home is held up to scrutiny and then let go. As postmodern and postcolonial subjects, we surprise ourselves with our detachment to the things we were taught to be attached to. (p. 200)

The South Asian-Australian writers' postcolonial and postmodern experiences as presented in the narratives analysed here support this statement. Further J. M Macgregor Wise (2000) observes that the idea of Home

> (...) is a collection of milieus, and as such is the organization of marker's (objects) and the formation of space. But home, more than this, is a territory, an expression. Home can be a collection of objects, furniture, and so on that one carries with one from move to move. Home is the feeling that comes when the final objects are unpacked and arranged and the space seems complete (or even when one stares at unpacked boxes imagining). (p. 299)

In relation to the issues and problems of setting up or shifting of 'home' to the hostland, the immigrants at every level confront the 'localised' (Bromley, 2000: p. 13) – be it in the form of people, places, names, and so on. And this confrontation with the localized often gives rise to a 'double representation' in the works of the diasporic authors.

It is interesting to note how diasporic authors represent 'home' in relation to where they come from and where they are now settling down. Throughout these stories, we can note that the characters are not stable in their present location, although there is a clear will to stay and make Australia their home. However hard the protagonists try to locate a sense of Australianness, it skips away from them or makes them first accept the challenges as a test of resilience. But this is just the initial stage for migrants in the process of settlement. There is always an aspiration nurtured by the immigrants to move on with life in this new home. The protagonists are put under predicaments that their authors might have gone through or experienced or dealt with in one form or the other during the process of settling down in Australia. Table 1 illustrates the five stages of development that immigrants go through and on which the stories studied in this chapter have been analysed. These stages can be seen in both the overall patterns of the development of the diaspora group and individual consciousness. Each new stage of cultural consciousness arises in response to conditions in the hostland and coincides with external pressures and internal development. It also develops in reaction to the preceding stage's negative values. The recognition of these stages by characters and their authors help in opening-up of Australia to its diasporas.

Table 1 *Stages of Cultural Consciousness*[1]

S. No.	*Stage*	*Attitude towards One's Culture*	*Attitude towards Other Cultures*
1	Control	Oblivious/Unclear	Curiosity/Excitement
2	Behavioural	Denial	Confusion/Helplessness
3	Reintegration	Idealization	Denigration
4	Pseudo-independent	Aware	Intellectual acceptance
5	Independent	Accepting	Accepting

The table clearly shows that the

> true acceptance of the host and the adoptive culture goes through several stages before it is incorporated into consciousness (...). The ability to grow, develop, learn and benefit from other cultures would naturally be reduced if the stages are not gone through progressively and acceptance attained. (Patri and Patri, 2002: pp. 14–15)

It can also be clearly noted that most of the acclaimed diasporic writers, who are writing about their own experiences, have in one way or the other reached Stage 5 – Independent with the ability to grow, develop, and accept the 'otherness' of the people of the hostland. However, this independence and the ability to accept otherness are often deliberately not provided to their characters as a solution of cultural difference(s). The protagonists/characters are shown to have retained many of their South Asian traditions in the hostland, a land 'alien' to them, in their original or a slightly changed form, while the South Asians living in the Indian subcontinent have long discarded or changed some of the norms and practices or modified them beyond recognition. So, the immigrants are shocked and surprised at the changes, as they were still preserving a set of cultural norm in the 'imaginary homelands' of their own that were created in Australia or any other foreign country or hostland.

Amitava Kumar (2004) observes that often it is 'the portraits of the lands in which they now live, portraits drawn by discerning outsiders, which represent the greatest achievement of the *desi* writer' (p. xvii). The concept of home and the process of settling down in the Australian outback, during the early 1900s, is seen from a child's perspective in Australian-born Mena Abdullah's collection of short stories *The Time of the Peacock* (1965) about which Bruce Bennett (2002) observes: 'Abdullah's stories of childhood exhibit a gentle, celebratory tone, mingled with a certain sadness at the loss of childhood harmony and innocence' (p. 158). Immigrants bring many things to Australia, but their lasting contribution to the country has always been their children. The family presented in Abdullah's collection consists of a Muslim father and an ex-Brahmin mother and their three children – Rashida, Nimmi, and Lal. Nimmi, the young daughter born and brought up in the outback, narrates these stories. Paul Sharrad (2000) in relation to the use of a child narrator has argued that 'with innocent, sometimes naïve ideas on life', a child narrator 'allows the white adult reader to feel benignly condescending towards all kinds of difference represented' (p. 253).

In her story *The Time of the Peacock*, Abdullah presents an immigrant Punjabi Muslim family living like exiles in New England, the Australian hinterland, which is their world now. This particular story exploits the Australian myth of the independent rural pioneer sweating it out in taming the land that is farming. This family is away from home yet the 'stories (from home) were alive in (their) heads' (p. 1). The family gets a pet from India – a white peacock fondly called Shah-Jehan but who 'will never open his tail in this country' (p. 3). For this family, being Australian is not as important as preserving their cultural heritage in an alien hinterland. The very process of preserving can be seen working internally in the family, as the narrator's mother, who was Brahmin before marriage and 'believed in the tales of Krishna and Siva' (p. 6), even now after getting married to a Muslim 'remembers her old ways' (p. 6). These religious beliefs, however small they are, such as the mother putting milk outside the house to satisfy and feed the snake, are dangerous in the unknown Australian hinterland. The narrator's father knows that it is foolishness to do such a thing and removes the bowl of milk without telling anybody or hurting his wife's belief. In this story, the peacock, Shah-Jehan's, opening the tail can be read as a symbol of joy and happiness, which this family is looking for in Australia. The peacock also becomes 'in all his grandeur' a symbol of the diasporic self and a link between 'the past and the present' (see also I. Hussain: p. 184). In one of the myths, the peacock is presented as 'the bird of the paradise' exiled from heaven for his sin of helping Satan (I. Hussain: p. 185). The family is exiled, just like this peacock, from their homeland into the vast hinterland of Australia, almost in total isolation from Australians, both individual and the society.

Similarly, in Abdullah's story "Kumari", there is only loneliness for these diasporic children, as they do not have other (white Australian, Aborigine, or other immigrant) kids as companions and playmates in the outback. The only pastime the family can think of is talking about India and naming the various plants, animals, and places in their mother tongue – Hindoostani – to continue or form new links with the past. This 'evocation of audio, alimentary and visual pleasures through the naming of places' according to Iain Chambers is coming 'across cities that are both real and invisible', a journey through places 'whose symbolic and real alterity provide another chance, a further question, a further opening' (1994: p. 28).

Another insight into the working of an immigrant's mind, language acquisition, and the process of creating stories or yarns is provided in Abdullah's "The Outlaws". It is only through stories or yarns, the very acts of exploration, that the protagonists explore what they have lost in leaving their homelands and celebrate what they have achieved in this new land. Here, Abdullah compares the story of an Australian bushranger, Thunderbolt, with the story of an Indian dacoit, Malik Khan. Migrant experiences are best reflected and preserved in stories where every individual shares their memories with others. For example, here, the stories of the narrator's mother are set in a mythological space and time and are the most fanciful. She acquaints her children with the 'gentle and strange, stories of the time when magic people walked through Hindustan, and everything they touched was right and good' (p. 42). Meanwhile, the 'father's stories were true and real' (p. 42), containing practical wisdom inside them, drawn from his experiences as a hawker in Australia. But, it is the stories of Uncle Seyed that give pleasure to the narrator and other children of the household because his 'stories were different – not always gentle, not always real (...) his stories were for grown-ups' (p. 42) and, most importantly, in the language of the new homeland – English, that can be read as an act of educating the children with the ways of the hostland or new home.

In Abdullah's story "Grandfather Tiger", from the same collection, Raj, a second-generation Indo-Australian and father of the young protagonist Joti, believes in a city-based Anglo-Australian education for his children, as opposed to his mother, a first-generation immigrant, who thinks it is not right for her granddaughter, as 'She will learn the white people's ways and think we are ignorant. She will call me stupid' (p. 94). Raj is optimistic and understands the value of English education for his children in a new land, as is disclosed in a conversation with Ram-Sukal, a fellow migrant and family friend:

> 'No, Mother, no,' said Raj. 'My children must learn to live here. They cannot stay in the house always. They must learn all they can. Then they can go to India and teach what they know'.
>
> They have never known India,' said Ram-Sukal. 'They may not wish to go.'
>
> 'But now that India is free,' said Raj, 'there is so much to be done. Schools to be built, and hospitals, and people will be needed to run them. India will be great again.'

> 'I thought,' said Ram-Sukal, 'that you were an Australian.'
>
> 'I am. I was born here,' said Raj. 'But my people – '
>
> 'Your people,' said Ram-Sukal. 'I have been back and I have seen your people. There is a line through your father's village. Where are your people? Are you Indian or Pakistani? They will kill you if you do not know.'
>
> 'Old friend,' said Raj, shamefaced, 'old friend, you are always right and always wise. But what are we to do? I belong here. I am an Australian, but who will believe me? My skin, my face, my thinking contradicts me, and who will accept me – or my children? He looked at Joti.' (pp. 94–95)

A discussion on the value of English education in Australia soon turns into a plea for acceptance or socialization of the family with the mainstream white Australians. On the subject of the socialization process, Milton Gordon (1964), in his seven-dimensional model of assimilation, postulates that the key to a meaningful relationship between people belonging to an ethnic minority and the majority is 'structural assimilation' – the large-scale entrance of ethnic minorities into the cliques, clubs, bazaars, and other 'primary-group institutions' of the 'core' sub-society (see also Cameron, 2006). In the story, Raj is a second-generation Indo-Australian, who is born and brought up in Australia. Raj fears that if he is still not being accepted as 'Australian', then the future of his children and all the third-generation Indo-Australians is bleak. His question is straight: does his colour and thinking make him un-Australian? But then what is Australianness? The answer to both the questions is that there is no single trait that can define someone or something as Australian (see White, 1985; Harper and White, 2009). Another important issue is the futility of returning to 'home' – post-partition India. As Ram-Sukal, the family friend, points out: 'They will kill you if you do not know' (p. 95) whether you are an Indian or Pakistani. Post-partition India is, to borrow a phrase from V.S. Naipaul (1964), 'an area of darkness' – a completely pessimistic world for some immigrants. This has also caused an acute sense of disillusionment and loss of determination to return to the homeland. Therefore, the return to the homeland can be equally futile and disappointing.

Similarly, Satendra Nandan, noted Fiji-Indian-Australian author, in "The Guru" (1988) presents people of Indian-origin looking for 'future possibilities' away from their motherland in the cities of Fiji, New Zealand, and Australia. Pundit advises the protagonist Beckaroo alias Beer Kuar Singh to not change his religion under any circumstances – because that would be, according to him, a 'political suicide' (p. 72). He does not know that Beckaroo has already converted to Christianity in Tasmania to marry his love, Wendy, and 'to get a good job in the civil services (as) a Christian from Tasmania would carry more weight than a local one' (p. 72). Beckaroo, looking at houses on the street on his way to his house, compares the lives of second- and third-generation migrants with those of their forefathers and reflects that the 'temporary shelters of the fathers had become the permanent homes of the children who had accepted their lot with deepening fatalism' (p. 70). One of the questions that such diaspora narratives constantly ask, according to Lin Ho, is: How much of an ancestral culture and hierarchy is 'preserved', 'transgressed', and 'transformed' in the passage of diaspora? It is the differences in power and status that characterize community networks and relations not just in the homeland but also its preservation in the hostland, thus providing class mobility and social capital in the host society through generations (see Lin Ho, 2000; Ballard, 2001; Levitt, 2009).

Fiji-Indian-Australian academic Brij V. Lal, in his short piece "Labasa Secondary" (2001b) notes how his indentured grandparents, pioneer labourers, and first-generation immigrants from a village in eastern Uttar Pradesh, India, must have felt upon arriving in Fiji:

> In India their lives had been defined by their caste and community, their place in society determined by past deeds and misdeeds. There was no possibility of change in their own lifetime. But crossing the *kala pani* (dark, dreaded waters) had disrupted the old structures, and the rigours of daily plantation life had further destroyed the basis of social hierarchy. The lowly leather tanners, skinners of dead animals, and the twice-born Brahmins were all equal in the eyes of colonial law. In these green islands, private enterprise and individual initiative rather than social status determined whether a person survived and prospered. (pp. 102–103)

It is a 'revolutionary realization' at that time too and with education, the young Indian-Fijians looked forward to a 'new more egalitarian world' (p. 103). As mentioned earlier, these migrants, who were part of the 'labour diaspora' as a result of the colonial system of indentured labour, created in Fiji a mini-India, which was their way of projecting a return to the past to get over their feelings of rootlessness and lack of a permanent home. This was to some extent also because the 'old diaspora broke off contact with India which, subsequently, existed for it as a pure imaginary space of epic plentitude' (V. Mishra, 2002: p. 236). Similarly, the protagonist of Nandan's story, "The Guru", Beckaroo, expresses an anxiety which most of the second and third generation feels, that is, not the sense of homelessness or nostalgia for home but change that one needs in their life towards improving one's lot rather than being stagnated in the old traditions of a lost homeland. He sees 'history (as) what one sees in the rear view mirror' (p. 70), and one wants to move away 'as far the windscreen presents new vistas, new perspectives' (p. 70). Beckaroo stands for change in both economical and social conditions of his villagers.

Second-generation Indian-Australian Rashmere Bhatti, a community welfare worker, in her autobiographical piece, "The Good Indian Girl" (1992), recalls her family background in Australia and the feelings of isolation, the lack of familiar comforts from India being available to the family. She also talks about the Punjabi women's role in the family, her exposure to both cultures (Indian and Australian), her early education, and tertiary studies. This piece discusses the Indian tradition of arranged marriage and career choices offered to girls in the Indian-Australian community. She also points out the significance of gender constructs in both cultures (Indian and Australian) in the third generation's lifestyle. She writes of her dilemma about being a third-generation Indian-Australian:

> I think sorting out whether I was an Australian or an Indian was one of the most crucial decisions of my life. It is difficult enough to get on with growing up, without having to cope with a culture and religion that demand much and which influence a large number of both important and everyday decisions. I am certain my life would have been different if I did not have to constantly juggle my

> thoughts, emotions and actions between two very different ways of life. (p. 131)

The spatial versus the sensory location and generation gap that we see in South Asian-Australian diasporic society emotionally and mentally puzzles the individuals, by further socially resulting in alienation, as Rashmere observes,

> Throughout high school, participation in social functions was not allowed. It was not considered right to go to school dances, to mingle with boys; there was no social mixing at all. So naturally I became alienated when all other children discussed the school dances – I had to make some lame excuse for not going. (p. 132)

She notes that while her parents were happy because 'They thought they had been granted a gift from the gods, to have the fortune to live in Australia – the Lucky Country' (p. 132), her father, who was born and brought up in India where he also got married and then migrated to join his father, who was already working as a pioneer farmer on a plantation, is particularly rooted in the old ways of India and also wants his children to grow up as Indians in Australia. Australia, and the Australian way of life, offers Rashmere and her elder sister the courage to revolt against him, thus 'creating something of a controversy in the community' (p. 132). Australia offers Rashmere not just freedom and confidence to rebel for her rights but also a career choice and self-confidence to feel proud in her 'new image' of 'Australian Indian' (p. 134).

In her narrative about her life experience as an Indian-Australian girl, we also get glimpses about her mother's life as a pioneering migrant woman in the Australian outback. Her mother 'came to Australia at the age of 22 after an arranged marriage, to live a lonely pioneer lifestyle with few Indians or Australians around her. Hers was a life of childrearing, cooking and enduring the primitive conditions of bushland Australia' (p. 131). For Rashmere's mother who must have spent her early life in India surrounded by relatives, neighbours, street-hawkers, and others, a pioneer's life is a lonely one. She misses 'her family and homeland' and so 'reminiscing about a carefree way of life full of chores, religion, girlish capers and dreams' tells Rashmere stories of her life in India (p. 132). Rashmere's mother can be compared with

Nimmi's mother in Mena Abdullah's collection *The Time of the Peacock*, who as a pioneer migrant woman is placed in very similar situation and reminiscences a lot about her life spent in Kashmir.

Rashmere has heard so much about India from her mother that when the time comes to look for a husband, she visits India. She writes:

> So I went to India with much hope. Having spent my entire life in Australia, I had a picture of *my homeland* as a backward place with only the bare necessities for survival. Much to my astonishment, there unfolded for me a diverse land alive with vibrant colours and people – full of a history and culture that I could identify with. I found that for the first time I completely belonged. I felt I had come home and I didn't quite realize till then just how much of an outsider I had felt in *my western world*. (p. 135; emphasis added)

She marries a 'lovely Indian man' and with him spends 'a glorious year exploring, getting to know India' before beginning their 'life in Australia' (p. 135). Rashmere's idea of an originary homeland leads her, as it does to some second-generation migrants, to actually temporarily migrate to the place where their parents are from. They expect to find the ideal homeland that had provided them with a strong sense of belonging during their transnational childhood and adolescence. This is the concept of 'roots migration' that is useful here to describe the migration of the second generation to their parents' homeland – although not a permanent one in Rashmere's case (see Wessendorf, 2007). The use of the possessive adjective 'my' with both India and Australia, and her return to Australia with her husband after an exploration of India, presents her comfortable adaptation and acceptance of the cultures of both the countries. She is happy in or with her hyphenated identity (Indian-Australian) and has learned to negotiate with the Indian and Australian spaces, community, and home.

Well-known Sri Lankan-Australian academic and author Chandani Lokugé in her short story "Alien", the last story in her collection *Moth and Other Stories* (1992), explores the issue of migration through the story of Ramya, who migrates from Sri Lanka to Adelaide in Australia. Her brother, Ranil, a well-known doctor, was brutally murdered by terrorists (the LTTE) for not following their orders and the whole family ostracized. She could not believe 'that a nation could be so oppressed – how mutely it executed any order issued by the oppressors. But this was 1989. The terrorists had broken the back of the people' (p. 95). The refusal to submit to terrorism cost Ramya's brother his life. The police did not investigate the murder and family members lost all hope for justice. It is under this 'reign of terror' in Sri Lanka that Ramya

> submitted her application for migration to Australia. (...) The application was processed in six months. She was granted the resident visa (...). Her parents had promised that they would join her. She knew that they would not. Her mother would never leave behind the memory of her son. Nor would her father. (p. 97)

She is lonely in Australia but glad to be here:

> Far away in the distance the lights of Adelaide's city twinkled as if to welcome her home .... Home – in Sri Lanka. Home now Adelaide. (p. 94)

Australia is a peaceful haven for her and she is at one with the trees, birds, water, and the sky here. Yet her reverie on which she builds her narrative eventually makes her realize, at the end of her story, that she is an alien in Australia.

> (...) her friends (...) whispered secretly with strange tongues. She suffered their exclusion of her. (...) And it came to her that they did not need her, had never needed her. Did they not resent her alien presence then? (p. 98)

She could not forget the happier times spent in Sri Lanka with her father, mother, and brother. Now, she longs for 'the time when she had *belonged* to that island in the sun that knew no winters' (p. 98; emphasis added).

Ananda Bandara in Sri Lankan-Australian Chitra Fernando's "Making Connections" from *Between Worlds* (1988) feels 'empty' and 'immobile' in Sydney. He immigrated to Australia from Sri Lanka but now wonders: 'What am I doing here? Why did I come?' (p. 92). To him Sydney (Australia) is 'a jumble of unconnected shapes and clashing colours' (p. 89). He feels cheated but doesn't know whom to blame. His home gives him the feeling of a confined space and at work he feels like 'a prisoner chained to his desk' (p.

94). He feels a sense of disconnectedness with Australia – his new home. He observes that Australia offered only

> material comfort – but man couldn't live by bread alone. He remembered his experience in the train, that sense of disconnectedness. What it told him was that he didn't belong here, there was nothing significant he could do. Yet he felt capable of doing something significant – but not here. (p. 95)

But, very soon he recognizes the problem behind his feeling of disconnectedness. Even now, he knew very little about the people he is working with and of the history of Australia. It is his lack of interest in their life and history that has caused his disconnectedness. In a moment of introspection standing near the Harbour Bridge, he feels that he needs to make connections with people and places around him.

> He felt exhilarated as he saw that this was the beginning of his double life: his external life of eating, sleeping, going to the office, mowing the lawn, vacuuming the carpet, putting out the garbage – the life of the house-holder; and his secret inner life of making new connections, creating new meanings and forms. (pp. 101–102)

His exhilaration is also because in immigrating to Australia he hoped something for himself – 'a widening of mental reaches' (p. 102), and now he knows how to attain it.

The immigrants have come to Australia (hinterland or city) with a dream – 'to learn, to earn (...) to save and return' (p. 83), as the protagonist in Manik Datar's "Point of No Return" (1995b) says very poetically. He came to Canberra because he wanted to do something for his country. This is the very nationalist ideology or cultural baggage in the heart of most of these immigrants (going for study) that is carried on in their cultural baggage. The protagonist of this story like the other immigrants is 'grappling with its world (...) have an urge to name all things (...) birds, plants, places, whims of weathers, foodstuff, objects of everyday use – for in naming them in Bangla (he) can testify their reality' (p. 84). He is in search of Indian names and definitions for things that are Australian. We often find him comparing the Australian things with what he has left behind in the homeland, a practice to legitimate the things he finds and thus legitimizes his presence in Australia. Nevertheless, in doing so he provides the readers with various images of Canberra – 'the bush capital' (p. 85).

In India, for his family and relatives the problem is where to place Australia or where it belongs in terms of cultural effects – East or West – as they have no stories, good or bad, of Australia and its impact on the immigrants and their culture. So, Australia fascinates them but this lack of stories or images of Australia makes it, understandably, 'not rate(d) highly as a foreign destination' (p. 85). On the other hand, on reaching the Indian Cultural Club in Australia, he finds that he can act as a bridge or a point of contact with the homeland for others because of his status as a recent migrant to Australia. But still, even here, he cannot stop himself from thinking in terms of Bengali and non-Bengali, that is, in terms of internal Indian regional or provincial divisions. The only option for him as a solution to his dilemmas is to 'make friends with Australians, White Australians' (p. 88). Again, he wants a choice in terms of friendship, thus excluding Aborigines and other migrants from the category of 'Australians', and the result of such a situation can only be 'loneliness' (p. 88). The solution for his problem too lies in his resolve to 'belong' to Australia from within.

The narrator in Australia-born Anglo-Indian Christopher Cyrill's "Dusk and the Public" (2000) has no knowledge about the native Australians. He says:

> I was so sheltered from the customs of native Australians, so sheltered from the people themselves, that in my childhood I believed they were from another country. I thought them immigrants, as my own family were, but I could never name their homeland. They did not resemble the Africans or Asians or Americans I had met or seen on TV, and they were unlike the Australians I schooled with or befriended. Their skin was darker than anyone I knew, darker than my own. Up until the time I first heard the word Aborigine, and had it defined for me, I presumed the people who slept beneath the palm trees of St Kilda Esplanade were homesick, as my own parents often complained of being. (p. 10)

Similarly, the narrator in Cyrill's "Pestlesongs" (1997) follows the route (in Australia) that his grandfather took before his death –

a kind of Aboriginal walkabout or spiritual journey. He travels along the highway in Australia and comes across towns about which he does not know anything – 'lost in the broader cartographies of state and country' (p. 179). He imagines his grandfather 'passing along his way mountains and deserts and rivers named in a language long forgotten even amongst its once native speakers (...)' – the Aborigines (p. 179).

An interesting perspective of an immigrant's engagement and understanding of Australian lifestyles is provided in Indian-Australian writer Chris Raja's autobiographical piece "White Boots" (2003), where he uses the Aussie Rules football as a metaphor for assimilation. Chris, the narrator, immigrated to Australia from Calcutta with his parents, when he was just 11 years old. To him everything is strange, new, and alien. Also, his idea of Melbourne, the one he always imagined, taking references from the model of American cities presented in Hollywood films, is shattered – 'Melbourne was clean and green (...) with not a person in sight on the road except for those who drive' (p. 98). He further notes: 'I found this place particularly quiet. But here, on television, at the football people seemed to come alive and their personalities shone through' (p. 98). It is only in football that his young mind can grasp the idea of multitude and an Australian national spirit.

> My eleven-year-old brain tried to grasp reality of being in Australia, of living in Australia for the rest of my life. I hadn't even been to an Australian school yet but still I managed to understand that this strange game, the roughness, the secret hidden rules, would be useful currency. It would help me integrate and come to terms with being a stranger in a new country that was now going to be my home. (p. 97)

The narrator as a 13-year-old boy, grappling with his new identity, idolizes Warwick Capper, the 'idiosyncratic footballer, in a strange and alien land' (p. 98), who in a way teaches the young migrant the 'importance of being an individual' (p. 98). The narrator notes that Capper with his tall height, blond hair, tight shorts, and white boots stood out from the rest of the players. To his surprise, he observes that 'not everyone in Australia was blond and blue-eyed as I was led to believe growing up in India in the seventies. Naively, the young me had expected to become blond and blue-eyed when I became an Australian' (p. 98). It is the notion of individuality and being different than the rest that the narrator learns from Capper. Nevertheless, the white students at school made fun of him, his accent, and his difference – 'Have you ever got on with someone?' 'You speak funny' (p. 98). It is his friendship with a white Australian boy Darren Carter and football that has helped him adapt to living in Australia. He notes, 'I was lonely and the football on television occupied me' (p. 98) and 'It was only after Darren Carter became my friend that I slowly began to feel accepted' (p. 98). Chris saved Darren from getting mugged by other white boys at school and therefore in their friendship, one can read the Australian ideal of mateship.

According to Wray Vamplew (2007), 'Sport has played a role in community formation and perpetuation; it has been part of the life of immigrants, providing a cultural link with what they have left behind (...)' (p. 370). Further, on using Aussie Rules as a multicultural suburban event, initiating the new migrants into the Australian way of life, Michael Atkinson, the Minister for Multicultural Affairs, Government of South Australia, says

> People coming to Australia already have a passion for sport, whether it is soccer, cricket or rugby. Football is so much a part of Australian culture it is important for our community that migrants who are interested in sport are introduced to our national game, to share with us the highs and the lows of following their local team. (quoted in Forrest, 2009)

Furthermore, according to Lieutenant Governor Hieu Van Le, Chairman, South Australian Multicultural and Ethnic Affairs Commission:

> Giving that extra support to migrants when they arrive in Australia will reap rewards in the future. It is important that new migrants are given every support to take part in activities that form the basis of our culture, so that they adapt more quickly to life in their new country. (quoted in Forrest, 2009)

The Australian government and its various agencies recognize sports culture as one of the major entering points for migrants into the country's national culture. However, John Kinsella (2002) sees Australian Rules football or footy as a sports culture that inculcates a lot of ugly and aggressive masculinity, sexism, racism, and animal cruelty. He observes that footy was used as a sign of 'cultural assimilation', of recognizing the power of Australianness, but somewhere it has also became the sign of 'blind nationalism' that has led to the propagation of the game through many strata of Australian society and migrants.

As seen from most of the cases above, diasporic writers are anxious to write and talk about their experiences in Australia and to reflect on both the past and present. As the above examples substantiate, it is clear that the diasporic writer, though presenting an image of Australia for the readers back home, still uses the Indian subcontinent as a comparative model or reference point. They present the place that is left behind and the potential that this leaving has created for their present and future. This is mainly because of the diasporic author's need to strike a balance between the two – one that is lost, that is, the homeland, and the other that still has to be gained or conquered, that is, the hostland. In these stories, the main attempt of the writer is to move away from South Asia and towards Australia. This movement of the diasporic authors away from the Indian subcontinent, in a sense, may be considered as the immigrants' 'farewell' to the Indian subcontinent and they, as Makarand Paranjape (2001c) observes, 'demonstrate a self-legitimating logic of leaving the homeland behind and therefore at least indirectly, of embracing the new diasporic home' (p. 167). So, the diasporic writing or literature in a way remains preoccupied with a sense of self-rationalization. Providing reasons for leaving the homeland, of being dislocated, of presenting a separate identity in the new homeland, of assimilating or integrating with the mainstream, and so on and so forth remains a common strategy amongst the writers of various migrant groups. A common strategy of

> diasporic communities (...) to 'make up' the culture, as a means of interacting with others, negotiating an image that gives them importance and value, even by 'inventing' traditions derived from local customs or events but appropriated and transformed in the new environment. (Coronado: p. 49)

The homeland like the hostland, still, remains a pervasive reality for them. And the process of grieving for the lost homeland ultimately leads to an acceptance of the new 'home', that is, Australia, happily or unhappily. It can be seen that in most cases this process takes place happily and not because of the involvement of economic and other privileges as incentives. Yet, in the acceptance is the exclusion of Aborigines and limited references to other migrant communities in Australia in these stories that make us wonder how the South Asian diaspora imagines these 'Others'. For in its imagining the other we can clearly glimpse its self-perception.

South Asian-Australian diaspora narratives – 'personal memories and private recollections of past experience' (Ganguly: p. 30) also act as 'written documents which give expression to the experience of living, or having lived, in Australia' (Castan: p. 65). In this chapter, I have analysed how these narratives about Australia represent some very Australian issues and spaces in a fascinatingly different perspective as compared to mainstream Australian literature. The first insight is into the populating of the Australian land by Indian subcontinental pioneer migrants. In Mena Abdullah's stories, we find a family making a home in the Australian hinterland, while in others it is the charm of the city – Sydney, Canberra, Melbourne, Adelaide, or other places. These characters are drawn towards Australia for economic opportunities. So, be it the Australian city or hinterland, filling the spaces and becoming part of a social change by bringing their economic logic to change their destinies is what matters to these immigrants. Second is the presence or representation of Australians – whites, Aborigines, or people from other migrant cultures. They exist but only on the periphery or just as references in these stories and do not an act as crucial participants. This can be seen as a test of adaptability not only for the immigrants from the Indian subcontinent but also for the Australians. The stories are inward looking in terms of both characters and situations. In these stories, the 'self' is not just the individual but also the collective identity of the community to which they belong. We can note that the diasporic community uses all the resources available

> to survive collectively in adverse conditions, reproducing, transforming and inventing specific forms of identity to make clear their distinctiveness, creating 'resistance identities' as cohesive strategies against the risk of cultural disappearance under the

> pressures of assimilation, or against a disadvantaged position in a country dominated by one culture-language-race. (Coronado: pp. 42–43)

The immigrants imagining Australia and resisting forced identities may vary within the individuals of a diasporic community. It depends on the conditions and space provided to them in the mainstream environment of the hostland and also on the immigrants' 'urge to appropriate space at home, and to use it for self-sustenance abroad' (Jain, 1993: p. 88).

Vijay Mishra (2007) constructs this relationship between the diaspora and the homeland in dialectical terms:

> diasporas construct homelands in ways that are very different from people of the homelands themselves. For an Indian in the diaspora, for instance, India is a very different kind of homeland than for the Indian national. At the same time the nation-state as an 'imagined community' needs diasporas to remind it of what the idea of the homeland is. (p. 424)

The stories of the South Asian diaspora in Australia make it clear that the idea of diaspora acknowledges that 'the history and culture' from which they have come 'is not an illusion', as 'histories are real' and the 'past still informs' who they are (Selvadurai: p. 5). These immigrants are now 'expert in crossing borders and performing identities, using, transforming and inventing new identities' (Coronado: p. 51). For them, it becomes necessary, borrowing a phrase from Gabriela Coronado (2003), to prove or to become a 'South Asian' outside the subcontinent and inside Indian subcontinental culture, which may also ultimately produce a new form of South Asianness. Therefore in Australia, as is felt by other migrants too, they become more 'authentically' Indians, Sri Lankans, Pakistanis, and so on or collectively 'South Asians' – contributing, understanding, and strengthening key elements of Australia's social, cultural, political, and economic foundations by transmitting the values of their homeland. Australian immigrant literature, according to Corkhill (1994), became 'specifically Australian, rather than merely an offshoot of its collective overseas homelands, from the moment it ceased to set its works solely in its multiple countries of origin and began to place them at least partially in Australia. This inevitability happened soon after the potential authors' arrival in Australia, since problems of settlement inevitably preoccupied the writers and these difficulties were communicated to their readers' (p. 73). As the relationship with a homeland does not end with the departure, it continues in diverse forms. Furthermore, the diasporan representations of the homeland are 'part of the project of constructing diasporan identity, rather than homeland actuality' (K. Butler: p. 205).

At the end, one central question inevitably arises: Is the South Asian diaspora's future built on nostalgic longing or progressive thinking? As noted above, there is naturally a sense of alienation, at the outset, where the mainstream or the 'others' stare and point out the difference – religious, cultural, and social. The process of integration may take some time according to the individual and the cultural baggage or cultural orientation he or she carries as well as the reception in the hostland. The migrants in Australia first encounter a harsh land – unknown and alien to them; second, they miss the old cultural values of the homeland and at the same time are attracted towards the new society, its values, and lifestyles; third, the sense of dislocation felt by the first-generation immigrants gets weakened in the subsequent (second and third) generations. For them, Australia is their home and they are Australians; and lastly, though they are Australians they carry with them hyphenated identities or bi-culturalness, which actually gives them an extra edge over the dominant others who have a monocultural identity, as now they can choose what they want to be, for example – South Asians, Australians, and South Asian-Australians or Australian-South Asians.[2] The stories point out both the global and regional realities and indicate that both South Asians and Australians require a cross-cultural understanding through the study of each other's culture and history. Through this medium of sharing, they can effectively make 'sense of the world' and the immigrants seem willing to aid this understanding, at least in the stories discussed here. For

> (T)he cultural maps we hold in our minds to make sense of the world are tangible maps which we often mistake as immutable truths. To dislodge the apparent immutability of our cultural interpretations of the world requires considerable effort. It

> requires educating the mind to identify cultural boundaries within which we operate and it requires the willingness to venture into the foreign and to potentially be changed by it. (Crozet et al.: p. 9)

As South Asian migrants cross 'cultural boundaries' and 'make a journey from their home over there in order to construct a home over here' (Kershen: p. 97), they venture into the foreign creating stories of spaces as well as spatial stories of a promising future for the South Asian diaspora in Australia.

Notes

1. J. Helms' "Stages of Racial Consciousness" (1966), modified and adapted by Vasantha R. Patri and Neelkant Patri (2002: p. 14).
2. See Uma Parameswaran's article "Ganga in Assiniboine: Prospects for Indo-Canadian Literature" where she identifies four phases of the immigrant experience to Canada (quoted in Paranjape, 2001c: p. 164).

CHAPTER 4

Real, Imagined, and Mythologized

(Re)Presentation of Lost Home

> A diaspora exists precisely because it remembers the 'homeland'. Without this memory, the image of 'their' India (Home), these migrants and settlers would be simply people in a new setting, into which they merge, bringing little or nothing to the new 'home', accepting in various ways and forms the mores and attitudes that already exist in their new country and society. (B. Lal, 2006a: p. 18)

As noted earlier, in Diaspora literature, most homes are constructed through the memories of the migrants. In relation to this, Manfred Jurgensen (1986) has argued that ethnic writers are 'monocultural writers whose creative imagination remains restricted to a native culture (home) in exile' (p. 81). This construction of home through memory raises an important question: How do representations of lost home shape the lives of the diasporans? The diasporans foreground an 'ongoing and contested construction of a transnational set of images, discourses, and institutions that engender what different people mean by "home"' (Mankekar, 2005: p. 197). Thus, migrant narratives need to be understood as inherently and essentially 'spatial stories' – stories of movement and stories of different *homes*. Rosemary Marangoly George in *The Politics of Home* (1996) claims that 'the search for the *location* in which the self is "at home" is one of the primary projects of twentieth century fiction in English' (p. 3) that is, in other words, a 'search for viable homes for viable selves' (p. 5).

Through the movement of people from the Indian subcontinent to the diasporic locations, homes are constantly re-narrated in migrants' stories. As a home – one's place of birth – is 'traditionally seen as a static place with a variety of positive and negative attributes, functioning as a shelter, but that is too narrow for self-realization' (Helff, 2013: p. 3). Home (real, imagined, and mythologized), as a place of origin, becomes a key site of a displaced migrant's experiences and connections with past. Home, the domestic and public space, also constructs the attitudes and behaviours of migrants towards 'Others' – people of the homeland and hostland. However, the migrants' search for the things lost and their efforts to rediscover, cherish, and bond with their past and culture alike often seems to the dominant majority, as nothing more than tactics of enclosure on the part of the new migrants. According to Anne J. Kershen (2006), for migrants 'home' or the idea of 'homeland' is a

> contested metaphor, a carpet bag of memories, emotions and experiences. It is now but it is then. It is over here yet over there. It is days filled with laughter, love and sunshine but it can be also darkness and threat. Real and tangible yet imagined and mythologized, home is deconstructed on departure and then constantly reconstructed as the migrant experience and life cycle evolve. (p. 97)

Let's look at the perceptions of re-visiting 'home' in some South Asian-Australian narratives. Satendra Nandan in his short story "First Flight?" (1993a) notes that 'there are other worlds and, once you have imagined them, the mind is forever restless like waves nibbling the shore' (p. 303). He further remembers his first journey to India, his ancestral home: 'I was going to India: a land of mystery, magic and ancient mantras, from where all our grandfathers and grandmothers had come' (p. 304). Similarly, in "The Road to Mr Tulsi's Store" (2003) Brij V. Lal recounts that growing up in post-war Fiji India for him 'was not just another site for fieldwork, not just another country' (p. 44). It was

> the land of my forebears. We grew up in Fiji with its myth and legends, its popular sacred texts, with sweet, syrupy Hindi songs and films. Our thatched, bamboo-walled huts were plastered with pictures of film stars and various multicoloured gods and

> goddesses. In short, India was an important *cultural reference point for us*. (p. 44; emphasis added)

The idea of home or a 'cultural reference point', according to Brij V. Lal in "Return to Bahraich" (1998), has another side to it that 'grows gradually and imperceptibly' and its 'influence is overwhelming and humbling' (p. 99). He further adds that the 'sheer variety of sounds and colours of various festivals, the shape of the landscape, people at home in multiple (but to me incomprehensible) languages is astonishing to some born (...) in (an) uprooted immigrant culture' (pp. 99–100). A journey through impoverished regions of Uttar Pradesh in India fills Brij V. Lal with 'renewed respect for those hundreds of thousands of men and women, ordinary people from all walks of life, who took fate in their own hands, shouldered their little bundles and marched off to the far flung corners of the globe in search of a better life for themselves and their children' (pp. 106–107).

For some, a journey back to home after a long fills them with disgust, like the recently immigrated expat woman in Manik Datar's "If I were a Teller of Tales" (2002). She feels that the life and activity in the homeland is just too chaotic and hard to understand:

> She looks around as though for the first time. Again, that kaleidoscope of expressions twirls across her face as she takes in the chaos of buses pulling up and leaving, passengers disembarking or jumping on the steps of moving vehicles, auto-rickshaws and even a bandy-legged camel erratically pulling its cart. Tourists and travelers each with their respective burdens of video recorders and backpacks or baskets of ripening guavas or wood apples to sell at the stalls bustle around. (p. 21)

For the expat woman, everything has changed and is so different. Throughout the story, her speech is interspersed with phrases that compare the present with the past, an India she lived as a little girl. Her Australian husband humourously says, 'Ah, your childhood. My poor darling. The country has changed too much for you, hasn't it?' (...) 'My *homeless* darling' (p. 22; emphasis added). The husband's use of the word 'homeless' to represent his wife's diasporic situation is quite interesting. While his Indian-Australian wife is just nostalgic about her childhood, he reads certain rootlessness in her yearnings. But to his surprise, a few moments later the woman finds her purse missing, from the *chay*-stall, at which she was sitting at. She shouts in disbelief: 'God, how I *hate this place*. You come to have a holiday and they bloody well fleece you soon as look at you' (p. 23; emphasis added). The husband, although surprised, calmly continues: 'Just think honey, 36 hours and you'll be in Sydney' (p. 23). All the nostalgia that she was feeling earlier vanishes, filling her with disgust and hatred for Indians sitting around her. She wants to leave India as soon as possible. On the other hand, the 'chay-wallah' is saddened because he knows what this expat memsahib (the Indian-Australian woman) will tell 'Others' about India and its people when she returns to Sydney – her home.

Similarly, the narrator in Grace Mackie's story "Of Jasmines and Jumboos" (1993) also narrates her return journey to Sri Lanka as an expat:

> (...) my first aerial view of this magical land – a land that had been haunting me for the last ten *unhappy years*. When I left it shores those many years back, it was on a dark monsoon night, when the lightning flashed, the thunder crashed and even the skies cried buckets at my departure. (p. 299)

Her first sights of home 'blot' out the intervening years and she is so excited to 'see old faces, old places and to feel warm all over once more' (p. 299). She as an expat can feel the changes that have taken place in the Sri Lankan society:

> The air smelt familiar and heavenly; lots of dark eyes and brown smiling faces – lots of changes too. New airport for one thing, the people dressed differently. They had traded their traditionally gaily coloured sarongs for more conventional trousers and frocks. I looked around disappointed – somehow I wished they had retained their individuality. (p. 299)

The narrator however is disappointed with the change, as from her memory she was still looking for a Sri Lanka that she had left on the monsoon night 10 years ago. She has come back as a tourist to 'devour' the scenery of the 'picturesque countryside' but is shocked on her arrival and narrates the city with disdain – 'buses rattled, trams clanged and trains whistled and roared under the bridge. Bullock carts, trishaws (the motorized rickshaw) and cycles joined the throngs and pedestrians were everywhere, literally taking their lives in their hands as they weaved and dodged among the traffic' (p. 299). Looking at this 'organized chaos', she despairs and for a moment the only escape is getting lost in her childhood memories. The narrator has returned to visit her family home, see the places where she grew up, and got married. In short, she wants a 'stroll down the memory lane' (p. 300). She has already prepared herself with gifts and extra baggage, even such basics as razor blades, to distribute among her friends and relatives who are facing hardships in Sri Lanka. For her, Sri Lanka has changed and she can feel that the people here, given the political and social conditions, are thankful everyday that they are still alive.

'Severance' from homeland is 'bitter sweet' writes Ruth Van Gramberg in her autobiographical piece "Immigration Dreams, Foundations and Formations" (1997). She further observes in relation to leaving the homeland:

> To leave a known environment, the dear familiar loved ones and the tranquil, sweet security of your home is particularly traumatic. There are the beloved faces that will be etched into your memory and the photos you store away to help you remember – are they sufficient? No, nothing can prepare you for this journey, as it is very, very frightening! (p. 209)

But then what would be 'sufficient' for a migrant to carry? Van Gramberg writes: 'The two crates, three or four boxes and suitcases are the ultimate sum of your past years, the rest lie in your *treasure chest of memories*' (p. 209; emphasis added). For her, the real home is lost forever and it can only be imagined through this 'treasure chest of memories'.

Michelle de Kretser in her story "Life with Sea Views" (2000) presents the life of a Burgher family in Sri Lanka. One of the sisters, Estelle, marries Harry, because he was a Sri Lankan-Australian, and his being an Australian citizen provided her with an escape route from the political tribulations (civil war and Emergency) and poor economic condition of her family. Kretser observes that during those days Sri Lankans preferred to migrate to Australia – 'Islands are the places you set out from. Continents are where you arrive' (p. 6). But for Estelle 'the promise of leaving', also brought 'the sadness of arrival' (p. 1). Estelle wrote to her sister, Monique, that 'things hadn't worked out with Harry' and promised to 'send a cheque as soon as she was back on her feet' (p. 9). In Sri Lanka, for this marginalized Burgher family things are not the same anymore. They depend on Estelle for monetary help. In Australia, Estelle can work, save, and also send a part of her income to help her poor family members. But for the conservative and traditional family members, Estelle's divorcing Harry and living with a Slovene migrant named Stefan represents 'living in sin with a communist' (p. 10). To the family, Estelle's life in Australia is an ambiguity. They find her letters too incomprehensible, obscure, and 'puzzling' as the family cannot understand the references to 'lamingtons', 'nature strips', and other markers of Australian way of life (p. 8). She never returns home and the family is destroyed by turmoil of civil war in Sri Lanka.

Indian-Australian writer Neelam Maharaj in her story "Festivals" (2004) looks back at life in India through the struggle of Kamala, who lives in an Indian slum. Kamala works as an 'efficient and capable maid' (p. 127) in 'the middle class suburb a few miles away' (p. 127). The responsibility of the family is solely on her shoulders. Her husband Ram, who has fully recovered from a 'bout of Tuberculosis a few years ago' (p. 128), is good for nothing and refuses to work and share the responsibility of the family. The daily problems in Kamala's life seem unending to her. The in-laws of her daughter, whom she married off at an early age, are pressurizing her over more dowry. Kamala as a slum dweller has to bribe the local police for carrying out construction in the house. In between the mention of all these hardships in the story are devoted paragraphs about festivals of India. Overall, though a depressing picture of India, the story presents how still, with all the hardships, people in India, particularly lower or lower-middle class, try to make things better to enjoy the small joys that festivals provide them. The descriptive paragraphs devoted by the writer in explaining various festivals, however, really make the story seem as if it were written to educate or inform 'Others' in Australia about the great Indian festivals, their importance in our lives, and civilization. As Kamala says, 'one had to preserve tradition, tradition was what kept us civilized' (p. 129). The reference to these celebrations at such a level is beyond doubt to offer a reflective feeling of 'rootedness' to the scattered Indian diaspora in Australia.

In her story, we can also read another dimension that is attached to the festivals in India. As Kamala narrates the incidents related to the celebration of the festival, it gives a sense of the ghost of poverty that haunts the central character. Festival brings into the life of her daughter Veena, the whole range of seasonal outpourings from her avaricious in-laws, starting from taunts to tantrums, because her mother is incapable to meet their demands. So, festivals, instead of bringing an atmosphere of bliss and ecstasy, only provokes anger towards the impoverished state of living as Kamala fails to gift *thalis* (platters) of sweets and clothes to her daughter's in-laws.

Kamala's problem is not festivals but the 'debt', which she will take to fulfil the demands of the family and relatives. She, in spite of being a woman and doubly marginalized because of her social and economic position, shows great goodwill to provide everything she can to preserve tradition and the joys of her family with it. The story, however, lacks subjectivity, which is an inalienable part of the Indian perspective. The sense of loss of 'Indianness' is represented as the voice of the narrator is that of a detached observer. This detached sense of belonging is amplified by the use of scientific outpourings that get enmeshed with the religious dimension of the festival. For instance, *diwali* is no more connected with religious rituals such as Lakshmi *pujan* but it becomes a means to relish scientific inventions such as 'marvelous pyrotechnical displays of fireworks' (p. 131). The language and style used in the story is deficient in capturing the class-consciousness or even the sociolinguistic factors that are important in relation to the representation of Indian way of life.

Similarly, Radha D'souza, in "Riding High" (1997), presents life experiences that relate to India and particularly to the life of its suburban middle-class people. She takes us on a 'thirty hour journey by train' (p. 94) with a story about a girl whose 'cropped hair stood out incongruously like an alien imposition' (p. 95). The hair on this girl's head 'looks (so) odd' (p. 95) to the narrator because for her it is the general opinion in India that in the world only '*angrezee* memsahib' (p. 94) or 'Christian girls had short hair' (p. 100). The girl's tale is interesting but an ordeal in itself. This girl 'had long luscious hair' (p. 95) that 'fell like a straight sheet of blackness right down' (p. 95) and her mother used to care about her hair. When her mother became ill and was not able to take care of her hair, she hired a maid to look after it. Her parents die leaving the responsibility of her two younger brothers and their education on her shoulders. With all her hardships she 'felt like a heroine in a Hindi cinema and that lightened (her) burden' (p. 98). But one day the tragedy struck, as on a busy day someone chopped off her long plait in the local train. She cried and on the advice of her colleague, a Christian girl, she went to a beauty parlour. Before entering the parlour, she felt like a 'harijan (who is) entering the sanctum sanctorum of a Hanuman temple' (p. 100). It is in the parlour that she is enlightened on the value of the Indian hair and their demand in the European and American markets. This also in a way is a solution to all her monetary problems and later becomes a source of extra income to fulfil her own wishes. She grows her hair long for about 10 months and then sells them off at rupees 500 to buy things she likes and needs most. This story is predictable by nature but it looks at the situation in not too funny or tragic a manner. It presents India as the chaotic and unpredictable land where anything is possible.

Life of the urban, highly educated and 'foreign returned' is presented by Sunitha in her story "Reminiscence" (1987). This story presents various issues such as Indian values versus the Western values, superstition versus Rationalism, and urban versus rural. Savitha, the protagonist, is an educated woman and earns as much as her husband. She teaches in a college but because of problems at her home she remains imprisoned 'amidst the four walls of her room' (p. 107). To her relatives and in-laws, her not conceiving a child even after two-years of marriage proves without doubt her infertility and gives rise to all sorts of speculations and superstitious methods to get over it. Her husband, who is 'foreign returned' and 'highly educated', is presented as a 'paragon of social responsibility' (p. 107). Savitha and her husband's modern outlook gives the idea of 'anglicised' behaviour to others (p. 108). Savitha feels that she who is educated 'was being pressured to move backwards to good old days of superstition, (and) blind belief in oracles' (p. 109), which she would never believe in her right senses.

In contrast to Savitha is her 'Americanised friend' (p. 111), who through her mannerisms shows that she is a *pukka* NRI. She constantly makes it clear that she will not be able to live in India for a second, 'she kept on commenting that India was full of dirt (...) infection (...). Horrible really (...) (with) so many problems like unemployment, poverty, dowry, rape and so on, whereas America is a land of dreams. It is a land of opportunities' (p. 111). She got 'married to a green card holder; a widower, who already had a five year-old son' (p. 111). But she doesn't mind it, as to her 'it is better to be a second class citizen, a second hand wife in a country like America than be a first class citizen in a country like India, where problems keep escalating one after the other' (p. 112). Savitha too has experienced life in America, and 'America was no doubt (a) beautiful land' (p. 112) but her own experience was of 'an alien in America (...) severed from her roots/people/country' (p. 112). And she chose to come back to India because for her 'India's poverty was far better than America's luxuries' (p. 112).

This story contains a message for all NRIs, and the message is not of rejecting the traditions of homeland but 'of blending the oriental and occidental ways of thinking' (p. 108) and bringing change in 'traditions that are decadent, rotten to the core' (p. 108). The story is full of sayings and anecdotes from *Bhagavad Geetha* that are related to customs and traditions. It also makes an appeal to all to weigh every option that comes your way before making a choice. India, here, is not only the land of traditions (and superstitions) but it has a modern face too. Savitha is a teacher and the two texts she teaches, Charlotte Bronte's *Jane Eyre* and Bessie Head's *Maru*, are both women centric. So problems presented here at one level have universal implications. Savitha as an earning member of the family feels she is equal and, therefore, independent in making her decisions. She is the face of the new, independent, and educated women in India. Western education and knowledge of Indian traditions and values allows her to take the best of both the worlds and she knows what she is doing and what she can do for her family and the society.

The life of the academics and their world view, various facets of the Eastern and Western society, marked changes in historical and contemporary relationships between the East and the West are one of the relevant themes encompassed in Yasmine Gooneratne's writings. She conveys several of her own experiences to present and make her points more personal and real to the readers. According to Meenakshi Mukherjee (2001),

> There is a continuity in everything Yasmine Gooneratne has written so far, whatever be the genre. Fiction and history get woven together, poetry permeates her prose, and as a literary critic her attempts to explore histories of exile and expatriation, the effects of imperial domination, and its aftermath encapsulate the concerns of postcolonial experience.

Gooneratne's "Masterpiece" from *Masterpiece and Other Stories* (2002) presents an East–West encounter in India. It is at a level about cultural clash and also about the issue of adaptation, commentary, and textual 'authority'. She uses a story within a story format and the central story is related to the ancient Indian legend about Sri Jayadeva's literary masterpiece *Gita Govinda* or 'The Song of the Shepherd' written nine centuries ago. The story presents proceedings of a seminar discussion going on the subject – *Gita Govinda*, 'its status in relation to India's classical heritage and to world literature, its literary qualities, and the process of its composition' (p. 199). On this latter aspect of the poem, a well-known storyteller had been asked to speak. While the storyteller narrates his tale about the composition of this great classic, there is present in the room an 'irrepressible questioner' – an Australian Professor (p. 202). He continues to interrupt the storyteller with his academic questions related to the writer's block, women's status in India, and his own theory about who completed the poem in the absence of Sri Jayadeva. In the original legend, it was 'the god (Lord Krishna) himself (who) descended in glory from his lotus throne in the temple, and climbed the hill to a poet's house in order to complete a classic poem' (p. 205). But on the contrary, the Australian Professor feels that the poet's wife completed the poem. To the storyteller, this is 'sacrilegious' because 'as a respectable young woman of twelfth century India, palm leaf and stylus would have been carefully kept out of her reach' (p. 205). The storyteller feels that the professor should study 'the art of interruption' and that too of the 'constructive interruption'. Because it is such 'interruptions (that) allow the story to move smoothly onwards, to a proper conclusion' (p. 206).

"Masterpiece" in a way is not just a story about the academic versus the nonacademic or believer versus the nonbeliever. It presents before the readers an unknown facet of India, that of the rich and vast classical literature of the Indian subcontinent, its readings, and interpretations. The villages of India where the roots of ancient classics and epics lie are 'unknown' to the West and have to be discovered in full. Gooneratne presents the conflict of East and West vis-à-vis a very witty yet serious authoritative tone that reflects ancient Indian legends and the contemporary Western experience.

This conflict is also studied in Suvendrini Perera's "Rejections" (1984). She reflects on her student life at a Sri Lankan university, although her description of the campus is a typical one: '(...) raw, freshly bulldozed roads, harsh green vegetation dotted with ragged children and dogs from the village – and particularly in the shabby and dust-ridden English department, rumoured to have once served as a cattle shed (...)' (p. 357). What is clearly noticeable is the strong radicalism, nationalism, and anti-English wave on the campus. The Resident Poet, writes Perera, 'had called (English) language' the language of 'the most despicable people on earth?' And had 'resolved his dilemma by deciding he would write only "destructively" so long as he wrote in English' (p. 358). This hatred of English becomes further more complex by a strong hatred towards affluent English-speaking classes of Sri Lanka, as Perera notes:

> (...) a majority of angry rural students who were hostile and mocking of our sheltered Anglicised backgrounds. Kadu-class they called us, the English-speaking classes. The word directly translated into swords. Our speech marked us out for the swords. (pp. 359–360)

The 'rejection' in the title refers to (a) the rejection of the first American Professor's attitude by his Sri Lankan students and in turn his rejection of the students and the campus; (b) rejection of their own multicultural history by the young Sri Lankans (particularly Sinhalese); and (c) rejection of Steve, the new vibrant friendly American Professor, who because of the 'fear of condescension' is sacrificed by his English class bowing to the pressures of Sinhala-dominated students and their 'moral authority' – resulting in poor attendance and aloofness of students in his class like his predecessor's (p. 360). In the background of this story, we can read the building social tensions that led to the rejection and exile of many of Sri Lanka's affluent and marginalized English-speaking classes.

Suvendrini Perera in her autobiographical story-essay "Dravidian Curls" (1999) on a visit to Sri Lanka as an expat on hearing a bomb excitedly asks: 'what was that, a bomb?' (p. 112). Her teenage nephew's reply to this question is sarcastic: 'That's what they sound like' (p. 112). Perera notes that as an 'invulnerable' expat, her question is a stupid one. She does not have any knowledge of the lived reality of their lives in Sri Lanka anymore, although as an academic she keeps track of everything through news channels and papers. Her expatriate gaze on return is more focused on the surface cultural changes, as noticed through food, behaviour, and dresses of her family members.

> In the household there are almost as many dress styles as ethnic and religious denominations: my mother sings her Anglican hymns and, these days, has taken to kaftans; my sister's wardrobe is full of Burmese lungis and Indian salwar-kameez; my young nieces are in round-the-clock black, a fact I know owes nothing to their Muslim father, and everything to their devotion to MTV. (p. 114)

She further notes that her house in Sri Lanka was a multicultural household, as reflected through the dresses – 'kaftans', 'lungis', or 'salwar-kameez'.

Nostalgia is associated with the pain of taking leave or parting. Perera remembers the play of language, in both Tamil and Sinhala, when taking leave from someone. It is never said that 'we are going' but we are 'going and coming back' (p. 114).[1] Questioning this use of words of parting, she writes:

> Is it because the concept of parting so pains us, so hurts and offends us, that we Sri Lankans try to erase the very words from our everyday vocabularies? (...). 'Varome', we announce in Tamil when, in fact, we are just leaving, not arriving; as in Sinhala it is correct to say 'we are coming' even as we walk out of the door. (...) Do we really aspire, by these reality-deceiving means, to cheat ourselves the finality of departures, to assuage the unspeakably crude act of separation, the emptiness one feels to be one moment inside the fraught circle, and the next – where? (p. 115)

Perera further observes how the notion of a good and bad migrant is developed, particularly in West, through the mannerisms of departure, arriving, and nostalgia. She notes that while a 'good migrant' is aspiring for 'a fresh start, a new leaf, another life' (p. 115), a bad migrant

> is the one who arrives without having left, or leaves never to arrive; the one who, as we say, doesn't know whether she's coming or going; whose baggage, tied up in awkward shapes and emanating struggle smells, is not to be tossed cleanly into the waiting bin at the customs terminal. He is the one on whom the sniffer beagle playfully pounces at the baggage carousel, followed by its polite, uniformed keeper: 'Excuse me, Sir, Madam, isn't there something you've forgotten to discard ...?' (p. 115)

Australia, like other destination nations, demands from its migrants 'letting go, of passions and engagements of the past, of history' (p. 115). And '(N)ot to let go, to insist on memory and the indestructibility of earlier lives and other places is to put on the black armband of history, stubbornly to fight against the forward-looking times' (p. 115). But for Perera, 'letting go' is not always a solution, as '(...) our history, the past surprises and confronts us. Like a phantom (...), all the way into the unpromising future' (p. 115).

Leaving the homeland and remembering it, as real, imagined, and mythologized, also provides a greater introspection into its workings. As Perera, a Jaffna Tamil Christian and now an academic in Australia, notes about the tribulations in Sri Lanka: the first reason for the conflict in Sri Lanka is the language – Sinhala versus Tamil versus English. Language is directly interplayed with ethnic identity and nationalism. The English language teaching and books, acted as

> (...) essential agents in the scene of violence, rage and terror (...). Our primrose path to the professional middle-class, our secure niche in the colonial *and* post-colonial scheme of things, the wider divide between ethnicities, peoples and classes that it signaled – all this was marked with just these volumes, and the privileged role of the English language in breaking open our lives, our understanding of who and what we had been, and had become. (p. 117)

As English language offered socio-political and economic opportunities to certain Sri Lankan ethnic communities on the one hand, it also gave rise to a fluent English-speaking class instilled with Western cultural values on the other hand. This widened the growing ethnic and religious divide between the Sinhalese and Tamils resulting in an ethnic strife. The severe contest for power between the various ethnic groups in Sri Lanka increased the sorrows of the people:

> Somewhere between the madness of our caste system, the poverty of an ungiving environment, the combined violence of the Portuguese, Dutch, British and Sinhala states, we have simply lost our bearings, cast off along an unknown coastline, face-to-face against some turbulent, rolling, unplumbable deep. (p. 123)

But can these differences of language and ethnicity be taken for granted. From her situation as a diasporic Sri Lankan in Australia, she speaks, about Sri Lankans and the mythical stories she remembers, using the pronoun 'we'. She knows that those who insist on separateness in Sri Lanka won't be happy with it, but she as an individual knows that separateness was a total of colonial authority and now the politicians are using this old trick with the 'ample collaboration from historians, anthropologists and other learned observers' (p. 117), that is, the native academia.

On the language and subject of her stories, she observes that

> In tracking the impossibility of a single mother tongue for my stories, in revealing the absence of a home ground that is unambiguously my own, by dwelling on the shared absurdities and longings of our languages, I am guilty of amalgamating what is easier kept apart. (p. 117)

Her stories are the stories she remembers – stories told to her from her childhood by women belonging to various ethnicities, religions, social classes, and so on. She observes critically that despite the government assertions of separateness, Sri Lankan identities have mixed, 'have leaked and flowed into one another, through the quotidian transactions of travelling and trading, eating and celebrating; of invoking, appeasing and casting out the same demons and deities' (p. 119). And it is this history of togetherness and ethnic cohabitation on this small island nation that she misses 'reading about in the textbooks and newspapers: the irrevocable mixing of our blood and our stories in war and love, conflict and coexistence' (p. 119). It is in this irrevocable mixing that she recalls her own hair style – curly ('Dravidian Curls') and suddenly remembers a work written about with all the 'painful longing, anger and obsessive detail of the exile' on Jaffna Tamil Christians.

Derek Bartholomeusz in "Tamil Tigress" (1997) narrates a tale of love in troubled times. Major Mahinda, a Sri Lankan army officer, and Ranji, a beautiful young LTTE fighter, both loved each other but unfortunately they belonged to different ethnic communities. Unable to meet, both part ways and in the end both die saving each other. Their tragedy, the writer notes, reflects the tragedy of thousands of young Sri Lankans, who are 'at the threshold of their lives, well-educated and talented' but the never-ending civil war has ended all 'their hopes and dreams' and 'seeing no further use of life' they have ended it (p. 263). He questions everyone – 'Who can one blame for a tragedy like this? Or for countless similar tragedies the world over (...)' (p. 263).

For South Asian diaspora writers, such as Adib Khan, writing about life experiences or the past and representing homeland through memory is a window to explore the self. Adib Khan discusses the process and motivation behind his becoming a writer in his autobiographical story "My First Love" (1995). He notes that it is the 'beginning of a long journey that will presumably continue as long as I am alive' (p. 25). He nostalgically discusses the experience of reading and learning at his school in Bangladesh that brought new meaning to his life as a writer. Thomas O'Linn, the teacher who inspired Khan, was an Irish-American Christian missionary living in Bangladesh. Khan writes that his teacher 'made no attempt to discuss or scrutinise what he had read to us. I suspect that he tried to reach out and make us feel the words and put us into direct contact with the experiences (...) swirling colors and the turbulence of life. (...) I learned to interpret and create, squeeze the words and drench myself with their possibilities' (p. 25). The story provides an insight into the makings and workings of a diasporic writers' mind.

According to Uma Parameswaran (2000), the diaspora writers often act as 'outsiders to the homeland, looking in at a part of a space that has changed in their absence'. The question then is: do these South Asian diaspora writers act as what Makarand Paranjape (2001a and 2007) refers to 'native informants' – 'seeing' the Indian subcontinent with all its faults and shortcomings on one hand and as an exotic and beautiful land on the other hand, and re-presenting what they see for Australians (or the West). Noted postcolonial critic Vijay Mishra (1996c) constructs this relationship between the diaspora and the homeland in dialectical terms:

> diasporas construct homelands in ways that are very different from people of the homelands themselves. For an Indian in the diaspora, for instance, India is a very different kind of homeland than for the Indian national. At the same time the nation-sate as an 'imagined community' needs diasporas to remind it of what the idea of the homeland is. (p. 424)

The stories of South Asian diaspora in Australia make it clear that the idea of diaspora acknowledges that 'the history and culture' from which they have come 'is not an illusion', as 'histories are real' and the 'past still informs' who they are (Selvadurai: p. 5). We here see a deconstruction of home and its realities. The style used is humorous, ironic, and sometimes even full of cynicism regarding the conditions prevalent in the homeland. Although they do not reject outright the homeland, the use of a comparative tone, that is, comparing South Asia with Australia makes it appear that they are somewhere constructing 'the image of homeland as not only an area of darkness, confusion, violence, but a hopeless and doomed country which must be rejected' (Paranjape, 2001b: p. 11). This is largely because of the rationalizing principle involved in the process of settling down in the hostland. And this imagining of 'home' on the part of the diasporans is therefore to be 'understood in terms of the logic of the dominant culture, of which it is an ambivalent or unwilling part' (Paranjape, 2001b: p. 10).

In conclusion, these stories present not fanciful re-creations of home but for a larger part the harsher realities in which millions of South Asians live every day. It does seem that through these stories the authors are sharing 'meanings as part of a diasporic community (to) make the process of settlement easier' (Coronado: p. 43) by nostalgically remembering the past. The constant 'looking back' and 'imagining the lost' may signify to some readers a complexity in interrogation where the 'dominant culture of the host country is not interrogated as consistently or rigorously as that of the homeland' (Paranjape, 2007: p. 351).

Indian subcontinent, as discussed above, is not just a construct in these stories but it sounds and feels real, bursting out with local details, variety of voices, and individual consciousnesses that are working in it. It is therefore also a celebration of certain aspects of the homeland, as can be seen from the visual images used to represent Indian subcontinent that are rich, varied, and colourful. These narratives do tend to simplify and to some extent homogenize the differences and similarities of the home, so that the people of same origin – Indian subcontinental – reading these stories do not feel alone and away from the familiar traditions, cultural, and religious rituals and its other aspects. This use of the familiar in these narratives helps the diasporans in moving, with their eternal diasporic cultural baggage, towards their Australian future.

Note

1. Coming and going are denoted by the same word even in languages such as Bengali and Assamese as in 'Aachi' or 'Ahisu' respectively.

Chapter 5

Acts of Remembering and Forgetting

Reflections through Nostalgia

> (...) it's my present that is foreign, and that the past is home, albeit a lost home in a lost city in the midst of lost time. (Rushdie, 1991: p. 9)

> And how shall I speak for myself without memory – my memory and the memories of my people, however dispersed, however distanced. (Alexander: p. 156)

Introduction

Satendra Nandan has written in his book, *Requiem for a Rainbow* (2001), that there are at least three ways of knowing a country: you are born in its landscape and are buried in its dust; you fall in love with a person of that country, or you read its literature or narratives (see also R. Sarwal, 2008). The first way of knowing has the concept of 'dislocation' acting as a key in the study of South Asian diaspora. And to think of diaspora as 'here and there', a dispersal marked by a displacement still assumes the predominance of an earlier placement or home, as the 'past continues to speak' to the migrants, but it no longer addresses them 'as a simple, factual past', as it is 'always constructed through *memory*, fantasy, narrative and myth' (Hall, 2000: p. 226). Similarly, Svetlana Boym in *The Future of Nostalgia* (2002) identifies two types of nostalgia that helps an immigrant in knowing his location. The first is 'restorative nostalgia', containing conspiratorial and blame elements based on strict binarisms (They vs. Us or the notion that 'They' have destroyed 'Our' homeland); the second is 'reflective nostalgia', leading to a 'sense of not being able to go home again'. Salman Rushdie in his article "Imaginary Homelands" (1985/1991) has set in motion a complex investigation into this condition (reflective nostalgia) of the diasporic writer. He eloquently puts it,

> It may be that when the Indian writer who writes from outside India tries to reflect the world, he is obliged to deal in broken mirrors, some of whose fragments have been irretrievably lost. (pp. 10–11)

Diasporic author who is unable to go back home again, views the past through the pieces of a broken mirror, which inevitably distorts the memory one has of a 'homeland', making it idealized so that only certain memories and ideas are highlighted. Further, in relation to the construction of a past world through memory, Bangladeshi-Australian writer Adib Khan, in his novel *Homecoming* (2003), observes that 'fragmentation, detachment and melancholy are inevitable conditions for the migrants', as they 'live with parallel worlds':

> One is a world in the *memory*, of what was and you cling to that because that sort of represents a pristine idea of life which is gone now. Everything changes and yet you cling to and retain a part of the past and you sanitise it. You remember the best bits and somehow or the other you hope that is still there when you get back and it is an impossible expectation. (p. 318)

Nostalgia, thus, is predicated on a selective remembering and forgetting of the past (see Berdahl: p. 198). This remembrance of 'the best bits' is a powerful impulse of the memory that awakens a longing for the past, about the unrealized dreams of the past in a lost home and often leads to the yearning for the lost homeland. It also stimulates the re-presentation or re-creation of South Asian spaces in Australia and a reflexive appraisal of the homeland, and its cultural values and norms.

According to Amitava Kumar (2004), there is another reason behind this yearning for the homeland in the South Asian diasporic writing, and it is a different kind of nostalgia – of not being an 'authentic Indian' – so the diaspora writers 'repeatedly make their way back to the Indian subcontinent' (p. xiv). All this, just to encapsulate the collective social and psychological anxieties of whole dispersed generations and their children. In an interview Arnold Zable (2008) explains:

> The current generation of refugees (and migrants) are experiencing the intense challenges faced by previous generations. We tend to forget, or fail to imagine, how difficult it is to start life anew far from the homeland. We forget also that nostalgia, the longing for the return to homeland, is a deep and enduring aspect of the refugee (and migrant) experience.

This diaspora consciousness, in the host country, shaped by 'nostalgia, the longing for the return to homeland', finds its way out through specific texts, discourses, practices, and institutions that were part of a migrant's life in the lost homeland. It is within this literature that 'diaspora is used as a social and political tool' for highlighting and expressing issues that are intimately concerned with diasporic identity, place in homeland, and the 'quest for individuality' (Y. Hussain: p. 3).

In this chapter, I examine the formation of ideas such as (lost) home, nostalgia, sense of belonging, and diasporic identity represented through the ideas of time and journeys of the authors through memory, that is, how 'roots' can be constructed by nostalgia for home. I further explore the melancholia of diasporic loss and the place of longing and memory in the renegotiation of lost home in the selected short stories of South Asian diaspora in Australia.

It was a Swiss doctor, Johannes Hofer, who coined the term 'nostalgia' in 1688, from the Greek 'nostos' – return home, and 'algia' or 'algos' – longing, suffering, or pain. Annette Robyn Corkhill (1995) explains 'nostalgia' as a

> form of melancholia or severe homesickness caused by prolonged absence from one's country or home. Inevitably, the literature produced by those who have left their countries of origin is full of this emotion. Because nostalgia really represents a longing to return to the land of childhood to revisit family and places of the past, it is generally a backward-looking or regressive emotion: rather, it is often a constructive feeling, unleashing creativity among immigrant writers as they struggle to describe and define their moods and reminiscences. (p. 45)

Thus, this intense attachment or nostalgia towards one's lost homeland is often seen as unnecessary and is dismissed as a primitive stage. David Lowenthal (1985) further observes that nostalgic longings are becoming increasingly common in Western societies, and he postulates that a mistrust of the future fuels much of today's nostalgia (p. 11). Yet he explains, 'If nostalgia is a symptom of malaise, it also has compensating virtues. Attachment to familiar places may buffer social upheaval, attachment to familiar faces may be necessary for enduring association' (p. 13). Daniel Francis (1997) reinforces this point when he writes, 'In an age of anxiety, it is not surprising to find nostalgia flourishing' (p. 176). Some recent readings of nostalgia also suggest that it is an emotional resource for insight and cultural production. Anthropologist Kathleen Stewart (1988) defines nostalgia as 'an essential, narrative, function of language that orders events temporally and dramatizes them in the mode of "that's that happened", that 'could happen', that 'threaten to erupt at any moment' (p. 227). She further notes that nostalgia, 'like the economy (cultural industries) it runs with, is everywhere. But it is a cultural practice, not a given content; its forms, meanings, and effects shift with the context – it depends on where the speaker stands in the landscape of the present' (p. 227).

Acts of Remembering and Forgetting

While nostalgia has traditionally played a central role in migrant literature, this longing has typically rested on a nostalgic desire to 'journey toward an originary home' (see Kamboureli: p. 132). The nostalgic desire that the diasporans display is often 'blended with fear – the fear of uncertainty and of facing the challenges posed by the larger world and the fear of the absence of the clarity and confidence provided by the past' (Jin: p. 22). These two primary causes along with dislocation promote insecurity in a migrant (see Bates: 8). However, nostalgia may be used as a tool 'to create that space, but it is not the heart of home' (Wise: p. 305).

Nostalgia is primarily associated with the pain of taking leave or parting. Sri Lankan-Australian academic Suvendrini Perera, in her nonfiction piece "Dravidian Curls" (1999), remembers the play of language, in both Tamil and Sinhala, when taking leave from someone. It is never said that 'we are going' but we are 'going and coming back' (p. 114). Questioning this use of words of 'parting', she writes:

> Is it because the concept of parting so pains us, so hurts and offends us, that we Sri Lankans try to erase the very words from our everyday vocabularies? (...) 'Varome', we announce in Tamil when, in fact, we are just leaving, not arriving; as in Sinhala it is correct to say 'we are coming' even as we walk out of the door. (...) Do we really aspire, by these reality-deceiving means, to cheat ourselves the finality of departures, to assuage the unspeakably crude act of separation, the emptiness one feels to be one moment inside the fraught circle, and the next – where? (p. 115)

Similarly, Indian-Australian poet and writer Subhash Jaireth, in "Remembering Dehlie" (2001), borrowing the idea of 'walking' (panoptic gaze) from Michel de Certeau (1988) observes that: 'Walking is one of those spatial practices through which people transform places into spaces by making them "their own" and by circumscribing them within their everyday living' (p. 20). The same applies to migration or crossing over or journeys through memory and spaces. Jaireth in "The Bridge near Firozepur" (2003) re-assembles the story from his memory, of his college friend, Sunil, who now lives in the United States. Sunil on one occasion tells the writer,

> Can you imagine (...) I have never 'seen' my mother in my dreams? I have had dreams about her, but she has never, ever been physically present in them. Sometimes when she is about to appear, the dreams abruptly come to an end. (pp. 68–69)

Sunil has for the last 20 years tried to 'see' in his dreams the face of his dead mother. The family once had several photos of her but 'they were either left behind in Rawalpindi or perished in the refugee train' (p. 69). In the absence of her photograph, he even 'dug up a few old photographs of his grandfather and grandmother and took them to one of his painter friends so that he could conjure a portrait of his mother from the photos' (p. 69). But to his disappointment, he still does not know what his mother looked like. For Sunil, who has a 'knack for telling stories' (p. 62), the dilemma of not knowing and remembering his mother is very much similar to not being able to tell her story.

Photographs, paintings, and other visual markers often serve as entry point into a nostalgic journey. Subhash Jaireth notes in "Maps, Photographs, Paintings" (1998) that looking at an old painting of a bridge in Roorkee, India, feels a strange romantic wonder. Because:

> (...) this bridge is no stranger to me. I have walked across it, have been pulled in a rickshaw over it, and have carried my daughter across on my shoulders. 'I know this bridge very well', I tell myself, but when I look at it in the painting, it appears to me unknown, novel and attractive.
>
> The bridge, by appearing in a painting, has become special. The painting has framed it into a relatively autonomous 'reality' outside the world that surrounds the 'real' bridge over which I have walked. But the painting has also made the surrounding landscape attractive, romantic and picturesque. (p. 257)

In his yearnings about his old home, Jaireth feels that he has somewhere in his search for a new home in Australia become a tourist: 'I have obtained my visa from the Indian High Commission. I am no longer Indian; the passport that I carry tells me so. Perhaps that is why I have started behaving like a tourist' (p. 264). For Jaireth, the gaze that looks at India has changed post-Australian citizenship. While Satendra Nandan in "Delhi: Among the Ruins" (1998) remembering India of his 'childhood imagination' notes that

> India which had seeped into my adolescent consciousness with immense force through her epics, songs, stories of grandparents, films, pictures of gods and goddesses, portraits of Nehru and Gandhi, colourful, mischievous posters of Lord Krishna in a kitchen stealing and eating butter, Ram and Sita in an idyllic forest – was quite different from the India and the Indians one jostled with on the cobbled streets of Delhi. Indian mythology, like the dust of Delhi, is so powerful that I think it prevents one from seeing the realities of India. (pp. 109–110)

Subhash Jaireth in "Cricket Ball" (2006) writes about a subject that is close to the hearts of both the Indians and Australians – Cricket. On a trip to India, he sees at his friend's house, a very old cricket ball – the same crucial ball that helped India win the 1959 test match series against Australia in Kanpur. For Jaireth, who since his childhood days in India was a huge fan of the Australian team, Australian players 'had a special place':

> We loved the Australian team, although its invincibility, professionalism and arrogance annoyed us. We wanted them to be like our Hindu gods, perfect, kind, but also fallible, frivolous and unreliable. (p. 83)

He is surprised that after so many years he remembers the details of the match. It was in this test match that the 'Indian team recorded its first memorable win' (p. 86) and then 'disappeared into the pages of the history' (p. 87) like its hero Jasu Patel, who gave a sensational bowling performance. For Jaireth, the old cricket ball is a point of entry into a nostalgic journey into his childhood he had spent with his friends playing cricket on the streets.

Sri Lankan-Australian writer Beryl T. Mitchell in her autobiographical account "Tea, Tytlers and Tribes" (1997) writes:

> When deciding what to bring to Australia we sold some very precious things at auctions, but the old long-playing records we brought with us. They still rest in a bottom drawer of an unused wardrobe – *memories we do not want to discard.* (p. 306; emphasis added)

The 'records' reminds her of the happier times that she and other young married couples – (mostly) plantation owners or administrators – spent in the Planter's Club at Patiyagama in Sri Lanka – 'we would have great all-night parties – the sort that one can only enjoy in the exuberance of youth' (p. 306). She not only brought her records but also booked her furniture on the ship to Australia – 'every family migrating to Australia in the sixties and seventies would send their special pieces of furniture by sea, even if they were travelling by plane' (p. 304). Every article of her household is not only precious but also carries with it a memory of happier times and a story. She further notes that in the process of settling down:

> I soon filled my garden with plants of any species I remembered from those other gardens tucked away on mountain sides in Ceylon, now growing only in my memory, but still as fresh as yesterday. (p. 308)

Her constant use of terms of longing such as musical records, garden, furniture, letters, gems, photographs, and others throughout her narrative shows her rootlessness in Australia. And, for her Sri Lankan garden to grow in Australia, she takes the help of her Australian neighbour, who helps her 'with advice on the seasons in which various flowers would grow and bloom' (p. 308). And finally her flowers of Sri Lankan variety 'grew and flourished right through the year' in Australia (p. 308).

It can be noted that however fervent be the migrant's dream of a return to the homeland is, the idea is a futile one as there is no point of return. Sri Lankan-Australian Shelagh Goonewardene in "A Migrant Dreams" (1997b), using the trope of 'dream' writes that she often dreams about 'a house' in Sri Lanka that they 'owned for many years, but never went to' (p. 283). She rhetorically asks, 'Why did we not go and live there, since it belonged to us?' (p. 283). This 'mystery of the dream' is also the mystery behind many a nostalgic journey that migrants take to their homeland. She dreams that her husband has agreed to leave Australia soon and once again live in their beautiful country house in Sri Lanka. But 'suddenly, the distant sounds of gunfire' invade her dream and bring her 'back in reality' (p. 283). The socio-political conditions of Sri Lanka because of which they left their home in the first place are still the same. Although migrants intend to return to their place of origin, the physical possibility of a return is rare. The only viable option for them is to make 'nostalgic returns' to their place of origin.

In Sri Lankan-Australian academic and writer Chitra Fernando's "Making Connections" from *Between Worlds* (1988), Ananda, the protagonist, feels a 'great loneliness' and 'resentment' for immigrating to Australia. He tries to remember, mostly through a comparison with his new environment, his old home in Beruwala, Sri Lanka. On looking at the 'confined space' of his flat, he longs for

> the wide open verandah of his Beruwala home, for those leisurely early mornings: the chants of fishermen pulling in their nets, loud and clear, then momentarily drowned by the roar and thunder of the Colombo Express flashing past between coconut trees, comfortable sounds of household activity, the clatter of crockery, Leela bargaining with a fisherman early with his catch, the deceptive hustle and bustle of an essentially slow-paced life. (p. 90)

In Sri Lanka, he used to dream of becoming a 'second Gandhi' by

> Dedicating his life to the education of the peasants: eating and dressing like them, sharing their miserable huts, sweating in the fields, the founder of a new movement sweeping through Lanka, India and Asia. (p. 91)

However, he never becomes a 'second Gandhi', having immigrated to Australia for a better life – 'food, clothes, employment, education' (p. 90) – especially the education of his children. Moreover, the early morning train ride to his office in Sydney, reminds him of a 'distant time and place, another train' (p. 93) and friends with whom the 'journey to Colombo was whiled away eating *vadei*, drinking tea and chaffing each other' (p. 93). In Australia, a journey from his home to office now gives him a 'sense of disconnectedness' (p. 95). On walking down the street in front of the offices and shops, that looks like 'multi-storied temples of fashion and commerce' (p. 95) to him, he longs to return to the bazaars of his home town. He cannot imagine a future for himself in Australia. On seeing a derelict old man, 'For one terrible second he saw himself in that old man – the girls married and indifferent, Leela dead' (p. 95). He feels a sense of urgency to return to Sri Lanka and start his social service and 'new' life – a life that he always dreamt of: 'I must go back, he thought, before it's too late, I have work to do. (...) setting Lanka alight. He would be a second Gandhi' (p. 95). But all his feelings and the urgency to return are only due to a 'sense of deflation and embarrassment' at not knowing where he is. He knows that he cannot return to Sri Lanka, as 'there was nothing of special significance for him to do there. If he did, then he'd very likely think longingly of his brick house in Epping with the tall gums at the back (...)' (p. 100). He now understands what his mother meant when he told her about their decision to migrate – 'the grass on the other side is always greener' (p. 100).

Shelagh Goonewardene in her autobiographical story "The Pain of Leave Taking" (1997a) on hearing the news of a bomb explosion in the business heart of Colombo is suddenly transported back in time. She writes, 'It seems that our memories and our emotional responses are very much bound to landscape' (p. 6). She has lived in Australia now for more than 10 years and feels that

Australia is her 'home' and 'country'. But the news of the bombing in a place where she had grown up and worked arouses 'horror, anger and grief', which made her realize that: 'the umbilical cord which binds me to the country of my birth is not easily severed. The pain of that separation will probably persist until the day I die, even though it might come in spasms or gradually diminish with time' (p. 6). Through her musings she narrates that the best years of her life were spent in her family house, which they disposed of because of conflict and immigrated to Australia. But in her dreams, down memory lane, she writes:

> I was back in its intimate and well-loved environment. I would walk down the graceful stairway, sit in the pleasurable comfort of the sitting-room, and listen to the heavy clock which was positioned on the top of a glass-fronted cabinet in the gracious dining-room. To this day, I can remember the patterns of curtains and the silky feel of leopard skin rug on an upholstered cane settee on the front verandah. (p. 7)

And when after many years on a visit to Sri Lanka, she is allowed to see her old home, by its new owner; she was unable to see the full house, as she can observe that in the house 'all was completely changed. (...) Only the basic shell had remained' (p. 7). For her now, the memory of the house and the happy days is the last resort, as the people who know about the old house are not there anymore and her children were too young when she left Sri Lanka. She feels that her children will never understand her nostalgia and longing for her old home, as her children have Australian sensibilities and they never get to know how it feels to come from a sad place.

On the other hand, Chitra Fernando's protagonist Rupa, in her story "The Birds of Paradise" from *Women There and Here* (1994), in her youthful days, longed for her return to Australia seeking individuality, freedom, and an escape from her family and their traditions in Sri Lanka. But, having lived all her life in Sydney and after her children have grown up and left,

> She thought of the continuity of life there (in Sri Lanka), of years of custom and tradition shaping every domestic event, major and minor, and grew affectionately nostalgic, as she re-knitted herself in memory to her family at 14 St Mary's Road. (p. 50)

Her remembering and longing for home at this stage of her life is a true longing of a diasporan and not a 'trick of memory' (p. 51). She can hear old voices and sounds of a distant time and land that are familiar to her but cannot return except through memory.

Chris Raja, a Melbourne-based writer of Indian origin, remembers nostalgically in his autobiographical story "White Boots" (2003), the time spent in Dalhousie Institute – 'an **old** remnant of the British Raj' (p. 97). In the postcolonial India, it has become a club for the middle-income professionals. He remembers 'swimming at the pool, while they (his parents) socialized with friends over drinks and Chinese food or played billiards and tennis or simply browsed in the library' (p. 97). He further writes

> Occasionally, we watched movies on the outdoor screen. (...) I remember sitting between my friends Nitesh and Brian, watching Bette Midler in *The Rose* as it caused some fuss by its screening. I can't remember the film but I remember Mrs Buttacharia, one of the really wealthy members of the club (...). (p. 97)

In his memory of the past, Raja uses selective remembering to compare Melbourne and Calcutta. He notes that Melbourne is a 'particularly quiet', 'clean and green' place (p. 98) while Calcutta with 'its heat, colour and noise' makes him yearn for it (p. 97).

Chitra Fernando in "The Chasm" from *Women There and Here* (1994) presents a small Sri Lankan community living in Alice Springs. The arrival of Vijay, a sociologist from Colombo on a study tour in Australia, in this community makes them elated, as he was from 'home' and 'they still thought of their former country as home' (p. 53). Vijay, as a Sri Lankan,

> roused in them a mixture of envy and self-satisfaction: envy because he hadn't chosen to subject himself to the pain of self-uprooting; self-satisfaction because there he was sweating it out in the Third World while they luxuriated in the sweet life here. (p. 53)

His critical observations as a nondiasporic or an outsider in this diasporic community present most of the happenings of their lives in the story. He sees that behind all the talk and show of success, these Sri Lankan migrants were:

> often overcome by starkness of their surroundings, so different from the land they'd left behind. A land of endless green expanses: paddy fields, palm-edged coasts, forests and jungles, tea-covered hill slopes, grassy plains; people everywhere, their houses, gardens and cattle. It was small, manageable and pretty. (p. 54)

The vastness and barrenness of the Australian landscape and the 'void outside transformed into a private panic' that the Sri Lankans living there 'couldn't explain to themselves or to anybody else' (p. 54). To Vijay, people of this small community look like 'primitives' as he says:

> No one at home in Sri Lanka will believe this (...). There was here the rage, the frustration of the disposed. The supermarket cornucopia and the electric plenty were there; they laughed all the way to the bank. Yet deep within, they were dispirited. The landscape, its endless flatness broken only by huge bumps of rock or deep clefts, overwhelmed them. They talked to people. An exchange of sounds with no engagement of the spirit. (p. 61)

These people still believe and think crudely about ancestry and class, values which, Vijay observes, people at home tackle with 'subtlety and finesse' (p. 63). These people live their lives in a strange land, on memories of good times spent, and places and people (belonging to high class strata) they knew in Sri Lanka. An invocation of a civilization that they have lost is for them a kind of 'self-assurance' that back home would be both 'mocked and contested' (see also B. Lal, 2002). They have in their small diasporic community developed a 'self-repair system' to assist each other to 'dispel the chill, the discrete distances' through a 'round of dinners, lunches and picnics' (C. Fernando, 1994: p. 64) and preserve in their consciousness memories of home.

In his story "Out There" (1997), Adib Khan's young narrator, who escaped with his mother from the war-torn homeland, feels an 'unspeakable yearning' (p. 85) for home and its:

> tatty memories of tropical trees and a hot sun. The sky (...) acres of blue, its innocence finally restored. Sweaty faces, that do not wish to remember, shoveling rice and dried fish into small slits. Water buffaloes and paddy fields. The land has stopped burning (...). (p. 86)

The war is over and he wants to return to his homeland – now 'a foreign country' or 'an imagined world' (p. 86). He feels trapped in this adopted country. For his college assignment, he writes a paper on 'Asia, a Threat or a Boon for Australia?' (p. 87). As a second-generation immigrant to Australia, he does not fit the bill of a stereotypical Asian migrant. As his silent interaction with a security guard makes it clear:

> My overcoat and shoes are relatively new. I don't look helpless enough to be bullied. It's not quite right in his scheme of a prosperous country he once knew. I suspect that he belongs to a desperate order that views the world with yesterday's eyes. (p. 85)

The narrator in spite of having grown up in this country feels that the security guard, an Anglo-Australian was looking for someone with a 'raggedly dressed – torn jeans, faded windcheater, and a frayed baseball cap' (p. 85) like the old times.

Uma Parameswaran (2000) notes that people who move away from their native countries 'not only occupy but also bequeath to subsequent generations a liminality, an uneasy pull between two cultures'. For a second-generation migrant, the place of his or her birth is home. In "Dreamless" (2001), a quasi-autobiographical piece written after Indian-Australian author Suneeta Peres Da Costa shifted to the United States for studies, the narrator talks about Australia as her home: 'A place unravaged by war but a place that nonetheless caused me anxiety when I thought about it' (p. 101). She observes:

> I had just moved from one country to another, one continent to another. In fact, my world had literally been turned upside-down because these two continents were also in different hemispheres, (...) it was with some bad feeling that I had left my *own antipodean home*. (p. 88; emphasis added)

The narrator, who is a second-generation Indian-Australian brought up in Sydney, probably didn't feel out of place or confused in Australia. It is in the United States that she feels like a migrant and notes that at the supermarket

> I became stupid and forgot the logical location of things. (...) I searched for these items because to me coffee meant Vittoria, and juice Sunburst and shampoo Pears, I immediately felt cheated by

> the fact that they weren't there; I imagined at once that the new and un-familiar product names contained ersatz commercial goods, that I was being set up or duped. (p. 91)

Her frustration and confusion are also due to the fact that even though she spoke 'the same language, some very basic things could cause bafflement and bewilderment to the people around' her (p. 92). One example of this was the use of the word 'trolley', which is called a 'shopping cart' in the United States. Another reason for her paranoia is despite having all the papers attesting to her 'legitimacy to be in the new country' (p. 93) she is unable to open a bank account easily. And to her own surprise, she finds it difficult to communicate her story and explain the situation to the authorities.

On leaving her family and home in Australia, the narrator says:

> It was not the calling long distance itself, but my ability to close the distance if I so wanted that comforted me more than the voices of those whom I had left and for whom I longed, because, it has to be said, I had left because they could comfort me no longer and, as for longing, *one longs only for what is impossible, for what is irrecoverable*. (p. 95; emphasis added)

However, she feels homesick as the 'new city was full of piercing contradictions' (p. 97). She also meets other migrants – two men from the hinterland of Venezuela, employed in the business of moving furniture. These two men 'had come for better opportunities, but because the degrees they held were quite redundant in the new country, they made their living moving furniture' (p. 98). It is with one of the two men, the narrator debates about 'whether it was possible to write without a home', and observes 'how the writing about one's home is often distorted both there and away from it' (p. 98).

Being at home or away from it, the point of reference always remains *home* – your own or your ancestors. For the narrator, the daughter of a first-generation migrant, there is another home away from home – India. And she goes on a holiday to the village in Goa where her father was born. She writes about this ancestral village:

> A village is a small thing, barely a smudge on the map of the world. At the time my father was born, the village and the territory in which the village was located was a part of Portugal. It was only

> when he was a young man that it ceased being so. On a particular day when he was a young man some soldiers from the larger land-mass which shared its borders took over the territory in which my father's village was located. There was no war, few reprisals and recriminations; very soon it was said that the territory, including the myriad villages such as the one in which my father had been born, had been 'integrated' with the larger sub-continental land-mass that adjoined it. But this integration in words amounted to very little in the minds of people such as my father. (p. 102)

The fate of her father and village to which he belonged occupies a 'mythic place' in her 'imagination' (p. 103). She does not know and was never taught 'the native tongue' of her father – Portuguese, and yet she continues, 'I had an intimation of *saudade*, that melancholy for lost things, often confused with nostalgia' (p. 103). Her family has lost many things in India and she loses her passport. She writes that she was able to convince the Indian authorities with a 'guarantee of returning', it is a guarantee that is 'always fantastic anyway' (p. 104). She knows that she won't return as no one returned to their roots permanently and this is one of the most dominant and distinctive characteristics of a diaspora (Mishra, 1996b: p. 75). Homeland or 'Watan' for the diasporans is thus not so much an actual place to which one must return at all costs but according to Marije Braakman and Angela Schlenkhoff (2007), 'the importance of the notion lies in the sense of identity and belonging it offers. It can serve to create a niche, a space of belonging, within another country' (p. 13).

However, a fictive return is possible only through memory. As Jaireth questioning the value of maps in "Remembering Dehlie" (2001) notes:

> It seems that the map we construct through acts of remembering and forgetting, and the topography this memory inhabits, has warps, crevices and valleys where daylights fails to penetrate. It needs the helping hand of time to unravel that which is hidden. I am not sure if that is how the memory functions but we always assume, hope and believe that it works like that. (p. 22)

It is through these maps or nostalgic reconstructions of home that the lost 'past serve(s) as the active ideological terrain on which people represent themselves to themselves' (Ganguly: p. 29). On the sense of loss, Roger Ballard (1994) writes:

> No matter how bad the social and material conditions they may have left behind, and no matter how great their achievements abroad, migrants invariably feel a grievous sense of loss. They miss – and therefore long once again to experience – the familiar sights, sounds and smells of their birthplace, and the warmth and conviviality of everyday domestic life. (p. 9)

These nostalgic yearnings to return to a lost home reflect the migrants' search for the home or a sensory location in which the self is comfortably secure, thus providing a therapeutic value. Memory and nostalgia play with concrete spatial histories in not just recreating the lost home but also in a 'cultural construction in which our very selves and sense are constituted' (Chambers: p. 22). Borrowing further from Braakman and Schlenkhoff, it can be said that the South Asian diasporans are rooted in the homeland 'discourse and its habits', but they also pursue 'Western routes through the education system and the perspectives opened to them' (p. 16).

South Asian diasporic narratives characterize bifurcated, dislocated identities that exist in a liminal space, in-between two identities, two cultures, and two histories. Yet, 'home' remains, through acts of imagination, remembering, and re-creation, an important reference point for these writers in the stories discussed here. As Aijaz Ahmad (1992), answering Salman Rushdie, writes: 'it takes a very modern, a very affluent, uprooted kind of person to give up the idea of home' (pp. 68–69). Similarly, Indian-Australian author Christopher Cyrill's narrator in "What Withers and What Remains" (1996) wonders: 'if people were preserved by the thing that they preserved' (p. 178), as in these stories the migrants carry over many markers to deal with identity issues and in doing so define the South Asian diasporic space.

Nostalgia then plays an important part in the immigrant condition as it acts as a 'desire to simultaneously embrace what is left of a past from which one is spatially and temporally displaced, and the recognition that nostalgia can overwhelm memories of the past, allowing the colors of history to seep out of the mind's eye' (Mannur, 2007). For the migrant, just as for the non-migrant, nostalgia is tied to the process of home-building as we seek to produce in the present what we feel we had in the past: the feelings of security, familiarity, community, and possibility. Ghassan Hage (1997) states,

> Nostalgia is nothing more than a memory of a past experience imagined from the standpoint of the present to be homely. Clearly, nostalgic feelings do not only abound in migrant life but in everybody's life. They guide home-building in the present because people seek to foster the kind of homely feeling they know. (p. 105)

Therefore, the longing for and thoughts about homeland, heritage, and a place to call home become the identity rather than merely the means towards it. The nostalgic subject often turns to the past to find or reconstruct 'sources of identity, agency, or community that are felt to be lacking, blocked, subverted, or threatened in the present' (Tannock: p. 454). Their frustrations and sense of irritability suggests their predicament as immigrants – search of home and self. Paul Carter (1992) endorses the truism that a sense of place is a highly significant factor in one's sense of self. In relation to the diasporans longing for home, he writes, it is 'a mothering space that both nurture(s) him and help(s) define his own difference' (pp. 12–13) and also helps in negotiating with the communities and of the new space the diasporans enter.

Conclusion

As discussed earlier, nostalgia and memory play a fundamental role in the way South Asian diasporans see themselves and also in how they structure their daily existence and the world around them in Australia. However, they know that being in the Diaspora marks the end of an easy relationship with the homeland. A question that begs to be asked here is – why would a diasporic writer who has 'willingly' or 'voluntarily' left home constantly portray that 'lost home' in his or her writing? Stephen Gray (1986) contends that the principal feature of post-colonial and immigrant writing is place or 'setting', and this

> one variable, assumes great importance for us as analysts, and we like to see it percolate through a work, conditioning plot,

> characters, actions, etc. and when that place is fully embodied in a work, when it affects every other element, (...) we say (...). It has some discrete identity of its own. (p. 7)

The other reason of course, and the most common one as discussed above in detail, is 'nostalgia' for the 'past', which is now like a land far-far away and can just be imagined through memory. However, language, literature, and certain norms of behaviour are traditionally valued and preserved by the South Asian Diaspora. Another issue and a very important one in relation to the politics of diaspora writing could be the readership. It can be seen that the writers of the diaspora generally come from an advantaged group or social background. They write in English and their target readership is English speaking both in the homeland and hostland. As the work of a diasporic writer

> attracts the attention of two different sets of readers (...). The culture of adoption wishes to see 'through' the text to the culture of the 'other'; the culture of origin wants to assess the authenticity of self-reflection. (J. Jain, 2001: p. 85)

This concept of readership has a flip side too. The writer, who is aware of the readership, has a very strong 'diasporic urge to appropriate space at home and to use it for self-sustenance abroad' (J. Jain, 2001: p. 88). This is because of a sense of alienation in their new 'home' and the corresponding need to belong and therefore to travel through the memory lane in search of known and familiar markers of home. Homeland and its various known and unknown facets presented in these works cannot be judged as valid or invalid, as they represent only a 'slice' of the Indian way of life, be it in India or in mini-India(s) established elsewhere in the country of their migration. So, while physical place may be important to a sense of continuity, cultural identity is finally an imaginative construct (the product of memory, fantasy, and myth) in which the land itself is only one factor.

In these short stories, we see various versions of the homeland where nostalgia is one major facet that makes the diasporan writers write, imagine, or present an image of the home in their writings. It can be seen that however strong the diversity of circumstances under which these authors came to Australia, there is an interesting parallel in the aspect in which their writing is concerned with presentation of the myths, legends, customs, festivals, and rituals of the homeland for the 'others', that is, the readers of the hostland. To make them informed about the various cultural markers that are related to persons of Indian subcontinental origin and sensitize them about it is a very significant factor in the writings of the diasporic authors. More often than not, it is the utter ignorance or lack of proper knowledge about the migrant's culture that frequently becomes the basis of unnecessary and avoidable misunderstandings, prejudices, indifference, and discriminations against them, these short stories employ long descriptive paragraphs and special comments about the socio-religious practices of the migrants home culture, which is in some ways the writers' contribution in creating a knowledge base. These authors act as source informants, 'authentic Indians', or what Makarand Paranjape (2001b) and some other scholars have termed as 'native informants' for the host country, and who provide the people of the hostland with 'knowledgeable' perceptions about their (lost) homeland (see pp. 1–13).

In this chapter, I examined how nostalgia is always already 'predetermined' in 'scripting immigrant attachment' to the past in the representation of home by the writers of the South Asian diaspora in Australia (see Mannur, 2007). This desire to remember home by recreating memories through various referents, in the words of Anita Mannur, cannot be 'understood merely as reflectively nostalgic gestures', rather such 'nostalgically-framed narratives must also be read as meta-critiques of what it means to route memory and nostalgic longing for a homeland' particularly through one's relationship to practices, which help in the formation of a national identity (see Mannur, 2007).

In conclusion, South Asian immigrants view home as both a concrete reality that is achieved physically or in relation with others and a symbolic reference point that moves beyond territorial boundaries. With reference to South Asian diaspora's conception of home, Reema Sarwal (2008) writes that:

> It is the revisiting of the old home – not physically but through memory and writing, which can make possible the acceptance of the new home. Words become essential for finding home, for a 'movement forward'. (p. 249)

These overlapping strategies allow the diasporans to imagine and recreate their sense of home and belonging – to both a past and present – that provide sources of stability used in dealing with life in the diaspora. However, these strategies also highlight a lack of desire to return to the old homeland as they illustrate how South Asian immigrants bring home to their new settings questions that relate to the idea of belonging and process of identity formation. Using the past and the present, diaspora writers keep an eye on the future and construct a narrative that tells the migrant's story (Kershen: p. 98). Diaspora writers once free from the problems of settlement inevitably also write about their spatial experiences in Australia – experiences of the place and the Australian 'way of life'. Thus, a nostalgic return to past/homeland, that is, an exercise of the imagination can be an important means of establishing roots in the hostland/new home/future.

Chapter 6

An Australian Learning Experience

Prejudice, Racism, and Indifference

Manfred Jurgensen (1986) claims that 'with the arrival of the white man', Australia 'became multicultural on a permanent basis' (p. 80). As discussed in the Introduction to this book, as a settler society, with the exception of 2.7 per cent of the Indigenous population, everyone in Australia is 'either a migrant or a self-conscious descendant of a migrant' (van der Veer: p. 2). Despite this ethnic and racial diversity, as a result of the White Australia Policy (1901–1973), Australia has struggled with racism or negative stereotyping of the 'Other' (Castles: p. 53). Jeremy Sammut commenting on the practice of racism in White Australia writes:

> In the light of prejudices that long lay behind the White Australia policy, the nation's transformation into a harmonious multi-racial society over the last fifty years is amazing. It appears almost miraculous that a country that for so long was determined to reject the mass migration of alien races has peacefully incorporated millions of new arrivals from an array of racial backgrounds. (quoted in Windschuttle: p. 29)

Today, as the certitudes of the nation state are eroded under the pressures of globalization, social prejudice and racism are prevalent in both multicultural and monocultural societies throughout the world. This might be seen as 'a communal reaction to fear, a backlash against globalization that is perceived to be a threat to national identity' (A. Khan, 2001).

In the aftermath of the highly publicised racist attacks or opportunistic violence on Indian students in Melbourne in 2008–2009,[1] many have struggled with the question: Is Australia a racist country? But first, let us understand: What is racism? S. Zelinka (1996) defines racism as:

> A belief in the superiority of one particular racial or ethnic group and, flowing from this, the exclusion of other groups from some or many aspects of society. This exclusion (and often exploitation) is seen as legitimate simply because of the difference or supposed inferiority of the other group's race, ethnicity or nationality. (p. 1)

B. Troyna explains in *Racism and Education* (1993) the complexity and contradictions of racism as an ideology:

> What is evident, then is that racism is an ideology that is continually changing, being challenged, interrupted and reconstructed, and which often appears in contradictory forms. (...) specific forms of racism can be expected to change, and inherited racist discourse are likely to be reconstituted. New circumstances are likely to lead to new formulations of racism. (p. 15)

Further according to noted Australian historian Marilyn Lake, these formulations of new racisms may be a result of the 'yearning for a White Australia' that has never died (quoted in Windschuttle: p. 28; see also Jayasuriya, 2012). Gweda Tavan has also observed that 'racism remains the skeleton in closet' and 'Its ghost arises with each new decade to haunt political debate, whether the issue is multiculturalism, asylum-seekers, Asian immigration or Indigenous affairs' (quoted in Windschuttle: p. 28). Further, Panikos Panayi (1994) has observed: 'All minorities in all societies in all historical periods have endured hostility from the government and the majority populations in the countries in which they live' (p. 102). Further, according to Gopalkrishnan and Babacan (2007), racism 'diminishes the social fabric of society, creates social tension, and perpetuates social inequality and impacts on the life chances of the people involved. Racism affects many sub-sections of society: those who perpetuate it, those who are at the "receiving end," and those who are not directly involved in the problem' (p. 1). Going back once again to the academic/scholarly definitions of racism, which I discussed in the Introduction, sociologists define racism as a system of 'group privilege'. Similarly, David Wellman has defined racism as 'culturally sanctioned beliefs, which, regardless of intentions involved, defend the advantages whites have because of the subordinated position of racial minorities' (p. x).

This chapter attempts to critique racism, prejudices, and indifference as represented in the short stories of South Asian diaspora in Australia as multicultural literature is an important forum for negotiating these issues.[2] It concludes with the assertion that for Australians and its various migrant groups, an understanding of their diversity and tolerance of difference is required to resolve racial tensions and build a stable and secure future.

Prejudice, Racism, and Indifference

Despite the development of many policy initiatives, racism remains a major concern. Historically and in more contemporary times, discrimination or indifference has emerged as a problem for the Australian government and the intelligentsia – creative writers and academics. There are many forms of racism or discrimination. Culture and race sometimes become intertwined and dependent upon each other, even to the extent of including nationality or language among the categories that 'race' covers to the set of definitions of racism. Some scholars believe that in Australian culture, racialization has been so normalized by stereotyping the 'Other' that it is deeply disturbing. Richard Delgado (1995) points out that:

> A culture constructs social reality in ways that promote its own self-interest (...). Our social world, with its rules, practices, and assignments of prestige and power, is not fixed; rather, we construct it with words, stories and silences. (p. xiv)

A case in point is Yasmine Gooneratne's story, "Navaranjini Takes Note of Signs and Visions" (1992b). Gooneratne describes Navaranjini's first cab ride from the airport to a suburb in Sydney or in other words her first brush with Australian society. The ride is imbued with Navaranjini's vision:

> I had decided, quite early on, that though I didn't know much about Australia to start with, I was going to learn. Part of the baggage I packed for our visit to Australia, I now realize, was a very strong determination to make a great success of the next five

> years, for my husband's sake. And so I decided to equip myself early for whatever Australia would put before us. (p. 36)

Navaranjini is confident about her preparation but is alarmed by the pace of the city, grim faces, stickers on cars, and racist graffiti on the walls – 'ASIANS OUT' and 'BASH A PAK A DAY' (p. 40). Her first impressions of Australia turn into fear as she realizes 'anything can happen in Australia' (p. 38). But she wonders about an Australian immigration poster – 'a smiling child with her woolly lamb' (p. 40) – that she once saw as a schoolgirl in Sri Lanka.

> I knew, then, that the welcoming smile on the face of that little girl in the poster at school had been meant for someone else. Whoever it was that she had held her flowers out to so invitingly, it could not have been for me. (p. 41)

Her initial confidence and self-determination of making this journey of relocation from Sri Lanka to Australia a success, seeing the strange gaze and racist remarks around her, becomes weak.

Similarly, Ruth Van Gramberg in her short autobiographical narrative "Immigration Dreams, Foundations and Formations" (1997) points out that once the immigrants have undertaken their journey and reached Australia, they are often subjected to racism in this adopted homeland:

> On the way you'll be misused, mistaken, confused, churned up, spat upon and sworn at. Your emotions will be ripped apart and laid bare, as you strive to survive and there will be occasions when you feel so lost and inadequate, you wish to run back to where you came from, to admit defeat. (...) you lose your equilibrium, as the earth has not even begun to stabilize beneath your feet and you don't know who or what you are (...). (p. 209)

The results of such racism and dehumanization can be very dangerous for a new migrant and emotionally he or she will feel drained out and the simple everyday happenings that one takes for granted, 'can develop into the most frightening, desolate and desperate situations' (p. 210). As

> The beginning of a new life in a new country can be very traumatic for any migrant. There are so many barriers to be overcome, largely the complete geographical, physical and

> cultural differences are intimidating. More so, if language is a problem. (p. 210)

Van Gramberg feels an advantage over other migrant groups and other people from the Indian subcontinent as her family is proficient in English. She was lucky that she did not face any problems in Australia because of her language. But for others from South Asia, she further notes, 'survival for the moment, for each precious day, constitutes a challenge' (p. 210). She observes that travelling is always a problem at the beginning for a migrant – be it the journey from homeland to hostland or to a destination within the hostland.

> Travelling was another nightmare without a map, as one only knew the name of the destination written on a piece of paper. How many stops between or beyond was part of the unknown, however once there, you felt it was another parcel of alien territory you had made friends with. (p. 210)

But once the migrant becomes self-confident and starts adjusting and familiarizing with his or her new environment, space, and people around him or her, gradually, 'a feeling of stability emerges' and each accomplishment is like 'a milestone, stored away for future reference' and looks 'forward to the future with enthusiasm and love' (p. 210).

Particularly following the 9/11 attacks in the United States, Muslim Australians have experienced a significant rise in Islamophobia and racism.[3] Such prejudice has manifested in the spectrum of violent attacks, mosque and other property damage, slurs, and in stereotyping in the mainstream Australian media.[4] Dr William Jonas, Race Discrimination Commissioner, after listening to experiences of Muslim community's members regarding discrimination and vilification post-/11, summarized it in his report titled, *Isma – Listen: National Consultations on Eliminating Prejudice against Arab and Muslim Australians* (2003):

> What we heard was often disturbing. Participants identifiable as Arab or Muslim by their dress, language, name or appearance told of having been abused, threatened, spat on, assailed with eggs, bottles, cans and rocks, punched and even bitten. Drivers have been run off the road and pedestrians run down on footpaths and

> in car parks. People reported being fired from jobs or refused employment or promotion because of their race or religion. Children have been bullied in school yards. Women have been stalked, abused and assaulted in shopping centres. Private homes, places of worship and schools were vandalized and burned. (p. iii)

The above paragraph best summarizes the reported incidents of discrimination experienced and a general rise in intolerance towards Muslim Australians following 9/11. They were attacked not because of their 'individual actions, but on the basis of a cultural stereotype portrayed as barbaric' (Griffiths: p. 161). These acts of racism and anti-Muslim prejudice in Australia can be linked to the Australian media's exaggerating information regarding Muslims in general, which is closely linked with the American media reports. This made the Muslim community in Australia more vulnerable and isolated. The question that arises here is: Was Muslim community in Australia always seen with distrust and fear?[5] Hanifa Deen in her autobiographical narrative "Curry, Crusades and Scripture" (1992) compares the 1990s with the 1940s and the 1950s, the time she grew up as a second-generation Pakistani and observes,

> When looking back at the Australia in which I grew up – the Australia of the 1940s and 1950s – a feeling of nostalgia for a bygone era is singularly lacking. The dominant feeling is rather one of relief that fifty years down the track, society has changed for the better, that our regional insularity has broken down and that cultural diversity is not the aberration it once was. (p. 139)

Hanifa notes that the place, an inner city suburb, where she grew up in 1940s and 1950s in Western Australia, 'was jokingly and sometimes affectionately called "little Italy," but it was also a "little Greece," a "little China," a "little India" and so on. The same area contained a Muslim mosque, a Jewish synagogue, the various Orthodox churches and the more "normal" houses of worship' (p. 139). As the daughter of a Pakistani-Australian herbalist, she was often teased by high school boys about the 'strange-looking herbs' at her father's shop. She further notes, that although at school the 'classroom was ethnically diverse, the school curriculum, especially social studies, was "true blue" Britannica' (p. 140). And as the only Muslim student in the school, she further notes, 'I writhed with vague feelings of injustice and persecution' (p. 140). School teachers, instead of enlightening her on historical and religious differences, added on to the confusion. But in the 1990s, the scene had totally changed for Muslim children in Australia. Although 'still a minority', they belong to 'communities which collectively have a much stronger presence in society' (p. 141). Her mother explained the earlier injustice and absurdity of White Australia Policy to the children in her colloquial way: 'If Jesus Christ wanted to come to Australia ... he wouldn't be allowed in' (p. 141). Similarly, impressions of rural life in Australia particularly of the Muslim family and children are provided in Mena Abdullah's stories from a Muslim and at times also from a Hindu viewpoint. These works from religious perspectives are, according to Annette Robyn Corkhill, 'a challenge to dominance' of Anglo-Australians and are 'made all the more remarkable and potent by the stories' gentleness, humour, subtlety and apparent guilelessness' (p. 72).

Anura and his wife, in Sunil Govinnage's "The Vanished Trails" (2005), migrated from Canada to Australia in the hope that they will get good jobs and secure future for their daughter. But 'despite the Canadian experience, Anura could not secure a good job after he arrived in Australia' (p. 75). While his wife is able to get a job as administrative assistant, Anura blames Australians for his plight – 'some employers are racists in Australia' (p. 75). Siri, his friend from school days, on hearing this wonders: '*Is Australia a racist country? Why are migrants not always treated properly?*' (p. 75). Anura's frustration and disappointment with himself has resulted in targeting others for his missed opportunities. In his daughter's view, her parents have changed a lot, but 'they're still more Canadians than Aussies!' (p. 78), as Canadians are more 'demanding', while the Aussies are 'more laidback and not aggressive' (p. 79). On the other hand, Anura's friend Siri, who is also struggling as a writer in Australia, cannot get his poems published in magazines, even after doing a university course. He notes: 'There is no place for migrants' writings in Australia. Everything has to be white and linked to their bloody convict past!' (p. 76). Siri, after all the rejections, loses all inspiration to write. He feels that since his writings deal with Aboriginal issues and deaths in custody, his themes are not good enough for white Australian magazines (p. 76). Anura too has a very strong feeling that behind the rejection of Siri's works, there is an element of racism involved. The daughter, on the other hand, has accepted the fact that she is an Australian, and 'Just like the white settlers, we have settled down in Australia. We need to accept things as they are. We can't change the past and history' (p. 79). Siri knows that he and his friend cannot 'become a part of the history' but can sure 'try to change things' for their small community and a better tomorrow (p. 79).

Sunil Govinnage's another short story "Black Moon", in *Black Swans and Other Stories* (2002), is set at the time when the One Nation Party, a Right-wing political party that advocates zero immigration to Australia, sweeps Queensland elections and is expected to get 25 per cent votes in the coming Western Australia elections too. Jayadeva's son, Asela, asks his father:

> Dad, what will happen to Asians if they (One Nation Party) come to power in Perth? Will we have to leave Australia? Are we Australians or Sri Lankans, Dad? Me, Sunitha and amma have Aussie passports, but you don't! Will they ask you to leave? (p. 94)

These questions are not troubling only young Asela, but every migrant's mind consequent to the rise of One Nation Party and Pauline Hanson. Jayadeva answers: 'Where can we go? This is our country. You're all Australians. Maybe this is the time for me to get an Australian passport as well' (p. 94). But why in the first place did Jayadeva not become an Australian citizen like his wife? The answer to this lies in his emotional attachment or the uncut umbilical knot that attaches him to his homeland Sri Lanka. He wonders: '*How can I give up my Sri Lankan citizenship? I was born there, grew up there, studied there, perhaps one day I may go there to die ...*' (p. 94). He left Sri Lanka because of terrorism and limited opportunities. Australia has been good to them but will Asians be able to 'continue to stay here with racism' (p. 95). The father–son discussion and their interaction on the issue of the One Nation Party, and prejudice towards the Chinese migrants in the restaurant, provide a humorous peek into 'the inescapable ramifications of multiculturality in Australia' (p. xviii).

Yasmine Gooneratne in her story "Bharat Changes His Image" (1995) provides the first impressions of the couple, Navaranjini and Bharat, who are impressed by the 'many fascinating things about Australia, its landscape, its wildlife and its people' (p. 45). The narrator, as if learning from a tourist brochure, learns two things about Australia that are also told to every new immigrant coming here:

> (...) Australia is very rich in unusual species of bird, beast and fish, there are some varieties of Australian wildlife which should be carefully avoided. 'Australia is the most dangerous country in the world,' said the brochure the Rentokil man left in our letter box when he came round to spray the foundations of our house against funnel-web spiders and redbacks. Those are the creatures every newcomer to Australia is warned about. (...) and told me to beware of jellyfish off Australian beaches in January, and sharks and stonefish all the year around.
>
> 'Better watch out for stonefish, they're poisonous, and very very dangerous,' Christina said. 'One encounter with a stonefish can be fatal.' (p. 45)

This information is mainly related to the natural dangers that lurk on the earth and sea of Australia. One thing that Navaranjini sarcastically observes about the people of Australia is

> (...) like the Australian stonefish, which lies on the bottom of the ocean floor like a harmless piece of rock until you step on it, Australian people can be endlessly surprising. One surprising thing about them is, that deep, very deep, a long way down, Australians are true Orientalists at heart.
>
> Of course like, like many Asians visitors to this country, I didn't find that out at first, because Australians hide their sensitive souls under a rough exterior. I was fooled, just like everyone else. Just like my husband. (p. 45)

Further, according to Susan Koshy (1998), some scholars 'treat South Asian color consciousness as equivalent to white racism and criticises the immigrant community for denying its own blackness' (p. 285). A point ironically expressed by Gooneratne's narrator, Navaranjini, in "Bharat Changes His Image", where she observes this in relation to how we perceive 'Others':

> You see, at home in Sri Lanka, and I suppose in India too, which is the centre, after all, of the *real* Asian world, we always called far Eastern people 'Ching-Chongs.' My husband says it's racist way of speaking, that we learned racism from the British in our colonial

> days, and must discard it totally now that we are free. But coming from such a Westernised family as his, he just doesn't understand. There's nothing racist about saying (...) that word; racism's unknown in India and Sri Lanka. Race and caste and colour just have their appointed places there in the divine scheme of things, in which everything moves in a beautifully regulated order. Everyone knows *that.* (p. 46)

The narrator, in her innocence, speaks from a position of a loyal subject and feels that if you are not malignant towards others and follow the 'divine scheme' of colour, caste, and race then you are not a racist. She forgets that following such an order of things without thinking about the consequences of its result in the larger plan of things is quite dangerous, as racial prejudices are certainly present even among the South Asians (see Schmidt-Haberkamp, 2004).

Gooneratne, in an interview (1994), has pointed out that when writing this short story she felt that, if 'her racist Asian characters were to come up against fictional Australians, racist themselves, largely due to their colonial hang-ups, maybe they'd cancel each other out' (R. Rama: p. 4). Australian racism and prejudices are interestingly presented through Professor Blackstone, a sociology Professor from the same university where Bharat teaches. Blackstone reminds us of Professor Blainey and the debate that erupted in Australia in 1984, when Blainey expressed fears on the size of Australia's migrant intake. Blackstone, like Blainey, questions the concept of multicultural Australia, which in turn has become more Asianized. His provocative statements make headlines and stir national debate. He in his speech on the radio lashes out at Asians:

> 'Asians,' he'd said on radio, 'pollute the air with the fumes of roasting meat. And we Australians,' he'd added, 'must be alert to the dangers involved for our society if we allow Asians in who cannot assimilate and accept our customs.' (p. 48)

Navaranjini, initially, is not bothered about Blackstone's remarks and says the same to Bharat, who is undergoing a postmigration identity crisis. She feels that Blackstone is talking about 'Asians' (Chinese) and not 'South Asians': 'Why should you care what Blackstone says?; I asked. 'Your eyes aren't slits and your head doesn't look slope. It's obvious he doesn't mean *you*' (p. 48). Bharat's conception of his identity is shattered and it is up to Navaranjini to save him. She engages in a verbal fight with Professor Ron Blackstone and blames him for Bharat's identity crisis. She also tells him openly in the university party:

> *You*, a so-called sociologist who should know that *real* Asians would die before they touched charred pig meat, *you*, polluting the air with meat fumes from your filthy, smelly Barbie in your weed-ridden backyard.
>
> (...) you ignorant, non-vegetarian racist? I am a Tamil, Professor Blackstone, and a Hindu. Pure veg, and proud of it. What do you take me for? A pork-eating Ching-Chong? (p. 53)

In the end with change of name, lifestyle, and language (Australian English), Bharat feels more comfortable in Australia and among Australians. As Navaranjini notes: 'He seemed much happier as a result of all these changes, and instead of standing about at parties with a glass of orange juice in his hand, sulking and reading insults into everyone's innocent remarks, he'd have a real beauty time' (pp. 50–51). Navaranjini is happy too as she has reformed a racist (Professor Blackstone) and forgives him graciously to send home a message – 'how well *real* Asians of culture and goodwill assimilate to the Australian way of life' (p. 53).

Are these stories pointing towards racism in Australia? If what is going on in these stories is not 'racism', but just 'indifference', or 'prejudice' (indirect racism) towards a particular group, as some of the writers analysed here have suggested in their narratives, then we are constantly reminded by the great philosopher-thinker Martin Buber that the greatest evil in the world comes not from bad deeds but from 'indifference'. Sometimes, deeply racialized aspects of Australian society and prejudices of South Asians towards others are played out in these texts. According to Stratton and Perera (2009), this is the 'everyday racism', the kind of 'unthinking racism' that is accepted as a general rule in our daily lives and that we do not consider it racism anymore that 'prevents us from seeing the racialised discriminations that happen all the time in Australia'. In this literature, sexually and racially abusive graffiti public places and media also play a crucial role.

Many people believe that racism only exists when it is accompanied by violence. They do not comprehend how emotionally and psychologically painful discrimination and prejudice can be to its victims in a society. David Carter (1997) has noted that 'literature is not just a set of individual texts or authors but rather a set of institutions and institutional practices which regulate the making and transmission of (literary) meanings in a given society' (p. 18). It also regulate the makings and transmission of racial meanings. Given the cultural dimension of racism in Australia, as seen in the above analysis, the institutional challenge – both political and literary – is to translate the acceptance of cultural diversity, implied in the public's support for multiculturalism, into a belief that this diversity can coexist with a commitment to shared political institutions and values (see Inglis, 2006).

Conclusion

Even if we assume that people of South Asian origin, particularly the second and third generations, have integrated publicly into the mainstream, while keeping certain aspects of their cultural life alive at home, what about the post-assimilation mainstream Australians attitude towards them? According to Fazal Rizvi (1996):

> Australians have been asked to make a decisive ideological shift in their thinking, away from the colonialist frame that has traditionally informed their perceptions of Asia to a post-colonial outlook which challenges the racist assumptions of cultural dominance and superiority. Yet most of their attempts to revise their thinking have at best been clumsy, with the new practices of representation failing to make a decisive break from the residual racist expressions that had rendered Asians as a homogenised mass, socially inept and culturally inferior. (p. 173)

So, the closest designation that we currently have for this attitude of prejudice, neglect, and indifference towards a particular community is 'racism' – 'a reduction of someone from a particular group to the stereotypes, negative or positive, we have of that group' (Chow: p. 27).

However, the present situation of 'racism' or 'opportunist violence' against Indian students is a passing moment and keeping 'Australia fair' and 'multicultural', instead of being 'disguised under' some 'euphemistic terminologies', is a challenge for the Australian government (Kinsella, 2003).[6] In this respect Hanifa Deen (2001) notes that unlike today, the earlier government agenda for multicultural issues was 'more rhetorical than real'. And, Dr Geoff Gallop, Premier and Minister for Citizenship and Multicultural Interests, Western Australia, observed that in 'a democracy such as ours, while difference need not always be reconcilable, through *dialogue* it can be negotiated and mutually respected' (p. ii; emphasis added). For these dialogues and multiculturalism to succeed, Australia needs genuine partnerships between all participants.[7] Through a dialogue between various communities, multiculturalism offers the opportunity to both embrace difference and to reproduce the nation. Multiculturalism in Australia has been seen to be more and more advantageous, especially if it is understood as diversity.[8] This is the focus of what Stuart Hall has called 'the multicultural question' (2000: pp. 209–241). It sets 'unity in diversity' as the dialectical relationship between universals and particulars.

Today, the Australian government with its various antiracism regulations,[9] multicultural projects, publication grants, and encouragement to writers from various ethnic backgrounds is dedicated to making the migrant's voice heard and their cultural aspects seen in a positive light.[10] Within the Australian history, the narratives of or by South Asian diaspora writers about their lives in Australia have a special value.[11] First, they are 'a shining example to those groups of Australians who suffer from any form of discrimination on grounds of ethnicity, race, religion, region, gender, sexuality, age, class, family and the like' (D'Cruz and Steele: p. 13). Second, they are able to help continue the dialogue between the two countries through their literature and narratives as they are able to perceive more sharply – being 'adopted Australians', according to A. Phillips (1973), they are knowledgeable about Australian past without having lost the special advantage of their South Asian viewing-point (p. 1). It is this dialogue and promotion of success stories by the Australian government and academia that has further helped in building an interest in the study of contemporary migration and settlement of people from the Indian subcontinent, their problems, and future expectations.[12] Similar views are expressed in the introduction to *Seeing It Their Way* (1973), a handbook designed to be used at any level of the school curriculum. David Dufty et al. noted that the materials collected in the volume aim to:

> bring a clear awareness that we are all conditioned by our culture, that we tend to judge other cultures by our own standards and that to be culturally mature we need to be able to understand and appreciate at least one other culture in some depth and to be able to imagine with some accuracy how others view their world: in other words, to develop an intercultural perspective – to try seeing it their way as well as our own way. (p. 2)

For Australians and its various migrant groups, an understanding of their diversity and tolerance of difference is required to build a stable and secure future. As Kessler (1991) has noted, 'it is only by engaging with difference, not simply intellectually within our own minds but in the pluralistic public or political world where difference has its origins and is upheld, that we can really understand ourselves' (p. 63).

In conclusion, the South Asian diaspora in Australia has seen good days and from their historical journey, it can be prophesied that they will cope with this passing crisis of racism and indifference displayed by a certain section of Australian public.[13] In light of the recent debates and issues related to racism, multiculturalism, immigration, diaspora, and transnationality, it is imperative to suggest that to co-exist peacefully there is a need for the edification of the dominant society about various minority groups. However, we still need a strong plan for South Asian-Australian diasporic area studies both in South Asia and Australia that is based not just on language, history, and material life but also on a critical bilateral dialogue between the two regions, as diaspora literature 'commands respect, not sentimentalization, exploitation, or neglect' (Newman: xiii). Gantner reminds us

> the challenge is to ensure that the next generation (of Australians) has the knowledge and understanding to get on with their neighbours, to solve global problems, and to build a shared and prosperous future. It must start in our own front yard – Asia. We don't need to 'Asianise' our curriculum. We need to 'Australianise' it. (quoted in Henderson: p. 6)

In this regard, South Asian diaspora literature has helped in the past and can help in the future too by opening up the space of the postcolonial world and 'the possibilities of alternative ficto-historical texts that can create a world in process while continually freeing themselves from their own biases' (Ashcroft et al.: p. 85; Chambers: p. 12). In Australia, there will always be celebrations of diversity, and South Asians will be remembered for what they have achieved. The proclamation of Leila, one of the protagonists in Yasmine Gooneratne's story,[14] can as well be borrowed and reversed for Australia and Australians – South Asians become an Australian Learning Experience. About South Asia. About Australia. About the world.

Notes

1. As an aftermath of 'race attacks' in 2010, Dr Helen Forbes-Mewett, a Monash University-based sociologist, was awarded a four-year Australian Research Council (ARC) grant to investigate the nature of these attacks, which have caused great distress in the South Asian student community and damaged Australian relations with India (see Healy, 2010).
2. The Scanlon Foundation, Australian Multicultural Foundation and Monash University, in a survey for the 2013 *Mapping Social Cohesion* report asked participants: 'Have you experienced discrimination because of your skin colour, ethnic origin or religion?' The survey concluded that the there is a large variation in the experience of discrimination within sub-groups and South Asian respondents recorded 42 per cent experience of discrimination (Marcus: p. 2).
3. In July 2007, Dr Haneef, an Indian doctor working at the Gold Coast Hospital in Australia, was held for 25 days, including 11 days in immigration detention. He was being 'framed' by the Australian police for the London and Glasgow bomb attacks and involvement in other terrorist activities. Widespread public concern in India about Dr Haneef's treatment by the Australian government and police forced Indian Prime Minister Dr Manmohan Singh to intervene, making a statement expressing the hope that Australia would extend 'all the facilities' to Dr Haneef 'fairly and justly under Australian law'. Mike Head notes that letters to newspapers and blogs indicate that broad layers of people (both white Australians and migrants) were disgusted with the Howard government's approach and Kevin Rudd's support for the government's conduct and actions taken against Dr Haneef (see Head, 2007).

4. For a detailed discussion on racism towards immigrants in Australia, see Griffiths (2005); Rasool (2002).
5. For a detailed discussion on various facets of Islam and Islamic terrorism, see Kundani (2008).
6. Australian Universities, with an impressive performance in the overall world university rankings, are once again attracting Indian students. There has been a 50 per cent increase in the number of Indian students joining Australian universities, for management and commerce, information technology, food, hospitality and personal services, engineering, and related technologies, in the first half of 2013 as compared with the corresponding period in 2012 (see V. Srivastava, 2013).
7. Recently, Australia has also agreed to a proposal for sending a group of Australian Youth Ambassadors to India in the near future to promote bilateral links between the two countries (see Bhandari, 2008).
8. According to the Australian government's immigration department, 'the planned 2002–2003 Migration Program, if continued over the next 10 years, is estimated according to preliminary modelling by Access Economics to provide net benefits to the Commonwealth Budget of around $30 billion (in constant 2002–2003 prices and without savings in Public Debt Interest (PDI)' (DIMIA, 2004).
9. The *Racial Discrimination Act* of 1975 protects individuals from discrimination on the grounds of race, colour, descent, or national or ethnic origin. In 1995, the act was extended to make racial vilification against the law in Australia.
10. One such programme is the DIMIA's 'Living in Harmony' programme. It is designed to bring into Australian sporting activity the excluded groups by 'aiding and encouraging a host of sporting bodies to promote racial and ethnic tolerance in Australia' (Vamplew: p. 371).
11. Australia has commended the growing Indian diaspora in the country for its contribution in enhancing bilateral links. In a statement, Foreign Minister Stephen Smith said that the 'Indian diaspora in Australia is making a tangible contribution to enhancing bilateral links' (quoted in Bhandari, 2008).
12. A good number of Australian scholars are working on Australia–India relations and cultural diplomacy at the moment: Professor David Walker, Professor David Lowe, Professor Bruce Bennett, Professor Paul Sharrad, Dr Kama Maclean, Professor Auriol

Weigold, and Dr Rick Hosking. Dr Maclean, a University of New South Wales based historian and India expert, is looking into the Indian impact on internationalism in Australia in the early twentieth century. Also, a TV series, titled *My Australia*, produced by ABC, was broadcasted by Australia Network to 44 countries in the Asia Pacific region. It looked at Australia through the eyes of people from South Asia and the Asia-Pacific region who are studying or living there.

13. In December 2010, Dr Haneef returned to Australia with his wife and child and noted: 'Coming back to Australia represents a very important step for me and for my family. I'm grateful to the Australian government and the Australian people for their ongoing support and I'm hopeful that the upcoming mediation will be an opportunity to resolve this matter and give my family and me a chance to move forward'. He further observed: Australia is 'a very fair place to live' (Trenwith, 2010).
14. Yasmine Gooneratne, "In the East My Pleasure: a Postcolonial Love Story," *Span* 34–35 (November–May 1992–1993): pp. 269–279.

CHAPTER 7

Another World, Another Future

> What you chart is already where you've been. But where we are going, there is no chart yet. (Lorde: p. 180)

The stories of the South Asian-Australian diaspora are fraught with experiences that are based mostly on dislocation, fractured identities, sharing, and adaptation or re-accommodation of social and cultural values. The complex location of diaspora influences the stories produced by diasporic writers, as pointed out by renowned author Salman Rushdie (1991), a migrant

> suffers, traditionally, a triple disruption: he *loses his place*, he enters into an alien language, and he finds himself surrounded by beings whose social behaviour and code is very unlike, and sometimes offensive to, his own. And this is what makes migrants such important figures: because *roots*, language and social norm have been three of the most important parts of the definition of what it is to be a human being. The migrant, denied all three, is obliged to find new ways of describing himself, new ways of being human (...). (pp. 277–278; emphasis added)

This disruption of place and roots makes it imperative that the migrant narratives must be understood as inherently and essentially 'spatial stories' – stories of movement and stories of different *homes*. This 'search for the *location* in which the self is "at home" is one of the primary projects of twentieth century fiction in English' (p. 3) claims Rosemary Marangoly George in *The Politics of Home*

(1996). This search, in other words, is also a 'search for viable homes for viable selves' (p. 5).

Migration in this rapidly globalizing world has not just spread the roots of diasporic literature deeper but also put it on a global level by concretizing it as a natural and inevitable result.[1] South Asian-Australian writers have played an important role in the spreading of new ideas and thoughts. Through their fictional and nonfictional narratives, these writers have presented 'the clash of the new and the old worlds' (Paranjape, 2007: p. 354). They are also making possible a more interesting and vibrant understanding of the immigrant culture, its outstanding contribution towards the cultures of both the home and the hostland vis-à-vis the diaspora cultures of the world. Thus, making it obviously positive, their works celebrate the achievements of the South Asian-Australians and others in their involvement in various forms to the process of building a liberal world.

According to Bangladeshi-Australian writer Adib Khan (2002), in the last two decades or so, the 'acceleration in the proliferation of cross-cultural voices in fiction' emphasizes 'the diversity that reflects the type of society that Australia is' (p. 3). The wide spectrum of writings that we see in Australian Literature today shows that it has come a long way from the days of Anglo-Celtic dominance to an era of a literary culture that is much more representative of Australia's migrant or multi-ethnic past and present. This has been made possible by multicultural writers asserting their own literary and cultural traditions in their work. These narratives/texts produced by authors belonging to diverse – both culturally and linguistically – ethnic backgrounds/communities have stimulated not only fascinating cultural dialogues but also a whole new area of critical perspective in diaspora and multicultural studies. What is also significant is that these writers have raised questions of re-defining and re-viewing the national canon through literature. They have also tried to abolish categorizations and compartments of majority and minority literatures by making the mainstream accept their work as part and parcel of the truly 'Australian made' experience (see Mycak and Sarwal, 2010). However, the 'voices' of the early Indian subcontinental 'coolies' or pioneer South Asian migrants, according to Marie de Lepervanche

(2007), who is an authority on migration from Indian subcontinent, are for the most part silent documents for researchers. She notes that the early South Asian migrants did not leave any journals, diaries, letters, memoirs, or autobiographies and their lives as pioneer immigrants in Australia were very hard, often lonely and isolated. Yet, she asserts, their contribution to the economic success of Australia's early industries, particularly pastoralism, must be acknowledged (see pp. 99–116). Post-2009–2010 racist/opportunistic attacks on Indian students in Australia, South Asian-Australian diaspora studies have become more important but the number of books, anthologies, and articles commemorating the South Asian diaspora and its presence in Australia only points towards a nominal recognition. We still need to know more about and highlight the development of South Asian diasporic literature in Australia as a key part of this knowledge building process. South Asian diaspora through its literature has strongly stressed the benefits of immigration to Australian society through its ever increasing ethnic diversity. It is their presence that has made Australia more dynamic and cosmopolitan (see Castles, 1992).

South Asian intellectuals with their understanding and exploration of socio-cultural issues and dilemmas have helped in highlighting South Asian diaspora creative writers settled in Britain, United States, Canada, and other countries of their immigration. Similarly, since 1965, beginning with the publication of Mena Abdullah's ground-breaking *The Time of the Peacock*, a literary discourse has developed in the South Asian diaspora in Australia that further adds to cross-cultural studies taking place in South Asia since in these instances 'critics "at home" and writers "in the diaspora" basically belong to the same culture' (Riemenschneider: p. 118; see also Malak, 1994).The narratives under study produced from Australia deserve a special status in analyses of the social-cultural-economical-historical 'narratives' produced by the South Asian diaspora around the world. The South Asian-Australian writers' postcolonial experiences as presented in the narratives and analysed in this book support this statement. Specially, when 'certain things and places' at first remind them of the homeland, then on visiting the homeland they are reminded of the adoptive home, that is, Australia, a hope for the future of the diaspora, and finally, when they are able to 'transfer at will' between the two now familiar cultures (see Bennett, 2007: p. 336). In this chapter, I analyse the selected narratives in the light of questions and issues concerning the spatial identities the immigrants carry. It also deals with the issues of complexity of setting up of home and how immigrants imagine themselves and their future generations in the present Australian social and national space the journey must start with the perennial questions: Where are you from? And, who are you? In "The London Link" (2002) Brij V. Lal, a Fiji Indian-Australian scholar, recounts a funny incident that happened in London. On his way to the market a bedraggled old man asked him:

> 'Where are you from?' Australia. 'But you don't look Australian.'
>
> 'What's an Australian supposed to look like then?' 'No offence, guy,' the old man said apologetically, 'I thought you was from India.' Before I could explain my genealogy, he said, 'Great country, India.' (p. 78)

And on his way back, Lal stopped at a shop with a 'South Asian-looking man at the counter' (p. 78). Lal couldn't help himself 'asking the perennial question immigrants of colour automatically ask each other everywhere' (p. 78):

> 'Where are you from?' (...) 'Sri Lanka', he replied. 'Murali is a genius,' I venture. Muralitharan, the ace Sri Lankan spinner. 'I don't like cricket. Englishman's game,' he replied sullenly. That peeved me. Cricket is the game God plays, and we all know that God is not an Englishman. And I thought, if the English are so bad, what are you doing here in their country? But there was no point arguing. 'You are hailing from where?' he asked me as I was leaving, 'Fiji,' I replied. He gave me a blank, unknowing look. 'Fiji,' I repeated. Still no reaction. 'Fiji Islands,' I said, 'in the South Pacific.' 'In Gujarat?' I gave up. (pp. 78–79)

Who is an Australian? or What makes a person Australian – Colour, Race, Ethnicity, or Language? These are some of the questions that Siri also grapples with in Sri Lankan-Australian writer Sunil Govinnage's "The Black Australian" from *Black Swans and Other Stories* (2002). On a visit to Europe, he is bugged by the 'usual question' – 'Are you from India?' (p. 6). He wonders:

> Should I say that I'm from Australia and that I was born in Sri Lanka, but am now living in Western Australia? Why bother? (p. 6)

It is a 'universal question' asked everywhere to him and other South Asians, but the trouble is 'whatever he did to be an Australian, it always produced the opposite result' (p. 7). During a footy (Australian Rules Football) match, a youngster from Melbourne pointed towards him and said, 'I didn't know the Eagles had supporters in India as well!' (p. 7). To avoid such questions, Siri has devised a solution: referring to himself as a 'black Australian':

> This is an honour. I'm a Black Australian! You need not be an Aboriginal to call yourself a Black Australian. The Aborigines must be called Native Australians, not Black Australians. (p. 9)

Instead of sticking with his Sri Lankan-Australian identity, Siri is in a state of irritability. He wants to be referred to as just 'Australian' – black or white should not matter. For him acceptance as an Australian is the imperative. But deep down, he knows he is faking his 'black Australian' identity: 'Siri saw his image in the mirror behind the bar. He saw himself as if he were wearing thick make-up' (p. 10). The ambivalence and complexity of his identity confronts Siri everywhere. His search then is for an image of himself as an Australian recognized by the world and people around him.

Similarly, Glenn D'Cruz, writing about images and perceptions, in "Beyond the Pale" (2004) observes that for his Anglo-Indian family, the future in Australia became clear when the racial and cultural scene changed in Australia post-1980s. His being an Anglo-Indian now was seen as an asset in the academia and his half 'Indian appearance' made people assume that he was an authority on India – a result of 'explosion of scholarly interest in empire' (p. 227). He notes that it is in Australia that his family 'managed ultimately to acquire the accoutrements of middle-class life – "respectable" jobs, houses, cars and so forth – all of which seemed beyond their grasp in post-independence India' (p. 230).

Sushie Narayan in "Asha's Story" (1994) writes that 'Coming to Australia was a choice she (Asha) did not make, but at that time it felt exciting. Her parents had decided to uproot themselves from their birthplace and start anew' (p. 136). For Asha, there was no option but to migrate. She leaves behind her love, whom she couldn't marry because of her parent's opposition. And the man she marries in Australia makes her 'marginally content' (p. 136). She notes at a very early stage, 'life was better in a new land, it would hold many new experiences' (p. 136). She starts observing the Australians at her workplace and notes their philosophy of 'work, live and play'. But she feels alienated, confused and pained as 'she didn't fit in' (p. 137) and felt that her culture was holding her back. To her, 'the thought of having a new Australian life felt so strange' (p. 137) and sometimes 'frightening'. But, the author notes that Asha after going through so much pain realizes that 'she is no longer a member of old culture and not yet initiated into the new. (...) she was in a vacuum' (p. 137). To exit from the vacuum and to assert her individuality, she rebelled against her parents and their culture. She distanced herself from them and wondered 'what a new Australian was supposed to think' like and also wanted 'to find her own roots in a new land' (p. 137). She has sacrificed a lot for others but now wanted to pursue her life as an Australian with 'her roots nestle(d) into Australian soil' (p. 138). Australia provides her the space to escape from her loneliness and devaluation that she suffers in social status.

Karobi Mukherjee, of Indian origin who immigrated from New Zealand to Australia, in her autobiographical story-essay "An Asian Migrant Woman's View of the City of Adelaide" (1994), wonders

> Was it wise to move from the friendlier and insular existence of Dunedin in the South Island of New Zealand, where everyone in the City knew us so well and we managed to develop a rapport with the City and its people but suddenly to leave behind all these relationships and migrate to Australia, severing all such friendships and securities and come to a new land which I knew so little about. (p. 126)

Remembering her first few days in Adelaide, she observes that it was only because of the wonderful people, particularly veterans of ANZAC, who gave her family a warm welcome and guidance thus removing all her apprehensions as 'a migrant from non-English speaking background and an Asian at that' (pp. 126–127). At this welcoming moment, she felt that 'we were here to stay and make it our home' (p. 127). Adelaide became her home and the people of this city, her friends – she now cannot bear the thought of parting with it 'in the near or distant future' (p. 127). Her choices point towards another reality and she notes:

> There are no forms of discrimination as regards one's choice from different religious freedom and hence for those migrants coming from religious background there is the choice of a Mosque for those of the Islamic faith, a Hindu Temple for the Hindus, a Buddhist Temple for followers of that faith. Even for smaller communities there is always a place where they are able to go and practice their own religion in whatever fashion they would like achieve their own spiritual requirements. Indeed there is always the feeling of open acceptance of all religions. (p. 128)

Apart from the free life style of Adelaide, it is also the religious diversity, tolerance, and open acceptance that attracts her to choose it. Looking back at her life and days spent in Australia, she feels that although the initial decision to migrate to Australia was made in haste, at the end it turned out to be the right decision for her and the whole family. As a migrant she never felt 'disadvantaged' and found a rich social environment to work in and a great community life. Yet, she notes that migration and 'Moving places is always a traumatic event for anyone, it is like uprooting a small shrub and transplanting it in a place where there is always the uncertainty of not knowing whether it is going to grow or whether it will wither away with the passage of time' (p. 126).

According to Stuart Hall (1987), 'Migration is a one way trip. There is no "home" to go back to' (p. 44). Even in today's globalized world, immigrants who stay far away from their homeland or roots seek to return or create routes of return to the day when they left it (Braakman and Schlenkhoff, 2007). Noted Sri Lankan-Australian writer Chitra Fernando focusing on the notion of 'return' for a diasporic individual, in her story "The Birds of Paradise" from *Women There and Here* (1994) provides the way for a future in Australia. Rupa Gomez, is a young teacher, who immigrated to Sydney from Sri Lanka and

> (A)fter two years in Sydney teaching English to Vietnamese migrants in Bankstown, Rupa Gomez felt she had to return to Sri Lanka. The insistent 'When are you coming back?' in every letter from her father, her mother and (...) from everyone (...) took on the collective force behind a battering ram. (p. 41)

Rupa feels happy to return, but is saddened by the death of her Uncle Anthony. On her return, she finds her old room 'unfamiliar' and 'uncomfortable' (p. 43). And soon she longs for the 'silence of her Bankstown flat' (p. 45). She is surrounded by relatives with strange questions about Australia – 'Did Australians keep kangaroos as pets? (...) Was Australia really such a big country?' (p. 44). The 'hum and buzz of voices around dazed her' (p. 45) and soon she craves for 'the roar of Sydney traffic' (p. 45). She also remembers with nostalgic pleasure 'the easy informality of her life in Sydney' (p. 45).

> She felt a sharp *longing* for Sydney. A longing for its roads and freeways with traffic zooming, morning, noon and night; for glimpses of the Harbour, that wrinkled expanse of slate-grey water, glinting and gleaming as you flashed past by train or car; for the half-built Opera House, its thin white shells slicing through blue air; for the surf-riding, sun-tippling bathers at Bondi, Bronte, Cronulla (...) the wine-bars and restaurants and the bold, impudent pigeons in Martin Place (...). All these spoke to her of progress, of modern civilization and its freedoms. (p. 46)

In her longing for Sydney, she moves beyond the nostalgia for an originary home and instead expresses nostalgia for origins in a new home. This complicates the rooted understanding of nostalgia as commonly perceived.

Beryl T. Mitchell in her autobiographical account, "Tea, Tytlers and Tribes" (1997), describes the motives and the process of her journey of immigration from a tea plantation in Sri Lanka to Australia. She writes that

> Race hatred had become a reality. The very benefit we had most enjoyed – the open spaces in the beautiful tea country – were now beginning to appear threatening because they offered no protection from unhappy or disillusioned party. (p. 309)

She further notes that 'the political turbulence was colouring every facet of life in Ceylon. (...) finally (the mother) decided that our future must lie Australia, not in Sri Lanka' (p. 310). But what did the Australian future hold for them? It is a question that so many migrants through the last 200 years have contemplated upon and arrived at different answers. The answer to this question is related to or lies in what kind of reception the migrant happens to get in Australia. Beryl is happy with her Australian friends, who from the beginning gave her first-hand information of life 'down under' and 'they took away some of the nervous apprehension most migrants feel on taking the enormous step of moving permanently from their known habitat to the mysterious unknown' (p. 304). These small gestures from the Anglo-Australians and also from the people of her small diasporic community made life easier and worth living for her family. Therefore, for Mitchell, the answer was in 'kindness', 'capacity to adapt', 'self-help' and following just 'one goal' and aim – 'make a success of this life. Australia was our home and we were happy we had made this choice' (p. 311).

At the end of her narrative in "A Family for Us" (2002), Madu Pasipanodya is still not sure where she will live in the future: Australia or Fiji?

> I love Fiji and, even though I wouldn't have as much freedom as I do here in Australia, I might go back there for a few years, then return. I'll cope with whatever comes my way. (p. 125)

For young Madu, who was adopted in 1989, at the age of 9, from an orphanage in Fiji the concept of 'home is a complex one. Madu has adapted to her new family and country and sounds like any other young Australian but she seems to be able to move between Fiji and Australia with ease – like a true transnational.

In Mena Abdullah's story "Grandfather Tiger", the protagonist, Joti, a third-generation Indian-Australian, discovers the strength to 'remain true to herself, to find the courage to resist the assimilationist trends she finds at her school – the tendency among other things, of the teacher to alter her name almost imperceptibly, to make it sound more British' (Corkhill, 1994: 71). Joti's imaginary friend, the Indian tiger, represents the wise animal from *Panchatantra* – a collection of popular animal fables, and advises her on various topics related to growing up and also helps with instructions on the different aspects of life.

> 'The lessons are good,' said the tiger. 'Your teacher is good.'
>
> 'Oh yes,' said Joti. 'I like the lessons. The teacher is nice. But she calls me Josie.'
>
> The tiger banged his paw on the ground so that Joti jumped. 'That is a different matter,' he said. 'You'll have to stop that or it will last

> you all your life. Your mother's name is Premilla and they call her Milly. Your Aunt Halima was called Alma. And your Uncle Shamshir' – the tiger shuddered – 'they called him Sam!'
>
> Joti giggled and the tiger glanced at her sourly.
>
> 'You may think it funny now,' he said. 'And another thing, I would not wear that dress again. Wear your own name and your own clothes and they will understand you better.'
>
> Joti came down to breakfast the next morning in her white sulwa. 'Look,' she said. 'I am me again.' (p. 98)

'They' in the above extract from the story are Australians. The tiger's advice, which is really Joti's own inner voice, is in favour of multiculturalism rather than assimilation.

In his short story "The Ganges and its Tributaries" (1993a), an example of second-generation postcolonial migrant literature, Christopher Cyrill, a well-known Anglo-Indian writer, uses 'ordinary language' to present a mundane local narrative 'of unsettled settling in' (Sharrad, 2009: p. 578) and exploring an Australian suburb. For example, consider Cyrill's description of the family moving from St Kilda to Dandenong and then to Oakleigh. On looking at the photographs of the newly built house at Oakleigh that his father had taken while it was being built, he observes:

> The house in Oakleigh was three storeys tall. The middle floor was level with the street, because the land that the house was built on sloped downwards from the street to the back fence. (... As) I opened the photo album I could see (...). The first photograph in the album showed an empty block of land with foot-high grass, three garbage bags dumped against the back fence and pieces of glass on the nature strip. The last photograph showed the porch lights without bulbs, the four rectangular front windows without curtains and the landscaped island of mossy rocks, pygmy shrubs and azaleas dug into the perimeters of the front lawn. (pp. 157–158)

This shifting of home/address, according to Paul Sharrad (2009), 'suggests not only the unstable newness of housing estates still under construction, but the sense of fixation on specificities of location to compensate for fluidities of movement, physical and mental, that have been shared by white settler and brown migrant alike' (p. 579).

Christopher Cyrill recalls a model of India that his father had carefully constructed after his migration from India to Australia. This model, according to Sabina Hussain (2004), metaphorically 'illustrates the construction and deconstruction of borders and consequently the deconstruction of a previously established space and its ceaselessly transformable reconstruction' (p. 104). In the story, in his version of (a model) India the father ignores 'everything outside the borders of India (...) omitted the neighbouring countries to banish Pakistan from the map of the world in his mind' (p. 162). He further marks with toothpicks 'the places on the map that interested him: his birthplace in Lucknow; Calcutta, where my mother was born; Bombay, where the great Sunil Gavaskar would bat on the streets with a plank of wood' (p. 163). He then places it in the backyard pond of his Australian house. Christopher narrates:

> He let the model drift in the water without securing it on the edge of the mould. It looked as if India had pulled itself away from Asia, bringing the Himalayas along with it, and was steering itself through the Indian Ocean in whichever direction it chose. The Ganges no longer flowed into the Bay of Bengal, but into all the oceans of the world. (p. 163)

The father's version of India, according to Sabina Hussein,

> signifies an imaginary which reflects his self-opted place of belonging, constitutes a stable core and defines spaces of Inside and Outside. However, the detachment of the constructed core from its specific geographical locality inaugurates a motion through which borders are blurred and spaces demand new definitions. The individualized model of India is constantly floating and drifting in the water. (p. 103)

In this story, Christopher's life is characterized by an upbringing in an Australian community in between his Indian relatives, and also a distancing from an Indian community placing him similarly on the margin of the Indian migrant community in Australia. He says,

> When my uncles began to sing in Hindi I left them and walked upstairs to third-floor bathroom. As I walked upstairs I heard them singing in the language that I have never learnt. (p. 160)

This reference to the 'third floor' at this moment is quite significant. The third floor acts as a *third space*, a term used to refer to social surroundings separate from the two usual social environments of home (India) and the outside world (Anglo-Australian). This third space – an 'interruptive, interrogative, and enunciative' space where negotiation takes place – is a mode of articulation, a way of describing a *productive*, and not merely reflective, space that engenders new *possibility* (see Bhabha, 1994). Christopher, born in Australia, is a second-generation Indian-Australian. He experiences through his parents as well as a constant flow of relatives from India, who are recent sponsored-immigrants to Australia, a presence of other places or other times or other worlds (see Longley, 1997). Therefore, Christopher's hybrid 'identity is *rooted* in more than one space and his *routes* develop from the intermingling of diversified worlds' (S. Hussein: p. 113; emphasis added) that construct and re-construct his identity.

It is, definitely, the uniqueness of the Australian land that has been the source of inspiration for these writers, making them explore home and local spaces. The local, here, referring to the 'Australian' for them because of their increasing proximity with the things that are Australian – economically, culturally, and politically. In this, however, the concept of 'otherness' has been simplified to some extent with an inward looking gaze because of the cultural (baggage) discourse. And therefore, as argued earlier, the question of identity becomes central to these writings, where this 'identity' works in both ways and is open ended like the hyphen (-) which looks at both the self and the other and homeland and the hostland. Still, this creates a third space or a diasporic space, which belongs to self-realization and the processes of rationalization for the immigrants, wherever they stay.

Another dimension to the future of the South Asian immigrants in Australia is the Australian outlook and attitude towards South Asia or the bilateral relations between the two great continents. This angle is explored in Mena Abdullah's story "A Long Way" from *The Time of the Peacock*, when Nazit travels all the way from her small village in Mooltan, first by train, to Ranipur and then walks to the big city Karachi alone. Her youngest son is in Australia and she wants to send a woollen jumper to him as a gift. Begum, a social reformer, has through the help of an Australian Government Plan sent a large number of Pakistani students, poor peasants, and skilled workers to Australia. Nazit remembers when

> (...) the Big Man had come to the village in the big black car (...). Then the Big Man stood on the great stone, and told the people that he had brought them a notice. (...) The notice told them of a plan.
>
> The Big Man explained that he was from the Big Government in Karachi and that there were other Big Governments in the world. He said that the Big Governments were friends, and they were friends who would help. (p. 103)

At that time, his words meant nothing to the villagers. Since Yaseem, Nazit's son had studied in the city, he is found to be eligible for an Australian scholarship – a 'gift of goodwill' (p. 104). According to Begum, 'We must let our children learn, so that they can teach others. We must let them go a long way, so that they can return. It is not a kindness, it is goodness' (p. 104).

The story in its representation of migration to Australia also traces internal migration within Pakistan and to other favoured international destinations. On her way to Karachi, Nazit meets a young Hindu couple, on their way to Ranipur: 'They had come a long way to Ranipur, because it was big and might want them. It might give them food and work' (p. 106). The couple is frightened of the big city as everything is new for them but are confident of a successful future. Nazit also meets a woman from low-caste – a *chamar* – whose son is studying to be a doctor in Canada. The woman is happy and proud for her son, and tells Nazit:

> 'Think of it!' said the woman. 'Such a long way! My son, too – the father of my grandchild – he is in Canada. He is learning too. Think of that! My husband was a sweeper. He and I were called chamars, we were untouchables. But our son can now be a doctor. Think of that! And his son – here with big eyes open – who knows what he can be?' (pp. 107–108)

International immigration and study abroad programmes opened doors of possibilities not just for the migrants and their dependent family members, no matter to which caste and class they belonged, but also for their coming generations. Migration in such a situation has also played an uplifting role in the South Asian society.

But the looming question of whether Australian Government's Plan would fail or succeed has made Begum anxious. She has received reports about the plan and its reception in Australia from her daughter.

> She wrote home often, but recently the letters from Australia had been full of worries. The Plan might fail, its good work be undone. There were critics who said that it was silly, wasteful, uneconomic; that the country had causes of its own, that its people needed houses, and that its people's money was being thrown around overseas. What, they asked, have foreigners to do with us? (p. 112)

Begum feels that probably '(T)he critics were right. Australians need have nothing to do with her people unless they wanted to be friends. And did they want to?' (p. 112). At the end, Nazit succeeds in handing over the gift to Begum and narrates how she was helped by strangers, who are 'all our people'. Begum is optimistic now and knows what to say to Australian people: 'I will go to the houses, the streets, the parks. I will find the people who are my people, and I will tell them how their people need' (p. 114). Because 'They are all our people, she thought, no matter who we are or what, no matter where they are or why, the world is all our people' (p. 114). The story ends not only on a note of optimism but also on that of a cosmopolitan future. Abdullah shows the strength of friendliness. The last echoing phrase: 'The world is our people', reminds us of the famous Greek philosopher, Diogenes of Sinope, who declared himself to be a cosmopolitan – 'I am a citizen of the world' – an ideology that all kinds of human ethnic groups belong to a single community – a move towards a truly transnational being.

Mena Abdullah also points out creation of a third space or a diasporic space, beautifully in her story 'Mirabani' from *The Time of the Peacock*:

> 'It is not India,' said Father.
> 'And it is not Punjab,' said Uncle Seyed.
> 'It is just us,' said Ama. (p. 31)

For the diaspora, the spatial identity or geographical location, where one resides is not important anymore, as pointed above, whether it be India or Australia or any place on earth. It is better for them, as Spivak (1994) notes, to make a sense of themselves and their situations to produce self-identity (p. 179) and to move around, maintain and sustain a network contact with both India and Australia and thus to act in prominence.

This constant confrontation with new spatial and social locations demands 'adaptation and creativity that often leads to invention and development' (Scott: p. 1). The diversity of experiences in these stories present the dynamic phase towards which the authors are moving. For example, Nandini, in Sujhatha Fernandes' "A Pocket Full of Stories" (1999), is robbed of her multi-coloured stories and Rajan in K.C. Paramanandam's "Of Human Infatuation" (1956) struggle to locate a sense of being Australian. And similarly, the narrator of Rani Jhala's "Life's Key" (1999) becomes a widow in Australia but she does not lose her faith and instead learns to 'give more meaning to the purpose in life' (p. 21). She comes to this 'another planet' (p. 21) that is Australia, after marriage and lives a happy life with her husband and children. After the loss of her husband, she makes 'this new country (her) future home' (p. 22) and is confident and prepared to take on 'the modern sprawling city that is Sydney' (p. 22). Australia not only takes away from her many things but also presents before her the challenge and opportunity to realize her potential in the absence of her husband; among other things, she makes herself socially and economically independent with the help of a job-oriented course. She belongs to Australia and to her towards the end of the story it symbolizes, like the plant she has grown, the 'love of today and promise of tomorrow' (p. 21).

This sense of 'belonging' according to Peter Read (2004) can also be 'intellectual' (p. 23). Manik Datar reflects on this in her writings as she feels a bond with Australia and its landscape:[2]

> because she had consciously grafted herself to Australia, because she liked the look of the land, because it gave her space as a non-Anglo-Celtic Australian; because she felt accepted by its people; because she held a commitment to its democracy; because of her memories, and because occasionally she felt an ache for the land. (p. 23)

A clear solution that she provides to the protagonists of her stories is that to search for return to homeland is pointless and to find space and identity or to belong in the diversity of Australia is a more desirable and a profitable aspiration keeping in view the future that lies ahead. Similarly, Sudesh Mishra in "Diaspora and the Difficult Art of Dying" (2004) observes:

> (...) india slipped through my fingers like silk, like silk it slipped through the fingers of three thousand seven hundred and forty eight girmityas, and many things were lost during that nautical passage, family, caste and religion, yet many things were also found, chamars found brahmins, muslims found hindus, biharis found marathis, so that by the end of the voyage we were a nation of jahajibhais (...) all for one and one for all. (p. 60; lowercase in original)

Being away from the homeland then is not always a depressing dilemma. It is here a positive experience too that has created spaces of equality among the indentured labourers. Conditions in the homeland have not changed, as on a visit to India, Brij V. Lal, in "The Road to Mr Tulsi's Store" (2003), discovers 'how un-Indian I was in my values and outlook, how much I valued my individuality and freedom, (...). The Indian obsession with status and recognition, the routine acceptance of a ritually sanctioned hierarchy, was beyond my comprehension' (p. 44; see B. Lal, 2001a).

South Asian immigrants are looking to make Australia their home and build a future for themselves and their families. Australian cities offer migrants an urban, industrial, and technological way of life. Some writers have commented that the feeling of dislocation that is so frequently a part of the immigrant experience can be overcome by 'an intense desire on the part of the new settler to come to terms with Australian life' and this 'can be achieved by virtue of a commitment to loving and working the soil of the adopted homeland' (Corkhill, 1995: p. 37).

Further, according to Chandani Lokugé (2008), the presence of South Asian in Australia is like that 'leit-motivic presence' of the South Asian 'immigrant mynah bird', in Yasmine Gooneratne's novel *A Change of Skies* (1991) which 'confidently makes its home in the lillypilly tree, sometimes resented by the owner of the tree but never aware of the resentment (...)' (p. 213). The longer the migrants stay, the more rooted and at ease they feel in their new home and environment (see Ballard: p. 12). These narratives make it clear that Australia and its literature are not just an Anglo-Celtic space but 'there also exists other voices, bodies, worlds' (Chambers: p. 5) and the 'possibility of another place, another world, another future' (Chambers: p. 5). However, young South Asian diaspora writers also need to build on the flexibility or the power of their narratives to challenge the readers about the complexities of life in diaspora and Australia – an experience that helps them cast a more critical eye on both the homeland and hostland.

Notes

1. The concept of globalization and diaspora formation is clearly an ongoing process related to global flows, for a detailed discussion, see Kelly (1998).
2. For a discussion on depictions of interactions between the landscape and protagonist in Asian-Australian women's writing, see Tucker (2003).

Chapter 8

Conclusion

Thoda Indian, *Thoda* Aussie[1]

> Ours is a nation of immigrants and Indigenous peoples. A new world with an ancient past. A grand symphony with many melodies. (Zable, 2001)
>
> (...) you should consider that immigration has made us the most ethnically diverse country in the world. Australians' roots run very deep and wide. That gives us a stake in all the world's cultural heritage. (Brooks: p. 24)

The above quotes, from Arnold Zable and Geraldine Brooks, two award winning Australian writers,[2] immigrants themselves, not only help us to understand the fraught and complex legacy of immigration but also best summarize the future of South Asian diaspora and its literature in Australia. Shirley Tucker (2003) has also pointed out that there is often an 'uneasy reception' of minority writing by mainstream critics in Australia, as it 'may be perceived as unwelcome, discomforting and illegitimate: straying into Australian spaces without proper credentials'. It must be noted that Australian culture has been enriched and expanded 'beyond all recognition by the impact of the cultures of the world', and most people will, who are anti-multiculturalism and migration, also soon come to recognize the immense benefit to be derived from 'an Australian inheritance which encompasses the diversity of many peoples, the wisdom of many cultures' (Corkhill, 1995: p. 143). And, it is hoped that the South Asian diaspora and its literature will enrich the Australian multicultural heritage.[3] Nevertheless, as noted in the stories and also the sociological studies, there are still significant difficulties, anxieties, maybe confusions, and an element of estrangement today among the South Asian diasporic community in Australia. However, South Asian-Australian writings, as important 'expressions' of Australian 'people's lives', may effectively help, as Lyn Jacobs (2002) points out, 'defamiliarise understandings of local conditions and encourage fellow Australians to see differently' (p. 211) within the cultural context of South Asia and Australia. It is argued that writers belonging to diverse literary groups also help the government and other decision-making bodies to make better decisions about their respective communities.

Today, Australian government with its various anti-racism regulations,[4] multicultural projects, and encouragement to writers from various ethnic backgrounds is dedicated to making the migrant's voice heard and their cultural aspects seen in a positive light.[5] According to Kateryna O. Longley (1997), the rich and diverse contribution of South Asian diaspora to the economic, social, cultural, and literary development of Australia is also highlighted as part of Australian history. As the 'history of every life lived in Australia is potentially part of the country's history as are all those lives' connections with homelands elsewhere, but only if they are allowed in, allowed to be written and published' (Longley: p. 219). As noted in Chapter 1, the South Asian diaspora in Australia came into being in the nineteenth century. Although a progeny of the labour or indenture diaspora, it turned out to be one of the most successful diasporas in Australia, playing an effective role in building the Australian nation-state. According to Vinay Lal (2002), the prospect for or of South Asians in the diaspora revolves upon two modalities of thought and action. First, the immigrants must

> without necessarily offering their allegiance to the idea of the nation-state, attempt a coalition-style politics with other communities and groups of those who are not only marginalized, peripheral, and disenfranchised, but whose knowledge systems have, through the processes of colonialism and management, and with the aid of Enlightenment notions of science, rationality, and progress, been rendered powerless and superfluous (...).

> Secondly, diasporic Indians cannot reasonably look to the Indian government for succor and assistance, and whatever the strength of the emotional and cultural ties between them and the 'motherland,' their center of being lies elsewhere. (...) diasporic Indians are in an in-between space, they may yet be in the position of trying to give society a new, at least slightly more human face.

The analysis of the short stories also clearly shows that many immigrants will always maintain ties to their homelands while becoming integrated into the hostland – *thoda* Indian, *thoda* Aussie, that is, a little bit of Indian, a little bit of Aussie (see Levitt, 2009; "A Little Bit Indian ...", 2012). As noted in Chapters 2 to 7, South Asian diasporic narratives characterize bifurcated, dislocated identities that exist in a liminal space, in-between two identities, two cultures, and two histories. Yet, 'home' remains, through acts of imagination, remembering and re-creation, an important reference point for these writers. We can see that the future immigrants wherever they are scattered may not actually want to return home, yet they 'retain a conscious or subconscious attachment to traditions, customs, values, religions, and languages of the ancestral home' (Ramraj: p. 215; see also V. Mishra, 1996a, 1996b). On the notion of 'no return' and the strength of emotional and cultural ties between the immigrants and the 'motherland', Makarand Paranjape (2000) notes that

> Indian civilization, however, has come to be identified with a particular geographical area which is today known as the Indian subcontinent or South Asia. From here the civilization moved eastwards, until it once flourished over much of South East Asia or Indo-China. Yet, its epicentre remained in South Asia. Similarly with the spread of the Indian diaspora all over the world, this civilization may venture into new areas and countries but its epicentre will remain India. (p. 242)

The search for the 'epicentre' and a sense of self in diaspora writing has opened up a space that invites movement, migration, and a journey to the 'motherland'. It also involves putting 'a certain distance between ourselves and the contexts that define our identity' (Chambers: p. 10). The South Asian diasporic writers with their worldview appear to be at the 'cutting edge of modernity and cultural life in their countries of settlement' and 'provide other ways of viewing the world' they are living in now (Karim: p. 6).

But why do so many migrant writers who talk of returning from their present locations to their old homelands never do so? Brian Penton tries to answer this in *The Landtakers* (1934). He writes: 'a man might want to go back where he had been happy, but it would stop at that. Where he'd had his hard times – that was where he would stay?' (p. 30). For South Asian migrants belonging to a 'home' – both sensory (imagined) and spatial (real) – is a matter of debate.[6] As 'belonging'

> captures more accurately the desire for some sort of attachment, be it to other people, places, or modes of being, and the ways in which individuals and groups are caught within wanting to belong, wanting to become, a process that is fuelled by yearning rather than the positing of identity as a stable state. (Probyn: 19)

Many writers discuss attachment, belonging, and 'the promise of leaving' and 'the sadness of arrival' in their works (de Kretser, "Life with Sea Views": p. 1). But 'for most individuals', as Satendra Nandan (2004) observes, 'leaving their country is never an easy decision: one gets used to one's country as one gets accustomed to one's mother's body' (p. 7). In the same way, one gets used to one's country of adoption too. As noted in Chapter 3, these immigrants are now 'expert in crossing borders and performing identities, using, transforming and inventing new identities' (Coronado: p. 51). For them, it becomes necessary, borrowing a phrase from Gabriela Coronado (2003), to prove or to become an 'Indian/South Asian' outside the Indian subcontinent and inside Indian subcontinental culture, which may also ultimately produce a new form of Indianness/South Asianness.

Further, the 'circulation of texts in transnational markets', that is, the 'ability of ink itself to travel' means also that 'a diasporic community is created through these literary acts' (Walters: p. x). Today, because of globalization, trade, tourism, academic contacts, and collaborations, and through various other organizations Australia has come close to India like never before. And the most important role in this coming closer has been played by the South Asian diaspora in Australia – carrying with it a new global Indian subcontinental identity, which has integrated both the cultures – by presenting a 'new' image of Indian subcontinental culture, economics, and politics. Stephen Alomes (2009) argues that our often overt critical concern with loss and exile should be balanced by noting that living in the diaspora might as well be seen as 'the Promethean journeys of liberation, and discovery, celebration and recreation' (p. 384). The immigrants, through their 'Promethean journeys', have played a major role in doing away with the negative stereotypes of the past about the peoples of the Indian subcontinent. At the same time, D'Cruz and Steele (2003) have noted that the South Asian community with all its professional standing in Australia has 'been largely *voiceless* in public debates concerning their disadvantage and vilification' (p. 61; emphasis added). And similarly, the power of literature, particularly South Asian diaspora literature, and the voices of its authors have not yet been fully exploited to bring Australia and the Indian subcontinent together.[7] Reading 'their stories, one cannot deny there is a strong Indian (and South Asian) voice waiting to be heard in this country' (Kannan: p. 7). Australia may find it more and more useful to highlight and strengthen the immigrant creative output by promoting young creative writers of South Asian origin.

South Asian-Australian diasporic literature, as noted earlier in this study, despite many awards and recognitions is still struggling to make a place for itself in academic circles as a distinct tradition in Australia, although it has carved a small niche for itself through some celebrated books. This is an acknowledgement of the fact that South Asian studies and dialogues are important for national productions and knowledge. Moreover, as noted earlier, studies of South Asian diaspora and its literature in Australia are not only important for literary studies but also for the policy makers of both India and Australia by providing unique avenues to key policy makers and helping them understand the dynamics of South Asian socio-cultural practices. Based on such theses on the literature of South Asian diaspora, its problems and *location* can be best reported. These studies and narratives, like images however humble and marginal in their origins, 'help us to think through things, not above them' (Kracauer: p. 192).

These South Asian writers, who come from varied backgrounds and many cultures, as Satendra Nandan (1999) has observed, belong to one country – Australia (p. 8). These authors have convinced their readers by the quality of their works that reveals the complexity of the migrant condition itself. As is evident from Thomas Shapcott's observation in his introduction to the 1992 edition of Mena Abdullah's *The Time of the Peacock* that it like Judah Waten's *Alien Son* is another 'landmark exploration of ethnic difference and family' and 'one of the turning points in our cultural development' (p. x). Shirley Tucker (2003) has observed that Abdullah's narrator

> responds to her physical environment with nurturing images of a safe place that has enabled the child's cross-cultural transition from immersion in the Punjabi culture of her parents to one that takes account of her Australianness.

A similar view is reflected in the sociological study conducted by Vijaya Joshi (2000). Through her interaction with the interviewed second-generation migrant Indian women in Australia, she notes that most of them described:

> the reality of having two cultures from which to construct an identity was a positive thing. Most articulated character traits, which they felt they would not have had, had they grown up in a mono-cultural environment. (p. 200)

These frank admissions and testimonies of second-generation migrant Indian women in Australia, and the analysis of some of the selected short stories here, show that 'migrant women construct their own cultural space' – what Homi Bhabha refers to as 'third space' (Joshi: p. 200).[8] Today, it is the young and vibrant writers such as Christopher Cyrill, Suneeta Peres da Costa, Chris Raja, Sunil Badami, and Manisha Jolie Amin, to name a few, who beautifully present the aspirations and changing nature of lifestyles of the second generation of migrants and a promising future for South Asian diaspora literature in Australia. These diasporic authors through their narratives are mapping and re-imaging the everyday lives, anxieties, frustrations, and happiness of the South Asian diaspora in Australia.

According to Vijay Mishra (2006), the literature, particularly the genre of short story by the South Asian diaspora, is 'an accomplishment worth noting and being placed alongside all the other successes of this diaspora' (p. 139). These stories by South Asian-Australians dynamically emerge out as an influential literary form in the Australian literary atmosphere thus exploring, on the one hand, the cultural diversity within the South Asian community in Australia and, on the other hand, their interaction with Australians and other migrant groups. It can also be argued that these short stories by South Asian-Australians have in some ways helped to situate the Australian short fiction in the world literature today by forming 'international literary links' (see Bennett, 2002), which are needed by any literary culture to be considered successful and worth critical attention. The narratives taken here are in addition 'an assurance of a dynamic, prolific and innovative group of writing' (Sareen: p. viii) that has been produced from Australia but is working towards the larger objective of a canon-making process in Australian, South Asian, and the world diasporic literature. Writing and reading about diasporic locations, then, is also part of the construction of community spaces and the 'search for viable homes for viable selves' (George: p. 5).

These stories then act like an instrument that fills meaning in 'both textual and extra-textual' discourses and in the 'unsaid' (D'Cruz and Steele: p. 29). This acceptance of 'silences', 'otherness', and 'multiple views' leads to the formation of an ideal nation. I would here love to quote the words of Gary Younge, a British feature writer and award-winning columnist for *The Guardian*, in which he describes what an ideal nation should be:

> It is a nation where citizenship is not undermined by the happenstance of race or choice of faith but is understood as a common purpose and sense of belonging. A country that celebrates diversity because it understands the distinction between discriminating between people and discriminating against them. It is a place where people are not demonised collectively because of who they are but judged individually by what they have done. A land, like any other, where the poison of racism will always be present but where the antidote of anti-racism will be always available for those who wish to use it. (quoted in B. Lal, 2002: pp. 82–83)

Younge's words are a philosophy that Australia as a country professes and the people of Australia are always ready with the antidote of antiracism. South Asian diaspora in Australia has seen good days and from their historical journey, it can be prophesied that they will cope with this passing crisis of racism and indifference displayed by a certain section of Australian public. In light of the recent debates and issues related to racism, multiculturalism, immigration, diaspora, and transnationality, it is imperative to suggest that to co-exist peacefully there is a need for the edification of the dominant society about various minority groups. There will always be celebrations of diversity, and South Asians will be remembered in Australia for what they have achieved. The proclamation of Leila, the protagonist in Yasmine Gooneratne's 'In the East My Pleasure: A Postcolonial Love Story' (1992), 'I become an American Learning Experience. About Asia. About Australia. About the world – the real world, which is outside America. (...)' (p. 274) can be borrowed and reversed for Australia and Australians too – South Asians become an Australian Learning Experience. About South Asia. About Australia. About the world.

I feel that the importance granted to 'non-literary' or sociological aspects of diaspora in this book, dealing with one or the other South Asian group of immigrants and the discussions on the positive and negative effects of diaspora, does not 'marginalize' the narratives or autobiographical essays dedicated to its literary representation. Rather, it will help in expanding the discourse on South Asian diaspora in Australia with respect to interdisciplinary issues of racism, South Asiannness, politics of location, and various Australian/multicultural immigrant policies. To sum up, this study's heuristic ambition was twofold: to fill the paucity of not just critical material but also lack of awareness about South Asian diaspora creative writing both in South Asia and Australia and to chart out the geography of South Asian-Australian fiction and locate it in the larger rubric of South Asian diaspora writing as well as the Australian national literature. Keeping in mind the previous research done in this area, we need to use interdisciplinary sources – both primary and secondary, especially official sources – archives, reports, and others – more critically and seek out new materials, in the forms of oral testimony and life experiences, that are often neglected in the case of South Asian diaspora in Australia.

In order to understand the current situation of South Asian diaspora in Australia, I feel that literary analysts, particularly related to diaspora studies, have an important task to play in shaping the hitherto under-researched area. These scholars can help the social scientists in a better understanding of South Asian diaspora narratives with their viewpoint and analysis of both the internal and external events, and by continuously questioning the narrative strategies employed by authors in their works that is influenced by/influencing the social reality of the larger world around them. As noted earlier in the Introduction, research on South Asian diaspora in Australia, in spite of a decent history of migration, is still 'a new, dynamic and developing field' that 'requires its own research methods' and 'tools and techniques' (Horst: p. 13) and which can develop only through an interdisciplinary model. Present studies of the South Asian diaspora in Australia have been greatly expanded in recent years by research and scholarship in areas such as sociology, history, and anthropology – as is evident in the discussions related to previous research and debate mentioned in the first chapter of this book. These researches with their extensive fieldworks not only act as a foundation for my own research, but also point out a path for future researchers and help expand and explore literary, cultural, and diaspora studies in Australia. Also, scholars who are concerned with South Asian migration and diaspora in Australia need to work on both sides of the ocean in alliance.

What I found particularly interesting, as mentioned earlier too, is that there is no exhaustive or authoritative account of the South Asian diaspora in Australia. The rarity and small number of critical material on South Asian diaspora and diasporic experience in literary criticism, both in South Asia and Australia, is daunting and yet a challenge for the new researcher at the same time. The most prolific of Indian expatriate cultural critics, Gayatri C. Spivak (1985), has expressed her doubts earlier about the value of academic work (teaching and writing) where the academic project becomes reduced to mere 'information retrieval' (p. 243). However, with a good number of research works being undertaken by scholars, to name a few – Glenn D'Cruz, Sisiri Kumara Pinnawala, Basundhara Dhungel, Sharmini Kannan, Mohit Manoj Prasad, Tamara Mabbott Athique, and Michiel Baas – and books and articles written and published by academics and literary critics – J.V. D'Cruz, Marie de Lepervanche, Brij V. Lal, Pamela Rajkowski, Laksiri Jayasuriya, Bruce Bennett, Vijay Mishra, Makarand Paranjape, Paul

Sharrad, Cynthia van den Driesen, Suvendrini Perera, R.S. Gabbi, Vijaya Joshi, Annette Robyn Corkhill, Sissy Helff, and many others – in South Asia, Australia, and other parts of the world, this situation is headed for a positive change and we can hope that these researches will make visible those particular threads – historical, social, cultural, and anthropological – in the formation of a South Asian-Australian canon.

Through this, South Asian diaspora will finally emerge as, what David Walker (1999) has termed, 'Australia's Asian future – who would develop the country' (p. 7) and that will finally lead South Asia and Australia into a more intellectual and socially constructive dialogue. For this to happen, it undoubtedly requires involvement and more of a collective effort on the part of South Asian and diaspora thinkers, artists, politicians, business people, policy makers, and concerned citizens. Therefore, every artistic involvement, testimonial on the subject, constructive dialogue, and discourse – academic, political, or public – in the present inter-linked world is merely a step towards forming a change in perceptions and attitudes by creating a knowledge and interest base in this field. And in this whole process, ultimately, the South Asian diaspora in Australia, with its continuous growth, prosperity, and an ever-increasing role and responsibility in all areas of Australian society, will be a dynamic key participant in the shift towards global peace and trade, a vital element of World reconstruction and an area of abundant cultural potential.

There is clearly further accommodation to be made on all sides but the story of the hitherto success of South Asian diaspora in Australia suggests we can perhaps be optimistic about the future (see De Lepervanche, 2001). But this success also depends on the proposed concept of *paraspara* – where migration is a two-way process that does not only involve the migrant alone, but also involve those who make up the environment (see also De Jong: p. 3). *Paraspara* then is also a sustained mutual interaction or connection between old home and new home where boundaries will have no meaning. Ultimately this transnational experience means crossing borders rather than creating them, which according to Gabriela Coronado (2003) is the 'dynamics of the diasporic experience (...) a continuous movement of being inside and outside, of belonging (...)'

(p. 51). So, this new environment, space, and age call for challenges to our methodology, institutions, and institutional practices and re-questions the ways in which we have negotiated with Australia and the South Asian diaspora in Australia. In an increasingly globalized world, as students of South Asian-Australian narratives and texts, we must be conscious of other borders that shape ethnicity and cultural identities. Finally, in the stories of South Asian diaspora we must recognize 'our stories' and 'other(s) stories' (Chambers: p. 25).

A key theme of this book has been the constitution of *location* through both movement (routes) and attachment (roots). I am still fascinated and intrigued by the ways in which the idea or politics of location circulates and the ways in which South Asian diaspora produces a politics of location that has multiple contexts or categories. Analysing the ways in which immigrants define themselves in relation to these locations helps us understand South Asian diaspora and its creative output better. And it is precisely through carefully situating the selected literary narratives in their literary, social, class, and other contexts that we can help 'capture both their specificity and their relevance to other contexts' (Hage, 2005: p. 495). By analysing and reflecting on these short narratives a clear impression can be gained of the present condition of the South Asian diaspora in Australia since the 'point of the author, the point of arrival, becomes the point of departure, and the boundary of the sentence is breached by the surplus of language' (Chambers: p. 11). These short stories are also a way by which authors try to explain the 'identity categories' that 'immigrants bring with them and those to which they are assigned' (Cornell and Hartman: p. 80). These stories provide the possibility of an enriching creative life in Australia with a utopian vision and possibility of being located at home while dislocated from the homeland to writers of South Asian descent. But at the same time, the South Asian-Australian authors must engage (critically) in the struggle for recognition and representation in which our diasporas are involved, thus creating positive scenarios of self-fulfilment, freedom, and opportunity, and presenting the fate of South Asian diaspora in Australia.

As also noted earlier, my purpose here in this study was not to define a rupture but to fill a vacuum and offer a constructive discourse on South Asian diasporic fiction in Australia. This study has raised a lot of issues pertaining to this complex phenomenon and attempted to deal and analyse most of them with reference to the narratives. This study has sought to show how multiple locations become part of the broader question of negotiation with the community and self. Furthermore, eliciting the views of these South Asian-Australian writers about the future of South Asian diaspora, I sincerely believe it might help us give an insight to determine whether they see a future with a bicultural identity or an integrated one as both these cultural capitals will increase in coming years.

After analysing the narratives, we are encouraged to consider that the future of literature of South Asian diaspora in Australia is 'pregnant with promise' (Chambers: p. 36). It can no longer be ignored or shunned or denied a voice because of its being in between. What I have suggested through the analysis of short stories of South Asian diaspora in Australia in this study is that we can read diasporic narratives through the literary construction of multiple *locations*. I have also analysed the ways in which these writers use fiction to perform their varied and multiple claims to old and new homes. Working on these short stories has been an exercise in redefining and reviewing my own thoughts about the process of writing and our diasporas across the globe. South Asian authors have in these short stories not just questioned the politics of *locations* but also transformed the imagined communities and homelands into real ones – as the diasporic paradigm enables a global approach and initiates a new perspective (Fludernik, 2003b: p. 283). Being part of the postcolonial migrant literature, these texts carry

> in one way or another elements of migrant experiences, that is (possible) feelings of dislocation and highly sensitive awareness of location and subject position within the native community, but these experiences and perceptions always include and are an amalgamation of political and historical connotations. (S. Hussain: p. 106)

These experiences and awareness of location of the diaspora writer, according to Rushdie (1991), is an 'access to a second tradition' (p. 124) and a narrative space that has been modified through 'narrations and diversified forms of imagining' (S. Hussain: p. 115).

The South Asian-Australian writers in their short narratives not just present the theme of politics of location – sensory, spatial, gendered, familial, and class, but also hold a mirror to both South Asian colour consciousness and social prejudices and Australian practice of 'insidious forms of racism' (D'Cruz and Steele: p. 19) that can harm the practice of multiculturalism. The noted American writer John Steinbeck (1976) observed that 'a novelist not only puts down a story, but he is a story. He is each one of his characters to a greater or lesser degree.' Since the stories are told from within 'the dominant culture', the hostland or country of migration, 'the engagement with the dominant culture describes the adaptation to dominant forms and its escape and modification at the same time' (S. Hussein: p. 107). These works also deepen our understanding of the ways in which South Asian diasporic communities define and use collective memory to negotiate a sense of origins.

Finally, the chapters also reveal the dilemma of the South Asian diaspora writers regarding the location, their 'inner turmoil and anxieties translated into and finding expression in their creative work' (Riemenschneider: p. 116). As discussed earlier in Chapters 1 and 2, the diasporic discourse with its four-part process of 'displacement, detachment, uprooting and dispersion' (Kirshenblatt-Gimblett: p. 339) becomes stronger in these narratives as the authors explore the processes of displacement and dislocation of identities through migration, journey, settlement, and nostalgic returns and their character's struggle to negotiate locations within Australia. All of the South Asian diaspora writers discussed in the present study are caught between two different cultures and reflect that they are fully at home in none of them. This is because the writers who are '(D)isplaced, uprooted and insecure', according to Terry Eagleton (2005), usually 'clung to the values of order, authority, hierarchy and tradition more tenaciously than some of their less unsettled colleagues' (p. 259). But when this is combined with the fact that they are now in the first world, a more cosmopolitan world if compared with the homelands they had left, it also becomes the source of a richer (multi)cultural tradition that is inextricably linked to a truly 'Australian made'[9] experience that helps them 'cast a more critical eye' on both the homeland and hostland (see also Eagleton: p. 259).

South Asian intellectuals with their understanding and exploration of socio-cultural issues and dilemmas have helped in highlighting South Asian diaspora creative writers who are settled in Britain, United States, Canada, and other countries of their immigration. Similarly, since 1965, beginning with the publication of Mena Abdullah's *The Time of the Peacock*, a literary discourse has developed in the South Asian diaspora in Australia that further adds to cross-cultural studies taking place in South Asia since in these instances 'critics "at home" and writers "in the diaspora" basically belong to the same culture' (Riemenschneider: p. 118). Although South Asian immigrant short story as a genre in multicultural Australia is certainly a great achievement, the present study concludes that it still has a far way to go when compared with writings belonging to other prominent diverse ethnic groups of Australia. Many young South Asian diaspora writers need to build on the flexibility or the power of their stories to challenge the readers about the complexities of life in diaspora and Australia. In conclusion, it can be said that these short stories by South Asian-Australian diaspora writers are no doubt a crucial link in the literary history of Australian immigrant writing and allow, through the politics of location, to secure the *roots* and *routes* of one's journeys and destinations.

Notes

1. The word 'Indian' is used here in the sense of 'Indian Sub-continental' identity.
2. Geraldine Brooks is the 2010 recipient of The Dayton Literary Peace Prize for Lifetime Achievement.
3. Speaking at IIFA ceremony in Sri Lanka, Shashi Tharoor (2010) said Hindi films embody 'the very idea of India's diversity' and are 'part of India's soft power in the world'. He further observed that 'Hindi cinema is perhaps India's most successful brand ambassador internationally. Bollywood is bringing its brand of entertainment not just to the Indian diaspora in the US or UK but around the globe (...)' (http://tharoor.in/press/international-indian-film-awards/).
   Bollywood has a marked and continued presence in Australia and experts see this as just the beginning of a successful long-term relationship between India – the most film literate – and Australia – a professional film industry (see "Bollywood in Australia", 2007; Sarwal and Sarwal, 2009: pp. XXVI–XLIX).

4. The *Racial Discrimination Act* of 1975 protects individuals from discrimination on the grounds of race, colour, descent, or national or ethnic origin. In 1995, the act was extended to make racial vilification against the law in Australia.
5. One such programme is the DIMIA's "Living in Harmony" programme. It is designed to bring into Australian sporting activity the excluded groups by 'aiding and encouraging a host of sporting bodies to promote racial and ethnic tolerance in Australia' (Vamplew: p. 371).
6. The works of South Asian diaspora writers often reflect a 'pervasive and unresolved biculturalism' (Paranjape, 2007: pp. 355–356). Borrowing further from Paranjape from what he observed in relation to the Indian-Canadian writing, the 'passages to India' or the subcontinent or homeland are actually going towards the hostland or Australia.
7. Noted scholar Vinay Lal (2009) observed that the diaspora Indians must display 'greater political awareness' and need to 'make ethical, sensitive and democratic choices, such as forging linkages with other disenfranchised and disadvantaged groups' in the countries of their settlement.
8. On the other hand, the ability of South Asian diaspora in Australia to retain, reconstruct, and revitalize some aspects of their culture and holding on to their cultural differences of race, language, tradition, and religion referred to in the study by R.K. Jain (1993), as 'cultural persistence', is evident because of their earlier isolation and victimization by social prejudices and racism.
9. 'Australian Made' is a label on products found on a supermarket shelf that most often refers to goods and services in an attempt to circumscribe their origins, that is, the item packaged and distributed in Australia.

Bibliography

"A Little Bit Indian, a Little Bit Aussie!" *The Indian Link* August 2012. Web. 15 August 2013 <http://www.indianlink.com.au/a-little-bit-indian- a-little-bit-aussie/>.

Abdullah, Mena, and Ray Mathew. *The Time of the Peacock*. 1965. North Ryde, NSW: Sirius, 1989. Print.

Ahmad, Aijaz. *In Theory: Classes, Nations, Literatures*. London: Verso, 1992. Print.

Ahmad, Rukhsana. "Narratives of Diaspora: Construction of Identity/ Identities in British Asian Literature." *Across Cultures: Issues of Identity in Contemporary British and Sri Lankan Writing*. Ed. Neluka Silva and Rajiva Wijesinha. Colombo: The British Council, 2001. 90–97. Print.

Alatas, Syed Hussein. *The Myth of the Lazy Native*. London: Frank Cass, 1977. Print.

Alexander, Meena. *The Shock of Arrival: Reflections on the Postcolonial Experience*. Boston: South End, 1996. Print.

Alomes, Stephen. "Colonial to Global: Expatriation in Australia's Diasporic Story." *Reading Down Under: Australian Literary Studies Reader*. Ed. Amit Sarwal and Reema Sarwal. New Delhi: SSS Publications, 2009. 381–394. Print.

"An Overview of Australia's Migration Program." July 2013. Web. 18 September 2013 <http://www.immi.gov.au/media/fact-sheets/#migration>.

Anderson, Benedict. *Imagined Communities: Reflections on the Origin and Spread of Nationalism*. 1983. London: Verso, 1991. Print.

"Anglo Indians Pioneers and Prodigies." n.d. Web. 16 March 2006 <http://www.indiaprofile.com/lifestyle/angloindians.htm>.

"Anglo-Indians—Family Tree." n.d. Web. 16 March 2006 <http://www.sumgenius.com.au/index.htm>.

Anthias, Floya. "Boundaries of 'Race' and Ethnicity and Questions about Cultural Belongings." *Racisms in the New World Order Realities of Cultures, Colours and Identity*. Ed. Narayan Gopalkrishnan and Hurriyet Babacan. Newcastle: Cambridge Scholars Publishing, 2007. 12–21. Print.

——. "Evaluating 'Diaspora': Beyond Ethnicity." *Sociology* 32.3 (August 1998): 557–580. Print.

Armstrong, John A. "Mobilized and Proletarian Diasporas." 1976. *Migration, Diasporas and Transnationalism*. Ed. Steven Vertovec and Robin Cohen. Cheltenham: Elgar Reference, 1999. 199–214. Print.

Ashcroft, Bill, Gareth Griffiths, and Helen Tiffin. *The Empire Writes Back*. 1989. London: Routledge, 2002. Print.

Assayag, Jackie, and Véronique Bénéï. "At Home in Diaspora: South Asia, Europe, and America." Introduction. *At Home in Diaspora: South Asian Scholars and the West*. Ed. Jackie Assayag and Véronique Bénéï. Bloomington: Indiana UP, 2003. 1–27. Print.

Assisi, Francis C. "Australia's Anglo-Indians Reclaim the Best of both Worlds." *Overseas Indians* (September 2006). Web. 7 May 2010 <http://www.overseasindian.in/2006/sept/news/11m1.shtml>.

Athique, Tamara Mabbott. "Textual Migrations: South Asian–Australian Fiction." PhD thesis. University of Wollongong, 2006. Web. 7 May 2010 <http://ro.uow.edu.au/cgi/viewcontent.cgi?article=1621&context=theses>.

Australian Bureau of Statistics, Commonwealth of Australia. *A Picture of the Nation*. 2006. Web. 19 April 2010 <http://www.abs.gov.au/ausstats/abs@.nsf/mf/2070.0/>.

——. *Cat. No. 2068.0—2006 Census Tables, Census of Population and Housing*. 2007. Web. 11 July 2009 <http://www.censusdata.abs.gov.au/ ABSNavigation/prenav/PopularAreas?>.

"Australians against Racism & Discrimination." Facebook Group. 20 June 2010. Web. 12 July 2010 <http://www.facebook.com/#!/group.php?gid=33035913111>.

Ayres, Rowan. Opinion piece. *The Weekend Australian* 15–16 November 1997: 7. Print.

Baas, Michiel. *Imagined Mobility: Migration and Transnationalism among Indian Students in Australia*. London: Anthem P, 2010. Print.

——. "Imagined Mobility: Migration and Transnationalism among Indian Students in Australia." PhD thesis. U of Amsterdam, 2009. Print.

Badami, Sunil. "Sticks and Stones and Such Like." *Growing up Asian in Australia*. Ed. Alice Pung. Melbourne: Black Inc., 2008. 9–15. Print.

Bailey, Adrian J. "Turning Transnational: Notes on the Theorisation of International Migration." *International Journal of Population Geography* 7 (2001): 413–428. Print.

Ballard, Roger. "The Impact of Kinship on the Economic Dynamics of Transnational Networks: Reflections on some South Asian Developments." Working Paper. WPTC-01-14. Oxford: Transnational Communities Programme, 2001. Web. 11 June 2010 <http://www.transcomm.ox.ac.uk/working%20papers/Ballard.pdf>.

——. "The Emergence of Desh Pardesh." Introduction. *Desh Pardesh: The South Asian Presence in Britain*. Ed. Roger Ballard. London: Hurst & Co., 1994. 1–34. Print.

Bammer, Angelika. Introduction. *Displacements: Cultural Identities in Question*. Ed. Angelika Bammer. Bloomington: Indiana UP, 1994. xi-xx. Print.

Banchevska, Rachelle. "The Immigrant Family." *The Family in Australia: Social, Demographic and Psychological Aspects*. Ed. Jerzy Krupinski and Alan Stoller. 1974. 2nd ed. Rushcutters Bay, NSW: Pergamon, 1978. 176–184. Print.

"Bangladesh Australia Association, Canberra." 12 March 2010. Web. 5 May 2010 <http://www.canberrabashi.org.au/>.

"Bangladeshis in Australia." 2 March 2010. Web. 5 May 2010 <http://en.wikipedia.org/wiki/Bangladeshis_in_Australia>.

Bartholomeusz, Derek. *Tamil Tigress*. Perth: Ambit, 1997. Print.

Bates, Crispin. "Community and Identity among South Asians in Diaspora." Introduction. *Community, Empire and Migration: South Asians in Diaspora*. Hyderabad: Orient Longman, 2001. 1–45. Print.

Bennett, Bruce. "A Family Closeness: Australia, India, Indonesia." *Australian Studies Now: An Introductory Reader in Australian Studies*. Ed. Andrew Hassam and Amit Sarwal. New Delhi: Indialog, 2007. 328–341. Print.

——. *Australian Short Fiction: A History*. St Lucia: U of Queensland P, 2002.

Berdahl, Daphne. "(N)Ostalgie" for the Present: Memory, Longing, and East German Things." *Ethnos* 64.2 (1999): 192–211. Print.

Bhabha, Homi K. "Cultural Diversity and Cultural Differences." 1988. *The Post-colonial Studies Reader*. Ed. Bill Ashcroft, Gareth Griffiths, and Helen Tiffin. 2nd ed. New York: Routledge, 2006. 155–157. Print.

——. *The Location of Culture*. New York: Routledge, 1994. Print.

Bhandari, Neena. "Indians Aren't the Only Ones to have been Attacked: Police." 2 June 2009. Web. 10 June 2010 <http://www.

thaindian.com/newsportal/world-news/indians-arent-the-only-ones-to-have-been-attacked-police_100199966.html>.

——. "Australia Commends Indian Diaspora's Contribution." 23 June 2008. Web. 10 June 2010 <http://www.thaindian.com/newsportal/world-news/australia-commends-indian-diasporas-contribution_10063280.html>.

Bhattacharjee, Anannya. "The Habit of Ex-Nomination: Nation, Woman, and the Indian Immigrant Bourgeoisie." *A Patchwork Shawl: Chronicles of South Asian Women in America*. Ed. Shamita Das Dasgupta. New Brunswick, NJ: Rutgers UP, 1998. 163–185. Print.

Bhatti, Rashmere, and Verne A. Dusenbery, eds. *A Punjabi Sikh Community in Australia: From Indian Sojourners to Australian Citizens*. Woolgoola, NSW: Woolgoolga Neighbourhood Centre, 2001. Web. 25 April 2007 <http://www.apnaorg.com/books/sikhs–in– australia/>.

Bhatti, Rashmere. "The Good Indian Girl." *Who Do You Think You Are? Second Generation Immigrant Women in Australia*. Ed. Karen Herne, Joanne Travaglia, and Elizabeth Weiss. Broadway, NSW: Women's Redress P, 1992. 131–136. Print.

"Bhutanese Community Profile." 5 June 2007. Web. 3 May 2010 <http://www.immi.gov.au/living-in-australia/delivering-assistance/government-programs/settlement-planning/_pdf/community-profile-bhutan.pdf>.

Bilimoria, Purushottama, and Carmen Voigt-Graf. "Indians." *The Australian People: An Encyclopedia of the Nation, its People and their Origins*. Ed. James Jupp. Cambridge: Cambridge UP, 2001. 426–434. Print.

Bilimoria, Purushottama, and Ruchira Ganguly-Scrase. *Indians in Victoria (Australia): A Historical, Social and Demographic Profile of Indian Immigrants*. Melbourne: Deakin U and Victorian Ethnic Affairs Commission, 1988. Print.

Bilimoria, Purushottama. *The Hindus and Sikhs in Australia*. Carlton South, Victoria: Bureau of Immigration, Multiculturalism and Population Research, 1996. Print.

Bitel, David. "Perceptions of Bangladeshis Living in Australia of Jews, Israel and the Conflict in the Middle East." Paper Presentation. Conference on "Anti-Semitism in the Contemporary World." Melbourne, 6–7 February 2005. Web. 10 March 2006 <www.parishpatience. com.au/immigration/antisem.pdf>.

Blunt, Alison. *Domicile and Diaspora: Anglo-Indian Women and the Spatial Politics of Home*. Malden, MA: Blackwell, 2005. Print.

Bolt, Andrew. "Racism is here, in many Guises." *Herald Sun* 29 January 2010. Web. 13 August 2010 <http://www.heraldsun.com.au/opinion/racism-is-here-in-many-guises/story-e6frfhqf-1225824479463>.

—–. "We're Not the Racists." *Herald Sun* 3 June 2009. Web. 13 August 2010 <http://www.heraldsun.com.au/opinion-old/were-not-the-racists/story-e6frfifo-1225720517445>.

Bonnett, Alaistair. *Anti-racism*. London: Routledge, 2000.

Boyarin, J. *Storm from Paradise: The Politics of Jewish Memory*. Bloomington: Indiana UP, 1992. Print.

Boym, Svetlana. *The Future of Nostalgia*. New York: Basic Books, 2002. Print.

Braakman, Marije, and Angela Schlenkhoff. "Between Two Worlds: Feelings of Belonging While in Exile and the Question of Return." *ASIEN* 104 (July 2007): 9–22. Print.

Braakman, Marije. "Roots and Routes: Questions of Home, Belonging and Return in an Afghan Diaspora." MA thesis. Leiden U, 2005. Print.

Brah, Avtar. "Diaspora, Border and Transnational Identities." *Feminist Postcolonial Theory: A Reader*. Ed. Reina Lewis and Sara Mills. Edinburgh: Edinburgh UP, 2003. 613–634.

—–. *Cartographies of Diaspora*. London: Routledge, 1996. Print.

Braziel, Jana Evans, and Anita Mannur. "Nation, Migration, Globalization: Points of Contention in Diaspora Studies." *Theorizing Diaspora: A Reader*. Ed. Jana Evans Braziel, and Anita Mannur. Malden: Blackwell, 2003. 1–22. Print.

Broinowski, Alison. Foreword. *Celebrations: Fifty Years of Sri Lanka-Australia Interactions*. Ed. C.A. Vanden Driesen, and I.H. Vanden Driesen. Colombo: Government Printer, 1997. xvi-xvii. Print.

—–. *The Yellow Lady: Australian impressions of Asia*. London: Oxford University Press, 1992. Print.

Bromley, Roger. "The Third Scenario." Introduction. *Narratives for a New Belonging: Diasporic Cultural Fictions*. Edinburgh: Edinburgh UP, 2000. 1–16. Print.

Brooks, Geraldine. *People of the Book*. New York: Penguin, 2008. Print.

"Burgher People." n.d. Web. 16 March 2006 <http://en.wikipedia.org/wiki/Burgher_people>.

"Burghers." n.d. Web. 16 March 2006 <http://www13.brinkster.com/tormel/burghers.html>.

Butler, Kim D. "Defining Diaspora, Refining a Discourse." *Diaspora* 10.2 (2001): 189–219. Print.

Cameron, Hannah. "An Examination of the Demographic Impact of 'Transnational Marriage' between Citizens of the UK and the Indian Subcontinent." Paper presentation. Conference on "Political Demography: Ethnic, National and Religious Dimensions." London School of Economics, 29–30 September 2006. Web.

Carter, David. "Literary Canons and Literary Institutions." *Southerly* 57.3 (1997): 16–37. Print.

Carter, Marina, and Khal Torabully. *Coolitude: An Anthology of the Indian Labour Diaspora*. London: Anthem P, 2002. Print.

Carter, Paul. "Lines of Communication: Meaning in the Migrant Environment." *Striking Chords: Multicultural Literary Interpretations*. Ed. Sneja Gunew and Kateryna O. Longley. Sydney: Allen & Unwin, 1992. 9–18. Print.

Casimiro, Suzy, Peter Hancock, and Jeremy Northcote. "Isolation and Insecurity: Resettlement Issues among Muslim Refugee Women in Perth, Western Australia." *Australian Journal of Social Issues* (2007). Web. 15 March 2010 <http://www.accessmylibrary.com/article-1G1-163197876/isolation-and-insecurity-resettlement.html>.

Castan, Con. "Ethnic Australian Writing. Is it Really Australian Literature?" *Outrider* 3.2 (December 1986): 64–79. Print.

Castles, Stephen. "The 'New' Migration and Australian Immigration Policy." *Asians in Australia: The Dynamics of Migration and Settlement*. Ed. Christine Inglis et al. Singapore: ISEAS, 1992. 45–72. Print.

Chambers, Iain. *Migrancy, Culture, Identity*. New York: Routledge, 1994. Print.

Chandrasekhar, S. *From India to Australia: A Brief History of Immigration; The Dismantling of the "White Australia" Policy; Problems and Prospects of Assimilation*. La Jolla, CA: Population Review, 1992. Print.

Chow, Rey. *Writing Diaspora: Tactics of Intervention in Contemporary Cultural Studies*. Bloomington: Indiana UP, 1993. Print.

Clark, John. "Australia's Recent Visual Art Exchanges with Asia." *Australia and Asia: Cultural Transactions*. Ed. Maryanne Dever. Surrey: Curzon P, 1997. 196–215. Print.

Clarke, C. et al. *South Asians Overseas*. Cambridge: Cambridge UP, 1990. Print.

Cleland, Bilal. *The Muslims in Australia: A Brief History*. Melbourne: Islamic Council of Victoria, 2002. Print.

Clifford, James. *Routes: Travel and Translation in Late Twentieth Century*. Cambridge, MA: Cambridge UP, 1997. Print.

——. "Diasporas." *Cultural Anthropology* 9.3 (1994): 302–338. Print.

Cohen, Erez. "Voices of Our Land—Ethnic Radio and the Complexity of Diasporic Practices in Multicultural Australia." *Migrants, Strangers and Purple Bananas: Latin American Migrants in Spain, Australia and the United States*. Ed. Peter Read and Marivic Wyndham. Spec. issue of *Humanities Research* 10.1 (2003): 17–40. Print.

Cohen, Phil. "RE-thinking the Diasporama." *Patterns of Prejudice* 33.1 (1999): 302–338. Print.

Cohen, Robin. "Diasporas and the Nation States: From Victims to Challengers." *Ethnicity and International Relations*. Spec. issue of *International Affairs* 72.3 (July 1996): 507–520. Print.

Commercial Wing, Bangladesh High Commission. "Trade and Investment Opportunities in Bangladesh." Seminar Report. Monash University, Melbourne 7 November 2005. Web. 10 March 2006 <users.cyberone.com.au/bdeshact/Monash%20Report.pdf>.

"Conference on Australasia's Diaspora." News Release. 7 July 2004. Web. 28 March 2005 <http://www.ausgovindia.com/public/news/2004/7july.htm>.

Corkhill, Annette R. *The Immigrant Experience in Australian Literature*. Melbourne: Academia P, 1995. Print.

——. *Australian Writing: Ethnic Writers 1945–1991*. Melbourne: Academia P, 1994. Print.

Cornell, Stephen, and Douglas Hartman. *Ethnicity and Race: Making Identities in a Changing World*. Thousand Oaks, CA: Pine Forge P, 1998. Print.

Coronado, Gabriela. "Crossing Borders and Transforming Identities: Encountering Diasporic Mexicanness in Australia." *Migrants, Strangers and Purple Bananas: Latin American Migrants in Spain, Australia and the United States*. Ed. Peter Read and Marivic Wyndham. Spec. Issue of *Humanities Research* 10.1 (2003): 41–52. Print.

Crane, Ralph. "A Raj Connection: Anglo-Indian Fiction in Australia." *Reading Down Under: Australian Literary Studies Reader*. Ed. Amit Sarwal and Reema Sarwal. New Delhi: SSS Publications, 2009. 371–380. Print.

Cyrill, Christopher. Interview with Tamara Mabbott Athique. 19 November 2003. "Textual Migrations: South Asian-Australian Fiction." Tamara Mabbott Athique. PhD thesis. U of Wollongong, 2006. 286–304. Print.

——. "Dusk and the Public." *Heat* 15 (2000): 7–18. Print.

——. "Pestlesongs." *Picador New Writing 4*. Ed. N. Jose and B. Yahp. Sydney: Pan Macmillan Australia, 1997. 178–182. Print.

——. "What Withers and What Remains." Ed. Matthew Condon and Richard Lawson. *Smashed: Australian Drinking Stories*. Milsons Point, NSW: Random House, 1996. 173–179. Print.

——. "The Ganges and its Tributaries." *Meanjin* 52.1 (1993a): 157–168. Print.

——. Interview with Steve Womersley. *Australian Book Review* 154 (September 1993b): 24–25. Print.

D'Cruz, Glenn. "Beyond the Pale." *Meanjin* 63.2 (2004): 223–230. Print.

——. " 'Representing' Anglo-Indians: A Genealogical Investigation." PhD thesis, U of Melbourne, 1999. Print.

D'Cruz, J.V. "White Australia and Indian Mutiny." *The Asian Image in Australia*. Melbourne: The Hawthorn P, 1973. 11–31. Print.

D'Cruz, J.V., and William Steele. *Australia's Ambivalence towards Asia*. Clayton: Monash UP, 2003. Print.

D'souza, Radha. '"International Community": What an Intriguing Idea!!', 16 April 2002. Web. 18 November 2008 <http://www.arena.org.nz/ vasudeva.htm>.

——. "Riding High." *Span* 45 (October 1997): 94–102. Print.

Dabydeen, Cyril. *The Wizard Swami*. Calcutta: Writers Workshop, 1985. Print.

Dale, David. "The Next Big Trend in Immigration: They're Indians." *The Sydney Morning Herald* (Weekend Edition) 22–23 January 2005: 11. Print.

Datar, Manik. "If I were a Teller of Tales." *Manushi* (December 2002): 20–24. Print.

——. "My Sister's Mother." *Quadrant* (October 1995a): 75–77. Print.

——. "Point of No Return." *Voices* (1995b): 83–88. Print.

Dayan, D. "Particularistic Media and Diasporic Communities." *Media, Ritual and Identity*. Ed. T. Liebes and J. Curran. London: Routledge, 1998. 103–113. Print.

de Certeau, Michel. *The Practice of Everyday Life*. Berkley: U of California P, 1988. Print.

De Jong, Tania. *Complexities of the Sri Lankan Migrants in Australia*. Pascoe Vale South, Victoria: Slam Publishing Service, 1987. Print.

De Kretser, Michelle. "Life with Sea Views." *Penguin Australian Summer Stories 3*. Ed. Clare Forster. Ringwood, Vic: Penguin, 2000. 1–13. Print.

De Lepervanche, Marie. "Early Indian Workers in the Australian Colonies." *Limits of Location—Creating a Colony*. Ed. Gretchen Poiner and Sybil Jack. Sydney: Sydney UP, 2007. 99–116. Print.

——. "Fieldwork in Woolgoolga." Chapter Four. *A Punjabi Sikh Community in Australia: From Indian Sojourners to Australian Citizens*. Ed. Rashmere Bhatti and Verne A. Dusenbery. Woolgoola, NSW: Woolgoolga Neighbourhood Centre, 2001. Web. 25 April 2007 <http://www.apnaorg.com/books/sikhs-in-australia/>.

——. *Indians in a White Australia*. Sydney: Allen & Unwin, 1984. Print.

——. "Australian Immigrants 1788–1940: Desired and Unwanted." *Essays in the Political Economy of Australian Capitalism*. Ed. E.L. Wheelwright and K. Buckley. Vol. 1. Sydney: ANZ Book Co., 1975. 72–104. Print.

Deen, Hanifa. "Courage in all Its Different Guises." Speech given at Islamic Women's Welfare Council AGM. 2005. Web. 12 April 2010 <http://www.hanifadeen.com/Musings_CourageInAllItsGuises.htm>.

——. "Travels Among Australian Muslims." Interview with Rachael Kohn. *The Ark* (Radio National) 24 September 2003. Web. 23 April 2010 <http://www.abc.net.au/rn/relig/ark/stories/s949099.htm>.

——. "On Reinventing Oneself." 2001. Web. 12 April 2010 <http://www.hanifadeen.com/Musings_OnReinventingOneself.htm>.

——. *Caravanserai: Journey among Australian Muslims*. St Leonards, NSW: Allen & Unwin, 1995. Print.

——. "Curry, Crusades and Scripture." *Who Do You Think You Are? Second Generation Immigrant Women in Australia*. Ed. Karen Herne, Joanne Travaglia, and Elizabeth Weiss. Broadway, NSW: Women's Redress P, 1992. 139–141. Print.

Delgado, Richard. Introduction. *Critical Race Theory: The Cutting Edge*. Ed. Richard Delgado. Philadelphia: Temple UP, 1995. xiii-xvi. Print.

Desai, Meghnad. *Development and Nationhood: Essays in the Political Economy of South Asia*. New Delhi: Oxford UP, 2005. Print.

Dhungel, Basundhara. "A Study of Nepalese Families' Paid and Unpaid Work after Migration to Australia." MPhil disst. U of Sydney, 2000. Print.

DIMIA. "Chapter One—The Policy Context." Web. 10 March 2006 <www.immi.gov.au/settle/settle_review/pdfs/chap01web.pdf>.

——. "Key Highlights: Economic Impact of Migration." *DIMIA Annual Report 2002–03*. 2004. Web. 17 July 2010 <http://www.immi.gov.au/ about/reports/annual/2002-03/report14.htm>.

——. "The Indian Born Community—Historical Background." *Community Information Summary*. Jointly produced by Multicultural Affairs

Branch and the Economic and Demographic Analysis Section of DIMIA. Web. 16 March 2006 <http://www.immi.gov.au/statistics/ infosummary/source.htm>.

——. "The Sri Lankan Born Community." *Community Information Summary 2003*. Multicultural Affairs Branch and the Economic and Demographic Analysis Section of DIMIA. 9 March 2006. Web. 11 July 2009 <http://www.immi.gov.au/statistics/infosummary/source. htm>.\

——. *National Agenda for a Multicultural Australia*. 1989. Web. 16 June 2010 <http://www.immi.gov.au/media/publications/multicultural/agenda/agenda89/whydowen.htm>.

Dixit, Sheryl, and Rajni Anand Luthra. "Record Number of Candidates in the Fray." *The Indian Link* (September 2013): 14–16. Print.

Docker, John. *1492: The Poetics of Diaspora*. London: Continuum, 2001. Print.

Dorais, Louis-Jacques. "Defining the Overseas Vietnamese." *Diaspora* 10.1 (2001): 3–28. Print.

Dufty, David, et al., eds. *Seeing it Their Way: Ideas, Activities and Resources for Intercultural Studies and Looking Around Corners—The Intercultural Explorers Guide*. Sydney: Reed Educational, 1973. Print.

"Dumb, Drunk and Racist." ABC. Web. 15 May 2013 <http://www.abc.net. au/tv/dumbdrunkracist/>.

Dunn, Kevin M. *Racism in Australia: Findings of a Survey on Racist Attitudes and Experiences of Racism, National Europe Centre Paper No. 77*. Sydney: U of Sydney P, 2003. Print.

Eade, J. "Roots and Routes: British Bengalis and Questions of Homeland." *Roots and Routes: Ethnicity and Migration in Global Perspective*. Ed. Shalva Weil. Jerusalem: The Magnes P, 1999. 23–44. Print.

Eagleton, Terry. *The English Novel: An Introduction*. Malden, MA: Blackwell, 2005. Print.

East Indian Club of Melbourne. *A Passage from India: Anglo-Indians in Victoria*. Melbourne: Immigration Museum, 2004. Print.

"85% Australians Feel Racism Exists in Australia." *Times of India* 24 June 2009. Web. 20 June 2010 <http://timesofindia.indiatimes.com/World/Rest-of-World/85-Australians-feel-racism-exists-in-Australia/articleshow/4696418.cms>.

Emirbayer, Mustafa, and Ann Mische. "What is Agency?" *American Journal of Sociology* 103 (1998): 962–1023. Print.

Endagama, Pandula. "Sri Lankan Material Culture in North-East Queensland—A Study of Acculturation." Certificate Diploma of Material Culture. James Cook University, 1981.

Evans, Stephen. "Is Australia too Immature to Examine its Racism?" *The Punch* 25 June 2009. 12 June 2010 <http://www.thepunch.com.au/tags/sol-trujillo/>.

Faria, Ana Ivete. "The Future of Indian Ethnicity in Australia—An Educational and Cultural Perspective." *International Education Journal* 2.4 (2001): 134–143. Web. 12 May 2009 <http://www.flinders.edu. au/education/iej>.

FECCA. "Pakistan." 2005. Web. 2 January 2006 <http://www.fecca.org.au/World%20Views/Countries/Pakistan.html>.

——. "Sri Lanka." Web. 10 March 2006 <http://www.fecca.org.au/World%20Views/Countries/Srilanka.html>.

Ferdinands, Rodney. *Proud and Prejudiced: The Story of the Burghers of Sri Lanka*. Melbourne: R. Ferdinands, 1995. Print.

Ferguson, Niall. *Empire: How Britain Made the Modern World*. London: Allen Lane, 2003. Print.

Fernandes, Sujhatha. "A Pocket Full of Stories." *Waiting in Space: An Anthology of Australian Writing*. Ed. Paula Abood, Barry Gamba, and Michelle Kotevski. Annandale, NSW: Pluto, 1999. 90–94. Print.

Fernando, Chitra. *Women There and Here: Progressions in Six Stories*. Stanmore, NSW: Wordlink, 1994. Print.

——. *Between Worlds*. Calcutta: Writers Workshop, 1988. Print.

Fijac, Bianca M., and Christopher C. Sonn. "Pakistani-Muslim Immigrant Women in Western Australia: Perceptions of Identity and Community." 2004. Web. 15 March 2010 <http://eprints.vu.edu.au/ 403/1/Fijacsonn.pdf>.

Flannery, Timothy. *The Future Eaters: An Ecological History of the Australasian Lands and People*. 1994. New York: Grove P, 2002. Print.

Fludernik, Monika. "The Diasporic Imaginary: Postcolonial Reconfigurations in the Context of Multiculturalism." Introduction. *Diaspora and Multiculturalism: Common Traditions and New Developments*. Ed. Monika Fludernik. New York: Amsterdam, 2003a. xi-xxxviii. Print.

——. "Imagined Communities as Imaginary Homelands: The South Asian Diaspora in Fiction." *Diaspora and Multiculturalism: Common Traditions and New Developments*. Ed. Monika Fludernik. New York: Amsterdam, 2003b. 261–285. Print.

Forrest, Simon. "SANFL Introduces Indian Migrants to Australian Rule." *Multicultural South Australia*. Government of South Australia. October 2009. Web. 15 April 2010 <http://www.multicultural.sa.gov.au/IndianIntrotoAussieRules.htm>.

Francis, Daniel. *National Dreams: Myth, Memory, and Canadian History*. Vancouver: Pulp, 1997. Print.

Friedman, Jonathan. "From Roots to Routes: Tropes for Trippers." *Anthropological Theory* 2.1 (2002): 21–36. Print.

Gabbi, Rajender Singh. *Sikhs in Australia*. Glen Waverly, Victoria: Aristoc, 1998. Print.

Gallop, Geoff. "Premier's Foreword." *A Changing People: Diverse Contributions to the State of Western Australia*. Ed. Raelene Wilding and Farida Tilbury. Perth: Department of the Premier and Cabinet, 2004. 2–3. Print.

Ganguly, Keya. "Migrant Identities: Personal Memory and the Construction of Selfhood." *Cultural Studies* 6.1 (1992): 27–50. Print.

Gantner, C. Opening Address. National Summit on "Studies of Asia in Australian Schools at a Crossroad: Strategic Directions 2004–2006." Canberra, November 2003. Web.

Gelder, Ken, and Paul Salzman. *After the Celebration: Australian Fiction 1989–2007*. Carlton, Victoria: Melbourne UP, 2009. Print.

George, Rosemary Marangoly. *The Politics of Home: Postcolonial Relocations and Twentieth Century Fiction*. Cambridge: Cambridge UP, 1996. Print.

Ghosh, Jaydeep. "Facebook Group Asks Immigrants to Leave Oz." *Hindustan Times* (*Sunday Times* supplement) 14 June 2009: 1. Print.

Gilligan, Chris. "The Racism that Dare not Speak Its Name." Rev. of Liz Fekete's *A Suitable Enemy*. *The Spiked Review of Books* 30 (December 2009). Web. 23 April 2010 <http://www.spiked-online.com/ index.php/site/reviewofbooks_article/7877/>.

Gilroy, Paul. *The Black Atlantic*. Cambridge, MA: Harvard UP, 1993. Print.

——. '"It ain't where you're from, it's where you're at": The Dialectics of Diasporic Identification'. *Third Text* 13 (1991): 3–17. Print.

Gooneratne, Yasmine. *Masterpiece and Other Stories*. New Delhi: Indialog, 2002. Print.

——. "Bharat changes His Image.' *Rubicon* 1.2 (1995): 45–53. Print.

——. "In the East My Pleasure: A Postcolonial Love Story." *Span* 34–35 (1992–1993a): 269–279. Print.

——. "Navaranjini Takes Note of Signs and Visions." *Wilder Shores: Women's Travel Stories of Australia and Beyond*. Ed. Robin Lucas, and Clare Forster. St. Lucia: U of Queensland P, 1992b. 36–41. Print.

——. *A Change of Skies*. Chippendale, NSW: Picador, 1991. Print.

Goonewardene, Shelagh. "The Pain of Leave Taking." *Australian Multicultural Book Review* 5.2 (1997a): 6–7. Print.

——. "A Migrant Dreams." *Celebrations: Fifty Years of Sri Lanka-Australia Interactions*. Ed. C.A. Vanden Driesen and I.H. Vanden Driesen. Colombo: Government Printer, 1997b. 283–284. Print.

Gopalkrishnan, Narayan, and Hurriyet Babacan. Introduction. *Racisms in the New World Order Realities of Cultures, Colours and Identity*. Ed. Narayan Gopalkrishnan and Hurriyet Babacan. Newcastle: Cambridge Scholars Publishing, 2007. 1–10. Print.

Gordon, Milton. *Assimilation in American Life: The Role of Race, Religion and National Origins*. New York: Oxford UP, 1964. Print.

Govinnage, Sunil. "The Vanished Trails." *Postcolonial Studies* 8.1 (January 2005): 75–79. Print.

——. *Black Swans and Other Stories*. New York: Writers' Showcase, 2002.

Gray, Stephen. "A Sense of Place in the New Literatures in English, Particularly South African" *A Sense of Place in the New Literatures in English*. Ed. Peggy Nightingale. St Lucia, Queensland: U of Queensland P, 1986. 5–12. Print.

Griffiths, Phil. "Racism: Whitewashing the Class Divide." *Class and Struggle in Australia*. Ed. Rick Kuhn. Sydney: Pearson, 2005. 160–175. Print.

Hage, Ghassan. "Multicultural Situations." *Postcolonial Studies* 8.4 (2005): 491–495. Print.

——. *Arab-Australians: Citizenship and Belonging Today*. Melbourne: Melbourne UP, 2002. Print.

——. *White Nation*. Annandale, NSW: Pluto P, 1998. Print.

——. "At Home in the Entrails of the West: Multiculturalism, 'Ethnic Food' and Migrant Home-building." *Home/World: Space, Community and Marginality in Sydney's West*. Ed. H. Grace et al. Sydney: Pluto P, 1997. 99–153. Print.

Hall, Stuart. "Thinking the Diaspora: Home-Thoughts from Abroad." *Postcolonialisms: An Anthology of Cultural Theory and Criticism*. Ed. Gaurav Desai and Supriya Nair. Oxford: Berg, 2005. 543–560. Print.

——. "Conclusion: The Multi-cultural Question." *Un/Settled Multiculturalisms: Diasporas, Entanglements, "Transruptions."* Ed. Barnor Hesse. London: Zed Books, 2000. 209–241. Print.

Haque, Md. Shahidul. "Migration trends and Patterns in South Asia and Management Approaches and Initiatives." Paper presentation. "Regional Seminar on the Social Implications of International Migration." Bangkok, 24 August 2005. Web. 18 July 2010 <www.unescap.org/esid/psis/meetings/siim/TrendsPatterns.pdf>.

Harper, Melissa, and Richard White. "Land of Symbols." *Symbols of Australia: Uncovering the Stories behind the Myths*. Ed. Melissa

Harper and Richard White. Sydney: U of New South Wales P and National Museum of Australia P, 2009. 1–12. Print.

Harvey, David. "From Space to Place and Back Again: Reflections on the Condition of Postmodernity." *Mapping the Futures: Local Cultures, Global Change*. Ed. John Bird, Barry Curtis, Tim Putnam, George Robertson, and Lisa Tickner. London: Routledge, 1993. 3–29. Print.

Hassan, Ghali. "Rising Tide of Xenophobia: Australia's Shallow Multiculturalism." *Global Research* 27 September 2005. Web. 23 April 2010 <http://www.globalresearch.ca/index.php?context=viewArticle &code=HAS20050927&articleId=1011>.

Hassan, Riaz. "Pakistanis." *The Australian People: An Encyclopedia of the Nation, its People and their Origins*. Ed. James Jupp. Cambridge: Cambridge UP, 2001. 615. Print.

Hassan, S.A. *Australia for Pakistanis: Where Cultures Meet*. Sydney: Tribune, 2003. Print.

Hayes, Brian. Foreword. *Colonial Cousins: A Surprising History of Connections between India and Australia*. Joyce Westrip and Peggy Holroyde. Kent Town, South Australia: Wakefield P, 2010. XI-XII. Print.

Head, Mike. "Australian Government's "Terrorist" Case against Dr Haneef Unravels." 20 July 2007. Web. 17 May 2010 <http://www.wsws.org/articles/2007/jul2007/hane-j20.shtml>.

Healy, Guy. "Sociologist Investigates Attacks on Overseas Students." *The Australian* 3 February 2010. Web. 15 March 2010 <http://www.theaustralian.com.au/higher-education/sociologist-investi gates-attacks-on-overseas-students/story-e6frgcjx-1225826089 308>.

Helff, Sissy. *Unreliable Truths: Transcultural Homeworlds in Indian Women's Fiction of the Diaspora*. Amsterdam/New York: Rodopi, 2013. Print.

——. "Locating Indo-Australian Fiction in Multicultural Australia." *Australian Made: A Multicultural Reader*. Ed. Sonia Mycak and Amit Sarwal. Sydney: Sydney UP, 2010. 128–150. Print.

——. "Indian-Australian Literature." *Muse India* 24 (Mach-April 2009). Web. 25 June 2009 <http://www.museindia.com/showfeature13. asp?id=1209>.

Henderson, Deborah. "Reconceptualising Our Cultural Maps: Teaching for Cross-Cultural Understanding through the Studies of Asia." *The Social Educator: Journal of the Social Educators Association of Australia* 22.2 (June 2004): 5–11. Print.

"Hindu Council of Australia." n.d. Web. 16 March 2006 <http://jains.australians.com/>.

"History of Immigration from Bangladesh." n.d. Web. 2 May 2010 <http://search.museum.vic.gov.au/origins/history.aspx?pid=4&cat=none&cid=0>.

"History of Immigration from Pakistan." n.d. Web. 2 May 2010 <http://search.museum.vic.gov.au/origins/history.aspx?pid=44>.

"HM Birthday Celebrations in Sydney." n.d. Web. 12 March 2006 <http://www.australiabhutan.org.bt/abfanews.htm#HM%20birthday%20celebrations%20in%20Sydney>.

Hodge, Bob, and Vijay Mishra. *Dark Side of the Dream: Australian Literature and the Postcolonial Mind*. North Sydney, NSW: Allen & Unwin, 1991. Print.

Horst, Cindy. "Transnational Dialogues: Developing Ways to do Research in a Diasporic Community." *Working Paper*. WPTC-02-13. Oxford: Transnational Communities Programme, 2002. Web. 10 June 2010 <http://www.transcomm.ox.ac.uk/working%20papers/horst1.pdf>.

Huggan, Graham. *Australian Literature: Postcolonialism, Racism, Transnationalism*. Oxford: Oxford UP, 2007. Print.

Hugo, Graeme. "Knocking at the Door: Asian Immigration to Australia." *Asian and Pacific Migration Journal* 1.1 (1992): 100–144. Print.

Human Rights and Equal Opportunity Commission. *Isma—Listen: National Consultations on Eliminating Prejudice against Arab and Muslim Australians*. Sydney: HEROC, 2003. Web. 17 August 2010 <http://www.hreoc.gov.au/racial_discrimination/isma/report/pdf/ISMA_complete.pdf>.

Hussain, Intizar. "A Chronicle of the Peacocks." 1999. *Individual and the Society: Essays, Stories and Poems*. Ed. Vinay Sood et al. New Delhi: Pearson, 2005. 181–193. Print.

Hussain, Sabina. "Label and Literature: Borders and Spaces in Postcolonial Migrant Literature in Australia." *JASAL* 3 (2004): 103–116. Print.

Hussain, Yasmin. *Writing Diaspora: South Asian Women, Culture and Ethnicity*. Hampshire: Ashgate, 2005. Print.

"I am Australian and I would rather Immigrants Living here than Racists." Facebook Group. 2010. Web. 17 July 2010 <http://www.facebook.com/#!/group.php?gid=121223051227626>.

"Immigration to Australia." 9 March 2006. Web. 10 March 2006 <http://en.wikipedia.org/wiki/Immigration_to_Australia>.

"Indian Arrival in Australia." n.d. Web. 16 March 2006 <http://indians.australians.com/INDIAN-ARRIVAL-IN-AUSTRALIA.htm>.

"Indian Arrival in Australia: Sikhs in Australia." 20 March 2003. Web. 16 May 2005 <http://www.sikh.com.au/inaus/index.html?arrival.html~bottomaus>.

"Indian Diaspora—A Short History." n.d. Web. 28 March 2005 <http://www.goacom.com/overseas-digest/Asian%20Diaspora/history.html>.

"Indian-born Community in Australia." n.d. Web. 16 March 2006 <http://www.sumgenius.com.au/indianborn_community_in_australia.htm>.

"Indian-origin Candidates in Fray in Australia Elections." *Economic Times* 7 August 2013. Web. 2 September 2013 <http://articles.economictimes.indiatimes.com/2013-08-07/news/41167727_1_wikileaks-party-senate-candidates-seven-candidates>.

"Indians in Australia (Anglo Indians)." n.d. Web. 16 March 2006 <http://indians.australians.com/anglo-indians.htm>.

Inglis, Christine, and Chung-Tong Wu. "The 'New' Migration of Asian Skills and Capital to Australia." *Asians in Australia: The Dynamics of Migration and Settlement.* Ed. Christine Inglis et al. Singapore: ISEAS, 1992. 193–230. Print.

Inglis, Christine. "On the Beach: Racial Confrontation in Australia." February 2006. Web. 19 April 2010 <http://www.migrationinformation.org/Feature/display.cfm?ID=377>.

Israel, Milton. "Transformations of the Sikh Diaspora." *Diaspora* 1.3 (1991): 373–384. Print.

Jacobs, Lyn. "About Face: Asian-Australians at Home." *Australian Literary Studies* 20.3 (2002): 201–214. Print.

Jain, Jasbir. "The New Parochialism: Homeland in the Writing of the Indian Diaspora." *In Diaspora*. Ed. Makarand Paranjape. New Delhi: Indialog, 2001. 79–92. Print.

Jain, R.K. "Culture and Class in Indian Diaspora: India vs Bharat." *Economic and Political Weekly* 28 April 2001: 1380–81. Print.

——. *Indian Communities Abroad: Themes and Literature.* Delhi: Manohar, 1993. Print.

Jain, Surinder. "Is it an Ancient Temple or Just Cave Rock Formations?—A Documentary." 2005. Web. 16 March 2006 <http://www. mosman.com/cavetemple/>.

"Jains in Australia." n.d. Web. 16 March 2006 <http://jains.australians.com/>.

Jaireth, Subhash. "Cricket Ball." *Conversations* 6.2 (2006): 79–89. Print.

——. "The Bridge near Firozepur." *Meanjin* 62.4 (2003): 61–70. Print.

——. "Remembering Dehlie." *Under Construction*. Spec. issue of *Meanjin* 1 (2001): 13–22. Print.

——. "Maps, Photographs, Paintings: A Story-Essay about Seeing and Telling." *Unfinished Journeys: India File from Canberra*. Ed. Debjani Ganguly and Kavita Nandan. New Delhi: CRNLE and PIP, 1998. 255–267. Print.

James, Sheila Pais. "Anglo–Indians: The Dilemma of Identity." Paper Presentation. "Counterpoints: Flinders University Postgraduate Conference." South Australia, 19–20 April 2001. Web. 10 May 2010 <http://home.alphalink.com.au/~agilbert/dilemma1.html>.

Jayaram, N. "Introduction: The Study of Indian Diaspora." *The Indian Diaspora: Dynamics of Migration*. Ed. N. Jayaram, New Delhi: Sage, 2004. 15–43. Print.

Jayasuriya, Laksiri, and Kee Pookong. *The Asianisation of Australia?—Some Facts about the Myths*. Melbourne: Melbourne UP, 1999. Print.

Jayasuriya, Laksiri. *Transforming a 'White' Australia: Issues of Racism and Immigration*. New Delhi: SSS Publications, 2012. Print.

——. "Australian Multiculturalism Reframed." *The New Critic* 8 (September 2008): 1–5. Web. 28 June 2009 <http://www.ias.uwa.edu.au/ new-critic>.

Jhala, Rani. "Life's Key." *Australian Multicultural Book Review* 6.1 (1999): 21–2. Print.

Jin, Ha. *The Writer as Migrant*. Chicago, IL: U of Chicago P, 2008. Print.

Jose, Nicholas. "Australian Literature Inside and Out." Barry Andrews Memorial Address. *Australian Literature in a Global World*. Ed. Wenche Ommundsen and Tony Simoes da Silva. Spec. issue of *JASAL* (2009): 1–13. Web. 7 May 2010 <www.nla.gov.au/openpublish/index.php/jasal/article/download/894/1752>.

Joshi, Vijaya. *Indian Daughters Abroad: Growing Up in Australia*. New Delhi: Sterling, 2000. Print.

Jupp, James. "Immigration, Asylum and Extremist Politics: Europe and Australia." *National Europe Centre Paper No. 70*. Paper presentation. International Conference on "The Challenges of Immigration and Integration in the European Union and Australia." U of Sydney, 18–20 February 2003. Web.

——. ed. *The Australian People: An Encyclopedia of the Nation, Its People and Their Origins*. 1988. 2nd ed. Cambridge: Cambridge UP, 2001. Print.

——. *Immigration*. Oxford: Oxford UP, 1998. Print.

Jurgensen, Manfred. "Multicultural Literature." *Outrider* 3.2 (December 1986): 80–90. Print.

Kallivayalil, Tanu. "The Work has Begun." *The Indian Sun* (September 2013). Web. 10 September 2013 <http://www.theindiansun.com.au/the-work-has-begun/>.

Kalra, Virinder S., Raminder Kaur, and John Hutnyk. *Diaspora and Hybridity*. London: Sage, 2005.

Kamboureli, Smaro. *Scandalous Bodies: Diasporic Literature in English Canada*. Don Mills: Oxford UP, 2000. Print.

Kannan, Sharmini. "Pappadums in Paradise?—Journeys of Indian Migrant Women to Australia." MA disst., Deakin U, 2002. Web.

Kanth, Emmanuel. "Does the Indian Really Matter in Australia?" *The Indian Sun* (August 2013). Web. 9 September 2013 <http://www.the indiansun.com.au/does-the-indian-really-matter-in-australia/#>.

Karim, K.H. "Mapping Diasporic Mediascapes." *The Media of Diaspora*. Ed. K.H. Karim. London: Routledge, 2003. 1–17. Print.

Karunarathna, Thishanka, ed. *Celebrations!—Sinhalese and Sri Lankan Women in Canberra: Testimonies and Memories*. Comp. Badra Kamal Karunara5thna. Canberra: Badra Kamal Karunarathna, 2008. Print.

Kelly, John. "Time and the Global: Against the Homogeneous, Empty Communities in Contemporary Social Theory." *Development and Change* 29.4 (1998): 839–871. Print.

Kenna, Len. "Indians are Not Ethnic Minority in Australia." *Bharat Times* (Online). Web. 22 March 2006 <http://www.bharattimes.com/BT_WEB/interview~month.htm>.

Kershen, Anne J. "The Migrant at Home in Spitalfields: Memory, Myth, and Reality." *Histories and Memories: Migrants and Their History in Britain*. Ed. Kathy Burrell and Panikos Panayi. London: Tauris Academic Studies, 2006. 96–113. Print.

Kessler, C.S. 'Negotiating Cultural Difference: On Seeking, Not Always Successfully, to Share the World with Others—or, in Defence of "Embassy".' *Asian Studies Review* 15. 2 (1991): 57–73. Print.

Khan, Adib. *Homecoming*. Pymble, NSW: Flamingo, 2003. Print.

——. "Trends in Australian Fiction." *Kosmopolis* 2 (2002). Centre de Cultura Contemporània de Barcelona. Web. 10 January 2008 <http://www.cccb.org/rcs_multimedia/Adib_Khan-eng.pdf>.

——. "In Janus' Footsteps." *Australian Humanities Review* (June 2001). Web. 15 March 2008 <http://www.lib.latrobe.edu.au/AHR/archive/ Issue-June-2001/khan.html>.

——. "Out There." *Westerly* 42.4 (1997): 85–93. Print.

——. "My First Love." *My First Love & Turning Point*. Ed. Graham Reilly. Albert Park, Victoria: Julie Morgan Marketing, 1995. 21–25. Print.

Khilnani, Sunil. "What is South Asian?" *No Man's Land—Exploring South Asianness*. 22 May 2004. Symposium Report. By Shiromi Pinto. June 2004. 18–25. Web. 28 June 2009 <http://www.akademi.co.uk/ download/NML_report.pdf>.

Kinsella, John. "Refugees and Australia." Lecture. "A Just Australia" Campaign. Canberra, 2003. Web. 10 April 2010 <http://www.johnkinsella.org/essays/refugees.html>.

——. "Why I Didn't Play Australian Rules Football." *Overland* 166 (Autumn 2002): 21–24. Web. 10 April 2010 <http://www.johnkinsella.org/ essays/footy.html>.

Kirshenblatt-Gimblett, Barbara. "Spaces of Dispersal." *Further Inflections: Toward Ethnographies of the Future*. Spec. issue of Cultural Anthropology 9.3 (August 1994): 339–344. Print.

Klimt, Andrea, and Stephen Lubkemann. "Argument across the Portuguese-Speaking World: A Discursive Approach to Diaspora." *Diaspora* 11.2 (2002): 145–162. Print.

Koshy, Susan. "Category Crisis: South Asian Americans and Questions of Race and Ethnicity." *Diaspora* 7.3 (1998): 285–320. Print.

Kracauer, Siegfried. *History: The Last Things before the Last*. New York: Oxford UP, 1969. Print.

Kudaisya, Gyanesh. "Indian Leadership and the Diaspora." *The Encyclopedia of Indian Diaspora*. Ed. Brij V. Lal et al. Honolulu: U of Hawai'i P, 2006. 82–89. Print.

Kumar, Amitava. Introduction. *Away: The Indian Writer as an Expatriate*. Ed. A. Kumar. New York: Routledge, 2004. xiii-xxvi. Print.

Kundani, Arun. "Islamism and the Roots of Liberal Rage." *Race & Class* 50.2 (2008): 40–68. Print.

Lake, Marilyn, et al. *What's Wrong with Anzac?—The Militarisation of Australian History*. Sydney: U of New South Wales P, 2010. Print.

Lakha, Salim, and M. Stevenson. "Indian Identity in a Multicultural Melbourne: Some Preliminary Observations." *Journal of Intercultural Studies* 22.3 (2001): 245–262. Print.

Lakha, Salim. "Regions and Communities: Australia." *The Encyclopaedia of the Indian Diaspora*. Ed. Brij V. Lal et al. Honolulu: U of Hawai'i P, 2006. 383–387. Print.

Lal, Brij V. Introduction. *The Encyclopedia of Indian Diaspora*. Ed. Brij V. Lal et al. Honolulu: U of Hawai'i P, 2006a. 10–18. Print.

——. Interview with Tamara Mabbott Athique. 9 June 2004. "Textual Migrations: South Asian-Australian Fiction." Tamara Mabbott Athique. PhD thesis. U of Wollongong, 2006b. 326–347. Print.

——. "The Road to Mr Tulsi's Store." *Meanjin* 62.4 (2003): 42–48. Print.

——. "The London Link." *Conversations: Occasional Writing from the Research School of Pacific and Asian Studies* 3.1 (Winter 2002): 78–83. Print.

——. *Mr Tulsi's Store: A Fijian Journey*. Canberra: Pandanus, 2001a. Print.

——. "Labasa Secondary." *Conversations* 2.1 (2001b): 96–118. Print.

——. "Return to Bahraich." *Unfinished Journeys: India File from Canberra*. Ed. Debjani Ganguly and Kavita Nandan. New Delhi: CRNLE and PIP, 1998. 91–107. Print.

——. "The Odyssey of Indenture: Fragmentation and Reconstitution in the Indian Diaspora." *Diaspora* 5.2 (1996): 167–188. Print.

Lal, Vinay, and Ahmar Mahboob. "The Politics of Identity among Diasporic Communities along the Pacific Rim: Indians in the United States and Pakistanis in Australia." Association of Pacific Rim Universities 2006. Web. 3 May 2010 <www.apru.org/_files/afp/LalMahboob.do>.

Lal, Vinay. "Diaspora Indians Suffer from the Anxiety of Invisibility." Press Release. "The Cultural Politics of the Indian Diaspora." Aspen Institute India. 30 July 2009. Web. 3 May 2010 <http://www.aspenindia.org/outreach/pdf/VinayLal_press_release.pdf>.

——. "Labour and Longing." Online Paper. "The Diaspora: A Symposium on Indian–Americans and the Motherland." June 2004. Web. 2 May 2010 <http://www.india-seminar.com/2004/538/538%20vinay%20lal.htm>.

——. "Diaspora Purana: The Indic Presence in World Culture." *The International Indian* 10.6 (February 2003): 29–31. Web. 2 May 2010 <http: //www.sscnet.ucla.edu/southasia/Diaspora/indic_presence.html>.

——. "Reflections on the Indian Diaspora, in the Caribbean and Elsewhere." *Manas* 12 December 2002. Web. 16 March 2006 <http://www.sscnet.ucla.edu/southasia/Diaspora/reflect.html>.

Lalthlamuanpii, Pauline. "A Study of Women's Characters in Yasmine Gooneratne's Novels *A Change of Skies* and *The Pleasures of Conquest*." MPhil Disst., Jawaharlal Nehru U, 2009. Print.

Langfield, Michele. "Bridging the Cultural Divide: Movements of People between Australia and Asia." *Australia and Asia*. Ed. Mark McGillivray and Gary K. Smith. Melbourne: Oxford UP, 1997. 28–55. Print.

Levitt, Peggy. "Roots and Routes: Understanding the Lives of the Second Generation Transnationally." *Journal of Ethnic and Migration Studies* 35.7 (August 2009): 1225–1242. Web. 10 June 2010 <http://www.peggylevitt.org/pdfs/Levitt-roots_and_routes.pdf>.

Lin Ho, Elaine Yee. *Timothy Mo*. Manchester: Manchester UP, 2000. Print.

Ling, Chik, Tseen Khoo, and Jen Tsen Kwok. "Chinese Voices." *Meanjin* 63.2 (2004): 149–159. Print.

Lokugé, Chandani. "'We Must Laugh at One Another, or Die': Yasmine Gooneratne's *A Change of Skies* and South Asian Migrant Identities." *Fact & Fiction: Readings in Australian Literature*. Ed. Anit Sarwal and Reema Sarwal. New Delhi: Authors P, 2008. 202–219. Print.

——. Interview with Tamara Mabbott Athique. 22 May 2004. "Textual Migrations: South Asian-Australian Fiction." Tamara Mabbott Athique. PhD thesis. U of Wollongong, 2006. 349–358. Web.

——. *Moth and other stories*. Sydney: Dangaroo P, 1992. Print.

Longley, Kateryna Olijnyk. "Little Histories: Diasporan Family Narratives in Australia." *Southern Review* 30.2 (1997): 212–225. Print.

Lorde, Audre. "Frontiers: Aydre Lorde Interviewed by Pratibha Parmar and Jackie Kay." 1988. *Conversations with Audre Lorde*. Ed. Joan Wylie Hall. The UP of Missisipi, 2004. 171–180. Print.

Lowenthal, David. *The Past is a Foreign Country*. London: Cambridge UP, 1985. Print.

Macintyre, Stuart. *A Concise History of Australia*. Cambridge: Cambridge UP, 1999. Print.

Mackay, Hugh. *Reinventing Australia: The Mind and Mood of Australia in the 90s*. Pymble, NSW: Angus & Robertson, 1993. Print.

Mackie, Grace. *Of Jasmines and Jumboos*. Northbridge, WA: Access P, 1993. Print.

Madigan, Michael. "Indians Brand Australians as Dumb, Drunk, Racist." *Winnipeg Free Press* 22 June 2012. Web. 26 June 2012 <http://www.winnipegfreepress.com/opinion/columnists/indians-brand-australians-as-dumb-drunk-racist-159983215.html>.

Mahanta, Namrata Rathore. *V.S. Naipaul: The Indian Trilogy*. New Delhi: Atlantic, 2004. Print.

Maharaj, Neelam. "Festivals." *Best Stories Under the Sun*. Eds. Michael Wilding and David Myers. Queensland: Central Queensland UP, 2004. 127–131. Print.

"Main Migrant source for Australia is India." *The Hindu* 4 June 2013. Web. 12 August 2013 <http://www.thehindu.com/news/international/world/main-migrant-source-for-australia-is-india/article4780674.ece>.

Malak, Amin. " 'The World is Your People': *The Time of the Peacock* and the Evolution of an Australian Identity." *Kunapipi* XVI.2 (1994): 43–47. Print.

Mankekar, Purnima. " 'India Shopping': Indian Grocery Stores and transnational Configurations of Belonging. " *The Cultural Politics of Food and Eating: A Reader*. Ed. James L. Watson and Melissa L. Caldwell. Malden, MA: Blackwell, 2005. 197–214. Print.

——. "Off-centre: Feminism and South Asian Studies in the Diaspora." *At Home in Diaspora: South Asian Scholars and the West*. Ed. Jackie Assayag and Véronique Bénéï. Bloomington: Indiana UP, 2003.52–65. Print.

Manning, Patrick. *Migration in World History*. London: Routledge, 2005. Print.

Mannur, Anita. "Culinary Nostalgia: Authenticity, Nationalism, and Diaspora." *MELUS* 32.4 (Winter 2007). Web. 14 May 2010 <http://www.accessmylibrary.com/article-1G1-173644213/culinary-nostalgia-authenticity-nationalism.html>.

Marcus, Andrew. *Mapping Social Cohesion National Report*. Melbourne: Scanlon Foundation, Australian Multicultural Foundation and Monash University, 2013. Web. 21 October 2013 <http://www.arts.monash.edu.au/mapping-population/—documents/mapping-social-cohesion-national-report-2013.pdf>.

Massey, Doreen. *Space, Place and Gender*. Minneapolis: U of Minnesota P, 1994. Print.

Mazumdar, Sucheta. "Race and Racism: South Asians in the United States." *Asian Americans: Comparative and Global Perspectives*. Ed. Shirley Hune et al. Pullman, WA: Washington State UP, 1991. 25–38. Print.

McLaren, John. "Dialect of the Diaspora: Sourceland, Empire and Homelands." *Regenerative Spirit. (Un)settling, (Dis)locations, (Post-)colonial, (Re)presentations: Australian Post-colonial Reflections*. Ed. Sue Williams et al. Vol. 2. Adelaide: Lythrum, 2004. 36–43. Print.

McMahon, Suzanne. "Overview of the South Asian Diaspora." 1995. Web. 4 May 2010 <http://www.lib.berkeley.edu/SSEAL/SouthAsia/overview.html>.

Melleuish, Gregory, and Geoffrey Stokes. "Australian Political Thought." *Creating Australia: New Essays in Australian History*. Ed. Geoffrey Bolton and Wayne Hudson. Sydney: Allen & Unwin, 1997. 111–121. Print.

Mellor, D. "Contemporary Racism in Australia: The Experiences of Aborigines." *Personality and Social Psychology Bulletin* 29.4 (April 2004): 474–486. Print.

Mishra, Sudesh. *Diaspora Criticism*. Edinburgh: Edinburgh UP, 2006. Print.

——. "Diaspora and the Difficult Art of Dying." *Regenerative Spirit. (Un)settling, (Dis)locations, (Post-)colonial, (Re)presentations: Australian Post-colonial Reflections*. Ed. Sue Williams et al. Vol. 2. Adelaide: Lythrum, 2004. 60–64. Print.

——. "Lila." *Meanjin* 53.4 (1994): 649–655. Print.

Mishra, Vijay. *The Diasporic Imaginary*. New York: Routledge, 2007. Print.

——. "Voices from the Diaspora." *The Encyclopedia of Indian Diaspora*. Ed. Brij V. Lal et al. Honolulu: U of Hawai'i P, 2006. 120–139. Print.

——. *Bollywood Cinema: Temples of Desire*. London: Routledge, 2002. Print.

——. "(B)ordering Naipaul: Indenture History and Diasporic Poetics." *Diaspora* 5.2 (1996a): 189–237. Print.

——. "New Lamps for Old: Diasporas Migrancy Border." *Interrogating Post-colonialism: Theory, Text and Context*. Ed. Harish Trivedi, and Meenakshi Mukherjee. Shimla: Indian Institute of Advanced Study, 1996b. 67–85. Print.

——. "The Diasporic Imaginary: Theorizing the Indian Diaspora." *Textual Practice* 10.3 (1996c): 421–447. Print.

——. "Satendra Nandan, *The Wounded Sea*." *Span* 32 (1991): 79. Web. 10 March 2006 <http://wwwmcc.murdoch.edu.au/ReadingRoom/litserv/SPAN/32/Mishra>.

——. "Ni Sa Moce/Salaam Fiji." *Meanjin* 48.3 (1989): 481–494. Print.

Mitchell, Adrian. Introduction. *New Directions in Australian Studies*. Ed. Cynthia Vanden Driesen and Adrian Mitchell. New Delhi: Prestige Books, 2000. 1–22. Print.

Mitchell, Beryl T. "Tea, Tytlers and Tribes." *Celebrations: Fifty Years of Sri Lanka-Australia Interactions*. Ed. C.A. Vanden Driesen and I.H. Vanden Driesen. Colombo: Government Printer, 1997. 301–312. Print.

Mohanty, Chandra Talpade. "Feminist Encounters, Locating the Politics of Experience." *Copyright* 1 (Fall 1987): 30–44. Print.

Moore, Gloria Jean. "A Brief History of the Anglo-Indians." 2007. Web. 7 May 2010 <http://angloindian.wordpress.com/history/>.

——. "Anglo Indians." *The Australian People: An Encyclopedia of the Nation, its People and their Origins*. Ed. James Jupp. Cambridge: Cambridge UP, 2001. 434–439. Print.

——. *The Anglo-Indian Vision*. Melbourne: AEP, 1986a. Print.

——. *The Lotus and the Rose: An Anglo-Indian Story*. Melbourne: River Seine Publications, 1986b. Print.

Mosselson, Jacqueline. "Roots & Routes: A Re-imagining of Refugee Identity Constructions and the Implications for Schooling." *Current Issues in Comparative Education* 9.1 (December 2006b): 20–29. Print.

——. "Roots and Routes: Re-imagining the Reactive Identities of Bosnian Adolescent Female Refugees." PhD disst., Columbia U, 2002. Print.

Mukherjee, Bharti. *Darkness*. Minnesota: Fawcett Publications, 1985. Print.

Mukherjee, Karobi. "An Asian Migrant Woman's View of the City of Adelaide." *Turn the Page: An Anthology by the Migrant Women's Writer' Group*. Ed. Migrant Women's Writer' Group. Elsternwick, Victoria: Migrant Women's Writer' Group, 1994. 126–134. Print.

Mukherjee, Meenakshi. "Yasmine Gooneratne." 2001. Web. 15 March 2010 <http://www.samvadindia.com/si-web/si-rra.htm>.

"My Australia." Australian Broadcasting Corporation. 2010. Web. 7 May 2010 <http://australianetwork.com/myaustralia/>.

Nagel, Caroline. "Questioning Citizenship in an 'Age of Migration.' " *Globalization and Its Outcomes*. Ed. John O'Loughlin et al. New York: The Guilford P, 2004. 231–252. Print.

Naipaul, V.S. *An Area of Darkness*. London: Andre Deutsch, 1964. Print.

——. *The Mystic Masseur*. London: Andre Deutsch, 1957. Print.

Nandan, Satendra. "The Migrant as a Metaphor: Life as a Text." *Multiculturalism in Australian Literature*. Ed. R.K. Dhawan and Suman Bala. Spl. issue of *Journal of Australasian Studies* 1 (2004): 7–15. Print.

——. *Requiem for a Rainbow: A Fiji Indian Story*. Canberra: PIP, 2001. Print.

——. "Migration, Dispossession, Exile and the Diasporic Consciousness: The Body Politics of Fiji." *Shifting Continents/Colliding Cultures: Diaspora Writing of the Indian Subcontinent*. Ed. Ralph J. Crane and Radhika Mohanram. Amsterdam: Rodopi, 2000. 35–54. Print.

——. Introduction. *The Universe We Are: A Multicultural Anthology*. Ed. Robert Verdon. Canberra: Canberra Multicultural Writers' Group and Aberrant Genotype P, 1999. 8–10. Print.

——. "Delhi: Among the Ruins." *Unfinished Journeys: India File from Canberra*. Ed. Debjani Ganguly and Kavita Nandan. New Delhi: CRNLE and PIP, 1998. 109–144. Print.

——. "Antyesti Samskara: The Last Rites." *Broken Hearts*. Spec. issue of *Meanjin* 55.3 (1996): 410–424. Print.

——. "First Flight." *Diasporas*. Ed. Vijay Mishra. Spec. issue of *SPAN* 34–35 (November 1992–May 1993a): 302–314. Print.

——. "Mangoes." *SPAN* 34–35 (1993b): 306–314. Print.

——. "Nandi." *Meanjin* 49.5 (1990): 619–633. Print.

——. "Ashes and diamonds." *Redoubt* 7–8 (1989): 58–66. Print.

——. "The Guru." *Encounters*. Ed. Bruce Bennett and A. Janaki Ram. Jaipur: Pointer, 1988. 69–77. Print.

Nandy, Ashis. "The Need to have Inferiors and Enemies." *Australia's Ambivalence towards Asia*. J.V. D'Cruz and William Steele. Clayton: Monash UP, 2003. 1–6. Print.

Narasimhaiah, C.D. "Notes Towards Exploration of Australasian Bonds." *New Directions in Australian Studies*. Ed. Cynthia Vanden Driesen and Adrian Mitchell. New Delhi: Prestige Books, 2000. 23–31. Print.

Narayan, Sushie. "Asha's Story." *Turn the Page: An Anthology by the Migrant Women's Writer' Group*. Ed. Migrant Women's Writer' Group. Elsternwick, Victoria: Migrant Women's Writer' Group, 1994. 136–141. Print.

"Nepal Australia Friendship Association." n.d. Web. 12 March 2006 <http://www.nepalaust.org/>.

"Nepal: Country Brief." February 2010. Web. 3 May 2010 <http://www.dfat.gov.au/geo/nepal/nepal_country_brief.html>.

"Nepalese Association of Victoria." n.d. Web. 12 March 2006 <http://www.nav.org.au/aboutus.htm>.

"Nepalese Australian Association." n.d. Web. 3 May 2010 <http://www.naa.org.au/>.

"Nepalese in Australia Protest against Laxampur Dam." *Peoples Review* (2000). Web. 12 March 2006 <http://www.peoplesreview.com.np/preview/2000/08/11082000>.

"Nepalese Student Bashed in Sydney." 2 February 2010. Web. 4 May 2010 <http://aussienepali.com/2010/02/02/nepali-student-bashed-in-sydney/>.

Northrop, Mia. "Vindaloo against Violence 24 February 2010." 25 February 2010. Web. 15 March 2010 <http://vindalooagainstviolence. wordpress.com/>.

O'Grady, John. *They're a Weird Mob*. Sydney: Ure Smith, 1957. Print.

Okpewho, Isidore. Introduction. *The African Diaspora: African Origins and New World Identities*. Ed. Isidore Okpewho et al. Bloomington: Indiana UP, 2001. xi-xxviii. Print.

"Pakistan Association of Australia." n.d. Web. 3 May 2010 <http://www.pakistanassociation.com.au/>.

"Pakistan Australia Friendship Association." n.d. Web. 3 May 2010 <http://www.pafa.org.au/>.

"Pakistani Australian." 2010. 3 May 2010 <http://en.wikipedia.org/wiki/Pakistani_Australian>.

Panayi, Panikos. *Immigration, Ethnicity and Racism in Britain, 1815–1914*. Manchester: Manchester UP, 1994. Print.

Papastergiadis, Nikos. *The Turbulence of Migration: Globalization, Deterritorialization and Hybridity*. Cambridge: Polity P, 2000. Print.

Paramanandam, K.C. "Of Human Infatuation." *Westerley* (1956): 16–19. Print.

Parameswaran, Uma. "Dispelling the Spells of Memory: Another Approach to Reading Our Yesterdays." *Proceedings of the Red River Conference on World Literature*. Vol. 2. Fargo, ND: North Dakota State U, 2000. Web. 8 February 2008 <http://www.ndsu.edu/RRCWL/ V2/uma.html>.

Paranjape, Makarand. "Mirroring Ambivalences: Resistance and Reconciliation in South Asian Australia." *Australian Studies Now: An Introductory Reader in Australian Studies*. Ed. Andrew Hassam and Amit Sarwal. New Delhi: Indialog, 2007. 342–359. Print.

——. Preface. *In Diaspora*. Ed. Makarand Paranjape. New Delhi: Indialog, 2001a. i-vi. Print.

——. "Displaced Relations: Diasporas, Empires, Homelands." Introduction. *In Diaspora*. Ed. Makarand Paranjape. New Delhi: Indialog, 2001b. 1–13. Print.

——. "One Foot in Canada and a Couple of Toes in India." *In Diaspora*. Ed. Makarand Paranjape. New Delhi: Indialog, 2001c. 161–170. Print.

——. "What about Those Who Stayed Back Home? Interrogating the Privileging of Diasporic Writing." Afterword. *Shifting Continents/ Colliding Cultures: Diaspora Writing of the Indian Subcontinent*. Ed. Ralph J. Crane and Radhika Mohanram. Amsterdam: Rodopi, 2000. 225–246. Print.

Pasipanodya, Madu. "A Family for Us." *Weaving a Double Cloth: Stories of Asia-Pacific Women in Australia*. Ed. Myra Jean Bourke, Susanne Holzknecht, and Annie Bartlett. Canberra: Pandanus, 2002. 113–125. Print.

Patri, Vasantha R., and Neelkant Patri. *Essentials of Effective Communication*. New Delhi: Greenspan Publications, 2002. Print.

Penberthy, David. "Are we Racists? Chk Chk Chk Boom We're Racists." *The Punch* 3 June 2009. Web. 12 June 2010 <http://www.thepunch.com.au/articles/are-we-racist-golly-gosh-goodness-gra cious-me-yes/>.

Penton, Brian. *The Landtakers*. Sydney: The Endeavour P, 1934. Print.

Perera, Suvendrini. "Dravidian Curls (Fragments from an Unfinished Narrative)." *Hecate* 25.1 (1999): 111–123. Print.

——. "Rejections." *Meanjin* 43.3 (Spring 1984): 357–361. Print.

Peres Da Costa, Suneeta. Interview with Tamara Mabbott Athique. 29 November 2003. "Textual Migrations: South Asian-Australian Fiction." Tamara Mabbott Athique. PhD thesis. U of Wollongong, 2006. 367–386. Web.

——. "Dreamless." *Fire & Shadow*. Spec. issue of *Heat* 1 (2001): 87–105. Print.

Phillips, A. Introduction. *The Asian Image in Australia*. J.V. D'Cruz. Melbourne: The Hawthorn P, 1973. 1–10. Print.

Phillips, Zelma. *The Anglo-Indian Australian Story: My Experience—A Collection of Anglo-Indian Migration Heritage Stories*. Keysborough, Vic: The Author, 2004. Print.

Pinnawala, Sisiri Kumara. "Sri Lankans in Melbourne—Factors Influencing Patterns of Ethnicity." PhD thesis. Australian National U, 1984. Print.

Pinto, Shiromi. No Man's Land—Exploring South Asianness. 22 May 2004. *Symposium Report*. June 2004. Web. 28 June 2009 <http://www. akademi.co.uk/download/NML_report.pdf>.

Prabhakar, Jyoti. "There's a Clear Bias against Us in Oz." *The Times of India* (*Delhi Times*) 4 June 2010: 5. Print.

Prasad, Mohit Manoj. "Indo-Fijian Diasporic Bodies: Narratives in Text, Image, Popular Culture, and the Lived Everyday in Fiji and Liverpool, Sydney Australia." PhD thesis. U of Western Sydney, 2005. Web.

Prashad, Vijay. "From Multiculture to Polyculture in South Asian American Studies." *Diaspora* 8.2 (1999): 185–204. Print.

"Pratibimb—Indian Cultural Community Australia." Facebook Group. 2009. Web. 28 May 2010 <http://www.facebook.com/group.php?gid=118558284832134>.

Probyn, Elspeth. *Outside Belongings*. New York: Routledge, 1996. Print.

"Queensland Aust-Ind Association." n.d. Web. 16 March 2006 <http://www.geocities.com/Nashville/Bluegrass/1513/>.

"Question on Notice—Bhutan Refugees." Question No. 1857. 15 March 2000. Web. 12 March 2006 <http://www.dfat.gov.au/qwon/1999_2001/000315e.html>.

"Racial Violence in Australia." 2010. Web. 10 April 2010 <http://en.wikipedia.org/wiki/Racial_Violence_In_Australia>.

"Racism Confined to 'Minority' of People: Australian Minister." *Times of India* 31 May 2009. Web. 25 June 2009 <http://timesof

india.indiatimes.com/World/Rest-of-World/Racism-confined-to-minority-of-people-Australian-Minister/articleshow/4600020.cms>.

"Racism in Australia." 2010. Web. 10 April 2010 <http://en.wikipedia.org/wiki/Racism_in_Australia>.

"Radha D'Souza's ZNet HomePage." n.d. Web. 10 March 2006 <http://www.zmag.org/bios/homepage.cfm?authorID=171>.

Rai, Sudha. "Beyond Place; Beyond Gendering: Reconstructions of Immigrant 'Third Space' in Diasporic Short Stories." *Gender and Narrative*. Ed. Jasbir Jain and Supriya Agarwal. New Delhi: Rawat Publications, 2002. 134–148. Print.

Raja, Chris. "White Boots." *Meanjin* 62.1 (2003): 96–99. Print.

Rajkowski, Pamela. *In the Tracks of the Camelmen: Outback Australia's Most Exotic Pioneers*. North Ryde, NSW: Angus & Robertson, 1987. Print.

Rama, R.P. "A Conversation with Yasmine Gooneratne." *SPAN: Journal of the South Pacific Association for Commonwealth Language and Literature Studies* 38 (1994): 1–18. Print.

Ramraj, Victor J. "Diasporas and Multiculturalism." *New National ad Post-Colonial Literatures: An Introduction*. Ed. Bruce King. Oxford: Clarendon P, 1996. 214–229. Print.

Rasool, Kay. *My Journey behind the Veil: Conversations with Muslim Women*. South Melbourne: Lothian Books, 2002. Print.

Rauf, Abdur. "Islam Enlightens Australia." 1994. Web. 10 March 2006 <http://www.renaissance.com.pk/jannevi20.htm>.

Ray, Manas. "Nation, Nostalgia amd Bollywood: In the Tracks of a Twice–displaced Community." *The Media of Diaspora*. Ed. Karim H. Karim. London: Routledge, 2003. 21–35.

"Regional South Asia." n.d. Web. 12 March 2006 <http://www.ausaid.gov.au/country/country.cfm?CountryID=28152753 &Region=SouthAsia>.

"Report of the Review of Settlement Services for Migrants and Humanitarian Entrants." Chapter One—The Policy Context. 23 November 2005. Web. 3 May 2010 <www.immi.gov.au/settle/settle_review/pdfs/chap01web.pdf>.

Riemenschneider, Jörg-Dieter. "Australia in Asia—Asia in Australia: An Intercontinental Cultural Discourse." *Asiatic* 2.2 (December 2008): 11–119. Print.

Rizvi, Fazal. "Racism, Reorientation and the Cultural Politics of Asia-Australia Relations." *The Teeth Are Smiling: The Persistence of Racism in Multicultural Australia*. Ed. Ellie Vasta and Stephen Castles. Sydney: Allen & Unwin, 1996. 173–188. Print.

"Routes to Roots." 2009. 8 June 2010 <http://www.routestoroots.com/>.

Rudrappa, Sharmila. "Disciplining Desire in Making the Home: Engendering Ethnicity in Indian Immigrant Families." *The Second Generation: Ethnic Identity among Asian Americans*. Ed. Pyong Gap Min. Walnut Creek, CA: Altamira, 2002. 85–112. Print.

Rushdie, Salman. *Imaginary Homelands: Essays and Criticism, 1981–1991*. 1985. New York: Viking, 1991. Print.

——. *Shame*. London: Jonathan Cape, 1983. Print.

Safran, William. "Comparing Diasporas: A Review Essay." Rev. of *Global Diasporas*, by Robin Cohen. *Diaspora* 8.3 (1999): 255–291. Print.

——. "Diasporas in Modern Societies: Myths of Homeland and Return." *Diaspora* 1.1 (Spring 1991): 83–99. Print.

"Sagarmatha Nepali Restaurant." n.d. Web. 12 March 2006 <http://www.sagarmatha.com.au>.

Salecl, Renata. *The Spoils of Freedom*. London: Routledge, 1994. Print.

Sangari, Kumkum, and Sudesh Vaid. "Recasting Woman: An Introduction." *Recasting Women: Essays in Colonial History*. Ed. Kumkum Sangari and Sudesh Vaid. New Delhi: Kali for Women, 1989. 1–26. Print.

Sareen, Santosh K. Introduction. *Contemporary Australian Short Stories*. Ed. Santosh K. Sareen. New Delhi: Affiliated East-West P Pvt. Ltd., 2001. vii-xii. Print.

Sarwal, Amit, and Reema Sarwal. "Creative Nation: Approaching Australian Cinema and Cultural Studies." Introduction. *Creative Nation: Australian Cinema and Cultural Studies Reader*. Ed. Amit Sarwal and Reema Sarwal. New Delhi: SSS Publications, 2009. XXVI-XLIX. Print.

Sarwal, Amit, ed. *Bridging Imaginations: South Asian Diaspora in Australia*. New Delhi: Readworthy Publications, 2013. Print.

——. "Roots & Routes: Politics of Location in the Short Stories of South Asian Diaspora in Australia." PhD thesis. Jawaharlal Nehru University, 2010. Print.

——. "Postcards from Trishankus: Images of India and Australia in South Asian–Australian Short Stories." MPhil disst. Jawaharlal Nehru U, 2006. Print.

Sarwal, Reema. "Lost and (then) Found: The Quest for Home in Benang, Tirra Lirra by the River and Requiem for a Rainbow." *Fact & Fiction: Readings in Australian Literature*. Ed. Amit Sarwal and Reema Sarwal. New Delhi: Authors P, 2008. 240–251. Print.

"Satendra Nandan's Profile." n.d. Web. 10 March 2006 <http://www.ce.canberra.edu.au/cc/profiles/Nandan.htm>.

Schmidt-Haberkamp, Barbara. "Cross-Cultural Experience and Existence in Yasmine Gooneratne's Novel *A Change of Skies.*" *Towards a Transcultural Future: Literature and Society in 'Post'-Colonial World.* Ed. G.V. Davis et al. Amsterdam: Rodopi, 2004. 215–230. Print.

Scott, Franklin D. Introduction. *World Migration in Modern Times.* Ed. Franklin D. Scott. Englewood Cliffs, NJ: Prentice-Hall, 1968. 1–8. Print.

Sellick, Robert. "Matthew Flinders: Naming the Diaspora." *Regenerative Spirit: (Un)settling, (Dis)locations, (Post-)colonial, (Re)presentations—Australian Post-colonial Reflections.* Ed. Sue Williams et al. Vol. 2. Adelaide: Lythrum, 2004. 1–5. Print.

Selvadurai, Shyam. "Introducing Myself in the Diaspora." Introduction. *Story-Wallah: Short Fiction from South Asian Writers.* Ed. Shyam Selvadurai. New York: Houghton Mifflin, 2005. 1–14. Print.

Shapcott, Thomas. Introduction. *The Time of the Peacock.* Mena Abdullah and Ray Mathew. Pymble, NSW: Harper Collins, 1992. Print.

Sharma, Pranay. "The Dominant Culture in Australia is a Racist Culture: Interview with Van Thanh Rudd," *Outlook* 8 February 2010. Web. 24 June 2012 <http://www.outlookindia.com/article.aspx?264017>.

Sharma, Renuka. "Paternity: A Study in Tradition and Modernity." *Turn the Page: An Anthology by the Migrant Women's Writer' Group.* Ed. Migrant Women's Writer' Group. Elsternwick, Victoria: Migrant Women's Writer' Group, 1994. 154–157. Print.

Sharma, S.L. "Perspectives on Indians Abroad." 1989. *The Indian Diaspora: Dynamics of Migration.* Ed. N. Jayaram. New Delhi: Sage, 2004. 44–65. Print.

Sharma, Shrishti. "Saying Goodbye to the Mango Tree." *Conversations* 3.2 (Summer 2003): 48–66. Print.

Sharrad, Paul. "Convicts, Call Centres and Cochin Kangaroos: South Asian Globalizing of the Australian Imagination." *Reading Down Under: Australian Literary Studies Reader.* Ed. Amit Sarwal and Reema Sarwal. New Delhi: SSS Publications, 2009. 571–582. Print.

——. "Mena Abdullah's Untranslatable Diasporic Identity." *The Literature of the Indian Diaspora in Criticism.* Ed. A.L. McLeod. New Delhi: Sterling, 2000. 252–261. Print.

Shukla, Sandhya. "Locations for South Asian Diasporas." *Annual Review of Anthropology* 30 (2001): 551–572. Print.

Singh, Gurharpal. Introduction. *Culture and Economy in the Indian Diaspora*. Ed. Bhikhu Parekh, Gurharpal Singh, and Steven Vertovec. London: Routledge, 2003. 1–12. Print.

Sivasupramaniam, V. "History of the Tamil Diaspora." Web. 10 March 2006 <http://murugan.org/research/sivasupramaniam.htm>.

Smith, Debra. "Out of Africa—Aboriginal Origins Uncovered." *The Sydney Morning Herald* 9 May 2007. Web. 21 June 2010 <http://www.smh.com.au/news/national/out-of-africa—aboriginal-origins-uncovered/2007/05/08/1178390312301.html>.

"South Asians are Forgetting Their Roots." n.d. Web. 16 May 2005 <http://groups.msn.com/AAPI/aresouthasiansforgettingtheirroots.msnw>.

Sparkes, Stanley J., and Anna Shnukal. "The Sri Lankan Settlers of Thursday Island." Chapter Seven. *Navigating Boundaries: The Asian Diaspora in Torres Strait*. Ed. Anna Shnukal, Guy Ramsay, and Yuriko Nagata, Canberra: Pandanus, 2004. 161–201. Print.

Spivak, Gayatri. C. *Outside in the Teaching Machine*. London: Routledge, 1994. Print.

——. "Three Women's Texts and a Critique of Imperialism." *"Race," Writing, and Difference*. Spec. issue of *Critical Inquiry* 12.1 (Autumn 1985): 243–261. Print.

"Sri Lankan Australian." 21 January 2006. Web. 10 March 2006 <http://en.wikipedia.org/wiki/Sri_Lankan_Australian>.

Srivastava, Roli. "We'll do Everything to Protect Indian Students: Oz PM." *Times of India* 24 June 2009. Web. 25 June 2009 <http://timesofindia.indiatimes.com/World/Indians-Abroad/Well-do-everything-to-protect-Indian-students-Oz-PM/articleshow/4697078.cms>.

Srivastava, Vanita. "Moving over US and UK, Indians Prefer to Study Down Under." *Hindustan Times* (online) 22 September 2013. Web. 24 September 2013 <http://www.hindustantimes.com/India-news/NewDelhi/Moving-over-US-and-UK-Indians-prefer-to-study-down-under/Article1-1125475.aspx>.

Steinbeck, John. *The Acts of King Arthur and His Noble Knights*. 1976. New York: Penguin, 2008. Print.

Stewart, Kathleen. "Nostalgia." *Cultural Anthropology* 3.3 (August 1988): 227–241. Print.

Stratton, Jon, and Ien Ang. "Multicultural Imagined Communities." *Multicultural States: Rethinking Difference and Identity*. Ed. David Bennett. London: Routledge, 1998. 135–162. Print.

Stratton, Jon, and Suvendrini Perera. "... Surely That's Not Racist?" *New Matilda* 16 Jun 2009. Web. 19 April 2010 <http://newmatilda.com/2009/06/16/surely-thats-not-racist>.

Sullivan, Gerard, and S. Gunasekaran. "Is there an Asian-Australian 'Brain Drain'?" *Asians in Australia: The Dynamics of Migration and Settlement.* Ed. Christine Inglis et al. Singapore: ISEAS, 1992. 157–192. Print.

Sunitha. "Reminiscence." *Hecate* 13.2 (1987): 107–112. Print.

Tannock, Stuart. "Nostalgia Critique." *Cultural Studies* 9.3 (1995): 453–464. Print.

"The Blainey Debate on Immigration—Newspaper Clippings." n.d. Web. 15 March 2010 <http://www.multiculturalaustralia.du.au/library/media/Image/id/635.The-Blainey-debate-on-Immigration-Newspaper-Clippings>.

"The Indian Diaspora." n.d. Web. 16 March 2006 <http://www.sscnet.ucla.edu/southasia/Diaspora/diaspora.html>.

"The Indian Diaspora: 2004–2005." n.d. Web. 28 March 2005 <http://www.theindiandiaspora.com>.

"The Urdu-Speaking Community in Australia." n.d. Web. 10 March 2006 <http://www9.sbs.com.au/radio/language.php?page=info&language=Urdu>.

Tinker, Hugh. *The Banyan Tree: Overseas Emigrants from India, Pakistan and Bangladesh.* Oxford: Oxford UP, 1977. Print.

Tölölyan, Khachig. "Rethinking Diaspora(s): Stateless Power in the Transnational Moment." *Diaspora* 5.1 (1996): 3–36. Print.

——. "Diasporama." *Diaspora* 3 (1994): 235. Print.

Trenwith, Courtney. "Haneef Happy to be Back in Australia." *Brisbane Times* 17 December 2010. Web. 21 December 2010 <http://www.brisbanetimes.com.au/queensland/haneef-happy-to-be-back-in-australia-20101217-190ad.html>.

Troyna, B. *Racism and Education: Research Perspectives.* Buckingham: Open UP, 1993. Print.

Tucker, Shirley. "The Great Southern Land: Asian-Australian Women Writers Re-view the Australian Landscape." *Australian Literary Studies* 21.2 (October 2003): 178–188. Web. 23 July 2010 <http://findarticles.com/p/articles/mi_hb6396/is_2_21/ai_n29051545/>.

Valentine, Lisa. "Australian Immigration Changes: Good News for Indian Students." 9 February 2010. Web. 21 June 2010 <http://www.embraceaustralia.com/australian-immigration-changes-good-news-for-indian-students-6399.htm>.

Vamplew, Wray. "Success for All?—Australia's (Un)Sporting Record." *Australian Studies Now: An Introductory Reader in Australian Studies*. Ed. Andrew Hassam and Amit Sarwal. New Delhi: Indialog, 2007. 361–374. Print.

van der Veer, Peter. "The Diasporic Imagination." Introduction. *Nation and Migration: The Politics of Space in the South Asian Diaspora*. Ed. Peter van der Veer. Philadelphia: U of Pennsylvania P, 1995. 1–16. Print.

Van Gramberg, Ruth (Ruth Marguerite Cruz). "Immigration Dreams, Foundations and Formations." *Celebrations: Fifty Years of Sri Lanka-Australia Interactions*. Ed. C.A. Vanden Driesen and I.H. Vanden Driesen. Colombo: Government Printer, 1997. 209–210. Print.

vanden Driesen, Cynthia, and I.H. Vanden Driesen. Introduction. *Celebrations: Fifty Years of Sri Lanka–Australia Interactions*. Ed. Cynthia Vanden Driesen and I.H. Vanden Driesen. Colombo: Government Printer, 1997. xix–xxiii. Print.

vanden Driesen, Cynthia. "Exorcising Alterity: South Asian Writing in Australia." *Multiculturalism in Australian Literature*. Ed. R.K. Dhawan and Suman Bala. Spec. issue of *Journal of Australasian Studies* (2004): 16–23. Print.

vanden Driesen, Ian. "The Sri Lankan Diaspora and the Academic Scene in Australia." *Celebrations: Fifty Years of Sri Lanka-Australia Interactions*. Ed. Cynthia Vanden Driesen and I.H. Vanden Driesen. Colombo: Government Printer, 1997. 341–343. Print.

Victorian Multicultural Commission. "The Pakistan-born Community in Australia." *Fact Sheet No. A-46*. February 2008. Web. 11 July 2009 <www.multicultural.vic.gov.au>.

Voigt-Graf, Carmen. "Indians at Home in the Antipodes: Migrating with PhDs, Bytes or Kava in Their Bags." *Culture and Economy in the Indian Diaspora*. Ed. Bhikhu Parekh, Gurharpal Singh, and Steven Vertovec. London: Routledge, 2003. 142–164. Print.

"WA's New Draft Charter of Multiculturalism." Office of Multicultural Interests, Government of Western Australia. 25 June 2004. Web. 23 March 2010 <http://www.omi.wa.gov.au/OMI_Charter.asp>.

Walker, David. "Survivalist Anxieties: Australian Responses to Asia, 1890s to the Present." *Australian Studies Now: An Introductory Reader in Australian Studies*. Ed. Andrew Hassam and Amit Sarwal. New Delhi: Indialog, 2007. 312–327. Print.

——. *Anxious Nation: Australia and the Rise of Asia 1850–1939*. St Lucia: U of Queensland P, 1999. Print.

Walters, Wendy. *At Home in Diaspora: Black International Writing.* Minneapolis: U of Minnesota P, 2005. Print.

Waten, Judah. *Alien Son.* 1952. Melbourne: Sun Books, 1968. Print.

Weerasooria, W.S. *Links Between Sri Lanka and Australia: A Book About the Sri Lankans (Ceylonese in Australia)—1788–1988.* Colombo: Government Printer, 1988. Print.

Wellman, David T. *Portraits of White Racism.* New York: Cambridge UP, 1993. Print.

Wessendorf, Susanne. "'Roots Migrants': Transnationalism and 'Return' among Second-Generation Italians in Switzerland." *Journal of Ethnic and Migration Studies* 33.7 (September 2007): 1083–1102. Print.

Westrip, Joyce, and Peggy Holroyde. *Colonial Cousins: A Surprising History of Connections between India and Australia.* Kent Town, South Australia: Wakefield P, 2010. Print.

"When did Australia's Earliest Inhabitants Arrive?" *University of Wollongong: Latest News* 17 September 2004. Web. 21 June 2010 <http://media.uow.edu.au/news/2004/0917a/index.html>.

White, Richard. *Inventing Australia: Images and Identity 1688–1980.* Sydney: George Allen & Unwin, 1985. Print.

Wilton, Janis. "From 'Culotta' to Castro: the Migrant Presence in Australian Writing." *Writing in Multicultural Australia 1984: An Overview.* Ed. The Literary Board. Sydney: Australia Council, 1985. 24–33. Print.

Windschuttle, Keith. "Why Australia is Not a Racist Country." *Quadrant* (March 2006). Web. 17 December 2010 <http://www.sydneyline.com/Why%20Australia%20not%20racist.htm>.

Wise, J. Macgregor. "Home: Territory and Identity." *Cultural Studies* 14.2 (2000): 295–310.

Wright, Erik Olin. "Reflections on Marxism, Class and Politics." Interview with Chronis Polychroniou. February 2001. 1–24. Web. 7 June 2010 <http://www.ssc.wisc.edu/~wright/Polyc-int.PDF>.

Wylie, A. "Why Standpoints Matter." *Science and Other Cultures.* Ed. R. Figueroa and S. Harding. New York: Routledge, 2003. 26–48. Print.

"Yasmine Gooneratne's Masterpiece and Other Stories." n.d. Web. 10 March 2006 <http://www.encompassculture.com/results/?qs=Yasmine%20Gooneratne>.

"Yasmine Gooneratne—Biography." n.d. Web. 10 March 2006 <http://www.english.emory.edu/Bahri/Gooneratne.html>.

Zable, Arnold. Interview with Mark Rubbo. *Readings.Com* 30 May 2008. Web. 7 May 2010 <http://www.readings.com.au/interview/arnold-zable>.

——. "Celebration: An Essay." 2001. Web. 7 May 2010 <http://museumvictoria.com.au/discoverycentre/infosheets/celebration-an-essay-by-arnold-zable/>.

Zelinka, S. *Understanding Racism in Australia*. Canberra: HEROC, 1996. Print.

Index